Wild
Mad wild
Pushing, pumping, beating
Blood wild

Fly oh bird-thing
Soar wind-like one

Fierce
Mighty
Swifter than the rays of the sun

Oh go straight my dream
Pierce the heart of god

The Arrow of Artemis
by Carol Marshall
1969

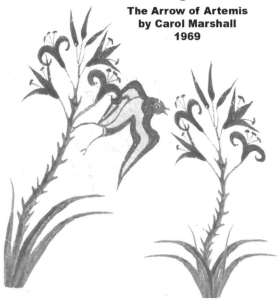

She Who Walks the Labyrinth.
By Kassandra G. Sojourner
Copyright © 2006 Kassandra G. Sojourner
All rights reserved.
Edited by Nan Brooks and Daña Alder.
Certain book design by Eva Bee.
Cover illustration by Vasilis Zikos.
Cover design by Anne Marie Forrester.
Copyright © 2006 *Creatrix Vision Spun Fiction LLC.*
All rights reserved.

ISBN–10: 0-9760604-4-2
ISBN–13: 978-0-9760604-4-4

Published by
Creatrix Vision Spun Fiction LLC,

A *Creatrix Books LLC* company

P.O. Box 366
Cottage Grove, WI 53527
Printed in the USA

SHE WHO WALKS
THE
LABYRINTH

by Kassandra G. Sojourner

Acknowledgments
What a long and involved process it is to actually write a book. This one had many incarnations over many years. Several people emerged as pivotal to my creative process and I would like to take this opportunity to thank them. Jade River offered unfailing encouragement and friendship over the years. My dear first Cella advisor, Emmie Harrison, read the roughest of rough drafts and even managed to smile while offering the truth about them. Gus and Linda provided space and love. Thanks to Tess my writing partner, Sage who provided valuable input, Daña and Nan my style editors, Eva Bee who never fails me, and Anne Marie whose magickal creations take my breath away. You all have niches in my heart and my eternal gratitude.

I offer special acknowledgement and gratitude to Bev who kindly pointed out the myriad differences between herons and cranes. I send a kiss and thanks to Marina at Knossos who serenely answered question after trivial question regarding the daily life of the Minoan people. And of course, I hold eternal gratitude to Carol who (more or less) patiently listened to me complain about every step in the process. Without you, sweetie, this book would never have been completed. Finally, I would like to thank the people (especially all the grandmas) of Crete – sorry about that olive tree; we promise to try to never drive on your lovely island again.

Dedication

Kvayn –

> *To the union of Love, Life and Truth,*
> *within and between us.*
>
> *Now it's your turn.*

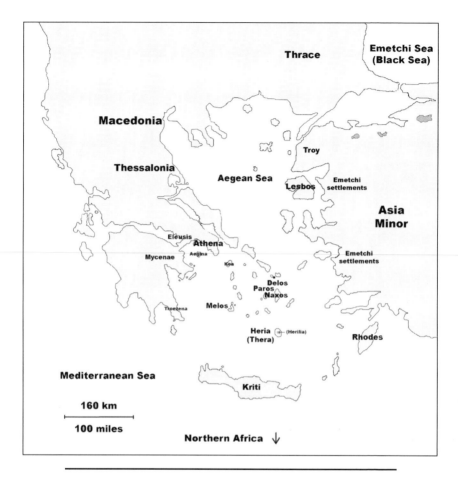

Thrace

Emetchi Sea
(Black Sea)

Macedonia

Troy

Thessalonia

Aegean Sea

Lesbos

Emetchi
settlements

Asia
Minor

Eleusis

Athena

Mycenae   Aegina

Kos

Emetchi
settlements

Delos
Paros
Naxos

Troezena   Melos

Heria
(Thera)

(Herilia)

Rhodes

Mediterranean Sea

160 km

100 miles

Northern Africa ↓

Kriti

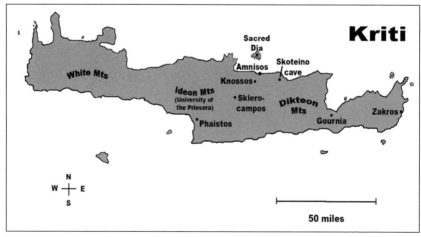

Kriti

Sacred
Dia

Amnisos

Skoteino
cave

White Mts

Knossos

Ideon Mts
(University of
the Priesera)

Sklero-
campos

Dikteon
Mts

Zakros

Phaistos

Gournia

N
W ─┼─ E
S

50 miles

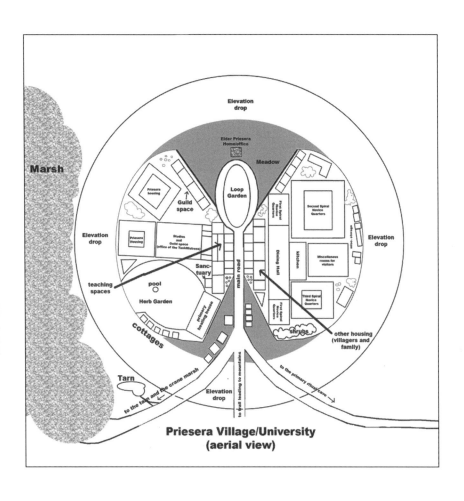

Marsh

Elevation drop

Elder Priesera Home/office

Meadow

Priesera housing

Guild space

Loop Garden

First Spiral Novice Quarters

Second Spiral Novice Quarters

Elevation drop

Priesera housing

Studios and Guild space (office of the Taskmistress)

Dining Hall

kitchen

Miscellaneous rooms for visitors

misc. storage

Elevation drop

Sanctuary

main road

teaching spaces

pool

Herb Garden

First Spiral Novice Quarters

Third Spiral Novice Quarters

primary Reading Room

cottages

shrubs

other housing (villagers and family)

Tarn

to the tarn and the crane marsh

to trail leading to mountains

Elevation drop

to the primary ritual cave

**Priesera Village/University
(aerial view)**

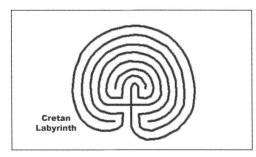

Cretan Labyrinth

SHE WHO WALKS
THE
LABYRINTH

Prologue

"I am the son of water and air!" proclaimed the slight, dark–haired boy. His patched woolen tunic was overly long, hanging below his bony knees. He waved his wooden herding staff menacingly, and it being heavy, somewhat uncontrolledly, over his head. Around him, several long–haired tan and black goats looked up and bleated appreciatively or perhaps indifferently – it was rather hard to tell. A number stared at him warily, the horizontal pupils of their eyes dull, before they resumed gnawing at the sparse hill vegetation. A couple scurried farther away, their hooves scattering some of the small squarish stones that covered the island. Theseus sat down hard on an outcropping of rock and, chin in hands, resumed his daydreaming. Told he was approximately ten turns old, Theseus looked even younger. He was skinny with delicate, almost feminine, features. His sleepy dark eyes, framed with impossibly long black lashes, looked huge in his finely boned face. His black hair was only slightly wavy, not tangly–curly like most of the other children who lived on the small fishing island of Paros.

For all Theseus knew he really was born of water and air. As a very young boy, he was found living all by himself in the dank treacherous alleyways of the mainland port city, Trozaen. The Kritin traderwoman who took pity on the filthy and starving youngster tried to find his family, but no one seemed to know where he had come from or whom his meter or uncles might be. None of the dockhands, fisherfolk and assorted transients seemed all that interested in finding out, either; "times are hard" they muttered, turning away. All Theseus remembered clearly was his name – Minos Theseus. About four or five turns old when first rescued, he said he had been surviving mostly by handouts or the occasional theft of a copper piece if he chanced upon an unwary sailor. He had been too ashamed to admit to anything else. The TradesKore, who had a toddler of her own and did not wish to bring another young child along the business routes with her, took the boy to her sisters and meter who lived in the rural hills of lonely Paros.

Though life was undeniably easier with his adoptive family – he knew he would be fed regularly anyway – young Theseus grew restless and bored with the placid life of a herder. There was a saying in the islands that once one got the sea in their blood, he would never be content in one harbor. Theseus supposed that since he had been found by the docks, it was likely that he had somehow gotten seawater in his blood. He even slashed open his forearm with a borrowed bronze dagger once, hoping to prove he indeed had sea water rather than blood in his veins, but to his disappointment, the fluid was just as red as anyone else's. When he tasted it though, he knew by the saltiness that he had been right all along – seawater!

"Some day," Theseus said aloud, "I will leave this island and travel. I will go to Sparta and Trozaen and even Athena! I will be a hero just like Heracles – no, even more famous than Heracles!" He jumped to his feet and excitedly began waving the stout wooden staff again. Several goats started and ran off. "I am a hero, goats! I am all–powerful, more than even Heracles! Do you hear me? You must bow to a hero!"

And when the closest goat stupidly refused to fall to its knees in reverence to all–powerful Theseus, the boy clubbed it hard on the head until it did.

Chapter 1

Ten turns later...

Somewhere off the Northern coast of Kriti, deep beneath the surface of the wine dark sea, the Great Bull stamped His mighty hoof. In response, She of Ten Thousand Names shuddered. A new wave was born from the womb of the ocean.

Huffing and red–faced as she trudged up the last few chiseled stone steps, Ansel bent over from her waist, hands on knees and panted aloud, glad to leave the steep rocky cliffs below her. When she caught her breath, she straightened and glanced back, shielding her eyes from the brilliant mid–morning sun. She inhaled the sea air deeply. *The ocean is the exact shade of serpent–stone this morning,* she thought. Serpent–stone was her favorite type of rock, soft green, sometimes with silvery white chips embedded in it.

From this height, the harbor town below, Amnisos, looked like a child's play village tucked cozily within the rocks where they rose above the sea. The beach glowed golden and the people bustling about on the sand below looked almost like the miniature images carved into the seal–stones her GranMeter pressed into warm, soft beeswax to stamp official scrolls.

A long line of brightly painted boats rested along the sandy stretch where they had been hauled from the water. Even more tiny vessels dotted the peaceful bay. Most were small rowboats of the fisherfolk from Amnisos, though as Ansel watched, a larger merchant ship unfurled its sail and set out for the open sea. She squinted into the sun, trying to pick out the little red skiff that held Uncle Psidoras and her cousins. They had gone out fishing at dawn.

The whipping winds were warm, but not yet the hot, dusty gusts of Metertide they would become later in the turn. Ansel tossed her head, allowing her long dark curls to blow into tangles, enjoying the air as it cooled her sweaty face. Just then, a tiny snake slithered over her open sandal. Startled, she jerked her foot back, nearly losing her balance. The snake disappeared into the greening meadow brush so swiftly that Ansel briefly wondered if she had truly seen it. She glanced around her feet. A gliding movement next to a stone, a jewel green head, and an impulsive red tongue confirmed her reflexes. *Snake omen,* she thought, *a warning to the wise. Meter will want to know. I should get home.*

She whirled away from the ocean intending to trot home, then quickly spun back, her attention riveted. Something was wrong with the bay; that was what she remembered first noticing. The waves had lost all rhythm; they slammed each other from all directions, creating white peaks like miniature mountain tops. The fishing boats rocked and slapped down hard on the ocean surface propelling eruptions of water to shoot from their sides. Some swamped, violently propelling the occupants into the sea.

Then the noise began. The earth bellowed and shook like some great, enraged animal. Ansel's legs trembled, then she lost control of them as the earth bucked and snorted and rumbled. Pitched hard to the rocky ground, she twisted her ankle sharply and her breath expelled from her lungs as an "oof". Around her, soil and stones rained down with such fury she threw her arms to her face in defense. *The Bull stamps again,* she thought. *Goddess, Meter, please make Him stop!* Ansel heard, then felt, a hollow roar as the ground near her ripped open. Another shower of stones flew at her prostrate body. Great slabs of rock crashed and bounced down the cliff face. Fearful the entire cliff side would collapse, she crawled away from the edge on bleeding knees. When she could not crawl any further, she wrapped her arms around her head, rolled into a fetal position and hummed a prayerful chant through clenched teeth. Though it seemed an eternity passed, the tremors finally eased to shudders, then ceased.

After a few moments of glorious quiet, Ansel straightened her legs from their cramped position and sat up, murmuring a prayer of thanks. Blood ran from her scraped palm where she had scrambled over jagged rock. Dazed, she sucked at the wound, a sharp metallic taste filling her mouth. Shaking the pebbles and debris from her hair and skirt, and with a rueful brush at her painfully scraped, dirty knees, Ansel tentatively stood, testing her ankle. It held, but felt oddly loose.

It is sprained, she thought, *perhaps even broken. Should I try to walk all the way home or should I go back down to Uncle Psidoras's house and ask them to help me with my ankle?*

She limped back to the cliff edge. A portion of it had indeed given way and the steps closest to the top had cracked, tumbling down the slope. Ansel watched as people gathered on the beach below. Something still felt very wrong. Even at this distance, Ansel sensed the fear of the villagers; their jerky motions, and the abruptness of their gestures bespoke panic. A woman cupped her hands and called loudly over the bay to the folk in the fishing boats, some of whom were clinging to the hulls of their overturned vessels. Ansel could not distinguish any words.

They are well in the boats. A shake is far worse for those on land. They all know how to swim; why are they so concerned?

A clump of men suddenly sprinted for the cliff path. Ansel watched from above as they shouted back to the people on the beach, then clamored for the steps as if the Bull Himself were after them.

Perhaps someone has been injured badly.

Thinking to meet them halfway, she hobbled to the cliff edge and reached a foot over, then stopped, wincing. Without the top steps, the descent would be treacherous. Many of the rocks could be loose and the earth was uneven. Besides, her ankle was already growing stiff. She flexed it tentatively, then rubbed as a jolt of pain made her catch her breath. *Ei, I am going to have to let them come to me. I hope they will help me walk home.*

A rolling sound, soft, then rapidly increasing to a roar, filled her ears. She looked out over the ocean again. At the shoreline, the shallow water rushed out exposing a long stretch of sand as a wave pitched into the bay at tremendous speed. Time slowed, and as she watched, the surge swelled to enormous heights as it gushed closer and closer to the shore. Horrified, Ansel could do no more than scream an incoherent warning, but it was drowned by the now earsplitting thunder of the approaching wall of water.

The people on the beach turned as one to face the onslaught as the swell reached its full height, many times that of the tallest man. Then, Ansel witnessed a nightmare almost beyond her comprehension; the fishing boats, some with fisherfolk still clinging to the hulls, lined across the surge crest as if gathered by an unseen hand. For an instant they balanced perilously before crashing upon the beach with the breaking of the wave.

As the wall of water slammed against the beach, some people, as if waking from a long sleep, began to run; others stood as if they had grown roots into the sand. It mattered not. Together, they bore the full wrath of the sea. Smacking the ground as a hand might an offending insect, the roiling sandy water rushed towards the little houses nestled into the cliff side, smashing them to splinters.

The surge continued to rise. The people climbing the cliff were about half way up. They had stopped to watch the wave and seemed affixed to the steps. "Climb! Climb!" Ansel shrieked. By some miracle, they heard her and looked up. "Climb! The water!"

The lead man bounded up the steps two and three at a time; others followed. In moments, the wave dashed against the rock face, shooting spray so high it soaked Ansel's skin. When it receded, the steps were empty.

My lungs do not seem to be working, she thought dully. Each tattered breath came and left in little sharp, painful gasps. Paralyzed, she stood far above the destruction, clinging to the wild hope that

Amnisos really had been a toy village; that she had not seen real people swept away in a violence of water. But her heart would not allow that phantasm to grow wings. Her legs clumsily gave way beneath her and she sat down hard, the still bleeding hand held over her mouth for a long moment. Dripping with salty water, she felt afraid to make an utterance, dared not draw attention to herself. The wind died and finally in the stillness Ansel heard a moan and knew it to be her own. From her throat ripped a keen akin to that a small animal makes when caught by a predator, a shrill of living anguish.

When she forced herself to look down again, she expected to see bodies and litter thrown upon the beach, but eerily, where the water had already receded, the sand was wiped clean as if the people and the boats had never existed. Numb, she looked outward to the sea, then passed her hand in front of her eyes in disbelief. An unbelievably huge woman, naked, her pendulous breasts swaying as she waded knee–deep through the waters of the harbor, cast out an enormous luminescent net. Ansel could see people in the net, the fisherfolk. They floated shimmering out of the water and into the woman's great web. There was no struggle, no turmoil, no sense of distress. Peace prevailed at the hands of the titanic woman. She paused and glanced up the hill toward Ansel. Terrified, Ansel threw her arm up across her face, but the woman only smiled. She locked her huge blue–green eyes with Ansel's.

"You see me, little one, but I cast not my net for your spirit. Instead, I cast to you my thoughts."

The woman's lips never moved, yet Ansel understood her perfectly, as if she had whispered intimately into Ansel's ear. She found she could not move nor break her gaze with the giantess. She swallowed convulsively in her parched throat.

"Kriti is challenged, child, and She of Ten Thousand Names weeps. The Bull, Her son, grows in strength but less so in wisdom. In these times of fate, the future is in the hands of the unexpected and the unexplainable. Tell the Sisters to study the signs as if the destiny of all Kriti depended upon them, for indeed, it does."

The woman drew up her net of souls, tossed it lightly over her broad back and vanished as suddenly as a snake in the meadow grass. Ansel found herself released. Like a frightened hare, she leapt to her feet and, heedless of her painful ankle, ran the many lengths back to her home at Knossos.

Chapter 2

Maidentide
last triad

The moon has cycled through full Meter into darkest Hag and round again to the Virgin's Bow two times since the great Bull roared. I could not stand to write of it before this. I do not even remember many of the days directly after. Meter says I am storm shocked. I told her there was no storm, only the great shake, then . . . then. . . no; I cannot write of it even yet.

My heart refuses to accept that Uncle Psidoras and his little boys and all the fisherfolk who were my friends are gone. We held a memorial rite on the beach for last cycle. Meter was not sure I should go, what with my ankle only now holding my weight again. I insisted I needed to go; how could I not? Xeronos carried me all the way down those awful steps. I hobbled back up with just a little help though.

They never found most of the bodies. I wonder if it is possible Uncle and the boys escaped somehow. Perhaps they rowed really hard and fast and made it to Dia or even Heria. Meter pats my cheek and tells me with sad eyes that this is unlikely. I know that, but maybe it is so anyway. She and GranMeter cry when they think I am not watching. I dream of Uncle and little Seus. He was only three turns old, still sometimes nursing at his meter's breast. They wave to me from the shore of Dia and I am so glad to discover they are all still alive. But I always wake.

Snakes haunt my dreams, too – wiggly green ones with jewel-bright eyes. I look through the slate pebbles under the brush and I know there is a snake there. I smell it or feel it somehow under a thorny bush with tiny leathery leaves. It will not move while I am watching. It waits for me to look away, and when I do, it slithers across my foot, quick as a just-caught scent, fleeting and elusive. I am terrified, though I have never been afraid of snakes before. I have heard that some snakes in distant lands render illness with their bite, but that is not true here on Kriti, or at least I have never known anyone to become ill.

I visited the beach with Geneera yesterday. It was the first time I went back to Amnisos, other than the memorial when many people were there. The beach is filled with splinters of boats. The homes are all shattered and ruined among the rocks. Sand and seaweed and muck are everywhere. I do not know why I remember the beach as so empty. I cried and cried. Geneera held me as I sputtered and sobbed until her shoulder was full of snot. She laughed and told me we were snot sisters. She dubbed me Priesera of snot, and she, my loyal cloth. I love her. She is my only, truest, best friend.

I finally told Meter about She-Who-Casts-the-Net. I feared telling her; I thought she might think the sea took my soul or tell me the shock made me imagine things, but she did not. She said the shock gave me "sight". She even asked me to repeat the message to the Priesera when they come for Festival. I asked her if she ever saw the Caster of Nets. She said no, but she sees some of the others. She said she would tell me about it sometime, when I am fully recovered.

But I fear I will never fully recover.

Ansel paused, absently chewing the end of her reed pen. She reached down to scratch her ankle. The shadow of a large yellow–green bruise still traveled up the outside of her calf. She picked up her pen again, but then heard footfalls.

"Ansel are you in here? Oh, there you are."

She glanced over her shoulder; Geneera leaned against the crimson painted door frame of their adjoining rooms. Her curly black ringlets were plastered against her damp olive skin.

"Writing again?" Geneera wiped her face with the back of her hand and shook her locks that were knotted carelessly atop her head.

Ansel shrugged, then, turning back to the scroll, carefully blew on the drying ink and placed her pen into its clay ink pot.

"It helps," she said quietly. Swinging her legs fully round to her friend, she forced a smile, taking in Geneera's sweaty appearance "Training again?"

"But of course."

Geneera stepped lightly into the room, graceful as a young gazelle. A single bead of sweat slid from her hairline down to her cheek, leaving a shimmering track as evidence of its passing. "The gymnasium was nearly empty. Everyone is preparing for Festival, I suppose."

She glanced at Ansel's scroll, then grinned and shook her head slightly. "Ai. Better you than me. Writing makes my head pound."

Warmth radiated from Geneera's body and Ansel thought her friend smelled faintly of the sea. Geneera shifted the sweat–soaked waistband of her brief white skirt. Bending over slightly, the lithe girl began to knead her long, upper thigh with slender fingers.

"How was your match this morning?" Ansel asked.

"I beat Carea in wrestling."

"The Bulldancer? Good for you. I wager she was roiled."

Geneera glanced up, grinning crookedly. "Not at all, actually. She does not respect anyone who cannot give her a tumble. She wants to be friends now."

"No!" Ansel's eyes widened. She smiled.

"Yes. She even invited me to meet some of the other 'dancers."

"Well, by the Goddess's teats, she is showing the other blade of the labrys." Ansel laughed clapping her hands together.

Though her eyes sparkled, Geneera bit her lips and her gaze slid down to her feet. Ansel peered at her friend more closely, then said, "There is more?"

Geneera merely shrugged; Ansel continued to probe. "Oh, give forth, Gen. You cannot keep a secret from your best friend. We have known each other too long."

Geneera remained silent staring at her sandal, then abruptly threw herself onto a cushioned bench across from Ansel and began tapping her foot furiously. "First, promise you will not tell my meter. Or yours either."

"I promise, I promise. Tell, for Rhea's sake." Ansel's voice rose.

Geneera took a deep breath, then said falteringly, "It is possible, uh, I might possibly be asked to join the Bulldancer troupe." She stopped tapping her feet and silence fell.

Ansel's smile froze upon her lips and the air between them turned thick. Geneera lifted her eyes and met Ansel's gaze. Ansel could see the muscles of her friend's square jaw flex as she clenched her teeth; her mouth was drew into a straight line.

"Ah. Wahall, that would really be an honor," Ansel said carefully. "You might possibly be asked? When will you know?"

Still holding Ansel's gaze, Geneera replied, "The truth is, I already know. I was already asked."

"And I assume you said 'Yes.'" It was not a question.

"I have not yet answered, but I want to join, yes."

Ansel's heart thudded, but she said in a steady voice, "Congratulations, then." She did not allow herself to break gaze with her friend.

Geneera's eyes grew wary. "You mean that?" Her foot resumed tapping.

"Of course. You are my friend. I know you have always dreamed of this. Just like Jerid, no? When will you move to the athlete's rooms?" Ansel forced her voice to sound cheerful.

Geneera's shoulders visibly relaxed. She closed her eyes and blew out a puff of air. When she looked at Ansel, her eyes again held a twinkle. She lunged from the chair and gave Ansel an enthusiastic and sweaty hug.

"I do not know yet. Soon, but not right away. Certainly not before Festival's end."

Ansel grabbed Geneera's hand and would not let go. "It will be lonely sleeping in these rooms without you. And to be alone in classes with your meter."

"It is hard to be in class with Meter whether or not I am there." Geneera pulled her hand away gently, then bent to kiss Ansel lightly on the cheek.

Ansel snorted overloud. "Well, true enough." Rising to her feet, Ansel turned her back to Geneera briefly both to roll up the scroll she had been writing and to hide the tears that had sprung into her eyes. When she turned toward Geneera again, she gave her friend a half–grin and said, "Your meter will fly with the Furies themselves when she finds out."

Geneera grimaced. "I know, I know," she said.

But her dark eyes danced with an inner light.

Chapter 3

"To our North, beyond steep Heria, lie the islands of the Cycliades in the center of which resides most sacred Delos. Even farther northward, we find the lands of Athena and Eleusis." said Priesera Vasilissa, sweeping her arm outward dramatically and gazing into the empty space before her as if addressing the heads of admiring multitudes instead of two rather inattentive girls. "Since the Achaean conquest, however, the world is less beautiful, less peaceful. Mycenae is a city seized in the bloody barters of war. The nations of the Aegean, over–eager to mimic the rest of the world, are in turmoil. Everywhere is conquest. She of Ten Thousand Names is displeased."

Ansel stifled a yawn, making her ears pop, and wiggled her foot in her sandal. Furtively, she glanced around. The white gypsum theater seats formed a semicircle around the sunken central stage upon which Vasilissa expounded endlessly. Though pretty, the gray–veined steps were remarkably uncomfortable on one's backside, and Vasilissa did not allow her students to bring cushions; she claimed such indulgences merely encouraged inattention and sloth. A scholar from the holy Priesera school and Elder Agronos teacher, Vasilissa rehearsed her oration for the festival debate, making it today's class for her two most advanced students, Ansel, and

Vasilissa's own daughter, Geneera. Her resonant voice boomed up from the center stage area.

Geneera, sitting well behind Ansel at the top of the theater steps, made not even a pretense of paying attention to Vasilissa. She sat with her long muscular back to both Ansel and the center stage, resting her chin on her crossed arms. She looked down over the edge of the west wall, scuffing her leather sandal as she kicked. Ansel could not see what her friend gazed at, but the lanky girl was clearly absorbed in something she considered more interesting than her meter.

Vasilissa, her eyes distant and her voice booming, would be droning on for a while yet. Sighing softly, Ansel resumed wiggling her toes as she lightly bounced her leg on her knee. She propped her chin on her hand and cast her thoughts adrift. Soon, the voice of her teacher merged with background sounds, of no more import than the buzz of a nearby fly. *It is hot sitting here on these wretched stone seats. And it is only just past mid–day,* Ansel thought grumpily. *There is not even a little maiden breeze blowing today. The sun is absolutely white.*

Across the theater to the east, Ansel's ears picked up a dusty whirl of voices rising up from the courtyard. Classes were usually held in that courtyard, in the shade of an elderly gnarled myrtle tree, but today they were moved to the theater area so the servants could set up for the opening feast that night. *Xeronos will have to wear those bull horns he hates so.* Ansel stifled a giggle. *He says "They look ridiculous and make my neck stiff for the entire Festival!" And me and Gen will see him having to eat with those stupid horns on, too, since we get to go the opening feast for the first time.* Ansel stuck her fingertip in her mouth and began chewing a nail. *And the Kore ritual. We have the Kore ritual this time. I hope I do not trip or say something really stupid. The Priesera are so solemn and scary. It is not until the end of the Festival though.*

"Ansel."

Jolted from her private musings, Ansel started and found herself looking directly into the stern face of Priesera Vasilissa, who had not only finished speaking but was now standing over her student and scowling darkly.

"Ansel, you have become senseless as a donkey with its head caught in a retsina jug. Did you even hear what I asked you?" Lowering her eyes, Ansel whispered, "No, Priesera. My apologies." Her throat closed on her.

Vasilissa grunted with a sound like "harmph."

Louder, she continued, "Perhaps, then, my daughter can answer the simple question I posed." Priesera Vasilissa pursed her lips and raised her eyebrows as if to imply she doubted her daughter capable of dressing herself. But no response came from Geneera. A stolen glimpse over her shoulder told Ansel her friend was still peering over the side of the wall, quite oblivious to her meter. Ansel winced and tried to silently warn Geneera with her thoughts.

Priesera Vasilissa quietly climbed the steps to Geneera. When she neared her daughter, she said simply, but with painstaking enunciation, "Geneera."

The girl visibly stiffened. With a deliberation matching her meter's, she turned to face Priesera Vasilissa. Ansel found herself holding her breath. *I hate it when they fight. What is Gen thinking? She is not usually this disrespectful during class.*

"How do you expect to become a teacher when you pay so little attention in class? Did you even hear one word I said throughout my speech?" Vasilissa's voice intimated a careful and infinite patience, yet Ansel knew her glittering dark eyes could cut more deeply than knapped flint.

Geneera's face was as if carved of stone. She murmured something Ansel could not hear, but whatever it was enraged Vasilissa. The woman whirled abruptly from her daughter, her face contorted as a gorgon's and said tightly, "I will not permit your insolence to upset me before the debate tomorrow. Class is over until the end of Festival." Drawing her light cloak carefully about her shoulders, Vasilissa marched down the steps and exited through the back of the theatre.

Not sure whether to be relieved or frightened by Vasilissa's abrupt exit, Ansel rose tentatively to her feet. Gen had resumed gazing over the side of the wall. Only the staccato scuffing of her sandal revealed any tension. Silent and catlike, Ansel approached her friend from behind, cautious of Gen's strange, fey mood.

Her back still to Ansel, Geneera motioned with her square chin to what held her interest on the other side of the wall, inviting Ansel to peer with her. On the field below, young women and men dressed in short tunics stretched, jogged or waited in line to vault over a stuffed bag of some kind. Ansel realized these were the Bulldancers, practicing for their Festival exhibition. No wonder Gen was fascinated.

The voices of the athletes drifted to her ears. They called out good naturedly to each other, encouraging and cheering as each in turn performed hand springs over the "bull" bag with calls of, "Good . . . Melanie," and, "You almost made . . . twist, Deena, do not . . . discouraged!"

Ansel stayed silent, waiting, not quite knowing what to say, while Geneera occasionally grunted and generally acted oblivious to Ansel's presence. Finally, Gen said, "They will take a break any moment while the handlers bring the bull. I wish I could speak to the trainer. I have decided I am ready to join the team."

"We could go down there if you like. Class is over anyway."

Geneera turned to Ansel with something that might have been surprise, or mayhaps cautious gratitude in her eyes. "Thanks, I would like that. We better hurry, though. The break will be a short one."

Gen's calculations proved correct. Shortly after the girls arrived, the trainer called for the athletes to take a brief break. Two of them, a compactly built girl and a tall, slender young man, waved and jogged over to Ansel and Geneera. With his twinkling dark eyes and cleft chin, the boy was beautiful. His short curly black hair had coalesced into sweaty ringlets at his brow, and his sleek, muscular torso gleamed with perspiration. But something about the girl made Ansel want to take a step backward. Short, yet powerfully muscled, she stood with her legs and feet seemingly planted into the very soil. Her glassy eyes did not reflect the smile on her lips.

"Carea," Gen smiled at the young woman, "and Garin, greetings."

"Greetings Gen; no class today?" Garin offered a brief hug that Geneera returned.

Pulling back, Geneera's face puckered as if she had been offered a citron. "We were given reprieve." She replied crisply. "Here, this is my friend, Ansel. And Ansel, here is Carea, the girl I told you about from the gymnasia, and Garin who is also a fine dancer."

"For a boy, anyway," Carea said with a tight grin.

Odd, her eyes do not smile though her lips do. Ansel thought.

"Greetings," Ansel said. "We saw you practicing from the theater. The exhibition comes soon, no?" Not wishing to invite a hug from either dancer, Ansel crossed her arms in front of her chest.

Garin smiled broadly, flashing strong teeth. "Ansel, grandaughter of Council Elder Thesmas, I know who you are, certainly." He bowed to her with a graceful flourish.

Ansel nodded politely, but felt even more shy than usual. Carea said nothing, just stood staring, her expression inscrutable. Ansel looked at her own feet then kicked at tuft of grass with her sandal.

"We were here practicing nearly every morn for the last several moons," Garin continued. "And now for the last third, we practice both morn and noon."

Looking up, Ansel found Garin was staring at her unabashedly and grinning. His gaze made her feel very self–conscious; her skin grew warm. *Of course you know my Gran. You likely know my Meter, too. The way you are staring, you probably wonder how I could even be related to someone as beautiful as Meta. I wonder if I combed my hair this morning. And was I getting a blemish on my chin? Oh, Goddess, his lips are still moving and I have not been listening. Did he just ask me something?*

"My apologies, what did you just say?" she asked, trying to shake the fog from her brain.

What ever is wrong with me? She glanced toward Geneera, but she and Carea were walking away toward the practice field, arms entwined as if they were the dearest of friends. Ansel gulped as some unidentifiable, painful feeling jabbed in her gut. She stared at their receding backs.

"I asked, 'will you be at the feast tonight?'" Garin repeated, reaching out to touch Ansel's arm.

He stood closer than she realized and she had to check herself as she almost leaped backward. She felt confused; his touch did not feel entirely unpleasant, but she did not trust him.

"Uh, yes, yes, I will. You?" *Geneera just disappeared, leaving me alone with this boy. Why did she do that? I only came out here for her sake. She knows I am not good with strangers.* Ansel swallowed the panic that was threatening to overcome her. Her armpits felt damp.

"Yes. Perhaps I will see you there." Noise erupted behind them. They turned to see the rest of the troupe waving and hooting. "I must return to practice. I will see you tonight then."

Turning, he jogged back to the field while Ansel exhaled in relief. Once, he looked back and waved, grinning broadly when he saw she still watched him. Reflexively, she raised her hand in a feeble wave.

Chapter 4

Late Maidentide is a particularly sweet time to live on the blessed isle of Kriti. With the lingering rains of Cronetide well over, the air feels cool and soft, yet the sun blazes not so intently as it will come Metertide. The ceremony of the Kore that turn was even more special because it fell during a Seven–Turns Festival. Every seven turns, the festival in Knossos became the most important gathering site across the entire island. Boats large and small crowded the beach at the small harbor just west of Amnisos. Any other turn, Amnisos would have been the docking place of choice, but it was not considered wise to spit in the face of the Fates.

Relatives not kissed for many turns embraced, while news was announced in full–bodied voices accompanied by excited arm gestures. Babes were fussed over and children soon tired of the exclaimations, "How tall!" "How beautiful!" Of course, as is true in the lives of humans, the specter of grief was also present. "La, la," clicked many a tongue. "He was too young, she was so beloved; I am sorrowed." Yet, all knew that Great Meter clasped the dead to Her generous breast and were comforted.

At the Seven–Turns Fest, the Priesera gathered from all across the island. They traveled from the University plain in the Ideon Mountains south of Knossos, from far Phaistos on the southern coast, fair Zakros of the east. From the caves came the seers, the strange ones with their wild eyes and loud ululations. Always they appeared old but perhaps this was illusion only, for the seers were touched sometimes even at an early age and marked especially for seeing visions from the Under and the In.

The traders, too, came from places far away to sell at the grand marketplace at Knossos center, also called the Agronos. They sailed from noble Libya and from Egypt, land of the cat peoples, hard Asia Minor, beautiful Athena, sometimes from even further, as the threads of the Fates guided. They offered for trade polished gems and rich gold, cloth of silk in rainbow colors, spices, sweets with exotic ingredients, fragrant perfumes – all manner of luxuries not often encountered in daily Kritin life.

And of course, with them they brought, (and often for free), tales of the wider world. New rulers reigned in Egypt; coarse shepherd kings. "Not good, not good," murmured the Egyptian papyrus seller. Though he spoke the Kritin language, his accent cast odd to the local ear. He waved his hands in a gesture of rejection, palms out, and would not say more of the southern nation from which he hailed. Others told of larger and larger groups of women warriors from the east gathering together. Fair of face they were, yet fierce in demeanor. They labored along side the traders, but kept their own council. Some came to the festival to trade in hides, cloth and pretty stones. They smelled strongly of horse – animals rare but not unheard of upon the Kritin homeland.

Whispers came too from Athena, northern neighbor and sometimes friend of the Kritin people. The latest Queen, (called a Helen), rarely appeared to the public, took only her own counsel and meditated deeply – and now the gossiper invariably lowered his or her voice even further – perhaps too deeply, with the Goddess of Poppies. The Poppy Goddess was a dangerous one to claim as personal deity. The soul could be lost within Her sweet embrace. Yet the faces of the traders broke into genuine smiles at the mention of the new Royal Consort to Helen Demetria, young Theseus. "Brave he is," they said, "a defender of Athena, one of Her own, truly." Against what he defended, no one needs remark.

Everyone knew of the danger, the shadow lurking on the outskirts of the land of the People: wandering bands of marauders. Some consisted of just a few strangers, large and strangely fair skinned. Others were a horde, nearly an army. They were rich with horses and wore thick leather as clothing and hard helmets upon their pale heads. Their weapons shattered bronze. It was a matter of grave concern. The GranMeters shook their heads sadly. The safety of the land was threatened.

"Close your eyes and lean forward."

Phoebe compliantly offered her face and the gooey whitish cream was slathered over it in brisk circular motions. It smelled minty and felt cool against her damp, warm skin.

"What is in this concoction, anyway?" Rheana asked as she dunked her hands in the warm bath water to wash off the cream. Fluffy white islands of glop floated off her immersed fingers. They lazily drifted away from the women who were seated facing each other in a large sunken bath. It occupied almost the entire whitestone paneled room and most of a morning was spent filling it, even with Kriti's famed indoor plumbing. It was a testament to Phoebe's importance that she and her apprentice could have the bath to themselves.

Phoebe leaned back carefully against the side of the pool where she was submerged shoulder deep. The whitestone lined tub wall felt cool and slick against her skin, and when she moved, the fragrance of jasmine wafted to her nostrils from the scented water. She inhaled deeply before answering.

"Oh, I do not know really, some medicinals, cream, honey, perhaps something to soften skin, I suppose."

"And here I thought my esteemed teacher knew everything." Water splashed hollowly as Rheana began to wring the creamy stuff from her hands.

Phoebe shrugged slightly. "Sorry. An herbalist I never was." A blob of the sticky mixture slid to her upper lip, and she licked at it tentatively. "At least this one tastes good. How long do I have to keep it on?"

"One–third hour."

"Ugh. Ah well, it is worth it. The sun does terrible things to your skin as you age. Of course, you need not worry about this yet, Rheana. You are not much older than my Ansel."

"I am five turns past Kore, Mistress."

"Young, indeed. Tell me, Rheana, did you always know you wished to be an Escort?"

"Yes, from the time I was a little maid."

"I did not. When I was young like you and Ansel, I wanted to be noticed by the boys and have pretty clothes and be well liked. I could not wait to be declared Kore and wear fancy dresses and be admired. I did not hear the call of Her until later."

"And now, Mistress, you are the Elder Escort of Knossos."

"Yes. Ironic, no? Although in my work I use many of the talents I developed before ever entering the, mmm, the Escort school. Only now I use them with knowledge and intention." Phoebe sighed, wrinkling her nose, staunchly resisting the urge to rub where the cream was drying.

"Do you know what my daughter Ansel calls my bath preparations?", she continued, 'Fish entrails; a waste of time and complete nonsense'. She is so very serious all the time, especially for a young girl. We are like mountains verses the sea: far, far apart."

"Ah, but Mistress, I hear that in the East, the mountains meet the sea. Someday she will understand."

"Perhaps. I am concerned for her, Rheana. Since the wave destroyed Amnisos, she does little each day but sit in her apartment and write. She grieves as much for my brother as I. She is one to keep her pain to herself. I tried to speak with her about it once or twice, but she is not open with me. She is of that age, you see, where I am regarded more with suspicion than with trust." Phoebe gave in and lightly scratched her nose with a long fingernail. She inspected the finger for a moment then plunged her hand under water. "To be honest, I have worried about Ansel since before all this happened.

She is alone too much. I made sure she had friends around the Center when she was a little girl, but in the last several turns she has not bothered. Do you know, sometimes she sneaks out of the Agronos late at night all alone and just walks? I thought perhaps she was taken with a young man or girl, but no, she stays all alone."

"You follow her?"

"Ah, Rheana, very little happens here that I am not made aware of sooner or later, especially as concerns my daughter. I let her go and keep her secrets. Goddess will watch over her."

Rheana nodded. "Does she have any friends at all?"

"Only little Geneera. You know, Priesera Vasilissa's youngest?"

"The athletic one, yes, I have seen her at the Gymnasia."

Phoebe leaned forward stretching the back of her legs momentarily then opened her eyes. The steam from the pool caused the plaster walls of the bathing chamber to drip with sweat. She stared thoughtfully at a painting on the far wall; carefree dolphins leapt through azure water, sea birds graced the air above them.

"Now that I think of it, Ansel reminds me of Xeronos."

"The Consort."

"Yes. He is a quiet, pondering soul, a man of solitude."

"Then she will turn out well, no? Consort Xeronos is both wise and honorable."

"Yes, I suppose I should not worry so." The mural was so incredibly blue; blue of sky, blue of water, and searing blue–white where the sun reflected. Her nose itched again. "Is it time for me to wash this *gadesh* off my face?"

"A thousand pardons, Priesera." Rheana waved her hand from forehead to heart in a circular motion, flicking water at Phoebe with her splayed fingers. "Yes, you can wash it off now."

Phoebe stuck out her tongue at her giggling student. "If you decide you do not want to be an Escort, Rheana, consider an occupation in driving goats." She dunked her face in the clear water then scrubbed at the congealed stuff with a square of linen. When finished, she said more seriously, "I do thank you for listening to my concerns, Rheana. But I must admonish you; even in private, even in jest, we must never call each other 'Priesera' here in the Agronos. It is too easy for it to slip out in public. People do not like to be reminded of who the Escorts really are. Besides, it serves our purposes."

Rheana nodded, suddenly serious. "Yes, Mistress, I understand. My apologies."

Rheana climbed out of the bathing pool. Dripping, she half walked, half slid on the tiles made slick with moisture to a pedestal in the corner of the room. She wrapped herself in a thick woven towel taken from the top of a stack, then offered some to Phoebe who also pulled herself from the water. Cotton was an expensive import from the south, but it was well worth it. Shaking a towel loose from its folds, Phoebe rubbed her wet hair to dampness. She twisted a second towel around her waist and padded carefully out of the humid bath chamber into the adjacent dressing room. She heard Rheana's footsteps echoing behind.

The small room felt pleasantly cool after the steamy bath. The wall murals of leaping dolphins were replaced with numerous sketches of the double–bladed ax, the holy labrys. Phoebe picked up an ornately carved ivory comb from the dressing table and handed it to Rheana with an audible sigh as she sat on a cushioned stool.

Rheana began to pick through Phoebe's hair with the comb. Phoebe winced as she struck upon a tangle. "Ai. Why does my hair turn into mattes of krikri fur whenever I bathe?"

"Madam, you have the hair of the ocean people – locks of seaweed."

"But luckily I have you to work your magic with it."

Rheana circled in front of Phoebe and dropped in an overly elaborate curtsy. "At your service, Mistress."

"Seriously, though, I am scheduled to meet the retinue from Athena directly after *eresti*. Their boat has already docked and they are being escorted here late this morn. As it cycles, I am to have an assignment for the Festival after all."

"Oh, I am sorry. I know you hoped to be free this Festival. Will you still be able to attend Ansel's Kore ritual?"

"Yes. I hope to slip away for that, though if absolutely necessary, I will ask Xeronos to go in my stead. This assignment came up rather suddenly, and the Council specifically requested I attend to it."

"It must be something important, then."

"Very possibly. We thought Helen Demetria of Athena was coming alone, but fate wove otherwise, and her Consort is accompanying her. I am to be his Escort."

"He will not spend his time with the Helen?"

"Hardly. It seems Helen Demetria and her new Consort do not care for one another's company. In fact, they are rumored to loathe one another."

"How interesting. I thought as Helen, she could choose as she liked. Can she not rid herself of him?"

"Apparently she would find herself facing turbulent winds with her people. The Consort, Theseus, is reputedly well–loved by the people of Athena. Demetria, alas, is not."

"So I have heard. At school, I once heard her called the sea prickle of Athena; ugly, slow and dangerous to come upon unguarded."

Phoebe felt her intended grin turn to a grimace. "Yes, I have heard that one, too. She is a worshipper of the Goddess of Poppies. The Houri of the Temple of Athena say she becomes ever more devoted to the *mekoi*, the essence of poppy, and ever less to her people."

"And there is nothing the Athenians can do since she is a hereditary monarch. How sad for them. Kriti is twice blessed for the Council." Rheana shook her head and clicked her tongue. "But what is so important about this Consort that the Council assigns you to escort him instead of an apprentice?"

"There are some on the Council who wonder if mayhap this Consort is a threat to us. I am to determine if there is any truth to this."

"A threat to us? How so?"

"He is a Warrior Consort and an unknown entity. It has happened before in lands not far from here where a warrior fights his way into power, then finds the life of a Consort exceedingly dull. Bored warmongers are dangerous folk."

"I can well imagine."

"As head of the Athenian army, Consort Theseus has already forcibly annexed all of the small towns and villages around Athena. The people of Athena love him for it, and why not? They get more resources. He brings glory to Athena. Bah!"

Rheana, finished with combing out Phoebe's heavy locks, opened a carved wooden box began sorting through the hair baubles and ornate pins it contained.

"Hmmm. He is undoubtedly a change for the better as far as the Athenians are concerned."

"He likely has some personal charm as well. They call him a 'hero'. Demetria was never a strong monarch and her power wanes the more she gives herself to her obsession. She is not being watchful of the actions of this Consort. Perhaps she underestimates him. If he grows more restless and more bold, who knows where his roaming eye will turn next?"

"And now they both come to Kriti for the Festival. Do we know why?"

"Demetria, yes. Her favorite trader is a renowned supplier of *mekoi* products. He is from Egypt and visits our area infrequently, but he will be present at the marketplace. She matronizes him whenever she can. As for why Theseus has chosen to accompany her, we do not know. Perhaps he just wishes for relief from his boredom. But it is a five–day sail from Athena to Kriti. Is his boredom so great that he would choose to sail with Demetria for so long? I should think even the largest craft would force them to be closer than either desires."

"If anyone can uncover the truth it is you, Mistress."

Phoebe half smiled as Rheana finished elaborately adorning her still–damp hair with strings of tiny white beads and spiral shells. "So the Council thinks." Phoebe scrutinized her reflection in a mirror of highly polished silver. "You have done lovely work, Rheana. I thank you also for your ear and your confidence. I may need your assistance again this evening after the feast."

"Of course, Mistress Phoebe." The young woman bowed her

head respectfully and left the bathing room while Phoebe picked up a charcoal stick and began outlining her eyes.

Chapter 5

Phoebe slipped silently into the waiting chamber via a little–used side entrance and slid into the long shadow of a huge cypress pillar, her Radiance wrapped tightly about her like a dark cloak; she did not want to be noticed just yet. On the other side of the room, his back to the pillar, stood a young man Phoebe assumed must be Theseus. He stood slumped with his hands thrust on his hips, seemingly absorbed by a gaily painted fresco featuring a line of ritually bare–breasted Priesera carrying amphorae of sweet oil to the bath.

Opening her *saria* vision, Phoebe observed Theseus. With enhanced awareness, she watched his Radiance grow bright and balloon outward from his back. *He is wary, this one.* She thought. *I will have to make my observations quickly. Already he intuits he is being watched.*

Theseus whirled around sharply on the balls of his feet, soundlessly, cat–like. Even from across the room Phoebe could see his muscles tense, ready to face the danger his senses told him lurked somewhere in the room. She held her breath. *He can not possibly see me,* she reassured herself. *Truly, what instincts this man has! Or boy, really. He is very young.*

Theseus jutted his head forward, straining to pierce the darkness of the room opposite himself where Phoebe was secreted. *A comely lad too,* she thought, intentionally relaxing into a posture she could hold absolutely immobile for hours if needs be. *I should have expected that, I suppose. It explains in part why he is so embraced by the people of Athena.*

Voices: a throaty chuckle, followed by a rumbling baritone. Arm in arm, First Elder Thesmas and Helen Demetria, hereditary monarch of Athena, walked through the main entrance across the room from Phoebe's hiding place, followed closely by the possessor of the baritone voice, the Consort Xeronos. Theseus turned to them and Phoebe began breathing normally. *That was too close,* she thought. *The boy is gifted with considerable latent talents.*

"Royal Consort Theseus of Athena, greetings to you," Xeronos said, inclining his head in the customary gesture of welcome. "I am the Consort of Kriti, Xeronos, and here is the First Elder, head of our Council of Elders, Thesmas."

"Greetings, First Elder Thesmas, Helen Demetria, Consort Xeronos," the lad replied in stilted Kritin. "I was admiring the beautiful paintings in this room. The colors are quite remarkable."

Phoebe was less interested in the conversation than the dynamics between the speakers. Her expertise was to gather information not spoken aloud; the secret motivations, alliances, dalliances, internal conflicts and hostilities that sit in the shadows of the consciousness, just as she sat in the shadows of the room. At this type of work, she was the best on Kriti.

Her special vision, the *saria,* wide open, Phoebe watched as delicate clouds of yellow and pink arose from Xeronos' head. *He must have steered the conversation to the architecture of the Agronos again; it is his favorite topic.* She smiled and allowed her eyes to linger on Xeronos, observing his familiar, lean frame as he grasped the much more petite Theseus' arm. He exuded warmth and kindliness. *Xero has come so far from the awkward boy he used to be,* she thought. But something about Theseus's Radiance disturbed Phoebe. It appeared to her strangely restricted and the colors were muted, even murky. When she reduced her vision to the normal range, it seemed Theseus was perfectly attentive and genuinely absorbed by the conversation he was engaged in with Xeronos. The *saria* told her somewhat differently, but she found herself reluctant to interpret what she was seeing.

One thing was certain; Demetria and Theseus genuinely hated each other. Even while pointedly ignoring his presence in the room, Demetria's Radiance turned prickly and flushed a deep angry red/orange when Theseus stood in her vicinity, and the feeling was clearly mutual. Demetria's Radiance appeared muddy. Looking more deeply, Phoebe perceived a tear in her essence about her middle torso. *The Helen is not well,* she thought. *She also desires the poppy,* she added when she saw the weak pulse of the Queen's Radiance. *She undoubtedly will excuse herself soon. I must make my entrance immediately.*

Noiselessly, she slipped from her shadowed perch and glided to the nearest entranceway. After first checking that her robes fell gracefully, she let loose her Radiance with a characteristic flourish, causing all heads to turn in her direction. It was gratifying to see their response to her hours of beautification. Xeronos smiled slightly, catching her eye and winking. *Thank Goddess he is not the jealous type,* Phoebe thought. Theseus stared unblinkingly, his jaw slack. She did not need *saria* to know he found her captivating.

"Greetings, First Elder Thesmas and Consort Xeronos. I was told you were here entertaining our guests from Athena and I thought to join you." Daintily she nodded first to Demetria, then to Theseus. In fluent Greek she said, "I am Phoebe, daughter of First Elder Thesmas. Welcome to Kriti, Helen Demetria and Royal Consort Theseus."

Demetria spoke first. "Oh yes, Phoebe," she said, "I know exactly who you are." The older woman cocked her head as if sizing up a worthy opponent and gave just a hint of crooked smile. *Sly but approving,* Phoebe surmised. She glanced briefly at Thesmas and the First Elder shrugged almost imperceptibly.

Demetria knows who and what I am, but she hates Theseus enough not to warn him. Ah well, the Escorts are an open secret anyway. All the better to have her as an ally. Phoebe met her eyes with a conspiratorial smile and said, "Yes, I expect you would, Helen Demetria."

Phoebe turned her smile towards young Theseus. She said warmly and with just a hint of tones in the seductive range, "I have been asked by the Elder Council to escort the Royal Consort of Athena during the Festival. I am told I am amusing company. Would that please you?"

Theseus bowed a bit stiffly. "It would be an honor, Mistress."

Expanding her *saria* slightly, she deliberately locked eyes with him. It took all of her training not to gasp aloud. *His eyes are made of stone!* She blinked, retracting her expanded awareness, then met his gaze again. *No, now they look quite normal, even softer than most.*

Her curiosity aroused, Phoebe smiled sweetly at Theseus, flashing her white teeth. He met the smile and Phoebe skillfully extended an energy tendril toward him. It reached its mark in the middle of his abdomen. She was rewarded when his face turned bright red. *Connection. Good.*

Offering her arm, she said, "Come, let me show you around our Agronos, Royal Consort Theseus. I am sure Xeronos has been telling you about our water system and light works. Let me show you these wonders and then it will be time for the opening feast."

"Yes, go, Theseus," Demetria encouraged. "I wish to tend to some business before the feast, and the First Elder and her Consort need to prepare also."

She is pretending to be sweet, the sly old cow, all the while salivating to get back to her poppy pipe, Phoebe thought. By the time they all left the room, Theseus by Phoebe's side, everyone was smiling. Their reasons, she supposed, were all of different origins.

Chapter 6

Ansel poked aside the thin goat hide shading the window of her suite and peered down at the meadow adjacent the Center. That afternoon, Knossos had ignited into a frenzy of festivity. Cloth banners tied to balcony railings snapped in the gusty breeze, the brilliant blues, greens, reds and yellows exciting the spirit as much as the eye. Everywhere people blazed about dressed in their brightest garb, for the Kritins loved color. Ansel recognized clan and guild attire from Gournia, Mallia, Zakros and even Phaistos, across the southern mountains. Revelers from prosperous Heria and the other Cycliades islands to the north had sailed in and she heard tell there were visitors from as far away as Egypt, Asia Minor, Libya and Athena, all many days' sail away. Voices crackled in the air, rising and falling as the afternoon turned toward evening.

Gaudy trading tents spotted the flat, rocky meadow bowl next to the Agronos; within, the traders undoubtedly were setting out all manner of wonderful and unusual items to touch and taste, smell or wear. Ansel bounced on her toes with anticipation. Meter gave her several silver rings to purchase a special Kore gift for herself. She could hardly wait to trade them for something extraordinary.

A gong clanged; the warning chime for the opening feast! This was an exclusive event, attended by the elite of Agronos Knossos and their families and friends. For the rest of the populace, the Festival would begin in the morn, though of course traders could often be enticed to give a preview of their wares even into the late evening of the night before if one proffered suitable reward. This was the first time Ansel and Geneera were old enough to attend the feast, as both girls had bled their first bloods since the last Seven–Turns Fest.

After the Bulldancers completed their practice, Gen had returned to the apartment she and Ansel shared. Gen was only recently back in the good graces of her friend, for Ansel had felt hurt at being left alone on the practice field.

"You just disappeared with Carea," Ansel had said, "holding her arm like she was your long–lost sister. Only a few days past, you despised the girl!"

"I am truly sorry, Ansel. I did not think of anything except speaking with the coach. Carea wanted to be there with me when I accepted the position." Gen's voice held a trace of bewilderment at Ansel's distress, and soon Ansel herself had wondered why she was so upset. It was not as if she did not know how to get back to the apartment without Gen.

She shrugged. "Let us forget it then, Gen. I was only, well, uncomfortable and to be honest, I do not truly know why," Ansel conceded.

Ansel and Geneera entered the central courtyard for the feast with their arms entwined. The courtyard was a rectangle many foot–lengths long, the floor inlaid with white slabs of veined gypsum tile and other pretty stone outlined with a vermillion grout which gave the overall effect of an intricate mosaic.

The courtyard perimeter was decorated with huge, gaily, painted ceramic pots filled with fragrant flowers. Small fruiting trees – olive, pomegranate, citron, fig and even a date palm imported from Egypt – were planted strategically to provide shade but not be in the way of dancing or Bulldancer exhibitions. The largest tree, a gnarled myrtle, was in the center of the courtyard and offered canopy even on the hottest afternoons. Though normally there were stone benches beneath the myrtle for sitting and enjoying the delicious cool of the shade, tonight a huge, long wooden table and many individual chairs replaced the benches. Each chair was ornately carved and held a soft cushion. The fragrances of jasmine and honeysuckle interwove with delicious food smells. Ansel's mouth watered.

The gong clanged a second time, signaling the beginning of the feast, and the guests who had been talking in groups began taking their seats. Ansel and Geneera were led to a smaller round table placed next to the long rectangular one where, it seemed, the rest of the guests were being escorted. "This is the table reserved for young people. You will have much more fun here, Mistress Ansel," the servant explained when Ansel began to protest. Geneera nudged her and pointed. "Look, the Bulldancers!"

In the far corner of the courtyard, the entire Bulldancer troupe lined up. They were being ushered to the same table as the girls. Satisfied, Ansel and Gen took their seats beside one another. A blur out of the corner of her eye told Ansel that the chair on her other side was abruptly occupied. She turned and saw Garin sitting next to her with a broad grin on his face.

"Greetings, Ansel. What great chance that I am seated next to you."

"Chance!" laughed a small, swarthy boy seating himself across the table. "You dove for that seat and we all saw you!" Garin's face turned red and he shrugged his broad shoulders sheepishly. "I knew I had better move quickly. Luckily, I am an athlete."

"Ho ha, that is a matter of opinion," retorted the other boy with a grin playing across his face.

Ansel smiled, then glanced toward the other table to see her meter being seated just a few chairs away from Vasilissa, toward the head of the table. Phoebe looked particularly beautiful tonight with her black hair pinned up into tight curls and her lips rouged the vivid red of pomegranate seeds. Her gown was a vibrant red and the neckline emphasized the deep cleavage between her full breasts.

To Phoebe's right sat a young man who looked as if he belonged at the young person's table with her and Gen. He was good looking in a girlish way. His sleepy eyes rested upon Phoebe's manicured hand as if he might offer to worship it at any moment. *Meta has worked her magic on him,* she thought, shaking her head slightly. *I wonder if he has any idea how foolish he looks to anyone who knows meta's skills?* Phoebe caught her eye and winked; Ansel could not help but grin and shrug her shoulders. The young man looked at her, too, but did not smile. His large, solemn eyes looked like he had a foot in the Underworld; positively haunted. *What a strange boy. I wonder who he is.*

"Ansel, are you lost at sea?" Garin touched her arm jarring her out of her musings.

"Uh, no, no, just watching people. This is the first opening feast I have been allowed to attend and I want to see who is here tonight. I recognize the Priesera from their open robes and hats, of course, and I recognize the faces of some of the administrators of Agronos Knossos, but there are so many people here I do not know."

"Oh, many are officials from the other Agronos. I hear they came especially for the all–citizenry meeting. I was talking to some folks from Delos earlier who came by to watch us practice after you left. Hoy, is it not wonderful about Geneera joining the troupe?"

"Ai, wonderful," she said, trying to mask the sour edge that threatened to creep into her voice. She looked tentatively over her shoulder, but Gen's back was turned to her and she was nattering animatedly with a whole group of 'dancers. Lowering her voice and leaning in closer to Garin so as not to be overheard, Ansel whispered, "Her meter will be angrier than a swarm of bees. Priesera Vasilissa never forgave the Bulldancer coach after Jerid died a few turns back. Jerid was Gen's brother, you know."

"Was he?" Garin matched her whisper. "I did not know. I was not a member of the troupe then, but I heard about it, of course." He paused, his face growing thoughtful. "They say it was not anyone's fault. The bull just went mad, and Jerid was gored. That happens sometimes. I mean, we raise them by hand from the time they are little calves, but they are still unpredictable."

"Neither Gen nor her meter ever really recovered. Jerid was Gen's only sibling. She loved him wildly."

"I can understand why her meter would not care for Gen joining us, though it is such an honor. I never heard of two members of the same family accepted into the troupe before."

A large triton shell was blown, its soft, clear tone echoing through the courtyard, and all of the guests were beckoned to rise. Straining to see through the throng, Ansel caught sight of First Elder Thesmas and her consort, Xeronos, parading into the courtyard from the entrance by the domestic apartments, followed by several other members of the Council of Elders.

Geneera, who had stopped talking at the sound of the triton, poked Ansel and nodded toward Xeronos. He was wearing huge, ceremonial bull horns; the symbol of the Consort. *Actually,* Ansel thought, *he looks pretty good in them.* She glanced toward Phoebe, whose eyes followed Xeronos. The strange boy next to Meter watched him too, his jaw moving as if he chewed something over.

With dignity, the council members took their places behind vacant chairs near the head of the long table. Thesmas stood at the head with Xeronos to her right. She nodded and everyone sat.

Thesmas raised an ornate earthenware chalice filled with wine and gestured to the rest of the people seated. "Honored guests," she began, "the Consort and I welcome you to the opening of this turn's Festival." She paused while the crowd applauded. The young Bulldancers cheered and whistled.

"Thank you," she continued. "This being a Seven–Turns Fest, Knossos is honored with the presence of many distinguished guests. I would especially like to introduce our visitors from Athena. Helen Demetria . . ." Thesmas gestured toward a robed and heavily jeweled woman seated in a place of honor next to the Elder Council. The Athenian queen's face was carefully made–up, but her neck was a swath of wrinkles bespeaking advanced years. She did not stand, instead bestowing a grimace that she may have meant as a smile and a wave of her hand.

". . . and her Royal Consort, Theseus." Thesmas indicated someone toward the middle of the table. *Why,* Ansel thought when he half–heartedly stood, *it is the young man who sits next to Meta. But he seems so young to be Consort. Surely he cannot be a member of the Athenian Council. Oh, but Athena does not have a Council like we do, does it?* She struggled to remember the governmental structure of Athena that Vasilissa taught several turns back. *So, then, he advises Helen Demetria? I wonder. Perhaps he functions only as companion?*

All of the young people at Ansel's table except Gen and herself suddenly stood as a group and waved while the adults applauded loudly. Ansel heard Thesmas say, "Be sure to see the Bulldancer exhibition this Fest. Then, at Festival's closing, upon the eve of Koretide, we celebrate the Kore, the ritual of blossoming womanhood, in which, I am proud to say, my very own grandaughter, Ansel, Phoebe's daughter, will participate."

Ansel felt her ears grow hot. Garin urged her to stand. She grabbed Geneera's hand and pulled her up, too. Thesmas added quickly, "As will her best friend and Priesera Vasilissa's daughter, Geneera." Ansel tried to squelch her embarrassment at being the center of attention, squeezed Gen's hand and pasted a smile across her face as the adults all applauded. The Bulldancers cheered merrily.

Finally, Thesmas finished talking and the food was served. Servants scurried about the tables offering dishes of grilled fish, squid and shrimp tossed with olives, chunks of lamb mixed with milk gravy and rice, gamebird stuffed with aubergines, mixed vegetables marinated in olive oil and aromatic herbs, mild goat cheeses, grains, and a crusty, rusk bread that was an island specialty. The thick Kritin wine flowed freely, but Ansel, having imbibed wine with meals from the time she was a little maid, drank as much spring water as spirits; she did not wish to risk making a fool of herself in front of the Bulldancers. Dried and honey–soaked sweets laden with figs, dates, citron and pistachios completed the meal.

"Ansel," Garin asked, "are you coming to the dancer exhibition? If you come early, you can sit in front and I could sit with you between events."

"To be honest, I have not thought very much about it before now. Gen will certainly want to attend and I suppose I will come with her."

"I will perform my best vaults just for you." He leaned toward her, smelling of amber and sea and placed a large, warm hand on her arm. His attentions made Ansel feel both nervous and flattered. *He perhaps thinks it would be a great tale to bed the First Elder's grandaughter for her Kore Festival. Perhaps I am some prize to be won and bragged about and he does not even really like me. It would not be the first time people pretended to like me but really just wanted to be seen with me. It is so hard to tell.*

"I will come," she promised.

We shall see, she added to herself.

The rectangular table, polished to a high gloss, was made of cedar wood imported from far to the east, Phoebe knew. The wood had arrived by boat as planks and still gave off a faintly exotic odor. While she nibbled at some flat bread and assessed her dining companions, she pondered how people's lives could be affected by objects and events so far away. For example, the man who traded in the poppy resin, *mekoi*, was one who affected untold lives indirectly.

Alekki was one of the ugliest men she had ever set eyes upon and yet she found him fascinating. His thick rubbery lips appeared the texture of octopus, and the red of his nose told tale of many nights upon open sea with perhaps only the resin wine, *retsina*, for company. Just then, Alekki paused in his conversation with Demetria, glanced at Phoebe and winked as if he and she were co–conspirators. Phoebe shuddered internally and redirected her attentions toward her work; Alekki had been invited to this feast for the sole purpose of pleasing Demetria. He, at least, was a known entity.

Not so Nikolas, the stout official from the Agronos of Phaistos. He sat across the table and two seats to the left of Phoebe. Presently, he was deeply engaged in conversation with Priesera Vasilissa who sat next to him. For some reason, Vasilissa had refused to enter and be seated with the rest of the Elder Council. She also no longer wore the open–breasted robe of the Priesera even at formal gatherings. Phoebe watched as the older woman self–consciously stroked the wide grey streak at her temple. Though Geneera and Ansel were the same age, Geneera was a child of Vasilissa's middle life. It was rumored that she had changed profoundly after the death of her son, Jerid, some seven turns ago. *In fact,* Phoebe suddenly realized, *he died at the last Seven–Turns Festival. Poor Vasilissa. I should be more compassionate.*

Meanwhile, Nikolas had slopped some gravy in his graying beard and Phoebe had to resist the urge to touch her own chin. She looked down at her plate and pretended interest in her grilled squid. She gathered her focus and soon could discern the voices of Nikolas and Vasilissa from the general clamor around her.

"They say, Priesera, that Mount Herilia rumbles now day and night, or so I heard last I spoke with my brother, Iphikeles, on Heria." Nikolas said. "He tells me She sometimes spits smoke, too. If one looks upon the northern horizon, does not the air look murky, as if cluttered with dust? I see this even as far south as Phaistos. And I feel considerable unease at the colorful dusks, though they are admirably beautiful."

"Indeed, Kourete Nikolas," Vasilissa answered in that annoyingly haughty tone she frequently used. "Everyone in Knossos and at the University knows of Herilia's unrest. Also you must have heard that less than a third of a turn ago, our port village Amnisos was devastated with another wave, this one bigger than any before in memory. This is why the ships were rerouted west to dock. We are all uneasy."

"Then, with all due respect, Priesera, what are the Sisters doing about this?"

"The Sisterhood is doing all we can. We have Priesera praying, dancing, and working spells all night and all day. We sought the seers of our community, but the answers they provide are unclear. It is as if they too must read the signs through murky air. But the problems are also political, I think. Perhaps the answer lies instead with our own Council. What are we doing to end the abhorrence happening all over the world?"

"Bah! Praying, dancing, magic and even the seers are not sufficient. No, Priesera, the deities want more, is this not obvious? Our pleas are no longer adequate."

"Well, is this not what I am saying? The Council must do something to change the blasphemy occurring in this region. The heretics who offer up the Son over His Meter must be stopped."

One sidelong glance told Phoebe that Demetria was far too involved in her flirtation with Alekki to overhear the conversation between Vasilissa and Nikolas. Phoebe exhaled quietly in relief. Vasilissa had no sense of how offensive she could be to others. After all, one of the "regions" she so despised was Athena. Had they not recently elevated their God, Zeus, to the same status as their namesake Goddess, Athena?

Nor did Theseus appear aware of Vasilissa's indelicacy. Perhaps this was because of his poor grasp of the Kritin language. Since she had strung a thread to him already, he was easy to tune in to. She briefly checked his emotional state, reading boredom mixed with a longing to be elsewhere. When he glanced at her, sexual energy flared. She felt faintly sorry for the boy; though the food itself was somewhat entertaining, he likely would not understand nor even care to understand much of the conversation of strangers taking place about him. *He would perhaps have been happier sitting over at the young people's table with my Ansel. She speaks Greek fluently. But I could not possibly sit there, too. I shall need to direct more attention toward him.*

But Nikolas was saying, "Is it not possible, Sister, that what is really needed is direct appeasement? I hear that in the East, they offer the very best they have to give when the Gods are displeased, sacrifices so precious that even an ill-tempered God could not ignore, up to and including their own citizens."

"In the East, they worship bloodthirsty Gods." Vasilissa replied.

"And She of Ten Thousand Names is not proving equally bloodthirsty? Does She not take untold lives on Her own when perhaps She could be appeased with only a few?"

"Blasphemy!" Vasilissa snorted, her face turning red.

Phoebe knew she could not stay silent any longer lest Vasilissa feel it was her solemn duty to share her opinions with the entire rest of the table. She stopped toying with her food and looked directly at Nikolas.

"Sacrifice, Nikolas?" she asked, pitching her tone to one of subtle command. "Are you truly proposing that the Great Meter, She–Who–Gives–Birth, would ask us to kill Her children to appease Her? Why? It makes no sense. Many of us do not wholly approve of even the occasional sacrifice of a bull."

"Pardon me," Nikolas said, his face flushing as he struggled against her light vocal control spell, "but I hardly think we should disdain out of hand what works for others. What is one life in return for the lives of all of us here on Kriti, not to mention the rest of the region? After all, these other nations are not without their most learned and holy religious leaders, *Mistress* Phoebe."

The way his harsh voice emphasized "Mistress" set Phoebe's teeth on edge. *Is he that much of a fool not to know I am also Priesera? Or does he realize I am in no position to rebuke him here in public?* Her hands tightened into fists underneath the table, crinkling her blue linen table napkin into a ball.

"Kourete Nikolas, you are quite mistaken," interjected a voice from somewhere farther up the table. "Sacrifice is only practiced in nations where their deities demand it as a matter of course. Our Goddess would be offended by a sacrifice of Her children. *Mistress* Phoebe is quite knowledgeable about the practices in foreign areas. I would listen to her if I were you."

Phoebe glanced up to see Elder Priesera Aluneia regarding Nikolas, her black eyes fixing him with an uncomfortably penetrating stare. *Blessings on Aluneia*, Phoebe thought.

Nikolas murmured something unintelligible, then said, "Of course Priesera, I would not presume to imply Mistress Phoebe does not know of what she speaks. Nevertheless, many of us at Phaistos are concerned."

"As are we all, Kourete Nikolas," Aluneia said returning her attention to her plate. Sweets were being served and the conversation turned to less controversial topics. Phoebe turned to Theseus, engaging him in small talk over honeyed figs and hot beverages.

A crash, then raucous laughter erupted. Demetria stood holding her substantial, double–handled wine cup aloft; her heavy wooden chair had tipped over in her abrupt rising. Like magic, a servant appeared to right it for her. "To Kriti!" she said, waving the cup in a somewhat alarming manner. "May She of Ten Thousand Names rule here forever!"

What is she doing? She cannot possibly be drunk; she barely touched her retsina. With a fluid motion, Phoebe grasped her cup and held it aloft to politely acknowledge the visiting monarch's toast. She glanced toward TradesKourete Alekki who wore a broad grin and was looking up at Demetria, his arms folded across his chest. In the flurry of servants who rushed to refill empty chalices, only Phoebe caught Demetria's cynical raised eyebrow and her sly nod toward Alekki.

Old sow, she is doing this for effect!

When Thesmas rose, cutting short whatever additional pronouncement Demetria was about to make, Phoebe revised her assessment. *Not for fun then, but to end the feast and get back to her mekoi. She must have had only a little of the poppy to be able to make this appearance or she would not be able to keep her head off the table. Ai, and this selfish ruler is the sovereign monarch of Athena.*

"Thank you, everyone, for your attendance," Thesmas said, "and you, Helen Demetria, for your kind words. There will be entertainment and dancing in the main hall shortly. Please join us if you so desire." She glanced at Xeronos, who donned his horns with only a little help from a nearby servant. They nodded and waved as they slowly walked together from the table and back into a private chamber of the Agronos. The members of the Elder Council stood next and walked in file from the table.

Phoebe turned to Theseus and said, "Are you interested in the entertainment tonight, Royal Consort Theseus? Helen Demetria, it seems, is likely to retire early and will need you not." Theseus smiled deeply and nodded. Together, they rose from the table. "A moment please, Mistress Phoebe?" Alekki stood looking at her expectantly. Phoebe turned back to Theseus and said, "If you will excuse me, Royal Consort Theseus, I will meet you at the east door." She pointed across the courtyard to the door closest her private apartment.

She turned to Alekki, who smiled openly at her, transforming his ugly face to that of a charming satyr. "Helen Demetria knows how to break apart a party, does she not?"

"Indeed, although I suspect it was more calculated than impulsive."

"Ah, you are as perceptive as your reputation and even more lovely. Would that you would escort me sometime."

Phoebe curtsied.

Alekki chuckled and continued, "The Trader's Code states that a trader should give aid to one who has been of assistance to them. I will make a fine profit from Helen Demetria and I know it was you who decided upon the invitation list. So, you have aided me, albeit inadvertently. In return, I offer information that I believe you will find interesting."

Phoebe inclined her head. "Information, TradesKourete Alekki?"

"Yes. Kouretes Nikolas, he is well traveled and asks interesting questions. Rumor is that he is involved in a new religion emerging on this island and others, especially Heria. The followers believe they gain the favor of the Gods through an offering of blood. He is closely related to a leader in the movement, his brother Iphikeles."

Phoebe caught his eye and stared at him deeply. "How do you know so much, Alekki?"

Smiling, Alekki broke away from her thrall spell as if snapping a thread. "Traders learn to keep their ears open. You may wish to feign ignorance, Mistress, but your true vocation is not a mystery to me. I wish you good evening." With unexpected grace, he turned his back to her and strode away.

Not many can break contact, Phoebe thought. *Interesting man.* She shrugged, made a note to herself to give both the proffered information and the curious dispenser of it more thought when she had time, then walked across the courtyard to meet the awaiting Theseus.

Chapter 7

Phoebe's private bedchamber was sumptuous; as Elder Escort, she required it. Elegant pottery embellished with painted spirals and olive leaves graced tables of glowing inlaid wood. The quavering flames of gypsum oil lamps added subtlety and depth to the room. A thick woven wool rug dyed a rich and rare purple covered the floor. Some of the gypsum walls were overlaid with woven wall hangings, warming the room from the chill of evening. She particularly favored sea motifs; an intricately stitched octopus eyed the room in surprise, while sea plants waved green fronds and schools of little silvery fish circled the walls.

With a graceful sweep of her arm, Phoebe invited Theseus to sit with her upon a cushioned bench. She snuggled close to him, lightly stroking his arm with her immaculately manicured fingers. He scrutinized the wall hangings, refusing to meet her eyes. She sensed his shyness.

"Do you like the tapestries?" she asked. "They come from a weaving village near Gournia, to the east of Knossos. I like them especially during the evening hours. The stone walls are beautiful, but so cold."

"They are magnificient." He paused and Phoebe inched just a bit closer to him, almost, but not quite, brushing her thinly draped breast against his bare arm. Though he pretended to be unaware, his Radiance told her differently. She directed her own Radiance towards his, gently, very gently, encouraging him to feel safe and reflective. He sighed, visibly relaxing, leaned against the wall warmed by deep sea tapestries and said, "She is a fickle Goddess, the sea, is She not?"

"Ai, yes. She nourishes with life abundant, yet She takes also."

"She can rip from you all you hold dear, without hesitation, without mercy. When I was a little boy, I thought Her my special Goddess. But today, I love Her not." He sighed again and shook his head slightly as if trying to clear it of a fog.

Phoebe rested a hand upon Theseus's forearm and softly pulsed his aura with her own, silently beckoning him to dive more deeply into his tidal pool of memory.

Slowly, as if in a light trance, he continued speaking, his voice barely above a whisper. "Once when I was a very young boy, I demanded the Caster of Nets bow down to me. Of course, She did not."

He paused briefly to run a finger lightly over the veined surface of a purple stone lamp next to the couch. The flame from the olive oil flickered softly. "I did not know Her vengeful side then; I was punished for my arrogance. My foster meter who rescued me from the streets, Karolina – she was of the fisherfolk on the island of Paros and the only Meter I remember – the morning after my foolishness, she and her brother paddled out far into the sea to catch fish before dawn. A tremendous wave, the likes of which was never seen before, crashed in. They never returned."

"Had there been a shake?"

"That is what the islanders say must have happened. A shake occurred somewhere way out in the sea that we did not feel on land. But I always knew better. I knew it was because of me. Because I dared challenge the Caster."

Phoebe placed a gentle hand upon his shoulder and enveloped him with a golden–honey comforting, compassionate Radiance. "I am sorry you lost your foster meter, but it was likely not due to your impiety. The Caster is not known for vengeance."

He shrugged. "You do not know the rest of the story. When we lost her and her brother, it left my many foster siblings and me without close family. They went to live with other relatives. None would have me. They said the Fates loved me not."

Again, Phoebe gently pulsed him. *Deeper,* she thought. *Tell me more.*

"Karolina owned goats for their milk and cheese since she had so many children to feed. I was youngest and tended the goats." Something red flared up in his Radiance and just as quickly died down. He continued. "After her passing, they sold the goats and needed me not. They drove me back to the streets from which I came. I was young and defiant and told them all I did not need them, that someday they would hear of Theseus the Hero. But every night I slept in the streets, I dreamt of the home I once had and awoke in the morning with my eyes swollen from weeping."

Abruptly, Theseus stopped speaking, straightened and dashed the tears from his eyes. "I do not know why I tell you this. You think me weak."

"No," Phoebe answered. "I think you young."

Theseus tossed his head and grunted as if slapped. His voice darkened, sounding insulted. "I hate the sea, yet also I do not leave Her. I am young in body, Mistress Phoebe, but my heart feels old indeed."

Phoebe caught his dark eyes and held them, risking opening her *saria* vision fully. The wall of stone was still there, but cracks showed in it. Deeply she searched, holding Theseus in a thrall she knew he would not recall. Carefully, tenderly, she probed into his spirit. Then, there it was, the thing she sought, the thing he hid; a terrible wound, red and festered, laid upon his soul, penetrating his very spirit. She gasped in surprise. Its shape looked like the sacred knot of the Priesera, the mark of Her chosen ones. Yet within him, it appeared as a thing of violence; inflamed, angry, furious, and vengeful. *Perhaps indeed the Caster has taken note of him,* she thought.

Unsettled, Phoebe withdrew and with an ease born of long practice, gently broke the contact. She hid the disquiet she felt. He was right. Here was not the young innocent soul she had expected to find behind the eyes. *I should have suspected*, she thought, *young souls cannot build nor maintain such defenses. His manner bespeaks depths, yet also something is terribly awry. Ah Goddess, this may be a thing more grievous than I had supposed. And yet, perhaps, too, more hopeful.*

Aloud she said, "Theseus, there are wounds only She of Ten Thousand Names can heal. Sometime, mayhaps you will seek and accept the grace of such a healing." She resumed stroking his arm, this time adding a pulse of orange–red sexual passion. She leaned forward and kissed him gently on the lips.

If Theseus understood her comment, he did not respond. Instead, he surrendered to Phoebe's touch, returning her kiss with fire of his own.

Chapter 8

Late that night, the feast and even the cleaning up afterward long since over, Ansel awoke to pale moonlight bathing her face. She had been dreaming vividly, yet the images ebbed before her waking mind, leaving only a trace of uneasiness in their wake. Shaking her head slightly, she sat up in bed. *I am not at all sleepy*, she thought.

Drawing back the linen bed sheet, she lightly swung her feet to the floor and stepped to the window. The scant maiden moon cast wan light upon the glittering whitestone of the courtyard. Empty tables still stood below, ghostly reminders of the lively meal they had hosted. Cocking her head, she heard the soft, even breaths of a sleeping Geneera in the next room. Ansel shuddered in lonely delight at her solitude. A longing to see the ocean by moonlight filled her heart. *What a lovely night it is and I have not walked the beach at night in so long, not since before Amnisos.* She hesitated at that thought, then set her jaw and decided it was long since time to resume her nightly wanders.

Even in an Artemis' bow moon, the sparkly whitestone path leading down and away from the Agronos reflected enough light for Ansel to see without a lamp. She knew it well anyway. Following the narrow trail, she carefully tiptoed over the jumbled stones so as not to turn her weak ankle.

The night air was deliciously cool and soft. Ansel hugged herself and hummed a cheery tune to suppress the feelings of grief that welled up in her as she neared the cliffs. Soon she stood at the edge of the foothill just as she had the morning the wave came. She heard the sea before she saw it; a sigh, then a rush, an inhalation and an exhalation. At night, the enchanting sea was some great breathing creature lying in wait in the darkness. More confidently now, like a wild mountain goat, she descended the shattered steps leading to the beach. In the semi–dark, she could pretend Amnisos was just at rest.

Ankle forgotten, Ansel ran lightly along the beach on the balls of her feet, digging her toes into the yielding sand, still warm from the day's sun. The muscles in her calves tightened as the sand gave way; it felt almost like running through the water itself. At the firmer water–smoothed shoreline, the tiny sand granules sparkled from the receding wave. Here and there, glimmering round stones graced the ground like fallen stars. The next wave rushed over her feet, cool and foamy. Despite the memory of Amnisos, Ansel was a child of the sea–blessed island, and the joy of feeling the ocean water again coursed through her body. She jumped back from the next wave, and on impulse began spinning on her toes in the soft sand, arms out from each side.

She began singing aloud an old sea melody her meter had taught her when she was little. Her voice, at first soft, then more loudly rose to the heavens as she lost herself in the lovely melody.

> *Goddess Moon, my heart turns to you*
> *and to your beloved, the shining sea.*
> *Meter Sea, my joy knows no bounds;*
> *I am a little child who wishes on stars*
> *that fell into your cup of plenty.*
> *Goddess Moon, I kiss my hand to your beauty.*
> *Meter Sea, Goddess Moon, bless me,*
> *for I am a child of your love.*

Tears rolled down Ansel's cheeks, belying the words of joy. Yet the acute pain of loss can blend seamlessly with ecstasy. Ansel did not know if she wanted to laugh or weep.

Dizzy and breathless, she stopped spinning. When she regained her balance, she began to dance, still humming the ages–old ode to Moon and Sea. Sway, step, sway, step, then cross one leg behind the other, Ansel imitated the ritual dances of the Priesera she had seen. She snaked out a spiral pattern in the sand, then stood still in the center and faced the sea, beginning another verse of the song,

"Goddess Moon, my heart turns to you . . . ," She stopped abruptly. Not twenty–five foot–lengths away, a glowing woman stood before her. Ansel was not sure if the woman was an apparition or flesh. Her skin glistened in the moonlight, but her long hair, hanging in strands like seaweed to below her waist, shadowed her face. Her garment, inexplicably flowing despite the water, draped over one breast and was pulled snug against her small waist. In one hand, she held a conch shell. The sea foam whirled dreamily around her knees. Ansel stood stock still, frightened and mystified at the woman's sudden appearance.

"Ansel, little one," the woman said, her voice husky and dark, "I claim you now as my own daughter. You must come to me when you are ready; there is much to do. Tell the Priesera. The sign is bestowed unto you." The woman raised a hand, palm out, to Ansel. She thrust a bright golden thread of light from her palm. When it touched her between her breasts, Ansel felt her heart surge in exhilaration and she gasped loudly.

"What? Who are you?" She gulped in breath for several moments before her heart returned to a normal beat. But Ansel was again alone on the beach, and the breath of the sea was all that responded to her voice.

Chapter 9

At dawn, Ansel woke restless and by habit, wandered over to her desk to write. She wondered if she had dreamt her encounter at the beach, if she had even gone to the beach at all, but when she scratched her head with her stubby fingernails, she felt gritty beach sand on her scalp. Surely, then, at least that part was true. When Geneera awoke soon after sunrise (as she always did for her morning run), she found Ansel still writing at her little, wooden table.

"My, you are up early this morn," the lithe girl commented between yawns.

Ansel shrugged. She felt hesitant to tell Gen of the woman at the beach; Gen might think she was losing her senses to the sea again, like after Amnisos, when she simply lost time. People worried about her, especially Meter and Gran. It occurred to Ansel suddenly that she might be losing her grasp of reality, really losing it – that she would become one of those people who does not know who or where she is at any given time, who talk to phantasms, shout to the sea and slap rocks until their hands are bloody and someone kind comes to walk them home. That thought threatened to throw her into a panic, so she forcibly pushed it back to ponder at a later time.

But other things preoccupied Geneera's mind. Grinning, she pounced on Ansel's sweet hay filled bed mattress and crossed her long legs. "Garin really likes you. He says you are prettier even than your meta."

Ansel looked up from her scroll, swiveled on her stool to face Gen, and forced herself to concentrate on her friend. "Hmm, that one I have never heard before. What does he want, do you think?"

"Silly, he wants to spend time with you."

"Gen, I do not even know him. Nor him me."

"So spend time with him and get to know him. He is considered one of the best of the 'dancers and he is very good looking. Do you not like him?"

"Ai, no, it is not that."

"Then what is it?"

"Well, boys have never before shown much interest in me and in honesty I do not trust his motives." Ansel wrinkled her nose and shook her head. "This is our Kore Festival, no? It is time to become women, to fling off girlhood, or so Meta and everyone keep tell ing me." She slammed her pen down on the table in frustration. Her voice held bitterness. "I have had many experiences with false friends, those who want to be seen with the First Elder's grandaughter yet care not for me. I do not need pretend interest from a false lover. Can you not hear the stories in the athlete's dorms? 'Oh Garin, you certainly did turn the head of the grandaughter. Did you take her in the meadow? Or did she bring you back to her private apartment? How was she, Garin? Was it worth it to have to spend time with her?'"

"Oh Ansel, I think you judge him, and yourself, harshly."

"Do I? Maybe. But Gen, everything is changing too fast. You are my best friend, my only friend in truth, and you are leaving me to join the Bulldancers. We are about to be declared women in front of all of Knossos, and I do not know who I am nor what I want." She glanced down at her chewed fingernails, then raised her head and looked Geneera in the eyes. "I envy you. You have always known you wanted to be an athlete regardless of what your meta wants. And now, you are joining the dancer troupe, just as you dreamed. I never had a goal like that. Now I am to become Kore and my future seems less clear to me than ever. I do not like change, Gen. I am plain scared."

"You could be a teacher, Ansel. You were always better at your studies than me."

"I could teach, but my heart would not be in it. Would I teach here at the Agronos? Then, for my entire life I could listen to people wonder aloud why I am not pretty like my meter, nor clever like my granmeter. And I would probably not be as good a teacher as your meter as well. I could spend my time apologizing for not being any of them." Ansel felt her eyes well with tears. She clenched her teeth trying to hold them back. It was no use though and the fat hot tears spilled over her cheeks. After a moment, she continued. "To make it worse, there is nowhere in this land I can escape, Gen. Both Meta and Gran are known anywhere I go." Ansel paused, ashamed at her tearfulness, angry with herself that she could not control them better. "I do not know how people know who they are, Gen. I am never sure of anything. I ponder and ponder, but still no answer comes to me. Sometimes I think I am going adrift. I really mean it."

Abruptly, Ansel stood and turned her back to her friend while rolling up her papyrus. She fumbled for a moment with a length of sinew, then wrapped and tied it around the scroll. Swallowing hard before she turned back to Gen, she said, "But let us talk about something else, yes? I was thinking... I was thinking... perhaps we could skip the opening of Festival and go directly to the market-place. If we go early, we will have the best selection. Later, it will be very busy."

Geneera nodded. "Agreed. Many will attend the opening. No offense meant to your granmeter, but she will speak for longer than I can listen."

A reluctant half–grin crossed Ansel's tear–streaked face. "Indeed. Gran can talk the length of many courtyards."

An hour or so later, the girls left the Agronos and began walking down to the large meadow bowl where the marketplace was held, south of the Center. It was a bright morn and a light, soft breeze blew their hair off their faces. Their feet kicked up a fine yellow dust from the dry rocky soil. Leathery–leaved plants lined the path as they descended in the meadow. As they approached the market, the sound of voices raised in dickering drifted to their ears. Others, too, had apparently decided to skip the opening of festivities in favor of shopping. Soon, their nostrils were assaulted with the odors of dung and unwashed bodies, as well as the more pleasing scents of baking bread, sizzling meats and exotic spices. The off–key clang of copper bells, accompanied by the lows and bleats of the various animals who wore them, could be heard mixed with the general din. Somewhere, someone was playing an eerie tune upon a reed pipe.

Traders intuited that the girls had the means to buy, perhaps based on the girls' dress, and Ansel and Geneera were eagerly courted from the moment they stepped foot in the dusty corridor between the many booths. "Girls! Girls! You must try my perfume!" called one peddler as he waved them towards his booth. Compliantly, the girls sniffed the proffered tiny ceramic pot of aromatic oil.

Geneera wrinkled her nose. "Ai, it is too sweet!" She pretended to gag, wrapping her arms around her slim waist and retching clownishly. The trader rolled his eyes, turned his back to Geneera and attempted to woo Ansel.

"It is jasmine, young Mistress, and the sweetness, that is what the boys like," the portly trader wheedled as he mopped his sweaty brow with a square of undyed linen. Ansel rubbed a drop of the oil onto her wrist while Geneera wandered away, her attention drawn to a nearby leather–goods stall.

Ansel's eyes followed the back of the rapidly disappearing Geneera, "Um, no thanks, I do not want the perfume, not now anyway," she told the trader hastily, then trotted to catch up with her longer–legged friend. The perfume peddler shrugged good–naturedly as he re–corked his pot of oil.

The girls quickly learned not to respond to the traders' calls. They scooped their hands into baskets full of slick obsidian beads and admired shell–encrusted bangles, looked at themselves in highly polished silver hand mirrors and cooed at brightly dyed balls of wool. Bronze charcoal braziers belched forth strongly–scented powdered incenses. Tubs of dried medicinal herbs and ostrich plumes were tucked between stalls of copper pots and ceramic vessels. Huge woven baskets overflowed with sea sponges or plant pods or drift wood. Geneera bought a seal stone carved from gypsum. It depicted a cunningly carved miniature Bulldancer springing through the air over a bull's head. Ansel bought a silver dolphin brooch for her meter. Both girls breakfasted on honeyed, goat–cheese pastries and pulpy fruit drinks as they meandered through the stalls and booths.

Next to a display of braided bread and green leaf vegetables was a booth where a stooped, elderly man was carefully arranging rows of short, broad–bladed bronze knives and swords with ornate sheathes of leather decorated with silver, gold and copper. As the girls approached, the man took out a cloth and began rubbing the blade of a knife. His naked belly jiggled in rhythm with his polishing. Behind the display of weaponry hung upon a pegged wooden board were coats of the sort one would wear for protection in a fight or battle. Some were jerkins of leather, others ringlets of solid bronze. Among them was a cap made of an exotic blackish metal.

"What is that?" Geneera asked the trader, pointing toward the cap. "I have never seen anything like that before."

The man took down the cap for the girls to look more closely. The metal was at least as heavy as bronze, but looked coarser and knobby.

Ansel asked, "Why would someone want to buy that helmet? Is it because they cannot afford bronze?"

The man laughed aloud revealing several missing teeth. "Little maidens, I would sell you that cap of iron for only about ten times the price of the bronze. For all its unsightliness, it can shatter a bronze sword." He bent close to them in a conspiratorial manner adding, "The making of iron is difficult and its recipe is a secret. Not that anyone here on the island is even trying to discover that secret. Bah! They think they are forever immune to what happens in the outside world. But those nomadic warrior ogres understand the value of iron. It is strong! And it is in the hands of the wrong people!" He shook his head in disgust, then ran a hand through his thinning gray hair. Pointing a gnarled finger at the girls, he said, "One day everyone will have iron weapons. When that happens, heed my words, girls, the world will change, the world will change."

"Ai, Good TradesKourete, you speak wise as the serpent. I myself bought an iron weapon just this past Cronetide," said a voice behind the girls. They whirled around to see a stout silver-haired woman, her hands on her hips, nodding her head as she talked to the iron trader. Next to her stood a tall, sallow man with extraordinarily fleshy lips. "Times grow dangerous for traders, especially the women. I feel safer with iron on my side."

"You are Melodia, the silver TradesKore?" the trader asked. "And of course, I know you, TradesKourete Alekki. Can I interest you in some iron weaponry also? Surely you need protection with the merchandise you handle. I have testimony to its efficacy, as you heard."

"No, friend, though I would indeed enjoy hearing more sometime. Melodia and I were just walking by and heard you speaking to the girls. I must be off to my own tent now, for I am on an errand for Helen Demetria of Athena."

"I would talk more with the iron TradesKourete, Alekki. Perhaps we can meet again to talk before the Citizenry meeting?"

"Of course, Melodia." Quickly he embraced her, kissing her on both cheeks, and then left.

Melodia frowned quizzically at the girls, then thrust a pointed her chin at Ansel saying, "Unless I miss my mark, you are Ansel, daughter of Mistress Phoebe. Do I win?"

"Yes," she replied, almost too wearily to be polite. Sometimes she wished mightily to have a less well-known face.

"Know your meta and Xeronos, and have met your granmeta. Saw you when you were a babe and not since. You look much like your meta though. Name's Melodia. I trade in Trojan silver mostly, gold, electrum and precious gems when I can."

Ansel warmed to the no–nonsense woman. "Delighted to make your acquaintance, TradesKore Melodia. Here is my friend, Geneera, daughter of Priesera Vasilissa."

"Geneera, delighted to meet you. I do not know your meter personally, but have heard her speak. But here, let me ponder for a moment; my youngest daughter, Dia, is a bit older than you, Ansel, so it must be, oh, close to fifteen turns since I saw you last."

"Indeed, I will have sixteen turns to me this Metertide."

"Ach, you are nearly Kore. How time flows."

"Yes, Mistress."

"Were you thinking of buying anything from our good TradesKourete? No? Then perhaps I may enjoin him. Please give my heart's blessings to your meta, Ansel. Tell her I will see her at the Citizenry meeting. Now, Good TradesKourete, what else have you in ironware?"

Just as she and Gen were retreating from the iron trader's stall, leaving Melodia deep in conversation with the trader, Ansel noticed two other people approaching – Carea and a man who turned out to be Carea's Uncle, Nikolas. Gen grinned and skipped over to them, excitedly kissed Carea on the cheeks and hugged "Uncle Niko" as Carea introduced him. Ansel tried not to feel left out when Carea did not also introduce her to Uncle Niko.

Nikolas was little taller than Gen and though stout, no doubt he was once as powerfully built as Carea was now. His balding head was more than compensated for by the rich black hair he grew everywhere else. His thick beard was liberally peppered with gray. His forearms and lower legs where they peered below his white linen tunic, even the knuckles of his square hands and the tops of his sandaled feet bloomed with lush black hair.

"Carea tells me you are to join the troupe, Gen. You must be excited. I remember when Carea told my sister and I that she had been accepted. My Carea whooped and danced for all of the weeks before she left for Knossos."

For all that Ansel did not like Carea, she could not help but warm to the idea of her jumping and dancing like a child. She smiled a little at Carea, but the girl was looking down at her own feet.

"Oh yes, I am breathless with excitement!" Gen confirmed. "But please, Uncle Niko, if I may call you that, I have not yet told my meter. If she were to find out from anyone but me..."

"Ah, I can see that would be most uncomfortable. You may count on me not to divulge your secret, Geneera. Some things a Meter must learn first from her daughter."

Carea looked up sharply and said, "My uncle wishes to speak at length with the iron trader, Gen. Where are you going? I hope to find some leather for boots. Would you like to come with me?"

Ansel held her breath. Gen turned toward her, caught Ansel's eye for a moment, then replied, "We, Ansel and I, are looking for a few things, too. Do you wish to join us?"

Carea looked at Ansel, her eyes hardening again, and said, "No, I think I will go quickly find the leather and then join the opening ceremonies. I will take time to peruse the market later." Gen shrugged her shoulders and hugged Carea farewell. The day was growing warm and the two girls walked slowly, pausing often to finger some new rarity. Ansel noticed that nearly every conversation she overheard, from the people milling around the refreshment booths, to some comments made to a traveling muse, to an earnest and somewhat heated discussion between traders, centered on unrest in the area. Some expressed concern about the great mountain peak, Herilia, rumbling on the nearby island of Heria. Others whispered about political and religious unrest on neighboring islands, and the northern mainlands. Many planned to attend the upcoming Citizenry meeting. For the first time, Ansel gave some consideration to attending herself, providing, of course, it did not conflict with something more interesting.

Finally, Ansel spotted a booth selling what she sought. Among trinkets of ivory and gold and boxes of a black wood, were bolts of orange and red cloth with fierce–looking, golden lions woven into the pattern. She had seen cloth of this type before in a market many years ago and had never forgotten it. Her meter had marveled at the texture of the material, soft yet tough, while the young Ansel had poked chubby little–girl fingers at the lions. To the young adult Ansel, the lion pattern of the cloth seemed random, yet still had a sense of rightness that spoke to her deeply. She had no idea how she might use the cloth, but she wanted it anyway.

"How much for the cloth, Good TradesKore?" she asked the tall, large–boned woman behind the booth.

"You have silver? It is two standard–weight rings for the length," she replied. When Ansel gasped at the price, the trader said, "Alas, young miss, the trade routes become more and more dangerous, and so I must ask more for my products to make the long journey profitable."

Geneera, who had been sifting through a display of wooden beads cunningly carved to resemble exotic birds, cocked her head in interest at the trader's words. "Why are the trade routes becoming more dangerous? I heard the weather has been particularly favorable.

"Indeed," the woman replied, gracefully turning toward Gen as she spoke, "the weather has not been the problem. You who reside on Kriti are isolated by the Meter Sea, and she continues to smile on your lovely lands." She flashed white teeth in a smile, but her eyes did not reflect amusement. "But alas, your neighboring countries do not share in your peaceful existence. Surely you have heard that in many of your neighboring lands there has been unrest – raids from light–skinned nomads who bear terrible weapons and worship a god who speaks in a voice of thunder and blood."

Ansel's heart thumped hard in her chest, then returned to normal. To cover her momentary confusion, she swallowed, then said, "No, we, uh, I had not heard."

"We think they come from far to the north. On the borders of Libya, my home, there have been battles. Everywhere is the rumor of war. The worst of it is spoken barely above a whisper; this god of battle commands his followers to sacrifice all the men and boys of the conquered lands to him, then to rape and enslave the women.

And so my business becomes more and more dangerous as even foreign traders are at some risk. Many women traders have already been forced to find less dangerous work, while others have given their sons or brothers or consorts a more active role so that the monsters and their vile followers will allow them to trade in peace."

The woman stood to her full height, her eyes full of flame. "My sisters and I also carry weapons now, and we have learned to use them. Never will we submit to the dogs." She spat on the ground and looked fiercely at the girls.

Abruptly the Libyan trader allowed her shoulders to slump a little and she chuckled. "Luckily for me, most of the gangs I run across are comprised of cowards, no more than little boys playing at defying their meters. The fear of She of Ten Thousand Names remains strong in them, and they know in their hearts they risk Her wrath. But I shudder to think what will happen if ever they lose that fear."

Ansel liked the trader woman and dickered with her just enough so as not to be offensive, then handed over her silver. As the woman wrapped the precious cloth with a length of cheap, clean linen, Ansel mused about the woman's tale of unrest in her home country. She privately resolved to attend the Citizenry meeting no matter what other interesting events might be happening at the same time.

Chapter 10

A Seven–Turns Festival lasted for thirteen days, the time it takes the moon to traverse through the final Maidentide bow into the initial full Koretide cycle of the turn. By the afternoon of the seventh day, the moon pregnant and ripening, Ansel had already attended the goat judging and the wrestling competitions and had seen the running tournaments and an enactment of the newest drama by Psiperia, a playwright and poet renowned throughout Kriti. This afternoon, the guildsfolk were meeting with others of their craft from around the island and surrounding lands to discuss new techniques and issues of their respective trades.

As promised, her meta had arranged for her to tell the Priesera about her visions. The meeting was in the guest apartments at the Agronos, on the third floor. She ascended the elegant, central whitestone stairs with a heavy heart, dreading to speak again of what happened at Amnisos. She had to go alone, too; the Sister had insisted. She debated whether to mention the second encounter on the beach and decided not to.

She gently rapped on the wooden door frame of the apartment. A young woman, barely older than Ansel herself, gestured for the girl to enter. Following her lead, Ansel thought, *She must be a novice Priesera. She wears the open robes of the Priesera, but she has no knot between her shoulders, and no hat.* Ansel took a deep breath and allowed herself to be guided to the cushioned bench in the apartment vestibule. A huge tapestry of orange lilies and blue swallows hung on the wall opposite her seat. She looked down at her hands folded carefully in her lap and resisted a sharp urge to chew her already ragged fingernails.

A tall, stern–looking woman dressed in the long, open–breasted purple mantle and tall hat of the Priesera stepped out to greet her. The formal garb cinched tightly at the waist, and when the Sister turned her back to lead Ansel into the room serving as her office, she stared at the looped fabric knot attached to the robe, just between the woman's shoulder blades. The knot of the Priesera was a symbol of prominence as significant as the double–headed axe itself. Only one who knew the mysteries of the net of life itself could wear it. It was rumored each Priesera undertook a dark and difficult journey to earn that knot.

Sister Aluneia, as the Priesera introduced herself, was not unkind to Ansel, but her demeanor was so severe and her eyes such an impenetrable black that Ansel found looking into them disquieting. The Sister stared, it seemed, long at Ansel without saying a word. Finally, her features softening somewhat, she said, "Tell me of your vision, child; what did you see at Amnisos?"

"Yes, Priesera," Ansel said. "I, uh, I was standing at the top of the cliff stairs, the ones carved into the foothill that leads down to Amnisos and the bay." She bit her hower lip, then continued. "I had just climbed them. I was returning home and turned around to look down upon the sea. Then the shake came and I was thrown to the ground. I hurt my ankle." Unconsciously, Ansel reached to her ankle and rubbed it, as if the action might help her thoughts flow more easily.

Aluneia said nothing, but nodded gravely, encouraging Ansel to continue.

"Just moments later, the wave came." The memory of the wave rushed back with astounding clarity. Ansel's breaths became short, and her heart pounded so fiercely she could hear it in her ears. She found herself unable to speak further. Aluneia reached forward and placed a surprisingly gentle hand on Ansel's arm. Warmth radiated through the girl, and her heart gradually slowed. She looked into the Priesera's gaze, surprised to see the solemn Sister's eyes widened with compassion. Unwittingly, Ansel's own eyes welled with tears and she felt her shoulders ease a bit, as if of their own volition.

Clearing her throat, Ansel continued, tears rolling slowly down her cheeks. "The Caster of Nets appeared after the wave receded. I watched Her gather the souls of the fisherfolk. I thought I lost my senses. Maybe I did. I still do not know sometimes."

Aluneia said with a wave of her hand, "Child, many people report visions after a shock such as you experienced. It is not a symptom of mind loss. Tell me, what did She look like to you?"

"Huge and naked. Her hair was long and covered Her face until She looked up and spoke to me. But, Priesera..." Ansel reached out in sudden desperation to the Sister; she felt inexplicably that this woman could save or destroy her with mere words. "Priesera, for a full half cycle, after...Amnisos, I heard voices and saw faces. My waking was all bad dreams, and my sleeping dreams, well, they were even worse. I could not talk. I could barely eat. People tell me I muttered and sometimes screamed for hours on end. My meter says I was storm shocked, but, inside me I felt like a clay pot dropped on a stone floor. I am afraid something within me truly shattered and that I can never again be whole."

A line appeared between the eyebrows of the Priesera and she bit her lower lip momentarily. It made her seem almost human. "Ansel," she said finally, "I have no simple reassurances for you; this would be dishonest. It may be true that some part of you broke that day and will never completely mend. But we are usually more flexible than we think. If you choose, you can heal and become even stronger for your experience. Also if you choose, you can let this tragedy claim yet another life – yours. The choice is truly your own, even if it does not seem this way to you now. No person lives a life completely free of pain and misfortune. What you make of that pain, how you use it, what you learn from it, these are tests of your character. You have received a dose earlier than many. No one but you will determine what you do with this wound you carry."

Ansel dropped her head. She had heard the words of the Priesera, but like the message from the Caster Herself, the meaning confused her. Still, Sister Aluneia had not said she was doomed to be mind–adrift as she had feared. She wiped her eyes and said, "I thank you for your honesty."

Priesera Aluneia made Ansel repeat the exact message from the Caster several times, asking her to think back carefully, to be as certain as possible she remembered every word correctly. Over and over Ansel repeated that the Sisters should study the signs as the destiny of Kriti depended on it and to know that the Bull Son was growing in strength. Finally, the Sister sighed and said, "Child, you were given a gift even at the moment of great disaster. Few besides the Seers are ever given a direct message from She–Who–Rules–the–Underworld. And yet so cryptic a message! What else can you recall? Perhaps the words are only part of the meaning She wished to impart. It is important, please try."

"The only other thing I remember clearly is the color of Her eyes. They were like the deepest sea, shifting from light blue–green all the way to deep violet. I could not turn away from them. It was as though She held me immobile with them."

"Ai, child. That is the Caster for certain. No other Goddess has eyes so remarkable." Aluneia tightened her lips into a thin line, looked thoughtfully at Ansel for several moments, then said, "You had another experience? Tell me about that."

Ansel gasped. "How did you know that? I did not tell anyone. Not even Meta."

The furrow between Aluneia's brows returned. She said, "I did not mean to frighten you, child. In my concern for the content of the messages, I neglected to tell you I spun a thread of connection when I touched you before. Each Priesera who receives Ariadne's thread is gifted differently. For some, the thread brings a knowing of important events of another's life. This is my gift. Though I cannot see exactly what this experience of yours was, I can see that it happened and was of importance to you. Please, do not be afraid to tell me of it."

Ansel nodded, feeling both reassured and nervous. "I woke up very late in the night, or perhaps early in the morn. The opening feast was the eve before. I could not sleep and I thought to walk to the beach. I like to go to the beach at night sometimes and just look at the moon and listen to the waves."

"The same beach near Amnisos?"

"Yes, it is the closest one to Knossos. The rivers surrounding the Agronos empty there."

Aluneia nodded and Ansel continued, "I walked the beach and then this woman appeared from the sea."

"She was human?"

"She glimmered like no human. She was draped in a flowing garment. Her hair was like seaweed, thick, and it waved with the rhythm of the sea. She moved silently. I...I am reasonably certain she was not human."

"And she just appeared? You did nothing but walk? Were you in *eukintos*, an altered state?"

"Um, I admit I was not just walking." Ansel suddenly felt foolish. "I was singing and dancing to the moon. I had seen the Priesera dance and was imitating one of the dances."

Ansel glanced up from her lap to see if her admission to imitating the Priesera was offensive, but the Sister gave no outward indication.

Priesera Aluneia said, "The dances of the Priesera give rise to *eukintos* and in late eve or early morn the net between worlds is tattered. Yes, the woman could have been a Goddess then, though I am not certain who from your description. Many arise from the sea. What did She say?"

"She said my prayers were heard and that I should come to Her when I am ready. And then she raised her hand and, well, hit me with something."

"Hit you with something?"

"I am sorry. That is a poor description, but it is how it seemed to me. I saw a thread come from her palm, and when it reached me, it felt like she hit me with it."

"Where were you hit? Did it hurt?"

"I was hit here." Ansel pointed to between her breasts, "and no, it did not hurt exactly, but it took my breath away."

"A moment please." Aluneia again stared at Ansel, but this time her eyes were unfocused. After a moment, she raised an eyebrow and looked directly at Ansel again. "You prayed to become a Sister? To be Priesera?"

"What? No." But she felt a sudden pang. *Maybe I did.* But a Priesera? Like Meta? Like Gran?

"You wear the mark."

"What mark?"

"The sacred knot in your Radiance. It is not visible to most people. Only those who also wear the mark can see it and only then when they are trained and hold the Intention to see it. Goddess marks those who are Her Priesera. It is Her promise to those who wish to dedicate their lives to Her service. You will need to come to the University for teaching. I will speak to your Meta, and we will discuss it further after the Kore ritual."

Chapter 11

Ansel was sorry she went to the Citizenry meeting; it was even more boring than one of Vasilissa's lectures. First, it was held during a beautiful morning, the next to last day of the entire Festival, inside the Agronos in the huge hall on the first floor. Phoebe told her it was easier to hear inside, but that did not make it any easier to miss the warm breezes and singing birds.

Second, Ansel was not sure anything worth hearing was going to be said. During the first half hour, the Council settled only two disputes. A very red–faced man sputtered about his goat–grazing rights. Then, the Council solemnly addressed some personal legal matter of a woman who owed this man something but did not think she did and who really gave a toot anyway? Now, the Council had just agreed to accept a new color of dyed cloth from some craftsman. The color was a beautiful red–purple and Ansel had enjoyed seeing the cloth, but really, she could be watching the Arista chorus, a popular singing and dancing group, instead of wasting her time here. At least the music was performed outside in the theatre. She had just stood up to leave when a muscular, gray–haired woman of middle years stood up to address the Elder Council. It was the woman from the marketplace, the one with the iron dagger. Ansel sat back down.

"I am Melodia, originally of Delos, but these last twenty turns I have called Kriti my home."

Thesmas smiled slightly. "Yes, Melodia. The Council acknowledges you."

The rest of the Council, many of whom had looked nearly as bored as Ansel felt, suddenly shifted in their chairs, sat up straighter and looked expectantly at the TradesKore.

Melodia continued in her curt manner. "I am a trader by craft. My specialty is Trojan silver, though I also buy obsidian and gems to sell to jewel crafters."

Thesmas nodded.

"I have been asked by the Trader Guild to approach the Council. I recently traveled north to Troy. I bring back concerns, not just for myself, but for many traders. I was accosted on my last journey."

"What? Accosted how?" Xeronos leaned forward in his chair and squinted toward the woman. His deep voice boomed through the hall. Ansel suspected Xeronos did not see well. He squinted a lot and she noticed he had to hold scrolls and other written materials very close to his chiseled nose when reading. Still, he was a handsome man and a clever one. Ansel could understand why her meter favored him.

Melodia continued, "I travel with my brother and second eldest daughter, Brita." She placed a hand upon the shoulder of a younger woman seated next to her. "We trade through a specific route, first sailing north through the Cycliades islands then west to the main port at Athena, then to my northernmost point at Thessalonia. I then head easterly to Troy and finally down through the coasts of the Emetchi homelands and sail home west to Kriti.

Ansel closed her eyes and tried to visualize the route. She mostly failed. *I will have to ask Vasilissa,* she thought, irritated with herself.

"Just east of Thessalonia, as we camped for the night, a group of young males, perhaps five or six of them, approached us. They were very light–skinned and I thought, hungry looking as young men generally are. I greeted them warmly and offered them food. I thought them perhaps kin of the sire of my youngest daughter, Dia.

But these young men were rogues. They wanted to rob us." The crowd murmured.

"Now, we have run into robbers before, mind you, and my brother carries a sword with him just for this reason. This was the first time he actually had to brandish it. My brother is a large man, and my daughter and I are both strong. I think the young men did not expect us to fight back. Anyway, they retreated long enough for us to sprint to our boat and row away. They got our dinner and our fire, but naught more."

"You say you encountered robbers before, Melodia. Why was this particularly troubling?" asked Xeronos. He rubbed his eyes and frowned.

The TradesKore grunted. "They were not ordinary robbers; they were at least as interested in threatening us, especially me and my daughter, as in our goods. At first, they assumed my brother was the leader of our group. When they realized I was leading, they became insolent and threatening. Although they did not speak Kritin or Greek, I understood their meaning well enough. They gestured threateningly at Brita and me and spat on the ground. They thought women had no business on the roads, and they would teach us a lesson." She chuckled. "I think, though, that the lesson went in the other direction. My daughter and I picked up flaming logs and pushed them into their faces. We shocked them."

"Still, we have heard of men being disrespectful to women traders before, especially in the north. It is unfortunate, but we cannot control the customs of the neighboring lands." Ansel noted that many of the Council members, particularly the female members, were glancing sideways at each other and scowling.

"Bah! Customs are one thing. Threatening the lives of honest trader women is another. I have taught many a young man a thing or two about respecting women in my day, but never have they banded together to attack like this before. This is new, I tell you. Allow me to finish my story."

Xeronos nodded.

"We then continued into the Emetchi lands. The women of that land are as close to warriors for She of Ten Thousand Names as I have ever encountered. They train with horses and wield swords. There I learned that new bands of people – or, I say people, but apparently they are all male – anyway, they are coming into the lands all around us. The Emetchi say this has happened before, when their nations first formed."

Turning to the rest of the crowd, Melodia explained, "The Emetchi are careful to maintain their history, you know. They teach their storytellers to retell the stories word for word." Turning again to the Council, she continued, "They tell tales of young men, often riding horses, though sometimes in boats, arriving from the north, who join together to invade local villages and even some cities. They are always light–skinned and often light eyed. They worship gods of war and thunder. Their gods order them to kill and rob. They believe their warrior knives to be holy."

Now the murmurs of the crowd erupted into exclamations of alarm. Thesmas had to stand, her arms out and gesture for them to quiet. Melodia continued, "The Emetchi do not know precisely from where they come. They think these boys have been displaced from their home tribes, perhaps due to hunger in their lands. I think they come from somewhere much colder since they hate the heat of Metertide and the sun blisters their skin. They keep their bodies covered in skins, too, even when it is very warm."

Ansel watched as Phoebe sat forward, pressing her chin into her palm. Her elbow rested on a table in front of her and she looked both grim and worried.

"The Emetchi say they have fortified their borders, patrolling night and day. There have been skirmishes. The route I take is no longer safe. They say we were blessed by the Goddess to have escaped, that some young Kore have been raped or abducted. Something needs to be done."

"What is it the Trader's Guild would have the Council do, Melodia? Thassaliona is a long way away." Thesmas pounded her fist on the table in frustration.

"We, the traders of Kriti, need to have safety in our journeys or we can no longer ply our business. Kriti is the most powerful trading and sea–faring nation on earth. Surely something can be done. These bands are only boys, but many boys in a group are still a threat. Do you want Kritin citizens to be hurt?"

We are a peaceable people. We do not even have a military. Perhaps we could appeal to the leaders of Thessalonia *to police these boys.* Ansel frowned thoughtfully.

Melodia continued, "If it were for myself only, I would be less concerned, but my daughter wishes to continue as a trader also; it is the only craft she knows, and she loves to travel. The men may not be safe either, though the Emetchi say the northerners nearly always target women. Perhaps that will change."

"The Council will discuss this, Melodia," Thesmas said. "Be assured, we share your concerns. We will find a way to exert influence. We recognize the importance of safety for our TradesKore." All of the Council Members nodded in agreement, many with their lips tightened into thin lines.

Melodia sat down and the Council called a recess for a third of an hour.

Phoebe watched as her oldest friend, Melodia, sat down and began gesturing emphatically to a younger woman next to her. *That must be Brita, Mel's second daughter.* Phoebe thought. *How grown up little Brita is! So much time has passed since the days when Mel and I endured classes together. How did we come to lose each other? Ach, how I miss the days when Mel and I were close. Still, she did not go to the University and I did. That changes people.*

Phoebe placed both her elbows on the smooth wooden table in front of her and rubbed her eyes with her knuckles. *Thank Goddess this Festival is nearing its end. I am getting too old to be up almost all night with a young man and then be attentive at meetings. I have had to use my glamour magic more than ever to not appear haggard. I will need to sleep for many hours once the Fest ends.*

Too soon, the short recess was over and the Council resumed. Phoebe noticed Ansel had slipped out. For a rueful moment, she wished she could do the same. Nikolas of Phaistos stood, drawing himself up self–importantly. "I have a concern, too, Elder Council." His booming voice belied his short stature.

"The Council recognizes Kourete Nikolas of Phaistos." Thesmas said.

"Thank you, First Elder. While I am, of course, concerned with the TradesGuild and their woes in distant lands, I wish to know what the Council is doing about the other, much closer threat from the north. Upon the island of Heria, the people tell me that the great mountain, Herilia, spews ash daily. The rumblings increase. Many of us lost loved ones not three cycles ago when Amnisos was swamped by a great wave. Clearly, She of Ten Thousand Names is displeased with us. What is the Sisterhood doing? What is the Council doing?"

Leave it to Nikolas to bring up the obvious. As if the Council could stop earthshakes! Phoebe absently scratched the nape of her neck where her hair was bound up too tightly. *Still, this does need to be addressed. It is like a great squid sprawled in the courtyard that everyone tiptoes around and no one dares kick. Better the Council defends the Sisterhood's actions in public than have the likes of Nikolas spreading rumors at the dinner table.*

Thesmas paused, possibly to think of what to say to Nikolas. Vasilissa pounced upon the moment and leapt to her feet to confront the man with whom she had lost the debate.

"Kourete Nikolas, you know full well that this matter is being addressed by the Sisterhood. However, I am in agreement with you that the Council should also take action."

Thesmas actually turned all the way around to face Vasilissa, who stood behind her. Phoebe would have given anything to witness the expression that must be crossing her meter's face at that moment. Vasilissa's face, which Phoebe could see, was stone–like. Only her glittering black eyes betrayed that she knew she was being openly defiant of Council protocol. To keep order, questions were always directed to and answered by the First Elder or the Consort. Other Council members were to join in the discussion either by invitation of the First Elder or by catching the attention of the Consort, who then invited them to speak. *I see where Geneera gets her rebellious streak,* Phoebe thought, smothering a chuckle. She leaned back in her chair and crossed a leg over her knee. It was always fun to see her normally unflappable meter a bit riled.

Thesmas, however, quickly and efficiently regained control of the meeting by saying; "The Council recognizes Member Vasilissa. Please, Priesera, tell us what you know of the situation and what the Sisterhood is doing. Then we can discuss what, if anything, the Council can do about this fundamentally religious matter."

Vasilissa cleared her throat, obviously satisfied that she had been able to pull rank on Kourete Nikolas and now had the attention of the floor. "As Kourete Nikolas has correctly pointed out, the peak of Herilia is throwing ash. Almost quarterly, the people of Heria feel small shakes. Sometimes larger shakes occur but these mostly seem to originate from the sea. Our Seers tell us there is danger, a terrible one, but it is still far off. We do not know if they mean far off in time or in distance. Seers have difficulty telling the difference. The Sisters have performed special rituals to aid the Seers' gift. Thus far, they have only been marginally successful."

Now Vasilissa spread her arms wide dramatically. "However, it is obvious to me that the source of Great Meter's displeasure is the elevating of worship of Her Son over Her. This is what I believe we on the Council should concern ourselves with. We must issue an edict outlawing the worship of Him over Her throughout our lands and people, and perhaps even pull in the nets on our neighboring nations. It is heresy to place Him over Her. She will continue to punish us until we take a stand."

Nikolas grew red–faced and began to sputter. His Radiance was red and angry looking. *I should really find an opportunity to make connection with him,* Phoebe thought. *I have not taken the time to think about what TradesKourete Alekki, told me about Nikolas. I must do so as soon as this Fest is over. If he is indeed a heretic, there could be trouble.* Again Phoebe rubbed her eyes and sore neck. *I am so tired and my head hurts. But I must not be lax in my duties to Kriti.*

Thesmas put up a hand and rose to her feet. "Member Vasilissa, this is entirely inappropriate for a Citizenry meeting. If what you say is true, it is a matter of the Sisterhood, not the Council." She turned to Nikolas. "Kourete Nikolas, we on the Council are concerned as well about the unrest of Herilia. We rely on the Sisterhood to communicate directly with Great Meter. Aluneia, the Priesera Elder, is attending this Festival. I will ask her to give the Council a formal report of what progress is being made, and then we will have the report rescribed and disbursed to each of the Agronos. I promise you it will be discussed, though what influence you think the Council has over doings of a fire mountain is obscure to me. She of Ten Thousand Names reigns over the land, not we."

Nikolas bowed politely and sat down, though Phoebe could see that he would have liked to have said quite a bit more on the subject. She wished her Meter would have allowed him to – it would make Phoebe's job easier. She found it distasteful to have to send out a connection to people she basically disliked. After all, connections went two ways and making one came with a price. In the past few days she had become truly fond of young Theseus, compassionate toward him in a nurturing way. She was finding it more and more difficult to keep her observations of him objective. She was becoming reluctant to press him further about painful issues. She needed to continue though. As always with the Escorts, personal feelings did not matter much when it came to serving Kriti and Goddess. It did not matter if she would have preferred to pat Theseus on the head than be his lover. It did not matter if she would prefer to love just one man rather than many. One could become bitter if one dwelled on this too much.

Chapter 12

The Festival reached its climax on the final day. Not only was the Bulldancer event to take place in the late morn, but the Kore ritual began at dusk, and the final feasting and dance commenced immediately after.

The Bulldancer event was very well attended. Crowds of people packed the perimeter of the courtyard both on the ground and on the first and second levels of the Agronos, shouting and cheering and waving colorful pennants representing their guild, family or village. Thesmas stood on the second floor balcony of her own personal apartment with the silver cone she used to amplify her voice. Even so, not everyone heard her announcement at the beginning of the event.

"The Bulldancers of Kriti are world renowned, and the troupe at Knossos is especially so," she began. "Today, they celebrate the vitality of life, passing through the horns of the Sacred Bull. Just as Goddess Herself possesses within Her the MoonBull, and just as She gives birth to Her Son, so the 'dancers are a living symbol of the fertility, abundance and passion for life that the people of Kriti personify." Cheers erupted from those who could hear Thesmas, causing the rest to suddenly be aware that the event had begun. Thesmas shouted over them, "Heradike, trainer of the 'dancers of Knossos, will tell you about today's exhibition." The crowd stomped and whistled as Thesmas handed her voice–amplifying cone to the Bulldancer's sprightly coach.

"Thank you, First Elder," Heradike began as the crowd quieted. "This exhibition of tumbling and skill is dedicated to the memory of a young man who unfortunately gave his life at the last Seven–Turns Festival. Jerid Ae–Vasilissa was a dancer of exceptional talent who was gathered from us too soon. We in the troupe honor his memory. We are pleased to announce today that his sister, Geneera Ae–Vasilissa, has been accepted into the troupe. May his memory live forever."

More cheers and whistles erupted from the crowd. Ansel gasped, turned to Geneera and asked urgently, "Did you know she was going to announce you joined the team?" Geneera's face was white as alabaster and she shook her head.

Ansel took Geneera's cold hand into her own and stroked it. "Your meta is not here though, right?"

Again, Geneera shook her head. "No," she choked. "She has not attended a dancer exhibition since my brother died. She is in her rooms, I think."

"That is fortunate. You are going to need to tell her as soon as you can. Do not allow her to hear it from someone else."

"I will have to find her. I will run to her apartment as soon as the event is over. Oh Goddess, I can not believe Heradike just announced to the entire crowd that I have joined the team."

"She undoubtedly assumes your meta would be proud. Anyone would think that."

"She does not know Meta."

The troupe entered the courtyard. The 'dancers wore very short skirts and loin girdles in bright shades of blue, yellow and coral. The bull, a huge brown specimen, wore a garland of flowers around his neck in colors matching the 'dancers' costumes. Three 'dancers led the bull to the center of the courtyard while the others took their places off to the side. A girl yelled "Aiyee!" and threw her arms over her head as she stood in front of the bull. Ansel recognized Carea as the dancer gripped the bull's horns. The animal tossed his head and Carea was thrust towards its back. She balanced herself upside down, hands still grasping the horns. The bull began loping slowly around the courtyard. Carea arched her back until her outstretched feet touched the bull's back, then planted her feet and pulled herself straight up. She stood balanced on its back, her arms extended from her side as the beast continued to jog around the perimeter of the courtyard. Finally, she did a handspring from the bull's rump into the waiting arms of another dancer. The crowd cheered wildly. Carea waved and ran to the sidelines to stand with the other 'dancers.

Next, Garin raised his arm high and shouted "Aiyee!" catching the attention of the audience. He cartwheeled and hand–sprung toward the waiting bull, then grasped the bull's horns and flipped onto the bull's back, using momentum generated by the animal's head toss. Landing feet first on the bull's rump, he somersaulted first back toward the bull's head, then forward to the rump, then hoisted himself to his hands and remained balanced there as the bull loped around the courtyard. He leapt off the animal to wild applause.

After Garin finished his performance, he came to sit with Ansel and Geneera in the crowd. He smelled somewhat of sweat and animal, but Ansel found she did not mind. He reached across Ansel's shoulders to thump Geneera on the back. "Great show, no? Carea's work has been superb today. Her uncle Nikolas is here all the way from Phaistos to see her. She really wants to impress him." Geneera just grimaced, her face still unnaturally white. She continued to stare intently at the dancer now on the bull's back, who was balancing upon one foot while arching her back and raising her arms.

"She has not told her meta yet about joining the troupe," Ansel whispered to Garin.

The boy winced. "Ach. She will need to tell her now. It is going to be difficult when she finds out, yes? That is regrettable." He paused, then said, "Will I see you at the dancing after the Kore ritual tonight, Ansel?"

"I will be there with Geneera."

"Ai, of course." He seemed about to say more, then checked

himself and watched the event for a few long moments. The tall, slender, dark girl was now dancing comically atop the bull to the amusement and cheers of the crowd.

Finally, Garin turned to Ansel and said, "Geneera is Kore, too. She will understand if we want some time alone."

"I may not be willing to leave her alone, Garin."

"But it is the last night of the Kore Festival. Everyone will be partnering. Will not Geneera find someone she wants to be alone with, too?"

Ansel shrugged. "I do not know. We have not spoken of it." Her insides felt funny again. She recognized a feeling of guilt, but whether it was towards Garin or Geneera, Ansel was not certain. Her heart ached, too. So many changes. So many losses. This might be one of the last nights she had to spend with Geneera before her friend moved to the athletes' house. It was not that she could not spend time with Geneera there, but it would not be the same as sharing an apartment. But Geneera seemed already so involved with the dancer troupe, maybe Ansel was foolish to think Geneera would even miss her.

Just then, Geneera grasped Ansel's hand and squeezed it. Ansel automatically stroked her friend's hand.

Garin frowned at the girls, but to Ansel's relief, said no more about the dance. Soon, he stood. "I must return now to the ring. I hope I will see you tonight," he added to Ansel.

Chapter 13

When the Bulldancer exhibition ended, Geneera closed her eyes, suppressing the dread that threatened to overwhelm her. "I need to go now and find my meta."

"Shall I come with you?"

Geneera thought for a moment, sorely tempted to have an advocate by her side, but then decided against it and said, "No. I need to find her quickly and she is likely to become quite angry. It is something better done by myself."

Ansel nodded slowly, her large, dark eyes widened, Geneera supposed, in sympathy. "Rehearsal for the Kore ritual will be early this afternoon. I will see you then?"

Geneera nodded curtly, squeezed her friend's shoulder for reassurance, then rose and left, slipping as unobtrusively as possible through the crush.

She trotted all around the Agronos, looking first in her meter's apartment, then, when it became clear that Vasilissa was not there, in all the likeliest spots. She finally found her meter at the perimeter of the courtyard not fifty foot–lengths from where she and Ansel had been seated during the exhibition. She was speaking with Nikolas. Carea was there, too. *Ai, Goddess,* Geneera thought, *I am too late.* Desperately she grasped at hope. *Maybe they have said nothing to her about me. Maybe if I hide somewhere and wait until they are through talking together, I will still be the first to tell her.*

But then Carea spotted Geneera and waved for her to join them. Vasilissa turned as her daughter approached. Her expression was unreadable, her eyes flat. Geneera's heart sank as she resolutely trod over to the group.

"Greetings, Geneera." Carea said as she and Niko flanked the girl. "We were just congratulating your meter on your having joined the troupe." She grabbed Gen's hand and whispered urgently to her, "Uncle Niko did not realize your meter still did not know you joined the 'dancers. I am so sorry." Geneera swallowed hard.

"Yes," Nikolao, said in an overly hearty voice, as he thumped Geneera on the back, "your meter is quite overcome, but we were telling her we are sure she will be delighted once she is over the initial surprise. We assumed she knew the news since Heradike announced it publicly," he said to Geneera with a note of apology in his voice, "but it seems we were mistaken." Turning back to Vasilissa, Nikolas continued, saying, "Carea's meta was concerned, too, Vasilissa, especially since Carea insisted on coming to Knossos to train rather than staying in Phaistos, but she is very proud now. We are, of course, sorry for what happened to Jerid, but to have two 'dancers from one family! Such an honor is unprecedented."

Geneera inwardly winced; then, as an increasingly uncomfortable silence unfolded, ventured in a small voice, "I was just trying to find you, Meta, to tell you. I looked all over the Agronos. I did not think to look for you inside the courtyard. I thought you had not attended the event."

"Indeed, I did not attend. Nikolas and I had an appointment to converse directly after the exhibition." Looking at him, she added, "You will have to excuse me though, Nikolas, I must now instead talk with my daughter. I hope to have a chance to speak with you before you must return to Phaistos."

"Of course, Priesera. I will be leaving for Phaistos the morn after tomorrow." He bowed slightly as he and Carea took their leave. Under his breath he added, "My apologies again, Geneera, and I wish you best of fortune with the troupe."

When Carea and Nikolas were out of hearing range, Vasilissa glanced coldly at Geneera and said simply, "Come to my office." She turned and marched ahead of Geneera, who followed her in grim silence, her head hanging. She knew she was in for punishment. Vasilissa would yell at the least. *I deserve this. I was too frightened to tell her before and now it is worse. She deserved to hear the news from me.* She sighed, shaking her head. *When this is over though, I will finally be free to pursue my dream.* This thought cheered Geneera considerably. She prepared herself to apologize quickly and thoroughly.

Once in her office, before Geneera could even open her mouth to speak, Vasilissa whirled upon her and said, "I absolutely forbid it."

Geneera felt her heart harden in the face of her meter's imperiousness; anger surged in Geneera's gut. She straightened her shoulders and glared back at Vasilissa, tossing her hair in defiance. "I am sorry I did not tell you sooner, Meter, but I do not need your approval. I have started training with the Bulldancers and will continue whether you permit it or not." She crossed her arms in front of her chest and grasped each bicep, digging into the soft flesh with her fingernails. The pain was reassuring, distancing. Vasilissa clenched her hands into tight fists, her knuckles turning white. The very room quavered with tension before Geneera's eyes.

"You think to be like your brother. I never should have let him join the '"dancers. Will you throw away your life frivolously, too, then?"

"No. You wish me to die of boredom instead." Geneera heard her own voice rising, but chose not to control it. "I do not want to teach. I never wanted to. I am not like you, Meter. I do not care to spend my life studying dull things and pretending I am smarter than everyone else." There. She had finally said aloud what she had thought for turns.

"Instead you will be the star athlete, yes?" Vasilissa's tone was fiercely mocking. "But what of when you are too old to dance the bulls, my daughter? What if you get hurt? What will you do then?"

"That is a chance I am willing to take." Geneera glared at her meta fiercely.

Vasilissa lost her cool demeanor. She began to shout, "Your brother took that chance. He is dead. It is a stupid path, a path of folly. He threw away the life Great Meter granted him, and for what, to be cheered by a crowd? To be thought a hero on this tiny island? There is more to life than what is here on Kriti, Geneera. Jerid never thought he could be injured either. He was wrong. You are wrong. I forbid it, Geneera, I forbid it!" Vasilissa shrieked the final words, practically cuffing her daughter with them.

"You cannot forbid me, Meter." Geneera shouted back as loudly as she could. She stomped a foot. "'dancers do not do this for the crowds. It is something I do well. I am good at this. My brother understood. He was like me. He would want me to do this."

Vasilissa strode the short distance to her daughter and slapped Geneera's face fiercely with an open palm once, then twice. Geneera's knees gave way, and she knelt hard to the floor, her ears ringing. Vasilissa stood over her daughter and spat each word as if her mouth was full of bitter herbs. "Your brother would beg, *beg*, you not to throw your life away like he did. He was young and stupid, as was I for allowing him to join the 'dancers in the first place. I will never forgive them, not the 'dancers, not their coach. They offend me – risking their sacred lives for thrills and adulation. The people cheer and scream, but they do not know what it is to sacrifice a child to the Bull of Thunder, the Bull of Blood Lust! They do not care that they leave behind meters who gave them life, who watched them grow, who had dreams for their children. I hate the Bull. He disgusts me. It disgusts me, too, that you want to be a dancer. I thought you better than this. I thought you understood."

Geneera, her palm over her cheek where it throbbed in dull pain, said in a voice so distant it seemed to emanate not from her throat, but from the Underworld, said, "Luckily, I care but little what you think, Meter."

For a moment, Geneera feared her meter would strike her again. Instead, Vasilissa's face slowly resumed its familiar cold, haughty expression. Geneera pulled herself to her feet. For several minutes, meter and daughter glowered at each other, stone to stone.

Finally, Vasilissa said, "Then so be it, daughter. If you choose to be a fool, no one can stand in your way. She turned her back to Geneera. "I suppose this means you will no longer study, since practice will take so much of your time."

Geneera remained silent and unmoving.

Vasilissa turned to face her daughter again, her manner a study in composure. With an outwardly casual wave of her hand, Vasilissa shook her head and closed her eyes. Her face suddenly looked much older, and drawn in pain. "You are Kore now. Perhaps it is time for me to resume my own life. Mayhaps I will leave Knossos and again teach at the University. The Priesera will be leaving with the end of Festival. If Thesmas agrees that my duties here are finished, I will join them. Go now; I have no wish to speak with you further."

Summarily dismissed once again, Geneera felt a familiar aching pain in her chest, and she swallowed hard to keep it from escaping as a sob. For an instant she considered flinging herself at her meter, hugging her hard and begging to be understood, accepted for herself, but she knew it would be an exercise in futility and humiliation. Biting her lips, she repeated her familiar mantra to herself: *I will not cry. I will not let her see me cry.* In silence, she pulled open the door and stalked out of the room, pretending she was as furious and uncaring as her meter so obviously was. *I will go and run,* she told herself, *then I will not hear her voice anymore.*

Chapter 14

Almost one hundred adolescent girls huddled just outside the entrance to the courtyard, giggling nervously among themselves and peering anxiously at the crowd. They were this Festival's Kore, young women, the pride and hope of Kriti. They each had bled the holy blood regularly for at least one full turn. It was both a time of honoring and a time of responsibility, for they were no longer little girls free to chase butterflies, but now must assume the mantle of power expected of adult women. Of course in truth, most had taken on responsibility before their Kore; this was just the official recognition of what was a practical truth. Girls of the fisherfolk already led boats in expedition. Girls of the farm guilds worked with their meters and uncles night and day to harvest grapes or olives or figs. Girls of the mason guilds were expected to have considerable expertise with stone; where to find the rare types, how to assess the value and use, and how best to extract it from the rich mountain veins. And some girls were of the Chosen Ones, those who would go on to the famed University of the Priesera where they would become the future spiritual and political leaders of Kriti.

The courtyard was a dance of color, scent and noise. Astounding numbers of people crushed into the perimeter of the courtyard, some waving red or blue or yellow scarves at friends and leaning over the upper–floor balconies, others sharing hearty laughter or gossip with those they were seated with, and still others standing and flailing their arms in an attempt to gain the attention of someone whose seat had been saved, at some personal risk from those who had arrived promptly. Everyone was dressed in their finest, for the Kore ritual was the climax of the entire Festival. Strings of flowers, many woven from the deep red blood–flower, and others containing white lilies, jasmine, and fuchsia were spiraled along the length of the vivid coral columns of the interior courtyard and atop the sea–green walls. Huge jars at the corners of the courtyard held elaborate arrangements of cut flowers and herbs. The aromas of basil, thyme, jasmine, rosemary, lavender and dittany scented the air.

The cacophony of sights and sounds swept over Ansel like an ocean wave and her stomach lurched as she peeked into the courtyard. Her hands were cold and clammy. Standing next to her, Geneera had been sullen since speaking with her meter, and while Ansel noticed that Gen's face was red and puffy, she could get her friend to say no more than, "Meter behaved about as I expected." Geneera rolled her eyes when Ansel tugged at the hem of her own loose, white robe once again.

"Stop that. You have pulled at that hem a hundred times."

"Well, it is not straight."

"As if anyone could see that from the sidelines."

"Hold this, will you?" Ansel pushed her lily into Geneera's hands and tugged at the cord around her waist. "There. Is this better?"

"Perfect." Geneera held out the flower for Ansel to take back. The long orange stamens wagged at her.

"You did not even look," Ansel said as she took the lily. That sounded pouty even to her ears. She looked around at her hem in back. Still not straight.

Phidra, the young novice Priesera in charge of coaching the girls for the ritual, had been staring fixedly into the courtyard. She whirled around and said, "I just glimpsed the signal. Now, line up and get ready to walk across the courtyard. Remember, watch your step and do not stop short to wave at your meters!"

Despite her nervousness, Ansel had to snicker. While they were rehearsing earlier, Phidra had told them about her own womanhood ritual where one of the girls had stopped suddenly, and the next few girls behind her did not. How embarrassing to have to pick yourself off the ground in front of the entire crowd!

A cheer erupted as the girls entered the courtyard. As instructed, Phidra led the girls to the center where they formed a circle. Five other Priesera joined the circle, led by the Priesera Elder, Aluneia, in a brilliant blue, slim–waisted ritual gown. Her tall rounded hat was imposing. The gown emphasized her powerful breasts and large nipples that were rouged a deep red.

One of the Priesera turned outward from the circle and began speaking, "Daughter winds, fair child–Goddess of whirling change and ocean currents, bless us with your presence."

The crowd rejoined with, "Bless us, fair wind." The Priesera turned back to the circle.

A second Priesera turned to the crowd. "Sister light, dancing Kore–Goddess of moon, sun and stars, bless us with your presence."

The crowd responded, "Bless us, dancing light."

The third said, "Meter sea, abundant woman–Goddess of deep waters, bless us with your presence."

"Bless us, fertile sea."

The fourth; "Wise earth, ancient GranMeter–Goddess of the providers, bless us with your presence."

"Bless us, provident earth."

Aluneia glided smoothly into the center of the circle. Lifting her arms above her head, palms out in a gesture of receptivity, she began to dance. She stepped and swayed, tracing a spiral with her steps, chanting softly. When she reached the very center of the circle, the other Priesera began to hum. Aluneia lowered her arms until they were straight out from her waist, her fingers splayed. "Britomartis," she said raising her voice to reach the ears of the crowd, "maiden bright, maiden beautiful, join us, we ask, and bless this time of transition. Girl becomes Kore; our community rejoices. Come to us now and guide their steps as they begin to dance their journey of adulthood." The humming of the Priesera grew louder, sounding like a swarm of bees, then stopped abruptly.

Phidra nodded to the girls, who linked arms and began to dance as they had rehearsed. The dance mimicked Aluneia's; step, sway, step, sway; a dance as old as the mountains and the sea. Ansel had seen it danced many times before, though except for on the beach the night when she had seen the strange Goddess, she had not done it herself and never with other women. It was sacred, mimicking the cadence of life, honoring the cycles of nature and of woman. Step, sway, step, sway, Ansel's feet followed the pattern of the spiral of her sisters and of life, the connectedness of the net, their steps circumscribing the very thread of existence. Step, sway, step, sway, deep into the heart of the circle, hands held out now, lilies extended, brushing palms with those of the other young women, a community of womanhood dancing the dance of life. Ansel felt a tingling sensation begin deep within her belly. It rose warm to her heart and her breath grew faster. The dance! The dance of women, midwives to life, made in the image of She of Ten Thousand Names, womb of the world, and she was now one; no longer a girl, but an adult standing upon the threshold of her life. Never before had she understood, but after today, never would she forget.

Aluneia nodded and Phidra raised her hand. The girl–women stopped dancing and reformed the circle; Ansel's head still tingled and buzzed. She could feel the Radiance pour from her body. Looking around her she was delighted to see the Radiance of all the others. Geneera's was a bright orange–red. Aluneia's was magnificent, deeply golden and full of sparks.

"With great pride," cried Aluneia, "we present to you, community of Knossos, of Kriti, of all the world, the new Kore!" As one, the crowd jumped to its feet, cheering and waving and stomping. The girls ran to the perimeter to toss their lilies to the crowd and receive hugs from proud relatives.

After several minutes and some coaxing from the Priesera, the girls re–gathered into a circle. Each Priesera took a group, and began addressing the young women individually. Phidra and the other novices stood at the elder Priesera's side, carrying a reed basket into which she dipped her hand and gave each girl a gift after speaking with her. Aluneia joined the group Ansel and Geneera were in. She spoke softly to Geneera, but not so quietly that Ansel, who stood next to her, could not hear.

"Daughter, how many moons have you bled?"

"It was nineteen this past time," Geneera replied.

"Good. And what plans have you for your life path?"

Geneera looked at her feet but her voice was unwavering. "I train with the Bulldancers, Priesera."

Aluneia nodded. Geneera steadfastly refused to lift her head. "But there is some difficulty involved?" the Priesera probed.

Geneera shrugged. Aluneia observed the girl for a moment then kissed her forehead. "Child, your heart knows the way. Listen more deeply to thine Inner Guidance." Geneera nodded and Ansel thought she looked like she might cry. Aluneia plunged her hand into the basket Phidra carried and pressed a small object into Geneera's hand.

Ansel was next. The tall Priesera turned her attention toward her and once again looked deeply into her eyes. Ansel saw this time that, like Priesera Aluneia's Radiance, her deep eyes were flicked with sparks of gold. Ansel was captivated. Aluneia began asking the ritual questions of Ansel.

"Daughter, how many moons?"

"Twenty–two, Priesera."

"Good. Are you ready to answer She–Who–Called?"

Ansel drew in a deep breath. "I have thought long and deep. The way is not clear to me, but I will answer the Call."

Aluneia took Ansel's hands and smiled kindly. "It is not necessary to know every step of your path in advance, Ansel. I am always content just to know the next step on mine. You come from a long lineage of Priesera. Did you know your meter almost refused her Call? You should ask her about that sometime."

Ansel barely felt the light kiss Aluneia placed on her forehead.

She glanced at the charm pressed into her palm. It was shiny gold with a dark red gem in the center, the charm of Kore; the gift of womanhood.

In time, the Priesera finished speaking with each girl. The five Sisters met at circle center and raised their arms to the sky. Chairs had appeared at the edge of the courtyard for the new Kore and they were led to them by the novice Priesera. Ansel sat down gratefully, relieved to be finished with her part in the ritual.

"We now thank Britomartis, Goddess of maidens and new Kore," Aluneia began. The crowd cheered, then fell quiet as Aluneia suddenly put out her hand. "Wait. There is a message to the people from Pasiphae, She–Who–Shines–for–All." The other Priesera suddenly flanked Aluneia. One produced a veil from the side altar and placed it over Aluneia's head and face. Another scurried to the periphery of the courtyard and whispered urgently to a servant, who quickly found an empty chair and set it near the front of the space. Aluneia was led to it by a third Priesera.

Except for some low muttering from the crowd, all were hushed for several moments as Aluneia sat in the chair, murmuring something to herself. Abruptly, Aluneia rose to her feet, only she was not Aluneia. Ansel could see clearly that the Radiance of the elder Priesera was overtaken by something much larger and brighter, a Radiance of bright yellow–white that Ansel found difficult even to peer at directly. When Aluneia again spoke, the voice was not hers.

"My children," Pasiphae/Aluneia said, "this age passes and the world changes. Bull gives way to Ram just as girl cycles to Kore. Some changes will gladden your hearts. Others will bring tears. Know that a noble loss is preferable to an ignoble win. There are few answers without, only within. Seek them and find peace. Blessings upon you, my beloved children. Know that She–Who–Shines–for–All remains with you always, even when all around you appears dark."

At the end of the message, the brilliant essence lifted from Aluneia, and the Priesera was quickly led out of the courtyard. Ansel could see Aluneia's Radiance had dulled and somehow knew the

Priesera Elder was exhausted. Aluneia needed to be somewhere quiet for a time.

The crowd began murmuring loudly. They had been prepared for perhaps a message of glad tidings and love from the Goddess as sometimes happens at important rituals. Even the Priesera who remained in the courtyard seemed disquieted. When whispers threatened to turn to roars however, a Sister strode to the center of the courtyard and announced, "Good people, the message from Pasiphae is a wise and loving one. We are a nation rich with blessings and have been given all one could hope for. She admonishes us to seek for our happiness within. It is just and holy."

The Priesera then raised her arms and said, "Pasiphae, She–Who–Shines–for–All, we thank You for Your message and Your presence and Your blessings upon Your people."

The crowd, upon hearing the ritual words, responded with, "May Your blessing enrich us and may we in turn enrich those things You hold dear."

Somewhat comforted by the routine of ritual, the disquiet of the crowd dissipated as the wind, light, sea and earth were thanked and released.

Chapter 15

The first full Koretide moon shone through the wispy evening clouds at dusk. *The final eve of Festival,* Ansel thought. *It went by so fast.* Though surrounded by people hugging and cheering the newest Kore, Ansel felt alone and abandoned in the courtyard. After the ritual ended, Geneera quickly ran off to greet Carea and the other Bulldancers who were loitering by a long table that was being laden with steaming plates of food at one end of the courtyard.

The crowd parted and an elegant Phoebe walked up and embraced her daughter. "You are a woman grown, Ansel. It is difficult for me to believe. I am so proud of you."

Ansel searched her meter's eyes, hoping to see herself reflected in them, but Phoebe appeared distracted. "Will you dine with me, Meta?" she asked. "I have things I need to tell you."

"*Mellia*, I cannot. I am still escorting until tomorrow. But then, I promise, we will spend time together, just you and me." Phoebe smiled, her eyes looking wistful.

Ansel nodded. There was no arguing when it came to Meta's duties. Phoebe embraced her daughter then walked back to the awaiting Theseus. The young man's face lit up as Phoebe approached, while Ansel felt her own light fade.

The closing feast in the courtyard, like the opening feast, was by invitation, but there were invitations within invitations. Most people were preparing to dine from several long plank tables weighed down with food and Ansel eventually wandered over to find Geneera there. Three tables laid end to end held many varieties of fresh fish dishes, roast mutton and fowls, basil and rosemary spiced grain dressing and porridges, and the freshest of the new green vegetables laced with pressed olive oil and sour wine.

As Ansel approached the feast, a group of young people seated at another long wooden table located next to the spread of food waved enthusiastically at her – the Bulldancers and Geneera, but Geneera was one of them now. Ansel waved back and walked over to the table.

"We did not go to the ritual," Garin said. He stood and smiled warmly, his eyes following Ansel's every movement.

"Ai," Carea added more expansively than usual, "we wanted to make sure we got good seats for the food!" Garin ushered Ansel to an open spot next to himself; he apparently had saved it for her. Geneera sat across from them, a short distance away with a group of female 'dancers, including Carea. Soon, the bell was rung announcing that the diners should serve themselves, and they all stood up to get into line.

Garin continued to be very solicitous towards Ansel during dinner. She still did not know quite whether she liked his attentions or not. She supposed he was trying to be gallant, but she felt awkward. "Shall I get you some more stuffed fowl, Ansel?" he asked when he noticed her plate empty.

"No, uh, thanks, Garin, I think I have had enough to eat, but thank you for asking." Ansel looked down at her lap. To her horror, she noticed that she had spilled some vegetable stew down the front of her white Kore robe. She tried to brush it off covertly with a linen napkin and was relieved when Garin got up to get himself more food.

Can my life really be changing as quickly as the time it takes to complete a Festival? Her heart longed for the comforting, familiar camaraderie of Geneera, but her friend was laughing gaily with the group of girl 'dancers, and Ansel leaned to overhear.

"You really should come and live in the athlete's quarters since you are one of us now, Geneera," Carea cajoled. "We all eat together and train together so we can work well as a team. It is hard to be a good 'dancer if you live outside the quarters. I have an extra cot in my room at the moment and I would be pleased to share my room with you."

Although the last statement was made casually enough, Carea blushed slightly. The girl sitting to her right, a lean, dark–skinned woman named Deena, elbowed Carea, remarking, "I do not remember you making *me* that offer when I came to live at the quarters." The rest of the girls snickered.

"That is not fair," Carea retorted with some heat. "You know that Sapha was living with me then!" Carea's defensiveness made the girls giggle all the more. Geneera grinned but did not respond. To Carea's obvious relief, Fatima changed the subject and soon the conversation was lightly buzzing again.

Garin returned to the table with a plate laden with sweets for all. As he offered a honeyed poppyseed cake to Ansel, he met her gaze and held it. How soft and dark his eyes were! Ansel squirmed and felt color rush into her cheeks. After finishing his own dish of liquored fruits over soft, sweet cheese, Garin inquired in a voice casual enough to have been rehearsed, "Ansel, will you meet me for the final dance, then?"

"Uh, I really had not decided." Ansel winced as she stumbled over her words, "I want to see what Geneera is going to do."

"The dance starts at nightfall. I would like to have a chance to know you better and this is the last night of Festival. Soon I will have to resume training, and that steals so much of my time."

The last night of Festival, she thought. She glanced over where Geneera had been sitting and saw to her chagrin that the chairs were empty. Geneera had left with her new athlete friends and had not even told Ansel where she was going!

"Oh, do not be angry at Geneera," Garin said when he saw Ansel's surprise at Geneera's sudden disappearance. He drew himself a little closer to Ansel and inclined his head toward her to share a confidence. "The girls wanted a chance to talk to her alone, especially Carea. I would not take it personally. They do this with all the new girl 'dancers."

It made sense, but still Ansel felt wounded. Could Geneera forget their years of friendship so quickly? What right did Ansel have to feel like Geneera had been disloyal, anyway? They did not own each other. Ansel felt suddenly very foolish; Geneera obviously did not want to include Ansel in her plans. Ansel said, "Why, yes, Garin, since I apparently do not have any other plans, I will meet you at the dance later this evening. Thank you for asking."

Night crept over the land gently and one by one, stars decorated the sky like some vast sparkling net of jewels. The yellow moon was already high in the evening sky. Ansel awoke from a nap she had allowed herself after dinner. She had hoped Geneera would come home, but found herself still alone in her room.

Ansel lit several olive oil–soaked torches from her brazier coals and thrust them into their wall pockets. Soon she would meet Garin. She could already hear the reveling of Festival–goers outside her window. She wondered that she had never before noticed how large and barren her suite of rooms was.

On a hook on one wall, a special dress was hung. Given to Ansel on the day of her first menses by her GranMeter, Thesmas, it was an adult party dress. As she lifted it off the wooden peg and held it against her body, she paused, wondering if she had something else to wear. The dress was beautiful. It reached to the floor in flowing layers of the rich blue color she favored. Bright embroidered orange–red poppies danced across the corset. It hugged her small waist tightly, emphasizing her new curves. It was cut low at the neckline, not revealing, but lifting and emphasizing her already ample breasts.

Ansel had only put it on once before and that was just to show her meter and granmeter. Breasts were an important symbol on Kriti, symbolic of power of She of Ten Thousand Names. Almost all women who bled, the Kore, wore clothing that emphasized their breasts. But Ansel had matured early. In her heart, she still saw herself as a shy, plain girl who found refuge in her writing. "Maybe I will just not go," Ansel murmured to herself. "I will tell Garin I felt ill and went to bed." But in the end, loneliness won out. *Geneera is off having a wonderful time with her new friends. She did not even think about me.* Ansel knew she would be too restless to return to sleep and at that moment, anything seemed better than lying alone in her darkened room listening to everyone else in the entire world have fun. Reluctantly, she stepped into the dress.

Chapter 16

"I hope Ansel is not angry with me for leaving her alone with Garin," Geneera said to Carea, Deena and Fatima as they strolled toward the athlete's quarters.

"Garin will see that she is not lonesome, Geneera," Deena reassured her. "He asked us to help him get her alone so he could ask her to the dance tonight."

"Oh, ai, I should have realized," Geneera said. Her stomach turned slightly at the thought that Ansel might want to be alone with Garin. He seemed like a nice enough boy, but why did he have to like Ansel?

The girls entered the athlete's quarters by a side door. Designed by the same architect who had designed the main Agronos itself, the quarters were in many ways remarkable, although not, to Geneera's relief, as labyrinthine as the Agronos. Like the Center, the dormitory hallway walls were interspersed with cut out places, lightwells, so that day light streamed into them. They also had indoor plumbing and pools for bathing.

Carea's room was easily large enough for two girls. Geneera turned all around, admiring the lovely paintings circling the plastered walls. Dancer teams vaulted bulls, their arms over their heads, the animals looking huge and fierce. Interspersed between the Bulldancer scenes were images of the double–bladed ax, the Holy

Labrys, as Bulldancing was not simply a sport, but a symbolic act of connection with She of Ten Thousand Names.

Behind Geneera, Carea uncorked a double–handled jug of wine. The ceramic jug itself was a work of art. A huge black octopus of the kind painted by the prestigious Stephanous Pottery Guild stretched its tentacles over the white ceramic surface.

"It is time to celebrate!" Carea announced, as she passed stemmed ceramic cups to the other girls. The cups, too, were painted in the octopus motif. "We have been training and training for this Festival exhibition. Now we can relax for a few days! I have been saving this jug of wine just for tonight, to share with dear friends, both old and new. I propose a toast; to Deena for winning the overall competition! Garin almost beat you, but you won the day. Next time it will be me!"

Deena laughed, shaking her head of black curls. "*Mellia*, you just do not give up, do you?"

"Never," Carea said. "It is what makes me a good competitor. I never give up."

Carea sounded a little tipsy already, although she had only taken a sip of the wine and her stomach must be still full from dinner. Geneera decided it was the exhilaration of the competition being over.

"To Fatima!" Carea continued, "the best spotter a girl could ask for. I apologize that I nearly kicked you in the head on that last roll-over." Fatima was not even twelve turns yet. She was not allowed to actually leap the bulls in competition since she had only been training for a year. Instead, she caught the other 'dancers as they jumped from the bull's rump.

"And finally, to Geneera, our newest member! May she dance the bull with ease and become the finest athlete we have ever had, except for me, of course!"

"I will drink to that," Geneera said, then tipped her head back and drained the cup of thick, sweet wine. Although she never drank much, Geneera was touched by the friendliness of these girls and felt at home with them in a way she had never experienced before.

Here were people who valued her athletic ability and did not criticize if she could not spout the names of the last ten rulers of Egypt. These were *her* people. Warmth filled her heart and for a moment she thought she might weep. Instead, she refilled her wine glass and laughed.

As the girls continued to toast each other and recount the highlights of the competition, Geneera silently raised her glass and thought, *To you, Jerid my brother. Now at last I truly understand.*

Sitting in Carea's room until the sun was beginning to set, the four girls had finished the jug of wine handily and Geneera was quite drunk. Then Deena remembered she had some mead in her room left over from a party the previous week. The mead however, was suspiciously off taste. The girls decided it was time to drop in on the revelries if for no other reason than to find more acceptable beverages. But first, they decided they needed to visit the baths. Fatima had spilled as much wine on herself as she had ingested. She and Deena went off to their shared room to find clean garments. Carea invited Geneera to share her bath.

"Does each room have a private bath?" Geneera asked in wonderment as they entered the large bathing room.

"No," Carea replied. "One bath serves five rooms. The rooms are connected like a star around the central bath. There are usually two girls or boys to a room." The older girl had slipped off her skirt and was testing the water temperature with a foot. Her powerfully built body made even her most casual movements appear exceedingly graceful.

Geneera pulled off her own skirt and waded right in, past Carea. She sat down on a smooth, white gypsum shelf that lined the perimeter of the bath and scooped up some herbal soap she found at the side of the pool. The bath was large enough for five or more people, but Carea, apparently satisfied with the water temperature, sat directly next to Geneera.

"Here," Carea said to Geneera, "let me scrub your back."

Geneera compliantly turned her back to Carea and felt strong hands begin to massage her shoulder muscles. "Mmm. That feels nice," she said.

Carea took some of the soap and smoothed it over Geneera's back, then used a wedge of sea sponge to gently rinse it off. Geneera became aware that Carea's face was near the back of her neck. The older girl began softly kissing the side of Geneera's throat, her arms slipping around Geneera's waist.

"Do you mind? It is the last night of Festival, after all," Carea breathed into Geneera's ear. Geneera found she did not mind at all. But as she turned to meet Carea's awaiting lips, her thoughts unexpectedly drifted to Ansel. Abruptly, Geneera realized there was something she needed to ask her oldest friend.

Moments later, Deena and Fatima burst into the bath and found Geneera and Carea still kissing. "Hey, Carea, we see you wasted no time!" Deena teased. The girls separated, their faces reddened. Geneera rose from the bath and grabbed a nearby towel. Carea splashed Deena and said, "You two had better get in here and get clean if we are going to make it back to that dance."

When they finished dressing, Carea took Geneera in her arms, looked in her eyes and asked, "Will you come back here to me after the dance tonight?"

"I would like that, Carea," Geneera replied. "I am thinking...I must speak to Ansel first. I need to know that she is ready to let me go."

"You are in love with her? It is unwise to fall for a girl who prefers boys."

"I did not say I was in love with her. I do not rightly know how I feel. She has been my closest friend for many turns. I must admit, for all our closeness, we never once spoke of the nature our relationship. I do not know even if she prefers boys. Just let me find out."

"I will be waiting, *mellia*, if you should decide you want me. Remember, I never give up." She gave Geneera a lingering kiss that caused Geneera's belly to tingle. *I love Ansel, but never have I felt like this*, she thought.

Somewhat later, with arms around each other's waists for support, the four girls tromped down the hallway, occasionally losing their collective balance and careening into a wall. Evening had fallen and the shadows of the lit wall torches wagged playfully as they progressed. Laughing wildly, they assisted whoever had stumbled and resumed their staggering progress. Together they rambled up the hill toward the lights and noise in the Agronos courtyard. They sang loudly, serenading all passersby with bawdy tunes like, "When Aphrodite Danced the Bull." Geneera laughed so hard, tears streamed down her face.

The dance in the courtyard was already in full swing. In the light cast by huge pillar candles and torches anchored deeply into the ground, people danced vigorously in a circle. A group of string musicians was located at one end of the dancing area. Those not dancing milled around the courtyard, talking, or snacking. Some were seated in chairs placed at area's perimeter listening to the music. A few people were smoking from carved wooden pipes. The fragrant dry herbs made the air cloud with a bluish haze. Most importantly to the girls, there was a line of revelers waiting to fill their mugs with fresh mead or diluted wine at large jugs opposite the musicians.

The girls slogged up to the line, still singing raucously, competing with the dancing music. As they more or less patiently awaited their turn at the barrel, Carea suddenly tapped Geneera on the shoulder and pointed to the dance floor. "Look, there are Garin and Ansel." The music had now changed to a slower, couples' line dance and through the smoke of the torches, Geneera could make out a petite form in an elaborately flounced dress, her hair piled high on her head, curls escaping around her forehead and neck. Geneera sucked in her breath. Ansel's fine pointed chin was lifted as she gazed up at Garin. Her curvaceous figure was hugged by the dress. Ansel was dancing with the taller, leaner figure of Garin, his arm around her waist. Geneera felt they were far too close to each other for her liking.

"See," Deena whispered in Geneera's ear, "we told you Ansel

would never miss you. She looks stunning in that dress. I am glad for Garin. He is a nice fellow."

Geneera felt as if someone had kicked her in the stomach, or maybe her heart. Sobering suddenly, she announced to the other girls, "I am sorry to be such a sea slug, but I do not feel very well. I think I will go back to my rooms and lie down for a time."

"I know how quickly drinking can go from fun to misery," Carea said, rubbing Geneera's back, "We are disappointed, of course. Try to eat some unsweetened bread. It will help sop up the poisons. Mayhaps you will feel better later tonight."

Geneera parted from her friends after a few more words, then crossed the courtyard and entered the Agronos. She walked past the dance floor and watched as Garin whispered something into Ansel's ear. Her heart thumped in her chest as Ansel cocked her head prettily and chuckled at whatever Garin had said, *Ansel does indeed look stunning. Why did it never occur to me before that I am in love with her?* Geneera was certain Ansel and Garin never saw her as she walked by.

"The musicians play beautifully," Ansel said to Garin as she took his hand to sweep down the center of a line of dancers. They were engrossed in a complex line dance. They separated briefly to perform a few steps with several other dancers then faced each other again. Garin met her eyes and gave her that engaging grin as he caught her by her waist. Ansel was a naturally good dancer. She was poised and had a keen sense of rhythm. Garin was a good dancer, too; he had an athlete's grace and a surety of movement. Arm in arm, they frolicked to the end of the line.

"You look very beautiful in that dress, Ansel," Garin whispered into her ear quickly just as they parted to reform two lines. Ansel blushed and found herself grinning. *Maybe it is not so bad to be Kore.* But her self–consciousness made the dancing less fun. She was aware that Garin was responding physically to her, and that knowledge caused her some panic. Many young women began their first love affairs on the last night of Festival – it was considered good luck. Only children slept alone on the last night of Festival! But Ansel did not know if she felt ready to be physically intimate or maybe it was only that she was not ready to be with Garin. She barely knew him.

"Ansel?" Garin's voice cut through her thoughts. "Ansel, what is the matter? Are you tired of dancing? It is almost over anyway. Do you want to leave the courtyard?" Startled, Ansel looked around her and saw that only a few couples remained on the dance floor. Some of the musicians had already packed up their instruments in specially carved wooden cases.

Maybe I am tired, she thought, then said aloud, "I am sorry, Garin, I was merely lost in thought again. Yes, maybe we should bid the moon goodnight."

Garin escorted Ansel from the dance floor where they took some empty seats. "It must be late," Ansel said. "Look, the moon is nearly setting. There are only a few of us left about."

Garin slipped an arm around Ansel's shoulders, lightly laying his hand just above her left breast. Nuzzling her neck, he said, "Most have merely adjourned to some more private place. We, too, could find somewhere to be alone for a while." He began stroking the back of her neck lightly with his fingertips, as his other hand crept over the thick layers of flounce to her thigh.

Ansel's body began to respond, and heat flowed from between her thighs. She could feel his passionate gaze, waiting for a response, but she refused to meet his eyes.

Perhaps it would be nice, she thought. *Maybe I could like him.* She began to lean into his encircling arms. Then she pictured him bragging to all of the other dancers about coupling with the First Elder's naive little grandaughter and whether it was good or not and how he had wooed her all night. She froze.

Garin stopped kissing her as she tensed. Rising a bit too abruptly and throwing off his arms, she said, "No, Garin, I am not comfortable. I hope we can be friends, but I need to know you better than I do now to be intimate with you."

She heard him inhale sharply, hold his breath a moment, then exhale a puff of air. "I understand Ansel. If you are not interested, I could just walk you to your apartment. Why have you gotten so prickly with me so suddenly? I would not try to force you to be intimate with me if it is not your desire. I thought we were having a good time."

Ansel sat back down, ashamed of herself. "I am sorry, Garin. I find it hard to trust. I have only known you for a short while, and we have not spent much time together." She hesitated, then added softly, "I wonder if perhaps you are interested in me because of who I am."

"I am sure you have many potential lovers fawning upon you, but no one can know you if you shut them out. Why not give me a chance?"

Ansel grimaced. "I do not have many potential lovers fawning on me. In fact, I have never had any lovers at all. Everything just seems to be happening so quickly, I hardly know what to think." She paused, placing a finger in her mouth. "You seem like a nice boy, Garin. I do like you. But I want return to my rooms now. No, no, please do not bother walking with me; the distance is quite short. I thank you for a pleasant evening." Ansel stood and strode as quickly as her long gown would allow, away from an open–mouthed Garin and toward the safe and nearly empty Agronos.

Chapter 17

Phoebe stretched her arms over her head and snuggled deeply under the bed covers. Her hair was mussed, but she knew it looked all the more seductive that way. It was their last night together before Theseus left to sail back to Athena. She had suggested they skip the dance and Theseus readily agreed. She needed to press him for more information. She rolled on her side to face him as he lay next to her on his belly. She drew a fingernail lightly down his naked back, taking note of several scars that were shiny against the golden tan of his skin. The young man shivered, laid his head upon his arm and smiled sleepily at her. Phoebe playfully kissed him on his nose as strands of his wavy hair tumbled over his forehead. She did not need to check his Radiance to know he was deeply enchanted.

"Tell me, Theseus, about living on the streets of Trozaen as a child. How did you find your way to Athena?"

He pursed his lips as if in thought before answering. "I was, as far as I know, born on the streets. I do not remember my true meter at all. Trozaen is a small city, but it has its share of harbor brats running the streets. Except for those few turns with Karolina on Paros, I never had a home."

Phoebe drew an arm around his shoulders. He breathed warm upon her breasts. "How difficult that must have been. How did you survive?"

"I joined a gang of youths. It is the only way to survive on the streets. I became the leader because I was smart." He shrugged slightly, then pulled away from her to prop himself up on his elbow, still facing her. "Actually, I was a slip, a cut purse. I could steal silver, or failing that, food. I was always small and fast. One day, we stumbled upon a cask of unattended ale on Cronos' Wharf. We decided to 'borrow' it." He half smiled. "We rolled it off the pier and into an alley we often gathered in. It was night, mind you, and no one seemed to be paying much attention. Anyway, the ale went to our tongues, and we began talking about rumors we had heard of bands of nomads from the North who raid towns, stealing everything they could carry, then making off quick–like." Theseus abruptly rolled over onto his back, flinging his arms over his head. Phoebe stroked his flat belly. "We began bragging to each other about how we could do that, too; get rich, then go to Athena, the big city. We were like goat kids. Stupid." He shook his head.

"What did you do?" Phoebe asked, her voice dark and rich.

Theseus inhaled deeply. "Just as we borrowed the ale, we borrowed a boat that night. We were full of spirits and thought we would just row to the closest town along the harbor and be a warband, just like the Northerners. I had the only real weapon in the group: a short, bronze sword, so heavy I could barely lift it, let alone control it. The rest had clubs or hatchets or heavy branches. We got to the shoreline and ran full tilt to the first hut we came across, burst in the door and demanded silver. I remember so well how clear the stars were that night. Breathtaking and, except for us, the night was so silent."

When Theseus hesitated, Phoebe reached out and stroked softly over his throat and chest area, releasing the blockage that had suddenly formed in his Radiance. There was no need to explain; he only noticed what she wanted him to. He coughed, then continued.

"We frightened the family in the hut nearly to death. They reminded me of my foster family, fisherfolk with lots of kids and a meter and her two brothers. One of the men pulled out a bronze fire poker and came at us with it. I started to back up just like the rest of the guys, but then the man called me some name, 'street trash' or something like that. Maybe it was because I was full of beer, I do not know, but anyway, I just snapped. I got mad, furious. I drew out my sword and threatened to hack his children to pieces if they gave us any trouble. They did not. He backed down right away. They did not have any silver. Why would they? But we took what copper they had and more beer, too. We laughed as we left. I had been so scared, but I came out the big hero. That was how it started."

"So, what did you and your band do next? Did you go back to Trozaen?"

"Not right away. We dashed into the woods and drank the beer we had stolen from the family. We could not even start a fire, we were so full of spirits. We told each other how brave we had been and how much fun we had. Even then I remember having a bad taste in my mouth about the whole thing, but the boys thought it was great fun. They all kept thumping me on the back, saying what a warrior, what a leader I was. We were a family."

"That must have felt good." Phoebe felt her heart ache for the lonely boy–child he had been, even as she felt compassion for the family who was accosted.

"Ai. It felt good. It felt like something I did not ever want to lose." He closed his eyes and sighed, running his fingers through his hair. "We planned our next raid on the outskirts west of Trozaen. There were more towns closer together, and we heard they were very rich. Turns out they were not, but soon we were in deep water. People heard about us, and we could not return to Trozaen anymore. The land north and west of Trozaen is full of caves and hills; lots of places to hide and easy to defend if it came to that. We began stealing any weapons we found, as well as beer and silver. We even got us a donkey, though then we had to worry about keeping it fed, too! We began practicing how to really use the weapons. None of us were any good, but then neither were any of the people we robbed. Our style was to attack quickly and at night or sometimes surprise a small group traveling on the road. A band of armed slips, that was us."

"You were heading for Athena?"

"Yes, though we stopped talking about what a great time we would have when we got there. We just hoped to make it to a city big enough to hide in. I wanted to stop raiding and robbing and so did some of the others, but we did not know how else to live. One day, we set up camp in a cave just outside the next town we were planning to raid, when up came a group of armed, uniformed men on horses. Athenians! We grabbed for our weapons, but we knew we were out–numbered. The leader approached the mouth of the cave and called out for parley with the leader of our group. That was me. I was shaking as much as if the Bull had stamped. I will never forget my first impression of that Athenian; tall and arrogant with a curling lip, and eyes that could pierce bronze. But he did not want to kill us. He said he admired our initiative. He wanted us to join the Athenian army, to help him win his campaign to unite the surrounding villages for Athena. Said he understood we were just a group of boys trying to survive and doing a fine job of it. I could not believe it. Of course, we jumped at the chance to be real soldiers with the Athenian army. His name was Andraphaedro. He needed experienced thugs. That was us."

"Andraphaedro was the leader of the army before you took over, correct?" *and Demetria's last Royal Consort,* Phoebe added to herself.

"Yes. I led my warband to Athena and we joined the Athenian army under Royal Consort Andraphaedro. He was a skilled man with a sword, but very cold. I learned all my real swordcraft from him. I both loved and hated him. I think he felt the same about me. When he was killed in an uprising, I became the next leader."

"So quickly?"

Theseus just shrugged.

Even then you must have worn the mark of a Chosen One. People respond to it even if they do not understand what it is they respond to. It is the only explanation why a mere boy would be followed so devotedly, promoted so quickly.

As Phoebe encircled him in her arms his voice grew distant and sleepy . "I understand Andraphaedro more now that I am Consort.

Helen Demetria is, well, difficult. Nothing is as simple as I once thought."

"Sleep now," Phoebe suggested, pitching her voice to a resonance to induce drowsiness. A receptive Theseus closed his eyes and almost immediately began to breathe deeply and evenly.

Phoebe stared at the ceiling in the dark and pondered. *What do I make of this information? Did the Caster, She–Who–Rules–the–Underworld, really choose you? If not Her, then who? And why? I have heard of males being chosen before, but only rarely. Never before have I met a male Chosen One. No male alive today upon Kriti is a Chosen One, though the great Architect, Daedalous, was believed to have been chosen by Dictynna of the Forge.*

After several minutes of contemplation, Phoebe felt herself starting to drowse as she listened to her companion's easy breaths. Suddenly, Theseus bolted upright on the bed, interrupting Phoebe's sleepy musings. He grabbed her hands and excitedly said, "I have had a true dream. I have them sometimes, but not for a long time."

Phoebe sat up and reached for the oil lamp at the side of the bed, then leaned against the wall at the head of the bed and crossed her legs. She cocked her head and looked into his face. "Tell me."

"There was a voice through the darkness, Her voice. She told me I must come back here to Kriti, that I must attend the University of the Priesera high in the mountains. She showed me where it is and what it looks like. There was snow all around it." He looked very earnest, his eyebrows raised and eyes dilated as if it never even occurred to him that he said something very, very peculiar.

Phoebe felt her jaw drop. When she found her voice, she said, "Theseus, the Priesera is for women only. We never admit males. Our men go to the Monestara. This is also in the mountains, but in the West. The brothers of the Monestara learn Her worship in the form of craft and guild leadership. The Priesera are given gifts that males are not given, gifts connected to Her worship and Her creative powers that only females can tap into. I believe that you are to study Her ways and Her worship, and even that you can be great in the powers given to males by Her. I see this potential in you, but

She must have shown you the Monestara, not the University of the Priesera. It is not possible for you to be Priesera.

He shook his head impatiently. "No. It was the Priesera I saw. She specifically told me to go to the University of the Priesera. Look, I will show you. I can prove my dream is true. Is there a pad and stick? I can draw what I was shown."

Phoebe set the oil lamp back on the nightstand, swung out of bed, and produced a wax pad and stylus from a stack on her desk. She handed these to him. He intently drew on the pad for a few moments, then showed her his representation.

Phoebe inhaled sharply. There could be no doubt from his drawing that Theseus had been shown the hidden, rarely described (and never in public) shape of the University of the Priesera. What could this possibly mean? Phoebe could only speculate.

Chapter 18

A tall torch lamp softly illuminated the apartment. The flame's shadow flickered against the wall as Ansel slammed the door open and entered her rooms.

"Ansel?" Geneera's voice came from her bedroom. "How did your evening go?" Her voice sounded slurred.

"Well enough," Ansel replied curtly as she entered her own bedroom and plucked at the fastenings of her dress as if the fabric burned at her fingertips. The gown slid down around her feet. She kicked out of it, then left it to lie in a heap on the floor as she slipped her worn linen sleeping dress over her head. "Where did you go?" she called to Geneera, trying hard not to sound as peevish as she felt.

Geneera did not answer immediately. Instead, she appeared at the entrance to Ansel's bedroom, then, at Ansel's invitation, sat next to Ansel on the bed. Ansel picked up a luminescent shell comb from her bed table, loosened her hair and began combing it. She refused to meet Geneera's eyes.

"I saw you dancing with Garin," There was an edge to Geneera's voice that Ansel did not understand. When Ansel did not reply, Geneera added, "The girls told me you and he wanted to be alone together, so I left with them. I thought they must have been right when I saw you two together later."

Ansel's eyes suddenly filled with tears and she threw the comb onto the bed. "You knew I did not want to be alone with him! How could you just leave me?" she asked accusingly. "He told me the girls wanted to talk to you alone. When you left without even telling me where you were going, I felt abandoned. I was telling him that I needed to ask you about your plans and then you just left me. I thought my choices were to be with him or stay here in my room alone. I decided I may as well spend the evening with him."

"Honestly, I meant to come back and see if you were all right, but then we all got to drinking, and I, uh, I must have lost the path of time. I am really sorry."

Ansel felt the hot tears spill over her lashes and roll down her cheeks. Brusquely she dashed the tears from her face with the back of her hand. "I enjoyed dancing, and he was pleasant company, but I could not relax with him. It is just, just, I had to wear that horrible dress." She knew she was making little sense, but the effort to make sense seemed an overwhelming task. She gave in to sobbing. Geneera put an arm around her shoulder. Ansel noticed her friend smelled strongly of drink.

"Garin must smoke poppies if he did not like the way you look in that dress."

"No, no, he . . ." Ansel could not continue. She buried her face into Geneera's shoulder and sobbed convulsively. Geneera embraced her friend and rubbed her back with an unsteady hand. She emitted something close to a growl.

"Ansel, I swear on the Meter's Teats, if Garin did anything to hurt you, he will meet worse than a bull at the next practice."

Ansel pulled away. "No!" she said. "You do not understand. He was very polite. I just did not want to spend the evening with him. I felt so alone, so lonely. I missed you. I thought you and I were going to you be together, and instead you left me for *them*."

"I am sorry, *mellia*. Carea and the others wanted me to see their rooms in the athlete's dormitory. Carea wanted to talk about the dancer exhibition and celebrate. Since I am one of them now, I felt I had to go. Besides, I thought you wished to be with Garin."

Ansel's sobbing slowed and she pulled back from Geneera's shoulder. She accepted a square of linen that Geneera drew from a pocket in her skirt and blew her nose loudly. "You are leaving me, Gen, and it hurts. You are my only friend, and I am losing you."

After a few moments, when Ansel's chest stopped heaving completely, Geneera turned to face her and cupped her shoulder with her right palm. "Ansel," she began hesitantly, "I need to know something."

"What is it?"

"Carea, I mean, Carea and I, we . . ." Geneera squirmed in frustration. Finally, her tongue loosened by the wine, she blurted out, "You say you wanted to spend the night of the dance with me? Ansel, what does that mean to you?"

Ansel felt confused. Clearly, Gen was asking something of importance, but Ansel was not sure what it was. "I do not understand, Gen."

Suddenly, Geneera embraced Ansel over–hard. She began kissing Ansel's hair, but Ansel, surprised, wiggled from Geneera's embrace, and pushed her friend away. "Wait, Geneera, what are you doing? Please, Gen, not you, too. Do not change on me. There is too much changing already. I do not know what to do."

Geneera pulled back out of arm's reach quickly and shook her head as if clearing it. "No? You mean you would not want me to love you, as you might want Garin. You do not think of me that way."

"Wait, Gen, I love you. I, honestly, I never thought about it before. Are you a lover of women, then?"

Geneera faltered, then caught herself. "I think, yes, I am."

"And you are wanting to be with me?" For an instant, Ansel felt only genuine surprise, then her heart thudded hollowly. *She does not want to be my best friend anymore. She wants something more.* Ansel gasped with a jerk of loneliness. In her pain, she could not feel compassion for Geneera. Aloud she wailed, "Oh, Goddess, is nothing like it was before this wretched Festival? I want everything to be the way it was before."

A plethora of emotions played across Gen's face, few of which Ansel recognized. Finally, Gen's face became expressionless, as if she were staring at her meter instead of her closest friend. Stiffly, she said, "Maybe it would be better for me just to leave. I can go to the athlete quarters and stay there. I certainly would not want to make you uncomfortable with my affections."

Ansel began to sob again. This time though, Geneera did not reach out for her friend.

Standing so abruptly that she needed to catch herself on the nightstand, Gen continued with a barrage of words so slurred Ansel was not certain she was hearing them clearly, "I am tired of my desires making everyone unhappy. First, my meter hates . . . hates my choices for my life . . ." a little gasp of breath obscured the next sentence, then Ansel heard, " . . . and now you, my best friend, judge me for who I am." She turned away from Ansel, grabbing the laces of her sandals and throwing them over her shoulder. "You think you are too good for everyone, Ansel. That is your problem. I do not know why I did not see this before. Poor Ansel with the famous Meter and Granmeter, everyone wants to use her. She could not possibly fall in love with a mere athlete. I shall have to go drink some mead with Garin and commiserate."

"No, wait, Geneera, just let me have some time to think. Please, Gen, do not leave!" Ansel cried.

But Geneera strode through the door without acknowledging she had even heard Ansel.

Chapter 19

Ansel just could not sleep. She thrashed about in her bed while Geneera's accusing voice played and re–played in her ears. "You think you are too good for everyone. That is your problem." The sound of Geneera slamming the door and her running footfalls echoed in Ansel's memory. *I will find her. Tomorrow I can go to the Bulldancer quarters and ask them where she is.* Sleep continued to elude her. Agitated, Ansel pulled herself out of bed and decided to walk to the beach again. *Mayhaps the Goddess will appear to me and I can ask her what to do.*

She did not see the Goddess, but she was not alone on the beach. A man, wiry and small, sat on the sand facing the sea, his back toward the path upon which she stood. His legs were folded up under his chin, and he was rocking slightly, like a child comforting himself.

He must have heard her coming, for he spun around abruptly. "Phoebe?" he asked into the moonlight.

Ansel recognized him: the young consort from Athena, Theseus. "No." She replied, "Phoebe is my meter. I am Ansel."

"Oh." His voice sounded disappointed, almost achy, like Ansel's heart had felt all evening. "I left her sleeping," he said. "I did not want to waste my last night here on dreams." He turned back to the ocean.

"Uh, I was just out for a walk. I will not bother you."

"No, wait. Could we talk for a few moments?" He turned again toward her, looking up from his seated position. His loose tunic flapped in the breeze.

"Certainly." Ansel felt uncomfortable looking down at him, and after a pause, dropped to sit next to him on the sand, cross-legged.

"I do not look forward to sailing home later this morn." His voice grew dreamy and soft. "Kriti is far more beautiful than I imagined."

"I have never been as far north as Athena. Is it so very different there?"

Ansel watched a wry smile play across his face. "No, the land is not so different, but my life is."

Ansel did not know what to say to that. Instead, she asked, "Did you enjoy the Festival?"

"Yes." Theseus turned to stare at her in the moonlight, seeming to study her. "You look much like your meter."

"Thank you." Ansel felt uncomfortable. The boy was so intense, almost offensive. Ansel dug her hands into the sand, then lifted them, allowing the grains to sprinkle through her splayed fingers.

Into the awkward silence, Theseus asked, "What can you tell me of the University of the Priesera?"

"What do you want to know?" Ansel stopped playing with the sand and looked over at the strange boy–man.

"Are they all women? I mean, will they accept only women?"

"Well, of course. Only women can be Priesera." Ansel dropped her eyes and resumed digging in the sand. *I wish he would not stare at me so. It is unnerving.*

"But what of the men called to Her service?"

"Why, I suppose they go into the Monastera. It is not really the same as the Priesera, I do not think. They are all skilled tradesmen though. Some become the heads of guilds. I have seen some of their work. It is beautiful. Others become officials in the different Agronos'. Our Consort here at Knossos, Xeronos, went to the Monastera."

"But what if Goddess called a man to go to the Priesera and not the Monastera?" he persisted.

Ansel raised an eyebrow. "I would say he needed to ask Her again. Only women can be Priesera because only women are connected to Her ways. Only women can bring forth life like Great Meter." When Theseus did not reply, Ansel continued, "Men do not desire to be Priesera. Men cannot understand the mysteries of women and cannot perform Her service. Men serve in ways appropriate to men."

The boy's face closed down as clearly as a hide window shade blocks the sunshine. It reminded Ansel painfully of Geneera's face right before her friend stomped out of the apartment. "I see," he said. "Well, thank you for the information, Mistress Ansel."

Theseus turned to face the ocean again, and Ansel felt his dismissal like the slap of a wave. *The nerve of the boy, to treat me as if I were one of his servants.* Ansel jumped to her feet, swiping her legs free of grit, and strode away, her toes digging into the soft sand.

Theseus was not *almost* rude. He was *completely* rude. In fact, he was the most bad–mannered boy she had ever met.

Chapter 20

Festival was over and multitudes of people were preparing to leave with first light. Everywhere collapsed tents were rolled up, banners were being folded and garbage was being collected to be taken to the dump site at the far west of the Agronos. But in an austerely furnished meeting room on the first floor of the Agronos, the nine Elder Council members gathered to discuss the business of Kriti. The sunlight streamed through open windows onto the glossy white gypsum wall panels. A heavy, simple rug of natural wool covered the white tiled floor while a plain, yet highly polished oval table of domestic cypress and matching sturdy wooden chairs dominated the room. Cups of water and small plates of the first Koretide berries, pears, and early grapes were placed on small side tables. The room was a silent reminder to the Council that they were servants of the people of Kriti, and that any privileges they derived from their status as Council Members stemmed from their dedication to this service rather than from a noble birth. Kritins were proud to keep with the traditions of their ancestors; they did not approve of the newer forms of government that called for hereditary rulers. "Goddess may choose a woman to lead, but may not choose her daughter," they affirmed among themselves.

They were joined by Priesera Elder Aluneia who was still at Knossos and by early afternoon, Phoebe was summoned to give a report. She spoke at length of her encounters with Alekki and Nikolas, but requested her appraisal of Theseus be left to the end as it would likely provoke much discussion.

Priesera Vasilissa surprised Phoebe with a vigorous defense of Kourete Nikolas. When Phoebe reported her suspicions that he was involved in a dangerous sacrifice cult, Vasilissa interrupted, "He has a fine intellect and cares deeply for Kriti. Alekki must be smoking too much of his own resin to suspect that such a brilliant orator would do anything to undermine the honor of our nation."

"Vasilissa, I am astounded. I thought you did not like the man. What has brought about such a change?" Phoebe asked.

"You think because I lost in the debate to him that I would hold a grudge? I am better than that Phoebe. I respect him and believe I could learn points of persuasion from him." Vasilissa countered with raised eyebrows. She patted a square of linen to her mouth, then coughed into it.

Phoebe shrugged. *Is Vasilissa wearing makeup?* Phoebe thought. *Yes, I am certain that is kohl around her eyes and her lips are stained. I do not believe I have ever seen her wearing cosmetics.* She made a mental note to herself to investigate the matter further.

"Now I must bring before the counsel a matter of great weight," First Elder Thesmas said. She closed her eyes for a moment as if to gather her thoughts, then broke the silence by breathing in deeply. "I have been approached by the Helen of Athena," she said. "Demetria offers alliance with Kriti, but for a steep price. She wishes us to rid her of her consort, Theseus. Quietly."

Many voices erupted at once and Thesmas raised her hand for silence. "Allow me to continue," she said, eyeing the more disruptive members of Council with irritation. "I of course asked her why she thought we would be interested in an alliance with Athena at all, let alone at such a price." The First Elder shook her grayed head slightly and paused to sip from a cup of water. Phoebe watched the spiral design on the cup tilt as Thesmas tipped it toward her mouth, her throat methodically moving up and down with each swallow. "I am afraid she made some valid points. As we heard at the All Citizenry Meeting, the world is changing, perhaps more rapidly than we believed possible. Egypt is now ruled by outsiders, shepherds. Though we once considered Egypt a friend, I fear it will not be so anymore. Our openness is also our greatest vulnerability."

Murmurs broke out. Again Thesmas found it necessary to raise a hand. This time, she motioned to Xeronos. "Please, Council, I know we all have opinions about this but we cannot discuss them all at once and expect to be heard. Xeronos, I recognize you first, and then Aradia of Phaistos."

Xeronos stroked his strong, clean shaven jawline in thought for a moment, then said, "First Elder, I agree the world is changing and not for the better. We must look to our future. Historically we have been provided for and protected by the Meter Sea. By Her grace, and also the grace of Her Daughter, Netted Dictynna of the Forge, we are the richest and most advanced of the nations in the world." He scratched his cheek in contemplation, and then continued. "The Achaean people, whom Helen Demetria rules, are little more than hut dwellers, First Elder. It is true they rule two great cities, Athena and Mycenea; however, these cities were not constructed by them but by those whom the Achaens conquered several generations ago." Xeronos paused, raising his cup of water to his lips, then set it down carefully. His thoughtful brown eyes looked troubled. "No, the Achaeans are advanced in one thing only – iron weaponry. This technology would be of benefit to us, but to what end? More and more, I become convinced this very metal is not of She of Ten Thousand Names. It brings the Achaeans wealth, but the once beautiful cities they conquered are now ugly fortresses. They look at warfare with enjoyment. They train a military in times of peace and conquer peaceful neighbors for sport. What kind of an alliance is this? How could it profit us? How could it not destroy us?" He raised both palms upward emphasizing his quandary.

Aradia was the member of the Elder Council who had traveled furthest to attend the Seven–Turns Festival. She hailed from Phaistos, on the southern coast of Kriti. Phaistos was not so long a journey as the birds reckon, but the center of Kriti is mountainous. Aradia and the others from Phaistos sailed all the way around the island to arrive at Knossos. She pointed a finger down the table at Xeronos. "You speak truly about the Achaeans, Xeronos," she agreed. "They are little better than the nomadi themselves just slightly more civilized now that they no longer follow the herds and live in caves. She glanced at Xeronos appraisingly, then continued when he nodded. "However, the Libyans are armed with iron and remain true to Great Meter. We in Phaistos trade with the Libyans regularly. We consider them our friends. They are alarmed at the changes in Egypt. They begin to watch the borders of their land. They are taking in Egyptian refugees, many of them noble people from the Temples." She snorted. "The Pharaoh of sheep wants all the Egyptians to worship only one god - his, of course. The Egyptians have always worshipped the Many. Now they are not even permitted to worship their own Great Meter, Mighty Isis and they are being persecuted in their own country. The Pharaoh begins to amass a large army. Will Egypt become aggressive? We are a ripe fruit to pick. Will they cast an eye our way?"

Herodious, a gray–bearded TradesKourete spoke next. "The days of our safe seclusion are passing, Thesmas. Kriti needs allies. Perhaps you think we are safe out here in the middle of the nowhere, but no one is safe from the nomadi. If merchants can sail here, what keeps invading ships at bay? We keep no army on this island and our cities are vulnerable."

"Bah!" Xeronos interjected. "As yet the nomadi do not even control a port. Nor is capturing an island so easy. No ship or fleet of ships, even bearing the fiercest warriors, could carry enough invaders to capture Kriti. First, we would sink them at sea. Even if they could land, they would have no resources to sustain the fight." Xeronos gestured an open hand toward Thesmas. "Fighting an island nation is not like fighting upon the mainland. There is nowhere to retreat and re–supply except by boat. Besides, as you well know, we are not at all 'in the middle of nowhere', but are within days' sailing to Heria and the rest of the northern isles as well as Libya, Egypt, Athena, and Anatolia. Who would attack us? We control the largest trading ports in the world. All nations would be our allies should the nomadi attack."

"There you are wrong, Consort," Herodious countered. "The nomadi hold the lands north of Demetria's Achaeans and seek to make alliances both south and east of Kriti. I hear they even entreat with these new Egyptian rulers. That would present a grave danger to us. We sit like a fatted calf that our potential enemies salivate to slaughter. The Athenians fortified themselves by uniting the surrounding lands, so the nomadi have little desire to attack there. Should the nomadi find a way to attack by ship, or worse, persuade the Acheans to ally with them, Kriti might well find herself friendless. We are an anomaly; a rich land where the old ways are honored. The nomadi see this as a direct challenge to their god's supremacy. They would love to see Kriti, and the worship of She of Ten Thousand Names, fall."

"But Libya and the Emetchi nations still hold to the old ways too," Xeronos argued.

"And they are besieged." Aradia interjected. "They will look for help from us sooner than we to them."

"The Emetchi are lawless," Vasilissa began loudly over the voices of several other council members.

Disorder threatened to overtake the querulous Council again. Phoebe was grateful when Xeronos interjected, changing the direction of the discussion. "Wait. Let us talk of the price, Council. It may make our decision easier. First Elder, why cannot Helen Demetria rid herself of Theseus?"

Thesmas rolled her eyes. "Because the people of Athena fawn over the handsome young man; they call him a 'hero'. It pleases them that he came from humble beginnings. They credit him with leading Athena to safety and prosperity by uniting them with the surrounding villages."

"But Demetria does not admire the boy's accomplishments." Xeronos sounded that dry only when he was being ironic, Phoebe knew.

"No, apparently not. She claims he is uncouth, arrogant, and dangerous. She wants her brother, Polymachos, to lead. She claims he was the one who set the unification in motion, that it was all his idea."

Unlikely, thought Phoebe, *Polymachos cannot unsheathe his sword in favorable winds.*

"First Elder," Phoebe cut in when Thesmas paused. "I think it unwise to make a decision of this magnitude out of fear. Our traditions teach us that good conclusions are always made from a place of faith in Her. I hear little faith in the trueness of the Achaeans and especially of the Helen of Athena. We all know she is treacherous."

"But would it not be better to have the Achaeans as allies rather than potential enemies? Being willing to use their army makes them respected by their neighbors. Think of the influence we could gain throughout the north with such an alliance. It could make the entire region safer for our Traders. This could be a solution for the Trade Guild's problems." Vasilissa said. "Why not consider Demetria's proposition. How much faith in them does it require for us to do them this favor?"

Phoebe narrowed her eyes and she almost growled, "It would be out of the question to murder the Royal Consort of Athena. Never have we considered such a thing and Great Meter would be outraged."

"But Phoebe," Thesmas said, "Demetria asks only that we rid her of him; it is not necessary to kill the boy."

"Surely you are not that naïve, Meter. This is exactly what Demetria asks of us!"

"Phoebe, you forget your place." Thesmas scowled at her only daughter until Phoebe lowered her eyes. More gently, Thesmas continued, "Need I remind you, daughter, that he is dangerous to us? These are not times in which to trust to luck. The nomadi are proving to be at least as aggressive as the Emetchi warned. News has also reached my ears that war has broken out in the east, beyond the the Emetchi lands.

Phoebe flinched. She had not known this. "The nomadi have invaded there too? I thought them only in the north."

"Babylon is besieged by her neighbors, not the nomadi. However, I think it is a sign of the restlessness of these times. Kriti must not reject out of hand those allies she can find."

"Even She of Ten Thousand Names seems to be feeling irascible, Mistress Phoebe," broke in Daphnia, a retired weaver who had been on the council longer than any of the others. "Witness the quakes and waves of late. Something is amiss."

"We are free to interpret Demetria's request as we choose, Phoebe." Thesmas ignored Daphnia and continued smoothly. "Would young Theseus like to study with a Guild perhaps?"

Phoebe caught herself chewing a fingernail and jerked her hand from her mouth. "Truly, First Elder, I was going to bring this to you in private." She hesitated, then drew her shoulders back and plunged on. "This will sound nearly unbelievable, but he carries the Mark of a Chosen One."

Vasilissa snorted loudly. "What? That cannot be possible. He is not even of Kriti let alone the right sex." Several of the other council members chuckled.

Phoebe clenched her teeth. This was exactly why she had wanted to tell Thesmas and Xeronos in private. Feeling anger rise in her chest, Phoebe forced herself to breathe steadily before answering. "I think I am capable of determining the presence or absence of the Mark of the Chosen, Vasilissa," she said in a quiet but forceful tone.

"It is not unheard of." Xeronos said. "It is however, exceptionally rare in a boy."

Phoebe flashed a grateful glance toward Xeronos for his support. "Yes, of course I know it is unusual. I was taken aback myself to see it, but I no longer doubt. He has spoken of contact with the Caster of Nets who is known to be eccentric in Her choice of followers."

"Still, it should be confirmed." Aluneia said. *They will not question the Elder Priesera's judgement about the Mark. Best to agree and try not take offense.* Phoebe swallowed hard, bit her lips and nodded.

"Well, perhaps then he should be allowed to study with the Monastera," Thesmas said, cupping her chin with her long–fingered hand. "We know that the Goddesses mark young women of other lands and then find ways for them to get to Kriti. Perhaps Demetria's request is in alignment with the Divine, though in as odd a way to arrange it as I have ever seen."

"He has requested to study at the University of the Priesera." Phoebe said it as quickly as she could to get it over with.

There was a long moment of astonished silence, then laughter erupted, filling the stone–panelled room. Some of the hilarity held an edge of hysteria. "The Priesera! He wants to study with the Kore? Is the boy *arsenokoites*?" Vasilissa made a rude hand gesture and snorted.

Thesmas once more had to hold her hand up for silence, though her own face was red with poorly suppressed amusement. Phoebe felt a flush creep up her neck and wondered why she had even bothered to bring it up. But, she knew the reason; the energetic ties went both ways and she was now Theseus' advocate.

"Phoebe, truly, are you certain he was serious?" Vasilissa snapped. "Perhaps he was making a joke with you. Does he not know the Priesera is only for the Kore?"

"He understands full well," she said, glaring openly at Vasilissa. "He claims he was called by the Caster long ago. It is possible that the Mark he wears is from Her. He knows he can dedicate his service to Her only if he studies at the Priesera. And, I doubt he is *arsenokoites*, Vasilissa," she added crisply.

"As you should know, Phoebe." Vasilissa replied too sweetly. She shook her head. "Oh this is outrageous. First we are asked to consider an alliance with *babels*, and then we are actually to consider allowing a boy, and a foreign boy at that, into the University? No doubt the Kore would have great fun with him, but will he not distract them from their studies? And how could the boy learn the blood mysteries?" She tittered into her sleeve.

Herodious said while stroking his beard, "Demetria warned us that he is delusional. Sounds as if she is right on this account."

"This is a dangerous game you play, Phoebe." Daphnia shook a finger at the younger woman. "Never have we allowed even one of our own men to enter the Priesera. Why would you suppose we would allow a stranger?"

"None of our men have requested it."

"Of course not." Thesmas said sharply. "Our men understand only women can know Her rites and mysteries. Women are made in Her image, men cannot possibly lead Her worship. This thing he asks is impossible. We cannot risk more displeasure from Great Meter."

"Obviously he cannot learn the blood mysteries since he does not cycle," Phoebe said. "And Vasilissa, the Kore already find a multitude of love interests at the University. What difference if they experiment with him or with each other? " Phoebe appealed to Thesmas. "But there is more to this Consort than you give talent for. First Elder, you know me. You know my skills, even if some members of the Council choose not to acknowledge them at this moment. I say in utmost seriousness that we should consider this boy's request, no matter how ludicrous it seems."

Aluneia broke the ensuing silence first. "Phoebe, does he truly understand the role of the Priesera on Kriti?"

"No, Aluneia, he clearly does not."

"Why are you willing to bring this petition before myself and the Council knowing the overwhelming probability he will be rejected?"

"I thank you for taking the matter, and me, with some seriousness, Aluneia. You ask a good question, but one I have only the vaguest of answers for." Phoebe sighed, looked down at her hands for a moment, then said, "He claims to have exceptional visions and dreams of Her. I believe him. You on the Council know who and what I am. I have been carefully trained in observation and to trust in what my spirit tells me about people. It is for this I am known and respected. See the boy, Aluneia. Talk to him."

Xeronos spoke. "I do not know the boy and do not understand his motives, but I do know Mistress Phoebe. If she says we should consider something, I think we should. Besides, it does solve our dilemma, does it not? The boy will simply disappear for many turns.

If Demetria decides to check upon his fate, she might think to have her spies look at the Guilds or in the Monestara, but the Priesera? Not only is it a University for Kore, it is secreted within high, secluded mountains. Her spies are unlikely to find him.

"No! I will not have this." Vasilissa nearly spat in anger. "It is a grave heresy. Goddess does not want boys to learn Her worship. He comes from people who want to usurp She of Ten Thousand Names. It is frivolous to even discuss it. At best he is simply seeking attention like a Bulldancer! Already She is displeased. I will not be party to such an affront."

Phoebe closed her eyes for a moment and a thought came to her. "Vasilissa, Council, First Elder, might we consult with a Seer? We could travel to the cave of the Eithyliad and ask She of Ten Thousand Names Herself if such a thing is allowable. If the Seer says 'no', then we must reconvene to resolve this issue. If the Seer says 'yes', then we know my thoughts are in rhythm with Goddess. What say you, Vasilissa, will you agree? Will we all?"

Though the thoughtful faces of the Council Members still looked skeptical, Phoebe knew they would eventually agree.

Chapter 21

Geneera could not remember ever being so happy. Every morning in the athletic dorm, she rose at dawn and kissed beautiful Carea to wakefulness. Together they tied on their specially constructed leather athletic shoes, stretched their legs, then sprinted across the meadow and up the steep rocky slopes of the hills south of Agronos Knossos, returning in the still early morning. Together they bathed, giggled and embraced. They ate a light breakfast with the rest of the Bulldancers, and then walked arm and arm to the huge underground storage room at the far end of the courtyard to lug out the equipment needed for the mid–morning practice. Once on the grassy field, Gen concentrated on the complicated gymnastic moves she needed to perfect before she was even allowed to go near a live bull. Although she noticed Ansel once, hovering alone around the edge of the field, she did not acknowledge her former friend. She had Carea now. Ansel's rejection still stung, but Geneera was determined to build a new life without Ansel and without her Meter. *False friends and false family are behind me*, she thought. *I am Kore now. I will live my life with those who understand me.*

Besides, there was a buzz around the Bulldancer dorm. Garin had not shown for practice. At first, Carea told Geneera, everyone just assumed he was taking a holiday with his cousin, a 'dancer from Phaistos, who visited during Festival. But when Garin did not show for the start of practice nearly a quartercycle ago, his apartment mate, Hermen, became concerned. No one could remember seeing Garin after the end of Festival almost a half moon past. He had been seen sitting alone after the dance and looking upset; some whispered he was crying. At Carea's probing, Gen admitted that Ansel had left Garin rather abruptly that night.

"She just abandoned him? Ai, he was crazy for her. That must have hurt very much," Carea said.

Gen bit her lips, torn between the desire to stand up for Ansel and the impulse to nurse her own wounds inflicted by that same friend. Finally she said, "Ansel can be really hurtful. I know, I," Gen's eyes filled with tears. She did not fully realize how deeply pained she still felt by Ansel's rejection.

"You too?" Carea put her arm protectively around Geneera's shoulders. "I knew I did not like the girl. She struts around like she is the First Elder herself. She stared at me as if I had three heads. I know her type. She pretends to be kind but when she is through with you she just walks away."

Gen wanted to defend Ansel, really she did. But then she found herself crying and not knowing what to say. Was it her fault if the other 'dancers assumed her silence was agreement? Besides, she desperately needed Carea and the other 'dancers to like her. If she spoke up for Ansel, they might turn against her. The things they were saying about Ansel were true sometimes. She *was* insensitive to others and wrapped up in herself. Gen wondered that she had not found Ansel annoying before.

Carea said, "We must find Garin. I have never known him to miss practice. During our break, I will bring it to coach Heradyke. I know she is already concerned, but we told her that he must still be visiting with his cousin Ganymede. I will go ask my uncle Niko too. I know he is returning with the rest of the Phaistos visitors later this quartercycle. He can find Ganymede and then we will know if Garin is with him."

Immediately after practice ended, Carea ran off to find her Uncle Niko. When she returned to their shared apartment, Carea had a peculiar look on her face. "Uncle Niko is spending time in the company of your Meter. Why did you not tell me they have become lovers?"

"Because I did not know. Are you certain? My Meter has not taken a lover in many turns."

"Oh, I am fairly certain. They were kissing when I entered his room. They looked rather put out at my presence." Carea broke out in giggles. "Your Meter tugged at her skirts and flushed. Both of them looked very embarrassed. I wondered why Uncle Niko had not yet returned to Phaistos; I never would have guessed this though."

Gen shook her head. "I have not spoken to my meter for many days; not since before the Kore ritual. We had a bad fight about my joining the 'dancers."

Carea took her friend's hand and kissed it. "Your Meter is so strange, Gen. Everyone else's family was so excited and proud that their child was selected for the troupe."

Gen changed the subject. "Were you able to find out about Garin?"

Carea shrugged. "Uncle Niko says he last saw Garin with Ganymede hiking toward the south several days ago, right after the end of Festival. He says they carried food and looked as though they were going to be gone for several days."

"They did not tell anyone when to expect them back? That was foolish." Gen frowned.

"Also not at all like Garin," Carea agreed.

"Someone should be out looking for them. I think I will go and tell Mistress Phoebe. Oh, she is away from Knossos right now." Geneera paused for a moment, and then added, "I know what her current apprentice looks like, though I do not know her name. I will find her."

With Phoebe away consulting with the Seer, it took many days for Rheana to hear the whisperings around the Agronos. Finally, Geneera found her to say that Garin, the handsome, young Bulldancer boy and his slender 'dancer cousin from Phaistos, Ganymede, were missing. Ganymede's GranMeter, Aradia of the Elder Council, was governor of Phaistos. Though she was needed at home, she refused to leave Knossos without him, delaying the entire group's departure. Garin's Meter, a daughter of Aradia, was frantic too. Garin had missed six days of practice, something unheard of and completely unlike him.

Finally, Rheana petitioned to see the First Elder herself and a half cycle after the end of Festival, was ushered in to speak with Thesmas. The First Elder looked tired as she sat at a scratched wooden table, scrolls of papyrus parchment, half empty pots of ink and warmed wax and numerous seal stones scattered around her on its surface. Thesmas gestured at a second chair near the table for Rheana to sit, but the apprentice Escort shook her head.

"First Elder, I have heard about the missing boys. I wish to offer my services to find them. I come from the people of the Mason Guild of Sklerocampos. I have traveled the mountain paths south of Knossos extensively as a part of my training. I have some tracking skills too, as we of the Guild hunt for our meals when we are on long journeys. It would be useful if others would accompany me, especially if there is a Priesera here connected directly to one of the boys who could sense his proximity."

"Yes, it is past time to start looking for them. Phoebe no doubt would have had us scouring the trails for them several days past, but I had so hoped they had simply wandered farther than anticipated and were late returning." Thesmas sighed deeply. "I know of no trained person who is connected to the boys, though of course their own relatives would be. None of them is Priesera however. I hesitate to send them because if they have met with harm, well . . . ." Thesmas grimaced.

"Yes, I agree." Rheana nodded vigorously. "We will have to track using our other senses then." She scribbled something onto the wax pad she had brought to take notes. "I heard that Nikolas of Phaistos saw the boys leave. Do you know anyone else who might know something?"

"Garin had been with my Grandaughter, Ansel, the evening before. Perhaps he told her where they were planning to go."

"I will speak with Kourete Nikolas and Ansel both. Perhaps one of them will want to accompany me on the search." Rheana retreated, determined to start the hunt as soon as possible. She stopped at the kitchen and asked the cooks to prepare travel food for several people for four to five days. "I hope we are back before then with the boys, but we must be prepared to go far into the mountains if need be," she instructed as the kitchen workers nodded and looked concerned.

Rheana found Nikolas on the practice field speaking with the Bulldancers. She nodded politely to a girl he introduced as his sister's daughter, Carea, and to Geneera who had her arm draped casually around Carea's waist. Rheana filed this information in her mind automatically as she had been taught by Phoebe. Nikolas could not offer more information about the boys' whereabouts than Rheana had already been told. Both girls, however, eagerly offered to accompany her in her search.

"We know some popular sites for camping and hunting," Carea said. "We 'dancers often hike or run into the foothills to strengthen our legs."

Nikolas, however, declined to assist in the search. "I am making the return sail to Phaistos early tomorrow morning. Aradia will not leave without Ganymede, which of course I understand. Still, Phaistos business must be resumed. I will be the governor while Aradia is gone."

The girls ran to their dorm to pack while Rheana went looking for Ansel. She found Phoebe's daughter in the courtyard curled up under the sheltering arms of the old Myrtle tree. She looked like she might have been crying.

"Hoi Ansel," Rheana said gently, squatting down to look directly into the girl's face. "I am your meta's apprentice this turn. My name is Rheana."

Ansel looked up at Rheana and nodded, but did not smile. Rheana *saw* that Ansel's Radiance was heavy and dull. The girl could barely move. Her large, dark eyes looked immensely sad.

"Ansel, I need to speak with you. Do you know that Garin is missing?"

She visibly flinched. "How could I not know? Everyone in the entire Agronos is blaming me for it."

"Blaming you?"

"Because I left him at the dance." Fat tears began to roll down the girl's cheeks. She brushed them away with the back of her hand as if they offended her.

Rheana allowed her Radiance to become embracing, just as Phoebe had trained her to. "Tell me about it." She said softly, extending a tendril of energy towards the girl's heart.

Ansel sighed heavily and slowly sat up, crossing her legs. Rheana noticed the bluish circles under Ansel's dark eyes. The girl looked like she had not washed her hair for some time; it hung in limp strands past her shoulders. Ansel brushed leaves from her skirt then, with her head bowed, said, "We were at the final Festival dance together. He wanted to spend more time with me than I wanted, if you understand my meaning. It ended badly." She looked up. "It was a wretched night all around." Ansel's voice grew harsh from poorly suppressed tears. "I do not want to talk about it."

"I understand." Rheana sat down next to Ansel and crossed her legs. As gently as possible, she pressed the girl. "Did Garin say anything to you about taking a hike or journey the next day?"

"No, he did not." She paused then blurted, "Everyone is saying I hurt him and it is my fault he ran away. Everyone assumes I did or said something really awful to him. They are talking about me and how terrible I am. I keep thinking about what I said to him over and over and over. I did not mean to hurt his feelings. Do you think it is my fault, Rheana?"

Rheana placed a kind hand on Ansel's upper arm and said, "No, *mellia*, I do not think so. No matter what you said or did to Garin, he is a young man who must make his own decisions." Rheana bit her lower lip thoughtfully and blinked her eyes several times, then asked, "Do you have any reason to think he would be reckless?"

"I did not think so, but to be honest, I do not know him very well."

Rheana nodded. "I am gathering a group to search for him. Do you want to accompany us? Geneera and Carea are coming."

Ansel looked momentarily hopeful, but then shook her head fiercely when Rheana mentioned who else was going. "No," she said, "I hear those two are the ones who blame me most and that they hate me." A sob escaped from her chest and the tears began to flow freely. "Please, just leave me alone, Rheana."

Rheana's heart ached for the girl, but she was eager to begin her search for Garin and Ganymede. She reached a hand to the Ansel's shoulder and gave it a gentle squeeze, then stood up to leave. She looked back as she left the courtyard. Ansel was again curled up under the tree, hugging her knees to her chest.

I hope Phoebe returns from her journey to the Seer soon. Her daughter really needs her, Rheana thought.

Rheana, Carea and Geneera searched in the foothills to the southeast and southwest of Knossos. They nearly went as far as the University of the Priesera in the mountains. But all their knowledge of good camping sites and likely caves proved useless. Late on the fifth day, when the sun of another long afternoon nearly touched the western waters, they finally gave up the search. As they carefully picked their way on the rocky path back down to the Agronos plateau, Rheana held out some hope that perhaps the boys had come back on their own. But the Fates would not have it so.

Hearing that her gransons had not been found, Aradia became frantic. "I can not leave here with out Ganymede. I must stay until he comes back. Please, send out more people to search!"

And so they did. A full cycle passed and the hot winds began. A rare red dust storm blew in from the south and covered everything with rusty grit. Still the boys did not return.

Chapter 22

Phoebe breathed in the fresh morning breeze as deeply as her lungs would allow. The air smelled green, perfumed with crocus and lavender and many herbs she did not recognize, their tiny blossoms dotting the tan soil around the rocks like multicolored gems. "I am glad we are making this trip together Xeronos. I miss you so. I cannot remember when last I had time to leave the Agronos grounds for even an afternoon." She placed her hands on the small of her back and stretched for a moment, allowing the constant cares of the Agronos to fall from her like so much dust, or perhaps like eggshells fall off a young bird who reaches out to greet the world anew.

Xeronos smiled. "When the Council agreed for you to speak with the Seer, I dove for the chance to accompany you."

"I wonder what Theseus said to Aluneia, or what she *saw*. She appeared shaken after her meeting with him. Why, she was ready to allow him entry into the Priesera right away. It was the Council who insisted we still query the Seer first."

"I wondered what it was you saw in the boy to persuade you to bring the matter before Council at all."

Phoebe shuddered, crossing her arms in front to grasp her shoulders and shaking her head. "I can not explain it, Xero. The boy is both young and old. I see violence in his eyes, but more too. He carries the mark like a festering wound. It worries me, Xero."

He pursed his lips and took her hand, squeezing it. After a few moments of silence, he said, "Tell me how our Ansel is doing. She looks so grown-up!"

Phoebe felt her heart warm and a small smile played on her lips. "You know she was called to the Priesera." Her chest swelled with pride. "She is much like you when you were a child, Xero. Remember how serious you were all the time? Always studying things you found – snail shells, bugs, plants. You would bring them back to the Agronos and ask every adult you could find to tell you about whatever you had in your hand, then you would go and write it all down." Xeronos nodded at the shared memory.

"No one was surprised when you entered the Monastera," Phoebe continued. "Ansel writes and wanders and questions, too. She prefers to be alone it seems, not at all like me when I was her age. I would flit around the Agronos soaking up the attention of anyone who would give it to me. I think she is every bit as introspective as you were." She stooped over to pick a white blossom and handed it to Xeronos playfully.

He took the flower and placed it behind one ear. "You were always such a friendly and pretty girl, I remember that."

"Of course, you would think so! Thank you for the kind words anyway." Phoebe laughed softly in amusement. "I annoyed Meter so. I loved attention and when I was Kore, I discovered sex. It always goaded Meter wild. She would insist I attend classes and wanted me to take everything so seriously. She lectured me over and over and over about the importance of learning to read and to write. I did, of course, but not willingly! No, I wanted to dance and sing and wear pretty clothes and chat with everyone."

"Ah, but it was that willingness to draw out even the quietest young men which brought us together." Xeronos reached out to her and drew her into an embrace. Phoebe loved his strong arms; she felt so safe, so nurtured, within them. In another moment, she reluctantly pushed herself away from him and continued to pick her way along the rocky path. It had been such a long time since she had walked so far. Her leg muscles felt warm and energized by the exertion. She sighed, "And even that is frowned upon. You should hear the whispers. 'An Escort, especially the Elder Escort, should not tie herself to one man!' You would think I have committed blasphemy. My work necessitates me to be intimate with many men. Can I not be allowed the luxury of only one lover in my personal life?"

Her stomach knotted. Being an Escort was so demanding. *Always I need to be paying attention, listening, on guard, always, well, 'on'. That is the worst of it. My meter expects me to have heard everything that is happening in the Agronos and beyond and to have taken care of any problems before they are even brought to her attention. On top of that, people would be scandalized if I appeared in public without my hair being perfect. There is so little to my life outside of being Elder Escort. Ansel paid a heavy price. I did too. I missed most of her Maidenhood and now will miss her Koretime too since she will be at the University. I once loved being an Escort. Now I am not so certain.* Phoebe suddenly stopped and drew Xeronos into her arms again, kissing his willing lips passionately, deeply probing his open mouth with her tongue. Drawing away, she breathed into his ear. "We should make another child. I could stop taking the Tea of Britomartis and do no Escorting assignments for a few moons. Surely being the Elder Escort can afford me that one privilege." Xeronos dropped his rucksack at his side and kissed his response to her.

When the fifth morning of the trip dawned bright, Phoebe and Xeronos began the final steep climb up to The Seer's cave halfway up Mount Skoteino. While Xeronos waited by some brush, Phoebe waded down through the loose stone to the narrow triangular rock entrance to kneel at the feet of the Seer, offering her gifts of fine ground flour and cheese. The cave, shadowy even during the brightest day, was softly illuminated with torches and candles. The inner rock wall glistened with a film of moisture. The cavern smelled damp, as if moldy secrets flourished in every crevasse and not all of them would be pleasing to the eye if held up to the light of day. The Seer sat upon a carved wooden chair, a cushion on the seat for comfort in her old age. Formally called "the Eilithyliad", she was wrinkled with years of wisdom. A huge beeswax pillar candle was always lit beside her. From the time of the first tiny white flowers of Maidentide, through the lush blossoming of Koretide, the dry hot winds of Metertide, and into the mutable early rains that foretold of Cronetide, the Seer Priesera of Eilithylia sat in Her cave, bound by sacred duty to answer the questions of all who asked. Only the piercing mountain cold of deep Cronetide drove her indoors to civilization. As a group, the Seers were known to be peculiar; the Seers who heard the voices of the caves were the strangest of them all.

Her black eyes sparkled oddly under her heavy, wild eyebrows, and she nodded for Phoebe to approach.

Phoebe cleared her throat and passed her fingers through her hair nervously. "Eilithylia, I have come from Knossos at the bidding of the Council to ask a question of She of Ten Thousand Names."

The shrunken woman squinted forward. "You are the Elder Escort, yes?"

"Yes, Eilithylia, I am Phoebe, the Elder Escort of Knossos."

"Why have you not come to me before this, Elder Escort Phoebe? Do you not know the time draws near? The One–Who–Brings–the–Change comes. The crone drew together her bristling brows, her unruly gray hair was a shock around her face.

Breathing in sharply, she answered, "I, uh, I had no cause before, Eldest One. I would not ask something trivial of you and I have held my own council."

Apparently satisfied, the hag relaxed abruptly, and said, "Give me your question then."

Phoebe, long trained in the art of calming herself, breathed in and out once. *You Seers make me too nervous to ask trivial questions*, she said to herself. *Besides, I cannot make sense of most of what you say.*

"There is a boy, a young man rather, from Athena." Phoebe began, her voice becoming stronger as she continued, "He wants to be educated and join in the Priesera Sisterhood. He has been touched by Her, GranMeter. He talks of visions from Her. I have heard. They sound authentic. At least, he believes them to be authentic."

The Seer frowned but did not seem astounded by the question. Perhaps she had heard too many odd queries to be overly surprised by anything posed to her. She closed her eyes. "What is his name? What know you of him?" She gestured impatiently.

"His name is Theseus. He is the royal consort of Athena. I have *seen* him and what I found disquiets me. His soul has known many lifetimes and he wears the Mark, but there is a wound upon it. I do not know its origin. He is a man of violence and I think perhaps this defect leads him astray."

The Eilithyliad opened her piercing eyes again and directed them like black daggers at Phoebe. "You hope the Priesera will heal him?"

Phoebe blinked at the question, then said her voice quavering slightly, "We wish to know if he will harm the Priesera or Kriti. We have never before considered making an exception. Yet if we do not, we could lose a valuable alliance or choose to take his blood upon our hands. We care about our safety."

"Such shortsightedness! Think you Kriti is the only nation Great Meter holds to Her bosom?" The old woman spit onto the ground. Phoebe flinched. "A soul healed is a sacred thing. Far greater than the safety of fair Kriti."

Determined to suppress her unease with the Seer, Phoebe steeled herself for an argument. "But, to permit him into the Priesera allows him access to Kriti's power should he choose to abuse what he learns."

"It allows him into the heart, soul and body of Goddess Herself." The Seer snapped. Abruptly, she rolled her eyes to the back of her head so that only the whites showed and her face melted free of expression. She began muttering incomprehensively.

Phoebe balled her hands into nervous fists wondering if the Seer was having some type of fit and if she should do something. But after a long moment the crone seemed to recover and she again looked at Phoebe thoughtfully. "This matter is between She and he, I think, but I will ask Her directly."

The woman gestured for her to come closer and Phoebe forced

herself to obey. The Seer pointed at a flat stone slab and said, "Slide this off the vent for me, daughter." When Phoebe dutifully pushed the heavy stone aside, fumes from deep within the cave seeped up from the crevasse in a plume. The hag leaned close to the smoke and inhaled deeply while waving Phoebe away. Soon the Eithyliad's head lolled to one side. Her eyes, though open, were unseeing, at least of the mundane world. She began murmuring, and Phoebe leaned toward her to hear.

"A bull paws the ground. In his wake, the ground groans and creaks. A woman stands, the holy labrys raised before the brutal beast. Can she stop him or will he run her down? There is blood and the pain either way."

"The cranes, I see their dance. Look! New flocks merge, one, then another and another in a line. Are they bird or human? Will they find solace or war?"

Suddenly, the seer sat bolt upright, leaning toward Phoebe. The unfocused eyes were directed toward her, but the sight was inward.

"The times are perilous, perilous. You think you know what is best for the land of your birth? You may be fooled. The path ahead is forked and in each direction are deadly obstacles. I cannot see which path leads to safety. Perhaps none do."

"Boats, I see many boats. The people flee. Fire, the very air is on fire. The earth is on fire, all in a circle around the people. The water is on fire. Where can they go to escape? How can such a fire ever be eluded? Yet they must flee, they must. Oh Goddess, She–of–the–Forge, how will they evade the blazing tongues?"

A boy enters the bosom of the Goddess, but will he use his gift for sacrament or sacrilege? He is called regardless and you cannot stop what She has set into motion. He is marked and so is she. The change begins. So be it."

The Eilithyliad abruptly stopped speaking. After several silent moments, she said in a more normal tone of voice, "That is the message from She–Who–Walks–the–Labyrinth. There is no more."

When Phoebe asked for clarification, the hag muttered, "Go child, I am exhausted. I do not ever attempt to interpret Her words."

Phoebe turned to leave, but the Seer called behind her, "Wait, daughter, one more message I have for you." Confused, Phoebe looked back. The Seer grinned revealing long yellowed teeth and said, "A challenge awaits thee too Escort. Where will your strength lay? Look inward, daughter. Remember the first edict of the Seers: Know thyself."

Phoebe scrambled up the loose rocks on the cave trail back to Xeronos, the bright sunlight nearly blinding her at first. He wrapped his arms around her, obviously concerned; her face must have reflected the distress she felt. Xero murmured, "You were gone so long, I very nearly came to get you. You are so pale, come sit with me and drink some water." She leaned on him heavily as he led her to an outcropping of flat rocks near a cluster of blooming pink flowers. She allowed him to care for her for many moments, relishing the attention and support. He asked about what the Seer said, of course, but was so obviously more concerned about her wellbeing that Phoebe nearly cried both from exhaustion and from gladness. It was such a relief to be taken care of once in a while.

Chapter 23

"Know thyself", Phoebe whispered to herself over and over. It was so easy, too easy, to get caught up in the intrigue at the Agronos. The missing boys still had not returned and Rheana confided that she had a bad feeling about it. Aradia, Ganymede's GranMeter, was in torment. She walked the Agronos, moaning and looking like death, frequently bursting unannounced into the First Elder's office searching for any glimmer of hope. Garin's meter was frantic too, but she was not visiting the Agronos at all, choosing instead to work night and day at weaving – or so Phoebe's contact at the weaving guild told her.

Upon her return to the Agronos, Phoebe had conveyed the Seer's words directly to Thesmas. The First Elder seemed perplexed by the messages – she kept calling Phoebe in to repeat them to her over and over. Finally, Phoebe suggested Thesmas do as she promised and have the message scribed in copies and sent to the rest of the council. "You do not have to make this decision alone, Meter, and in fact should not. Consult the rest of the Council. Ask them for a simple yes or no. Demetria is expecting us to respond to her offer before next Maidentide. That is enough time to have each council member read the Seer's words and respond. You have support Meter, use it."

Phoebe found that she needed to follow her own advice. She was perturbed that Nikolas returned to Phaistos as temporary governor in place of Aradia. She shook her head when she heard that Vasilissa accompanied him. *I do not trust Nikolas, regardless of how fond Vasilissa has become of him,* she thought. *Perhaps I need to go to Phaistos to keep watch there. But I promised Ansel we would spend time together before she leaves for the University in a few short quartercycles. How can I be in two places at once?* Then Phoebe remembered that she, too, was not alone. She smiled and called for Rheana.

Rheana had warned her, but Phoebe was alarmed when she saw Ansel. She immediately renewed her vow to spend time with her daughter before she left for the Priesera. *We have only this final triad of Kureide and the first of Metertide before she must leave. I will need to think of some way for both of us to get away from Knossos, maybe even Kriti itself.* Phoebe paused biting her lower lip, then snapped her fingers. *I know, it is but a short sail to Heria and Ansel has never even been there. They always have a marvelous Metertide ceremony – they celebrate the founding of Daedalos and almost the entire city attends. Ansel will enjoy it and we will both be able to forget the worries of Kriti for a while.* And, she added to herself hopefully, *Nadia is there.*

"Here," Phoebe said, offering a string of pearls for her daughter to entwine in her hair. "We must keep your hair pulled back so it does not tangle like this again." Phoebe yanked clumps of long dark hair out of the shell comb, then replaced the offending tool into her kid skin bag. Ansel tearfully nodded as she twisted the ornament into her somewhat less knotted hair.

The sail to the island of Heria took two full nights in the Agronos' second largest boat. They sailed past the tiny, uninhabited island of Dia, called "sacred Dia" because from the bay of ruined Amnisos, it looked like a huge Goddess lying on her back in the calm waters. The first day, Ansel discovered that far from being dismayed at losing all view of land, she loved being surrounded by water. The gentle waves soothed her heart and the warm wind, though it blew her tresses into awful tangles, kept her stomach settled. She enjoyed the breeze throughout the long afternoon. When she had to comb her hair out at night, however, she found it far less pleasant. Still, she was away from Knossos and the accusations that she was the reason Garin left. It hurt her heart that people, especially Geneera, could be so cruel.

The titanic peak of Herilia, the sole mountain that formed the island of Heria, loomed large in the distance by nightfall of the second day. Though it was fair and warm, Ansel shivered at her first sight of great Herilia. "Look Ansel," Phoebe said as she beckoned her daughter to the bow of the ship. We are in luck, the skies are clear. Often the heights of Herilia are covered with clouds but this eve we can see to the very summit." Phoebe put a comforting arm around her daughter's shoulder as they both gazed at the mountain. Ansel was surprised that she was nearly as tall as her meter. She tilted her head into her meter's neck and slipped her arm around Phoebe's waist. The sky was an exquisite pink–orange. The pinnacle of Herilia, white with snow all turn long, glistened purplish against the darkening sky. "It is so beautiful, Meter," Ansel whispered, awestruck. "Is it higher than any mountain on Kriti?"

"Yes." Phoebe hugged her daughter closer to her side. "There are supposed to be some very high mountains on Kriti far to the east of Knossos, but even they are not as high as Herilia. This is what I have been told by the Mason Guild folk, anyway."

That night, as Ansel tossed in her cot, she thought about what she had heard at the Seven–Turns Fest about Herilia; that the vast mountain was feeling restive of late, that she threw ash from her high vents and hot gases hissed through cracks in her great flanks. People had been injured by being too close to the gasses when they erupted. The biggest and best known city on Heria, Atalancia, was closer to the summit than the others and was being deserted. Ansel felt sadness about this. Atalancia was reputedly a city filled with amazing things. Many artist and architect guildsfolk had settled there, creating some of the most breathtaking sculptures and artistic buildings known anywhere. It was all being covered with ash.

Heria, and the mountain Herilia, had never been real to Ansel before. Now she scoured her mind for any lore, any tales, anything at all she could remember being told about the island. She remembered that Vasilissa taught her the people of Heria were the same people as lived on Kriti – they had all come from the northeast together long ago and some people had settled on the large island of Kriti, while others had settled on tall Heria and still others had founded cities on sacred Delos, Lemnos, and other islands. Heria consisted of one huge mountain with several peaks. By far the highest was the one called Herilia. The cities were built on lofty plateaus. There were only three that Ansel could name: Akrotiri, on the south side of the mountain, Atalancia, and Daedalos, where she and her meter were going, on the southeast plateau. She supposed there were other villages and cities, maybe even Agronos. *No, I think they do not have Agronos here,* she corrected herself.

In the bright cool of early morn, they disembarked the ship. Ansel was delighted to discover that instead of climbing the very steep and rocky trail to Daedalos, they would actually get to ride donkeys. A small team of village men were waiting with three of the gray–pelted beasts. The huge brown eyes of the donkey Ansel was to ride reflected unflinching patience. It graciously accepted a small slice of apple the herder had handed Ansel, reaching for the sweet with velvety lips. She patted the animal, then gratefully swung a leg over its withers. The donkey felt lumpy – maybe muscular – and bony. It was a strange feeling to Ansel's thighs. She had never ridden an animal before, though she had seen people riding donkeys and once a horse even, at the Agronos Knossos. As the donkeys began to lumber up the stony trail, the last one in line carrying their rucksacks, Ansel leaned forward and concentrated on keeping her balance.

Daedalos was built on a vast plateau high above the inlet. A high stone wall, raised as a wind break and to keep unwary toddlers from tumbling down the cliffs marked the edge of the plateau. As the riders approached the wall, the trail ended with a wooden gate. It slid open to admit the travelers, their escorts, and the donkeys.

As Ansel dismounted, a stout woman a full head shorter than

Ansel's meter hastened over and embraced Phoebe, who had already jumped off her donkey and was rubbing her hip.

"Phoebe!" the woman exclaimed after she had kissed her cheeks, "I am so happy to see you. It has been many turns since the University, has it not?"

Phoebe returned the kisses and smiled, "Nadia, it is lovely to see you. Thank you for agreeing to house us on such sudden notice." She looked over at Ansel and gestured for her to join them. "Here is my daughter, Ansel. Can you believe she just became Kore?" Ansel curtseyed, "Greetings, Mistress Nadia. It is good to meet you." Nadia embraced Ansel warmly, "We do not stand on formalities here, Ansel. Please just call me Nadia." Her body felt warm and comforting. She smelled of sweet clover. Ansel inhaled deeply and felt her insides relax. Here was a different sort of Escort than her meter. Nadia made people feel cared for.

Daedalos was not constructed like most towns on Kriti, where the buildings were erected around a large centrally located Agronos with a courtyard. Instead, although the dwellings were all connected with shared walls and flat roofs like at Knossos, they lined narrow stone–cobbled streets. Ansel found this confusing. Where were the communal kitchens? Where did the First Elder live? Ansel soon discovered that instead of having community meals in large rooms where everyone in an Agronos came to eat, people lived more separately on Heria. Nadia lived in a dwelling with several other women, some Priesera and some not, including Nadia's sister and their frail, white–haired meter. They ate meals together that one or another of the women cooked. Ansel was not certain she would like such an intimate eating arrangement every day.

There was more strangeness to Daedalos. Each building was somewhat self sufficient, with a large kitchen area featuring a huge cooking brazier that also provided heat when needed. The cities were elevated higher than most on Kriti and needed a source of warmth during the height of Cronetide. The wealthiest parts of town were built up and into the hillside so that residents had a breathtaking view of the ocean. These homes had indoor water systems similar to that at Knossos; a mountain stream had been diverted with clay pipes. The less wealthy people lived on the flat of the plateau proper and had to haul their water from one of several mountain–fed streams. Farmers and herders lived on the outskirts of the plateau beyond the town, where their animals had room to roam and graze.

After a late brunch, Nadia led Phoebe and Ansel to a main street several blocks from her home. "Phoebe," Nadia said, "I know you will want to visit the home of the Elder Priesera for a few hours. It is just three streets away and to your left. I am hoping Ansel and I might visit some shops."

Phoebe nodded, "Yes, I must tell the Elder Priesera that I am here. Ansel, I will not be long. Daedalus has craftsguild people living all up and down these few streets. I think you will enjoy visiting their studios."

The shops were fun. They visited the leatherworker, the smithy (who was too busy arguing with a strange man to show Ansel his wares), the shipwright, a potter, and a lantern maker. The last made beautiful lamps of stone especially for wealthy patrons. Ansel loved looking at the exotic purple, green and red rock the GuildsKourete was carving.

That evening, just as Phoebe and Ansel were preparing for sleep and saying their good nights to Nadia and the other women, the room began to tremble. Ansel, holding a cup of hot tea in her hands, saw the surface of the liquid break into tiny agitated waves. She shrieked and dropped the cup. It shattered on the stone floor leaving an exclamation of hot water in a puddle, scalding Ansel's foot. She jumped back, panicked, almost babbling, but then the trembling ceased.

"Only a little shake, Ansel" Nadia said, reaching out to the terrified girl while her sister grabbed a nearby linen cloth. The woman knelt carefully on the floor and picked up the shards of the cup while wiping up the spilt tea.

"Oh, I am so sorry," Ansel said, though she was still trembling. "I, uh, shakes frighten me." She allowed Nadia to wrap an arm around her shoulder and lead her to a couch. Nadia exuded kindness.

"My daughter had a terrible experience with a shake not long ago." Phoebe said, taking the pottery shards from Nadia's sister and throwing them into the brazier, then sitting down on the other side of Ansel from Nadia. The sister left the room, fetched another cup of tea which she offered to Ansel, (who was now feeling more embarrassed than frightened), then sat on a chair opposite the couch. "She witnessed the entire tragedy at Amnisos last Maidentide. She was lucky she came away with only a sprained ankle and bruises." Phoebe concluded.

"Oh my dear, how terrible, will you not tell us about it?" Nadia's eyes had grown large and moist. Ansel did not want to talk about it but did not see how she could reasonably refuse such a kind woman. She began softly, thinking to merely summarize the shocking scene so Nadia would allow her to go to bed. But then it began to feel good just to tell the tale in detail to this caring, compassionate woman. *Why not tell her everything?* Ansel found herself thinking. *She is so interested, so intent. I feel so safe with her; she cares and wants to know.* Soon Ansel was crying hard, choking out the entire tale in horrible detail, remembering aspects she had not even shared with her meter, while Nadia stroked her back and hair, nodding and encouraging her tears. Phoebe held her daughter's hand and passed linen squares to her when she needed to blow her nose. As she finished her long story, Ansel gave in to a desire to wail and keen while Nadia and Phoebe held her. She rocked in their arms for a long time and for the first time in many moons, Ansel felt a small wave of peace well up in her belly. She began to hope that she just might survive the shock of Amnisos.

Chapter 24

If she could not sleep in her own bed in her own room, Ansel surely could not sleep in a strange bed in a strange villa. Her head ached from crying. The moon, though still several days before full, beckoned to her through the window. Her meter's even, resonant breathing from the adjoining room told Ansel that Phoebe was sleeping the slumber of the utterly exhausted. Ansel felt weary too, in her bones and muscles, but her thoughts continued to whirl.

I will walk around just a little, she thought. *Maybe then I can sleep.* Stealing down the steps in her soft leather slippers, Ansel welcomed the gust of fresh air that greeted her at the doorway. Inhaling deeply, she felt her mind clear and the throbbing in her head recede. She wrapped her thin shawl tightly around her shoulders and stepped into the street. She looked up and down the lane, but no one strolled along the narrow slate path save a cat who ducked into a street level window when it spied Ansel. The air felt slightly cool upon the lofty mountain dale in high Metertide. Knossos was built within the low foothills, not nearly as high as Daedalos. *I wonder how cold Cronetide is here,* Ansel thought somewhat absentmindedly as she looked around. She turned down a wider path of stone, one not as carefully kempt as the lane her meter's friend lived on. It seemed to be a main road that led downhill to the flat of the plateau. She needed to watch her step so as to not stumble on uneven patches where the slate had cracked or slipped. *I should have put on my sturdy shoes* she thought, wincing as she stepped on a sharp pebble.

The road descending into the flat land was long but relatively straight. After many lengths' walk, the smell of animal reached Ansel's nostrils, then she heard a snort and shuffling noises emanating from an opening down the lane and to her left. Curious, Ansel crept to the doorway and peered in. The moonlight was bright enough for her to discern a large donkey. No, not a donkey, but a horse, tied to a wooden stake on the far side. Horses were rare on Kriti, but occasionally one was stabled at the Agronos. Ansel had always wanted to see one up close but had never had the chance.

Ansel stole into the room. Straw and wood shavings were scattered along the floor and the scents of hay and animal were strong. "Greetings, horsey" Ansel whispered in a voice as reassuring as she could manage. She felt a little nervous – she was not certain how much horses liked strangers. The animal turned its great head to look at her sidelong and stamped a foot. "Hoerrrr", the horse uttered while shaking its thick neck, then it snorted again.

Ansel decided the horse did not look too scary and tiptoed a little closer, still speaking soothing nonsense, asking if it was comfortable and if this was its home. Soon she was close enough to reach out and touch its neck. It accepted the pat calmly, regarding her with one large, glistening, dark eye. She reached to touch the soft nose, but the horse jerked back its head and whinnied loudly in alarm. "Sorry, sorry," Ansel said, backing up a few steps.

"Who is in here scaring my horse?" a rough voice demanded from behind Ansel. Spinning around, Ansel saw a tall shadow looming in the doorway, blocking her exit. Ansel felt the danger; she instinctively knew, even without being able to see, that the owner of the horse was armed and ready to defend the animal.

"I am sorry," she repeated. Her voice cracked a little and she suddenly needed to cough badly. "I just wanted to see a live horse." Her words stuck in her throat, and when she attempted to clear it, she spurred a coughing fit. She leaned over and hacked loudly. *Oh for Meter's sake,* she thought, *if the horse's person does not kill me, I will just embarrass myself to death.*

The figure strode out of the shadows then and slapped Ansel's back a few times. While Ansel's coughing fit gradually subsided, the owner walked to the horse and patted his neck. Through streaming eyes, Ansel saw that the horse's rider was a tall, leather–clad woman. She turned back to Ansel once she had checked that the horse was not harmed. Even in the near dark Ansel could make out her handsome features set into stern lines.

"Who are you?" The woman's deep voice was calmer now, but still sounded suspicious.

"My name is Ansel. I come from Kriti, at the Agronos Knossos. I was just out walking and heard your horse. I wanted to see him. I am very sorry. I will leave now."

"Are you alone?"

"Yes."

"Well that is a stupid thing. It is the middle of the night." Ansel flinched but did not reply. The woman took a deep breath and let it out again. She sheathed a dagger she had held in her left hand and visibly relaxed. Apparently she had decided Ansel posed no threat to herself or her horse. "How old are you Ansel?"

"Ummm, sixteen turns. I just turned Kore at the last Seven–Turns Fest, on Kriti that is." She sounded ridiculous to herself. This woman would not care to hear her prattle.

"Do you not know it is dangerous to walk alone at night?" the woman interrupted. "People have been disappearing. So far only boys, but do not take that to mean you are safe." The woman stared at her so intently Ansel felt disconcerted and suddenly realized her bladder was nearly full. She shifted from foot to foot.

"I did not know. What do you mean that boys are disappearing? Where are they going?"

The woman shrugged, then leaned back onto the shoulder of the horse. The horse bumped her shoulder affectionately with his cheek. "That is what I am here to find out. My name is Devra. I am a tracker with the Emetchi. I was hired by the meter of one of the boys to discover what happened to him." She scratched her jaw casually. "I knew some of the fisher and herder boys had gone missing. Whoever is doing it made a mistake and took the son of someone wealthy enough to find out what is happening."

Ansel's thoughts flew to Garin. "Have there been boys missing on Kriti? I know a boy who is missing."

Devra shrugged again. "Had not heard of anyone missing on Kriti, but I do not know too many people from there. I have kin here on Heria; that is how this boy's meter knew to hire me." She patted her own thigh rhythmically for a moment, apparently thinking, then added, "Could have spread to Kriti though, easily. I will have to think about that."

"What do you mean 'spread to Kriti'?" Ansel asked. She was becoming afraid for Garin.

"I think there is a sacrifice group here on Heria. Sickest, craziest notion. They believe if they kill a young man ritually, give his heart to the Bull God or some such nonsense, then Herilia will quiet down."

"Goddess Meter" Ansel gasped, "how horrible! Oh I hope this is not why Garin disappeared." Ansel clasped her hands over her mouth and shook her head in disbelief. "How do you know this has been happening?"

"Told you, I am a tracker. Here, follow me." Devra motioned for Ansel to follow her out into the street. There, she pointed to Herilia and said, "You can not see it in the night, but about two thirds of the way to the top of that lower peak, there is a morass of caves." Dropping her arm and leaning closer to Ansel, she continued. "Some of them are blowing fumes, but others are not. I think there is a particular cave up there the Bull religion people are using for their sacrifices." She dropped her voice even lower. "When it was just happening to the poor boys, the news was not spread far and wide. Now that it has probably happened to a wealthier boy, maybe someone will care enough to confront the people who are doing this."

"Do you know who they are?" Ansel breathed into the woman's ear.

"I have my suspicions. Once I am certain, I will tell my employer." The woman abruptly turned her back to Ansel and tramped back inside to the stalls, her rugged leather boots making a dull clopping sound.

Ansel followed her in. "My meter is Elder Escort at Knossos. She should know about this. May I tell her?" Ansel paused, then added "She might have questions I cannot answer. Maybe you can come and tell her yourself?"

Devra stood silent, then said, "Your meter would be a good person to tell. Where are you staying?" When Ansel pointed uphill, to the more affluent section of Daedalos, the woman said, "Tell your meta she will need to come find me. I am sleeping right here with Dolphina." She thrust her chin toward the horse. "I am not leaving my horse unattended and an Emetchi can not just openly walk through those parts of town without drawing a lot of attention. I wish to remain low key. Makes it easier to do my job."

They agreed that Phoebe and Ansel would meet with the Emetchi woman after the upcoming ceremony, a few days hence. "I must go into the mountains to check my suspicions tomorrow," Devra said. "It will take at least two days, maybe more. I will skirt the town which will add length to the journey. Besides, sometimes the best occasions to pass information are after the big rituals when there are many people around – it will not be so noticeable that your meta is talking to me."

Phoebe tried not to feel annoyed that Ansel had slipped out in the middle of the night. *I slept right through it,* she thought, *I must still be overtired.* Aloud she said, "Ansel, it is too dangerous for you to be walking the streets in the middle of the night in a strange town. I know you feel safe at Knossos, but here no one knows you. You could have been robbed or hurt." Phoebe felt her mouth tighten and turn down and she reflected that she probably looked just as cantankerous as her meter, Thesmas, had when Phoebe had displeased her. She tried to lighten her expression with a rueful smile.

Uncharacteristically, Ansel brushed off Phoebe's concerns with a wave of her hand. She looked irritated at hearing Phoebe scold. "Meter, this is important. Yes, yes, I am sorry I was not more careful, I will be in the future. I have something pressing to tell you." Ansel related her encounter with Devra to Phoebe.

When Ansel finished her tale, Phoebe huffed, then said, "Yes, I suppose you are old enough now that you need to learn of such things. This sacrifice 'religion' as they call it has been in existence for several turns. It is blasphemy." Phoebe felt anger rise in her. "I wish they would just sacrifice themselves and be done with it. Unfortunately they have conveniently decided they need to offer other people's children to their bloodthirsty Bull God. I wonder if they even know they are emulating their enemies, the nomadi. Apparently killing is uncivilized if one's enemy does it but sacred if you do it." Phoebe glared at Ansel, then abruptly the rage drained from her. "I am sorry, *melliu*. The religion has become more popular again these last few turns because of Herilia's increasing restlessness. They believe that the Bull God rules earthshakes and that he will be appeased with blood."

"What do you believe, Meter?" Ansel asked.

Phoebe remained silent for a few moments, considering her daughter. In the last few turns Ansel had blossomed from a mousey little maiden to a beauty. Gone was the shy, chubby child with wild hair. In her place stood a young woman who was growing into her features and promised to be both elegant and graceful. *Ansel is Kore now. And is one of the Chosen. She will know the truth soon enough anyway,* Phoebe decided. "At the University we are taught that the land we live on is borrowed from She of Ten Thousand Names. Sometimes She needs it back and Her people must move on. We of this region always knew this land was ours only for a time. Our storytellers teach us that we needed to move before, long ago, and that is why we came to this area. The Sisterhood prays Great Meter will change Her mind or find some other way, but many of us are reading the signs to mean that we will need to pick up and move again."

"Soon? I mean, in our lifetimes?"

"Yes, very likely. Just as the Caster warned, we are watching the signs closely. Herilia rumbles, the Seers' have become less and less clear, the earth shakes, the wild animals become more and more nervous. These are all signs. We wait for just a few more and when they come, we will need to leave."

"What are those signs, Meta?"

"The keepers of the tales say our Seers will suddenly receive very clear visions of destruction. Some will die just from the vision. There will be a great shake that kills many, there will be fire. That is the last sign, the fire."

Ansel gasped. "Why do we wait until these terrible things happen if we know they are coming?"

Phoebe sighed and lifted her palms. "Do you want to leave, Ansel? Where will we go? What will become of our way of life? Where is there land for us to claim? The Sisterhood has scouts – many of them – who are looking even now for a new home for us. The nations around here are hostile to our religion, our way of life." Phoebe allowed herself to collapse into a chair. She could not remember ever feeling so tired. "Some of our people are leaving already, but we think simply moving to other islands is not far enough. We will begin to leave when we have answers."

Ansel looked frightened and suddenly very young again. "Leave Kriti?" she asked. "So, the changes at the Festival were just a beginning then."

Phoebe gathered her only daughter into her arms and hugged her hard.

Phoebe had only been able to steal away a few days from Knossos. Together she and Ansel visited more shops, chatted with people over meals and admired the ocean views. The full moon shone soon enough, bringing the celebration of the founding of Daedalos and the last night of their trip to Heria. All day there had been festivities in town. Vivd flower garlands were twined around the shop facades, people stopped to visit friends, special meals and sweets were prepared. Nadia served a sumptuous meal for several neighbors, including the local Priesera. The golden honey wine caused Ansel to giggle when she drank too much. Phoebe, Ansel, Nadia, and the other women left the dwelling dressed in flowing robes and dainty sandals just before dusk.

They walked arm in arm toward the edge of town in the uplands. The ceremony would be held in a cave above the town. Even though they were early, a line had already formed at the point where the stone–paved town road dwindled to an earthen trail. A novice Priesera was handing out clay pots with rolled beeswax candles stuck in them. "You will light the candle wick at a torch further up the path," she instructed. Ansel gazed at the trail leading up to the cave. Along the side every few lengths were copper torch sleeves with the torches inserted, soaked in oil and ready to be lit. They would illuminate the path. A few moments later, another young Priesera jogged up the street from town with a lit torch, entered the trail, and began igniting the torches as she followed it up to the cave.

The sun set reluctantly in the mid Metertide sky painting the heavens in breathtaking shades of brilliant pink and orange. However, once the sun finally sank below the left side of the mountain, it grew dark rather quickly and the torches were the only light. As the ceremony began, the townspeople lined up to light their candles and began sauntering up the trail. Ansel was familiar with ceremonies in caves; there were several at Knossos each turn. The trails leading to the ritual caves had many switchbacks for ease of walking and were invariably wide enough to allow people to travel in both directions. Many also had a steeper and more direct back route to the cave for the Priesera to carry ceremonial items in and out more quickly. Nadia hung back, waiting to give her own meter an arm as they walked the trail together. Phoebe and Ansel went ahead. The lit candles and torches lining the mountainside glimmered in the moonlight and the people advanced in silence. As they approached the cave, they heard the eerie tone of a single reed flute. The simple melody made Ansel's heart ache as it echoed in the cave, stirring in her yearnings that seemed to emanate from the very ancestors themselves.

The ceremony was elegant and simple. The shallow cave, illuminated with torches and candles, was decorated with flowers and fruit. The Elder Priesera stood just inside holding a huge basket filled with grapes. As each townsperson took a grape, the Priesera said, "Taste the abundance of Daedalos," and the person replied, "It is good." The Priesera then anointed the forehead of each participant between the eyes, with a spot of red ochre paste. The townsperson then retraced his or her steps down the path, gave the clay pot back to a waiting Priesera keeping the candle to use in personal prayers during the turn. Ansel understood that a minimal ceremony was needed for such a large group of people. Afterward, many revelers would gather into groups, singing, dancing, and drinking far into the night.

Just as Phoebe and Ansel were beginning to stroll back down the path, they were intercepted.

"Ansel, bring your meter and let us take the short cut down," a tall hulk of a woman said as she stepped out of the shadows.

"Devra," Ansel whispered, "how did you find us?"

"I am a tracker, remember?" the big woman grinned, obviously pleased.

Ansel took Phoebe's hand and together they followed Devra around to the far side of the cave. As they scrambled down this much steeper trail, Ansel introduced her meter to Devra.

At the bottom of the hill, Devra bowed low to Phoebe, and said, "I am honored to make your acquaintance, Mistress Phoebe. Your daughter tells me you are Elder Escort at Knossos. It is not often an Emetchi such as myself gets to meet so prominent a person."

Phoebe smiled and replied, "Ansel tells me you are a tracker, therefore I believe our interests coincide. I learn what I can, but my position can make it hard to know what is happening on the other side of town, so to speak. " Ansel felt surprise at her meter's candidness. At the Agronos, she was much more demure about her true work, which was, of course, to spy.

Devra merely bowed again. "Let us go somewhere more private to talk, Mistress Phoebe. My horse is tied to a shrub over there in the bushes. I can not leave him alone much in Daedalos – he draws attention. An animal of his value invites the curiosity of many people." She threw a sly sideways glance towards Ansel who felt her face go hot.

"Where shall we go then?" Phoebe asked

"I have discovered something I believe you will find interesting, Mistress. Can you walk as you are dressed or do you need to change shoes? I need to take you up further into the mountains and the trail is somewhat rough."

Phoebe looked at her sandals and sighed, "Though we both should probably change, I am eager to hear your news. Let us take the path now. Does that suit you Ansel? Will your ankle be well?"

Ansel nodded. "My ankle is almost as good as new. This robe does not constrict my movements and the sandals are as good as anything I brought to walk in. Let us go."

Devra led them up a path that began close to where they had stood. It quickly became steep. She had not lied, the path was very rough in some places with loose stones and thorny bushes. The moon was full though, and cast enough light to see well enough. Both Phoebe and Ansel were born in the rugged mountain lands. Their leg muscles were strengthened with walking and their feet calloused from stone. If their sandals were not comfortable at least they were better than bare feet, and to Ansel's delight, Devra actually invited her to climb up on Dolphina's back. In the moonlight, Ansel scrambled up a flat boulder and was able to swing her leg over Dolphina's withers. It was much higher up than the donkey.

After about an hour of slow hiking, Devra signaled for them to stop. As Phoebe on foot and Ansel on horseback waited in silence, Devra crept around a rocky outcropping to the right. Soon she returned and after helping Ansel off Dolphina, she tied the horse's leather harness to a small thorny tree and beckoned Ansel and Phoebe to follow.

On the other side of the rocks were several cave openings, one after the next. Devra pointed to one that was elevated above the others. "That one." She said. "That cave is where sacrifices are happening. I climbed all around here yesterday. That cave is far deeper than the others and contains several hidden rooms. They have set up an altar to the bull, and there are blood stains on it. I also found a rhyton to transport blood, from the body to the altar, I assume. Some of the back cave rooms stink of blood and decay."

Ansel caught her breath. Phoebe began asking questions.

"Where do they dispose of the bodies?"

"There are cairns around the other side of the cave. I tore one apart and found human bones."

"Is this the only cave?"

"I do not know. This one is easy to find and reasonably close to the town, but that does not mean there are not more than one. I suspect there is another near Akrotiri and I have heard the sacrifice cult is popular in high Atlancia in the mountain valley, but that is beyond the scope of my employment."

"Ach, and we must leave tomorrow. Devra, when your employment ends here, will you come to Knossos and do further work for me? I am truly alarmed."

"Meta, do you think Garin and Ganymede have been, I mean are they . . . ?" Ansel found she could not vocalize her question.

Phoebe shook her head slowly and stroked her daughter's hair. "I do not know, Ansel. I do not know."

Chapter 25

Rheana found herself in constant confusion about directions. The sun was supposed to rise to her right when she looked at the ocean. Here in Phaistos it rose to her left. The sea too was darker and it behaved differently–the waves were rougher and their rhythm more erratic.

She always supposed Phaistos would be another Knossos. However, the people of Phaistos quickly, and most emphatically, dispelled this notion. "We are *not* Knossian," Rheana was informed. "We Phaistians are modern. We have more spacious rooms and more decorative pottery, more beautiful wall art, more wonderful, well, everything." Phaistos traded extensively with Libya and Egypt. Rheana could see the southern influences everywhere: in paintings of exotic animals with broad snouts or long necks; in sunnier, more golden colors and in striking cloth patterns never seen in Knossos. Rheana found the attitudes of the Phaistians somewhat distressing. "Knossos is the age–old center of the world," she was told. "but here in Phaistos, we are worldly and new. We do not need or want the dreary traditions of Knossos."

Still there was an underlying, if grudging, respect for things of Knossos. It was no secret that Knossian Bulldancers were the finest in the world. Phaistos had their own 'dancer troupe, of course, but the finest athletes invariably left to join the troupe at Knossos. During the Kore– and Metertide she spent on Kriti's southern shore, Rheana came to understand that Phaistos' people felt they lived in the shadow of Knossos. Like an adolescent daughter, Phaistos struggled to be different from the older Agronos, yet also deeply desired the approval of Knossos. The relationship was love and hate. *The Knossians think they are so wonderful* was the message spoken aloud, while the message underneath was, *we wish Knossos would recognize our greatness too.*

There was unrest in the lands to the south of Kriti and many people from the vast nation of Libya and from the ancient civilization of Egypt immigrated north to Phaistos. The Libyans were a tall and beautiful dark people with shining eyes and skin. Their tight curly hair was smoothed with oils and braided into ornate styles or, for the warrior clans, allowed to grow in naturally knotted tendrils that jutted in many directions. The Egyptians were a golden people, many with eyes the color of amber resin. They brought with them exquisite and friendly cats whom they considered sacred.

The peoples of Kriti believed that cooperation with the others who came to live among them made their nations stronger. Their rememberers told stories of how long ago, ancestors from the east joined with the cave dwellers of Kriti and together they built their great civilization. The Labrys, holy double axe of netted Dictynna of the forge, symbolized cooperation between peoples. She of Ten Thousand Names brings abundance and together we are better, they affirmed to each other.

Rheana quickly made friends with one of the young Priesera, Thalia, who, though born in Egypt, had immigrated to Phaistos with her meter and family when she was but an infant. Thalia worked as a scribe for the administration of the Agronos Phaistos and she often spent time in company of Kourete Nikolas, even more so now that Aradia was absent.

"It is as though he forgets I am there," Thalia giggled to Rheana as the young women sat together on a large flat slab of granite under the shade of a cypress tree watching the sea. Rheana sipped fresh squeezed pomegranate juice from an ornately painted cup and watched the succulent sea grasses bob in the wind that blew in from the sea. The breeze was cooling – it was considerably warmer and dryer in the south and Rheana wished she had thought to rub olive oil on her face and lips before venturing outside.

Thalia continued. "And now that Vasilissa is here, it is worse than before. Honestly, I do not know what to write sometimes. I am sure they do not want every intimate comment and caress recorded into the official scrolls! Should I write, 'and then he pinched her behind and commanded her to get him some wine'?"

Rheana chuckled. "I am surprised at Vasilissa. She always seemed so proper and stuffy. This is a side of her I did not suspect existed."

"Oh, I know the type." Thalia flicked her hand in dismissal. "The fussier they are with everyone else, the more submissive they are with their own lovers. He orders her around like a servant and she just looks at him with cow eyes and does it."

Rheana grimaced. "I fear she is incautious about what she tells him." She suddenly lowered her voice. "This is sister to sister only." Thalia nodded, acknowledging the sacred Priesera bond between them. "The Elder Council is allowing a male to enter the Priesera training sometime in the next few turns. This information is only to be shared with the Priesera and the Council, but I overheard Vasilissa tell Nikolas. I almost ran into the room to confront her, but I did not want them to know I listened in and it was too late anyway."

Thalia's eyes grew large and she thrust her palm to her mouth shaking her head. "What news though! Why would the Priesera ever allow such a thing?"

Rheana shrugged. "I do not entirely understand either but Mistress Phoebe and Elder Priesera Aluneia both advocated for him and that is good enough for me. They say he is marked by She of Ten Thousand Names. Vasilissa was furious at the decision. I have never seen her so angry. I think everyone at Knossos felt relief when she decided to come to Phaistos with Nikolas."

"How long will she stay I wonder? Nikolas has other lovers here at Phaistos. For the life of me, I do not understand what women see in him, but they are often quite jealous of his attentions. Why once two of his women accidentally met in the hallway outside of his door and . . . ."

The young women continued to gossip for several more minutes in the shade while the sun burned furiously overhead, until Thalia suddenly sat up and cupped her hand above her eyes, looking out toward the sea.

"Why, that is my uncle Alekki's ship!" she said. Thalia jumped to her feet and dashed to the water's edge several lengths away, her toes kicking up little puffs of sand as she shouted back over her shoulder, "I was not expecting to see him for several cycles. Rheana, come meet him!"

Rheana picked herself up and followed her impetuous friend at a more leisurely pace. The gritty sand was hot under her bare feet. Thalia was up to her thighs in the aquamarine water, helping a familiar–looking man with a leathery face and full lips pull his long green boat, its sails flagging as the gusty breeze abated, to security onto the sand.

"Uncle Alekki, this is Rheana of Knossos. She is visiting for several quartercycles." Thalia beamed at her uncle; obviously she was very fond of him.

The man smiled as he bowed, the corners of his eyes crinkling good–naturedly. "Greetings, Rheana. I believe we were introduced at the last Seven–Turns Fest, although I spent most of my time with Helen Demetria."

Rheana returned the bow and the smile. "Yes, of course. You are the opium trader. Mistress Phoebe introduced us. I did not realize that you and Thalia were family. How does your weather fare, TradesKourete Alekki?"

"Well enough, my thanks. I have come to spend some time with my favorite sister–daughter before I go to spend Cronetide in Athena with my meter." He turned to Thalia. "She is unwell, your Gran-Meter, "I must go to help your other uncles care for her. I do not know how long I will need to stay in Athena, so I thought to spend a cycle with you first."

Thalia's face crumpled and she said, "I am sorry to hear this. Should I go also?"

"No little one, you are needed here. Your GranMeter has lived a full life and she will be embraced by Goddess in her own time. We will witness her passing when it comes and tell the spirits of the goodness of her soul."

Thalia looked all the world like a little girl, her wide, dark, eyes soft, a finger in her mouth, as she nodded. Alekki sighed softly, then smiled again, though perhaps a touch more grimly as he turned his attention to Rheana. "I must admit that I am pleased to see you Mistress Rheana. It tells me your mentor has paid attention to my warning to her. Perhaps you and I might find some time to speak in the next few days; I have information I believe you will find interesting."

They arranged to have dinner together the next evening, when the hot sun was finally hanging low in the west turning the sky a brilliant orange–purple. The communal kitchen area of Phaistos opened toward the ocean, and the people dined upon a huge patio of white stone tiles interlaced with red mortar. The terrace was covered with tables and chairs and the air danced with lively conversation between elegantly dressed Phaistians discussing everyday activities or perhaps politics. Alekki led Rheana to a sea–facing bench just wide enough for two that had an equally small table in front of it. The back of the bench abutted an old cypress tree growing at the edge of the patio. It was a private table used most frequently by new lovers. Rheana and Alekki raised a few eyebrows as they brought their dinner bowls to the spot, but the far older Alekki just grinned and winked conspiratorially at anyone who stared, while young Rheana blushed prettily.

"I hope this table is acceptable to you, Mistress Rheana," Alekki said close to her ear. "It is the most private eating area here and so it would be considered terribly bad manners to listen in on our conversation. The people themselves will make certain no one is eavesdropping."

Rheana smiled and said softly, "It is the perfect place. I am an Escort, TradesKourete Alekki. No one should think twice that I have taken a lover, even if I am not from Phaistos. Escorts are not known to be alone wherever they go."

"Please call me Alekki, Rheana." He chuckled. "Ah, the irony; I am mostly a lover of men, you know. I make exceptions for certain women, but alas Rheana, I choose women closer to my own age, such as Mistress Phoebe. No offense meant against your own beauty, my dear."

"No offense taken. Goddess allows for all choices that bring love and pleasure." Rheana took a sip of wine and leaned back on the bench, "Still, let us keep up appearances, shall we? Here, slip an arm around me as we speak. Let us make certain to laugh and touch casually."

Alekki's eyes sparkled as he obediently tucked his arm around her waist and turned toward her. "I agree. However, I must ask that you do not try your Radiance connection trick with me. I can fend it off, though not easily, I admit. I promise to tell you what I know; there is no need to manipulate."

Rheana laughed aloud and agreed. "Now," she said, "what is it that you think I should know?"

"Do you know of a man named Iphikeles? He lives upon Heria in the city of Atalancia."

Rheana shook her head.

"I am certain Phoebe will know who he is. He is a leader of the sacrifice religion. It started on Heria, possibly even founded by Iphikeles himself. He is a genuinely pious man who, had he been born female, would no doubt be Priesera. He is also the elder half–brother of our Kourete Nikolas."

"Ah," Rheana said. "Are they close, these brothers?"

"Very close. Nikolas idolizes his brother. It worries me because I heard Nikolas speak favorably about the sacrifice religion at the Seven–Turns Fest. This is Iphikeles' influence, no doubt."

"Is it likely that Nikolas will bring it here to Kriti?"

"I do not believe so. Niko is not a mystic, but a politician. His life is that of an administrator." Alekki paused. "Still, I am troubled. I saw something I do not yet understand at the Seven–Turns Fest. Early morning of the day after the Fest, I was restless and decided to go for a walk. I followed the path down to Amnisos. It was almost deserted, of course, since those who had come by boat were using a different harbor after the Amnisos tragedy. But there was one boat I saw, sailing away from the bay. I knew I had seen it before, I know nearly all the boats of the traders by sight, but I could not place this one. I put it down to failing memory and old age at the time." Rheana reached over to brush his leg lightly with her hand and he grinned at her. "But that night, I suddenly remembered who owned that boat: Iphikeles. It was a wonder really that I put that together, since Iphikeles is not a trader and I have only seen the boat once before, but I am quite certain."

"So Iphikeles was at the Seven–Turns Fest?" Rheana asked.

"Not that I saw, though I suppose I could have missed him in the crowd. I wonder though why, if he attended the Fest at all, he would have docked at Amnisos."

"Hmmm." Rheana stared at the sea, pondering. After several thoughtful moments and a few bites of her dinner of grilled octopus, she said, "Why do they sacrifice persons, Alekki, do you know? It makes no sense to me."

"People do very strange and upsetting things when they are frightened, Rheana, and the peoples of Heria are very frightened – for good reason. The threat of the fire mountain, Herilia, is real. Atalancia is being abandoned. Its streets are covered in ash. Do you know, ten or more people were scorched to death from a cloud of hot fumes not two cycles ago."

"And so they sacrifice their own citizens? Why do they think this would please Great Meter?"

"Ah, but it is not to Great Meter they sacrifice. They believe the Bull Son, Minotaur, is enraged. They attribute all the restlessness of the land to Him, the shakes, the waves, the ash, the rumbling. Some of them claim He wants to wage war against the nomadi and their thunder gods. They teach themselves the ways of iron and talk of building an army. Others believe the sacrifice of young men will appease Minotaur and He will again let the people live in peace. It is fear that drives the sacrifice religion."

Rheana shook her head sadly. "Here is a piece of news. Did Thalia tell you that Council member Aradia's grandson, Ganymede, is missing along with his cousin Garin of Knossos? They were seen leaving to hike in the mountains and did not return when expected. Aradia has refused to leave Knossos until Ganymede is found. That is one of the reasons I am here. Phoebe felt Niko needed watching especially since he is in charge of governing Phaistos in Aradia's absence."

"Thalia did indeed tell me. Phoebe is wise to send you here. Has Niko done anything untoward?"

"No, unless you count embarrassing himself and Priesera Vasilissa with public sexual displays."

Alekki snorted. "So I have heard. Perhaps we are giving Niko too much credit. He may be too preoccupied with sexual conquests and self promotion to make mischief with the sacrifice religion."

"I am sure I do not know." Rheana said as she scraped the bottom of her dinner bowl with her wooden spoon.

Chapter 26

The journey to the Priesera village was difficult for Ansel, not because of the weather since the parching winds of Metertide had finally subsided, nor was it because of the extremely rocky and mostly uphill climb through the mountains south of Knossos. No, it was her traveling companions who made the journey decidedly difficult. Vasilissa, back from her Metertide tryst in Phaistos, was even more cold and distant than usual, snapping orders to gather firewood or to load the donkey quickly, when deeming to speak at all. Her lips were two thin lines, her eyes murky pools covered with ice.

Ansel was not the only novice joining the Priesera this side of Metertide. Vasilissa told her Joli and Beryl were both about sixteen turns, the same age as Ansel. They were from nearby farms where their families raised goats and barley for the Agronos. The girls claimed they practically drew their first breaths together. Joli, the petite one with enormous dark eyes and a cleft chin stared unabashedly at Ansel during the journey, but when Ansel smiled a little and said, "Greetings", the girl did not smile or respond. Ansel felt her face redden under the other girl's gaze. Beryl, who was at least as tall as Geneera but more coarsely boned and with slightly protruding teeth, never even looked at Ansel except from the corners of her eyes when she probably thought Ansel did not notice.

The girls never got any friendlier during the day. They said little to Ansel, but she could feel their eyes burn into her flesh. They giggled to each other when she turned to face them. Once she overheard Beryl whisper, "That cloak she is wearing is probably worth more than what my family grew all last harvest." The jeering behind her back felt all too familiar to Ansel. She had faced the jealousy of other girls when she was younger. Some hurts never went away entirely.

Then Ansel rubbed up painful blisters in the arches of her feet. Vasilissa grunted when she saw them and, rummaging through her leather pack, found some ointment. But while the salve soothed her feet, it could not soothe Ansel's heavy heart. She had never been this far from home before all by herself. She thought about her Mata and Geneera and even Xeronos all the time. As she lay with her head upon a rock, her favorite red woolen blanket pulled close around her face, she looked up at the stars and thought, *Do you even miss me Geneera? Do you even know I am gone?* Tears burned her face at night.

In the morning, Vasilissa led the girls up yet another winding mountain trail. Just when Ansel, her calves aching and blisters burning, thought they would never stop climbing, Vasilissa abruptly held up a hand, then disappeared into some thorny brush. Just as quickly, she returned and gestured for the girls to follow her. Ansel pushed up from the back of the line where she had been taking her turn leading the pack donkey. "Look," Vasilissa said, pointing from a ridge. "There is the University village. The trail now winds down the side of this mountain and into the valley. We will arrive before the sun reaches her apex."

Shading her eyes with the palm of her hand, Ansel squinted down from the crag. Before her was a vast green bowl–shaped valley with a large flat–topped hillock in its center. The clang of animal bells drifted up to her ears. She could just make out long–haired goats – krikri, the native mountain goat, she presumed – scattered around the bowl's meadow and clinging to the rocky sides of the hill. Upon the summit of the hillock sat the famed *Karthea* Priesera – the University of the Priesera.

To Ansel, the village looked small and primitive compared to the magnificent, towering Agronos home she left behind in Knossos; just a scattering of interconnected, flat–roofed structures huddled atop the rocky plateau. A wide, bright white road split the University town in two with the buildings located on either side of the broad road. They were arranged in a peculiar way, flaring out from the road to a semi–circular curve at their far ends. "What does it look like?" Ansel muttered aloud to herself.

She was answered by Vasilissa, "Long ago, the Priesera decided to build their home in a way that honors She of Ten Thousand Names. They wanted to create a symbol that represented Kriti and also the Priesera themselves. The walkways inscribe the double blades of the holy Labrys." Ansel peered more carefully at the layout. Yes, Vasilissa was right. The buildings and walking paths were arranged to look like the Labrys.

Vasilissa continued. "Look carefully at the road. It represents the Labrys handle, but it is more too. See the loop at the far end? That is called the "loop garden". We hold many classes there in nice weather. And at this end, the one closest to us, the main road splits into three. Can you not see that the road looks like the sacred Priesera knot?

"Oh yes, I see the Priesera knot," Ansel said. "So it is both the Labrys of Kriti and also the Knot of the Priesera, only put together. It is an interesting symbol. It almost looks like a person with wings."

"It has come to be considered our holiest symbol. No one outside the University is permitted to use it and it is not even known by most. We do not speak of it, and it has become one of the Mysteries of the Priesera." Ansel and the other girls nodded solemnly, understanding that their training had just formally begun.

As they hiked down to the plain where the village lay, Ansel could not help but feel anxious and even disappointed. The village was so much smaller than Agronos Knossos. It seemed to the homesick girl like an assemblage of rustic shacks compared to the bright, well–kempt, multistoried Center at Knossos. Surrounded by high mountain peaks, the sparse green plain and plateau upon which the Center squatted looked desolate and isolated from the rest of the world. There were Priesera who lived their entire lives here Vasilissa told her. Doing what, Ansel could not even imagine. "We live simply here," Vasilissa said, as if the lack of indoor baths and plumbing were an asset.

The jagged, steep path down to the valley followed a mountain stream. This time of the turn the creek was shallow and gentle as it wound its way down into the valley, but Vasilissa assured the girls it could engorge to a raging torrent in early Maidentide. When the ground leveled and they entered the bowl, a cobbled street emerged that ran more or less parallel to the stream which now meandered in gentle curves through the valley. It soon broadened, bisecting the bowl's meadow, and then wound off to the left while the path continued to the central road up the hillock. Several krikri scurried off the road as the party approached, though a couple of braver ones stood in the center looking at them curiously. "Baaaah!" they protested throatily when Vasilissa waved her arm and said, "Shoo!"

"Silly things, tame as kittens they are and twice the nuisance. No, Ansel, do not dare give that goat any bread!" Vasilissa said as Ansel was about to offer one a morsel from her pack, "They will follow us all the way into the village if you do!"

Ansel stuffed the treat back into her rucksack and looked apologetically at the disappointed animal. "Sorry," she whispered. The pack donkey looked at the goats disdainfully as it passed.

Finally, they reached the wide middle road at the bottom of the knoll. The mosaic of stones was so clean it appeared to have been vigorously scrubbed. Mostly comprised of white gypsum, the paved street was decorated with green, silver–gray and reddish stonework that created a twisting inlaid pattern.

Now that she was close, Ansel was surprised to see how truly beautiful the buildings were. Unlike the Agronos Knossos, the colors of the buildings were muted, mostly the whites and grays of the natural stone. But each window and doorway boasted wreaths of flowers and brightly painted symbols.

Joli, walking in front of Ansel, pointed to a building with a wall painting of graceful women dancing in a circle with poppy pods in their hands. Jars of late blooming flowers graced walkways with perfumed blossoms of yellow and purple. Vasilissa gestured toward almond, fig, pomegranate and gnarled olive trees, obviously planted by the residents, which lent a bit of shade to the street. One almond tree was half stripped of its leaves. "The woman who lives there makes dyes. She gets yellow from the almond leaves," Vasilissa said casually. Since reaching the top of the hillock, Vasilissa's mood had improved and once she almost smiled. A hunched woman paused from gathering fallen locust tree pods to wave at the travelers.

"Ai, you must be the first group of new novices, then," the woman said, nodding her head. "And Vasilissa, is it you? It has been so many turns."

"Lyssa! Greeting to you old friend. Yes, I have returned from teaching in Agronos Knossos for twelve full turns."

"Ai, Vasilissa, the turns do have wings. Aluneia just returned herself not a full cycle ago. She will be expecting you no doubt. She lives in the apartment at the tip of the loop where Odelia once was."

Vasilissa grunted. "Of course. Aluneia is Eldest now. My thanks to you, Lyssa."

To the girls she said, "When I was here last, Odelia was Eldest. Aluneia was her apprentice. Odelia returned to the arms of Great Meter a few turns back and Aluneia was elected Eldest."

"But Priesera Aluneia is not old." Ansel said.

Joli snickered. Vasilissa turned to frown at the slight farm girl, then said, "No, she is not. While the Elder Council is, for the most part, comprised of those elder in turns, here 'Elder' is only a title. We elect a leader based exclusively on her gifts and talents, not the amount of gray in her hair."

The office and home of the Elder Priesera stood alone and

opened to the beautiful garden within the loop of the road. It had bright white plaster walls and a flat roof. Aluneia, dressed in formal Priesera robes, stepped out of the square stuccoed doorway to greet the party. Ansel recognized the tall erect woman with solemn features.

"Vasilissa. How glad I am you decided to return to the Village." Aluneia turned to the girls and said, "Joli, Beryl, and Ansel, welcome. You are the first to arrive, but we expect the rest of the class to arrive in the next few days. You will be staying in the novice apartments at the far end of the village. I will have someone show you your rooms."

"Where is your scoundrel advisee? Is Diatima too indisposed from a late night of singing and mischief to show the novices around?" Vasilissa asked, her face genuinely merry.

Aluneia snorted and tried to suppress a smile. Ansel noticed the woman's eyes twinkled. It made her look much younger and nearly pretty. "No, though that would certainly not be beyond her, Priesera Diatima is still on her journey turn." Abruptly she sobered. Lowering her voice, she said "We have had no news and she is gone over long." Ansel, not understanding anyway, pretended she had not heard.

Speaking again to everyone, Aluneia said, "I have need to speak privately with Vasilissa. I must find someone else who can show you the village."

Vasilissa said, "We passed Lyssa on our way here. Perhaps she will show the novices to their quarters."

"Yes, that is a fine idea. Girls, go back down the road and ask Lyssa to show you the way. Take beds there and settle in. You will find the communal dining room next door and I will meet you there shortly for the midday meal."

Chapter 27

Ansel, Beryl and Joli were shown to a large room with many narrow cots.

"Choose beds quickly now and settle in. The privacy room is out that door," Lyssa pointed a finger to the far end of the room, "and straight down the little trail." The girls all nodded obediently. "I must go to the kitchen now to help with the midday meal. Come to the dining room down the hall and to your left when you hear the bell clang."

The girls had no more than set their packs down on their chosen beds when they heard the sharp chime of a bell. Instantly sounds of chairs scraping stone, feet shuffling and giggling voices filled the hallway outside the room. Beryl and Joli, who had chosen beds next to each other, linked arms and strode out the door, leaving Ansel quite alone. She had chosen a bed in the other corner as far away from them as possible. Fortunately, it did not prove difficult to find the dining hall; everyone was heading in only one direction.

A tall, wiry woman with unusually pale skin and a shock of hair the improbable color of ripe pomegranate seeds slammed into the dining hall during the meal. A flaccid child was tucked under her muscular arm. "I need a healer! Kai, are you in here?" she hollered.

The girl–child was limp and her long dark hair hung down over much of her face. Was she asleep? Unconscious? Injured? Ansel strained to look around Beryl to get a better view while next to her, Aluneia jumped to her feet and motioned to someone at the far end of the great hall.

A diminutive but strongly built woman, presumably Kai, was already on her feet and hurrying toward the girl. "Dia, who is the child and what is wrong with her?" she asked brusquely of the flame–haired woman as she swept the tresses out of the child's face, then felt her forehead. "Her name is Uazet." Ansel thought the name, 'oo–ah–set', very odd – but then the girl appeared odd too, all spindly limbs and heavy straight black hair. She moaned and looked up for the first time. She possessed the queerest eyes Ansel had ever seen, yellowy gold, almost glittering like the eerie glow of an animal's eyes in the torchlight.

Dia put her down gently. She stood, but leaned heavily on Dia. Kai murmured to the girl for a moment in a voice inaudible to the room, then announced, "All right, all right, you all can go back to eating. The girl is fine." No one dared disobey the healer; Ansel returned her attention to her bland porridge dotted with smoked fish and chopped green onion. From the corner of her eye she watched the Priesera Healer help the girl limp out of the room, presumably to the Healing House. The red–haired woman, relieved of her charge, pulled out a chair noisily, scraping it on the stone floor, and sat down heavily. "I am back! Was I missed?" she announced loudly to the room in general.

The dining room erupted into laughter and greetings spiked with hoots and cheers from everyone excepting the newest novices and some of the more disciplined Priesera. Even austere Aluneia smiled. Several of the older students jumped from their chairs and hugged or thumped Dia soundly on her back. Ansel found herself grinning.

So that is Diatima, she thought. It was hard not to stare. Lean to the point of boneyness, Dia had to be a full head taller even than

Geneera, and her white skin! Her orange–red hair! Who had ever seen anything like her before? After the initial greetings had subsided, Aluneia crooked a finger at Dia, who responded with exaggerated haste. Cocking a grin at Aluneia, the lanky woman loped over to the table. Close up, Ansel saw that her light, grayish eyes were underscored with dark rings. Her skin looked almost yellow beneath golden brown spots across her upturned nose. With a flourish belying her obvious exhaustion, she bowed low in front of Aluneia and said, "Your unworthy apprentice returns from beyond the waters, oh adviserly one."

Aluneia sucked in her cheeks, but Ansel saw her eyes were twinkling as she retorted, "I need your report immediately, apprentice, then you are off to bed. No, no, do not argue with me, I can see you are barely able to stand. Get yourself a plate of food and meet me in my office."

Dia grabbed a small stringed instrument that hung unnoticed around her broad shoulders, strummed a quick and only slightly off–key chord and sang, "Your wish is always my command, your wish is my command!" Aluneia raised an eyebrow and said "Then, apprentice Diatima, I suggest you sing less and move faster." Dia yelped as if pinched and dashed into the kitchen. Only when she was out of sight did Aluneia's face break into an unabashedly relieved smile.

Several minutes later, Dia sank her lanky frame onto a cushioned stone bench in Aluneia's office. She had charmed the cooks into giving her extra fish to help her recover from her journey and balanced her overloaded plate along with a huge bowl of barley precariously on her lap. Gently, she peeled her *kithara* from her shoulder and leaned it against the bench leg, ever ready when needed.

"The peoples to the east of the Emetchi borders are dangerous," she said to Aluneia past a mouthful of grain. "We cannot travel there safely any longer. The Emetchi watch their borders constantly for bands of warriors who come down from the mountains." She broke into a grin, suddenly, and pointed a chunk of bread toward

Aluneia. "Good folks, the Emetchi. Those women swing a sword as well as any nomadi and I would not want to vex 'em. They ride horses like they were born with four legs. An impressive group." Dia paused to cram bread into her mouth.

"The girl, was she waiting where the Seers predicted?" Aluneia asked.

"Yes. They got it right to the last detail. I found a boulder that looked like a vulture's head next to the curve in the river and there she was, tucked in a cave underneath it, lying next to the body of her nursemaid. Or at least I assume it was her nursemaid. That is what the Seers said I would find. The girl herself did not say much."

"Is she ill then?"

"Hard telling. Mostly she seems, well, odd, even nyxed. At first I thought she just did not understand Kritin or Greek. I am pretty poor at Babylonian proper, let alone any of the dialects, but I tried to make her understand I was there to take her to Kriti. Turns out she speaks a fair bit of Kritin, and well too."

"So what makes her nyxed?"

"She just stares into space for long periods of time, saying nothing, not even blinking. Then suddenly like, she will turn to you and start jabbering fast and fluttery as a butterfly. She will go on for quite a little while, then suddenly nothing again."

Aluneia touched her finger to her head. "Do you think she is *pesari*, touched, then?"

"Oh, she is touched all right, but then, I have been described that way too." Dia shrugged, grinning.

"Yes," Aluneia replied, not allowing herself to take the bait, "but at least you are minimally functional."

Dia laughed aloud. "Ei, advisor, you go a bit overboard there now." She grabbed her *kithara*, and swung into a jaunty beat,

> My granma was an houri,
> Or so the people say.
> By day she was a fury,
> But she drank the night away.
> She smoked some poppy at a fest

The people did say later,
And many swore her late night guest
Did look to be a satyr.

"Wretch!" Aluneia laughed. "Go sing your bawdy songs somewhere else."

Dia rose to her feet with her usual grace and said, "Shall I take that as a formal dismissal, Mistress?"

"No, not yet, sit down; I have some other things to tell you."

Aluneia had not meant for her tone to betray her misgivings, but apparently it did. Dia sat down again immediately, her face sober as she waited for the news.

"First, now that you are back from your journey, I would like you to take on an advisee of your own for the time you remain. I think you would be a good influence for young Ansel from Knossos. She is from the Agronos and educated, more so than the other novices anyway. She needs some fire in the belly, I think."

Dia nodded but said nothing.

"Secondly, we are likely to have a very unusual novice coming to school here later this turn or next."

"Surprising? How?"

Aluneia sighed. "First, the novice is male." She noted the sharp intake of breath from Dia, but quickly spoke over it. "And secondly, he is from Athena, not Kriti. He is Theseus, the Royal Consort of Helen Demetria."

"I do not understand. Why would he be coming here to the Priesera?"

"He considers himself called. I have spoken to him. I see that indeed he is called, and more I cannot explain. I have a *knowing* that he must be here and soon. Apparently the Eilithyliad thinks he should be here too. That was enough for the Council."

"But called to the Priesera? How can it be that he is called here?"

Aluneia shook her head. "The times grow ever stranger, Dia. I unmistakably saw the signs in him. I suspect the Council has political reasons for not objecting; my reasons and those of the Seer are spiritual. Change is coming."

"Of course. I foresee trouble from this, though. Many of the Priesera will not like it at all."

"I know. He does not even know the most basic of our teachings. My thought is to have him privately tutored as much as possible. I shall have to think upon how this is to be handled." She grimaced at Dia and shrugged her shoulders. "This goes as She will have it, not I. You may go now, Dia. Go to bed and sleep if you can."

Dia bowed deeply as if dismissed by First Elder Thesmas herself, and turned to leave. As she reached the door, she turned back and said, "You should know, the child, Uazet, she has horrible nightmares. Wakes up screaming and shaking."

"Undoubtedly she will stay at the healing houses for some time before formally starting as a novice, Kai will help her."

Dia nodded and left, shutting the door to Aluneia's office behind her.

Chapter 28

Already the skies around the University village were overcast as the threat of the Cronetide rains approached. It was much cooler high in the mountains, certainly chillier than Ansel was accustomed to. Perhaps the Cronetide rains came earlier here. Anxiously she scanned the sky as she hurried to the small two–story building at the end of the narrow street.

Most of the village buildings were attached and one could move from one to the other from the inside, but Ansel did not know her way through the labyrinthine University buildings yet and decided it was easier to find the office of the TaskMistress from the street. She was several minutes late as it was – the walk from the dining hall was longer than she anticipated. Hastily she sought to mingle with the cluster of girls who had already arrived. A stern Priesera, her long grey hair pulled back severely from her face, stood with her hands on her hips ushering the girls into a line. She had been previously introduced to Ansel and all the novices as the Priesera who would assign them chores to do at the University village, the infamous Priesera TaskMistress.

"You are not here just to study," Aluneia had explained at dinner several nights earlier, "but to add to this community. This village is run by all of us. You novices have now been here for over half a cycle. You can find your classes now. As of next quartercycle, we expect that before and after classes you will do chores as well. "

The Elder TaskMistress, her formal purple robe open to the waist and her huge breasts pointing to the ground, placed her hands on her hips. "Most of you come from farms or craft guilds and have vital skills. We do not assign chores merely to keep you all busy and out of mischief, though this is certainly warranted." She frowned and looked over them all. "We need your expertise to keep things running smoothly. Then, if you prove yourself diligent, you may request to learn new skills if there is something you fancy to study."

She took a wax tablet and sharpened stick from the deep front pocket of her undyed linen apron. Though an unusual accessory to the formal Priesera robe, the patched apron was, like the TaskMistress herself, eminently practical. "I am here to assign your duties. Each of you will be instructed all morn after your first meal and into the early noon until midday meal. You then report directly to your tasks and work until evening meal. Kitchen helpers may be required to work before the morning meal or after the evening meal. Is that understood?"

Some twenty young heads nodded sincerely. The other new novices had arrived within a few hours or days after Ansel, Joli, and Beryl. They all lived together in the one large novice dormitory. They would not have more privacy until the next turn when they would choose apartment mates. Ansel was disconcerted to find she had little in common with most of the other Kore who could not read or write well, but had other skills she had never before appreciated.

"Good. Now, get into a line. You," the TaskMistress pointed a stubby finger at the girl closest to her, "What is your name and where are you from? Do not dawdle girl, my time is precious."

The slight girl with wide–set eyes and a prominent eyebrows shifted her feet and clutched her hands behind her back. Her tunic was a beautiful shade of sky blue. "My name is Lidah and I am from the dye clan of Phaistos."

"We do not do much dying here, only for special ritual cloth. Do you spin or weave?"

Lidah nodded her head so vigorously her curly hair bounced on her thin shoulders. "Yes, Priesera. I am good at spinning and I know how to weave. I am small for a full loom, but I do stick weaving fairly well."

"Good. Then wool spinning you shall do and you will be consulted when we do any dying of ritual cloth. You are the only one we have from the dye clan at present." The TaskMistress scratched some markings in the wax tablet. "Now, how about you?" She pointed the sharpened stick at the girl behind Lidah. "What is your name and where are you from?" She in turn paled and gulped visibly.

And so the process went. Ansel was positioned nearly all the way at the back of the line, just in front of the fragile Uazet who had come in even later. When Ansel turned around to greet Uazet, the tiny girl was staring with wide golden eyes at the gruff TaskMistress; she did not acknowledge Ansel's greeting. Ansel felt unnerved herself. She racked her brain, but could not think of a single task she was capable of doing. Beryl was assigned to help farm the village's land while Joli was assigned to milking and animal tending.

Inevitably, the TaskMistress turned her attention to Ansel. Her frown deepened and she looked as if she doubted Ansel's ability to speak coherently. "Your name girl and where are you from?"

"Ansel. I am from the Agronos at Knossos."

If Ansel felt momentary pride that her voice did not quaver, it was quickly squashed.

"Ah, yes, I heard we had one from the Agronos. I do not suppose they bothered to teach you anything of use young Ansel?"

Ansel swallowed and said, "I know how to fish and repair nets, my Uncle taught me."

"Do you now? And do you think we are within spitting distance of the sea?"

The girls all giggled as Ansel shook her head. "No, TaskMistress." she answered meekly.

"All fish come to us already caught, gutted and preserved. We use nets to catch birds here, but many know how to repair them. Do you know how to take down a bird? No? What else do you know?"

"I can read and write very well. I could teach."

The woman glared at Ansel as if the girl suggested she could be Elder Priesera. Raising both eyebrows, she looked down her long nose at Ansel and sniffed. "May I suggest to you, novice, that you are here to be taught and not to teach. Clearly you have much to learn."

Ansel hung her head. "My apologies, TaskMistress."

"You Agronos girls think you can come into the village and be pampered just as you were at your private apartments. You have no understanding of work and that other people do it, do you girl?"

"Yes Mistress, I mean, no Mistress, I mean I would be happy to contribute to the village, Mistress, doing anything I can." Ansel fought back her tears.

"Do you know how to tend horses?"

"No, Mistress."

"Can you hunt?"

"No, Mistress."

"Can you harvest herbs properly or make medicinals?"

"No, Mistress."

"Can you cook?"

"No Mistress." Ansel's voice grew softer and softer and tears rolled down her cheeks. "I can sew a little," she whispered miserably.

"Can you now. That might be useful. Show me." From the pocket in her apron the woman withdrew a square of linen and tossed it at Ansel. From her bodice she removed a long copper needle with flaxen thread dangling from the eye.

With trembling hands, Ansel took the needle and drew a few clumsy stitches into the cloth. She knew they were bad. She could barely see through her tears.

"Humph", the taskmistress sniffed as she inspected Ansel's work, "I could take better stitches when I was still in nappies. Still, you must do something. Perhaps the elder seamstress will think you fit to repair tears or some such. Report to her."

Uazet, it turned out, knew much about herbs and tonics, though she had trouble speaking loudly enough for the TaskMistress to hear her. After much fuss, she was assigned to the healing houses to help the herbalists. The girls were finally released from the tender ministrations of the Elder TaskMistress who had proven to be even worse than her reputation suggested.

The Elder Priesera of needlework and weaving had as little use for Ansel's sewing as the Elder TaskMistress. A few days later, Ansel was assigned to bringing water to the kitchen workers. Later in the turn she would be taught to harvest olives. Anyone could learn to shake tree branches, she was told, and many hands would be needed when the olives turned ripe in deep Cronetide. There was much work for even the most untalented of novices – wool to be washed, pomegranates and figs to be picked, baskets to be carried – it was just that the village children were usually given these tasks. This knowledge did not make Ansel feel better, but if she wept at night in her cot, she was careful that no one took note. She was determined to abolish her reputation as "that spoiled Agronos girl."

That quartercycle and for several thereafter, Ansel lugged water in a heavy clay jug from the spring fed tarn at the far end of road. The double–handled jug was created from the red earth found around the village and though not painted, it was inscribed with waves and spirals. On the bottom, some spell markings had been scratched into the terracotta to protect the jug from cracking or being smashed. The clay felt rough to her fingers as she traced the outline of the spirals. It was well made and had a solid balanced feel.

The pool at the bottom of the hillock was deep and the water very cold. Ansel balanced herself carefully on a flat boulder as she squatted to dip the jug into the dark waters. It took both hands and a fair amount of determination to lift the full jug out of the water and back onto the rock, and Ansel was quite wet from the effort. She briefly despaired of lugging the full, heavy jug back to the kitchen, then she shrugged her shoulders. I have the whole afternoon to get it back, she thought. She squatted again down to the cold water, cupped her hands, and drank deeply. "Thank you, Lady of the Well, for this sweet water," she murmured aloud.

Every morn of Ansel's first triad of Cronetide at the University she awakened long before breakfast, sprinted to the kitchen while the sky was still dark and the weather rainy, and grabbed the jug waiting for her faithfully by the enclosed hearth. It would be warm to the touch from a night of sitting by the fire. In Cronetide, the kitchen workers tended the fire all long night. Sometimes it even snowed. Ansel skipped down the road, which was always wet unless it was icy; she slipped a few times and learned quickly to be more careful. She hummed to herself and watched her breath freeze into the air. Each morn she made sure to thank the Lady of the Well and sometimes left a bit of bread or porridge for Her animal children. The kitchen women were kind to her, smiling and teasing her when she brought back the heavy jug of water she had learned to balance on her head.

"Little Ansel," they called, "how strong your arms are getting – and your skull too!"

Ansel knew they meant no harm and soon learned to laugh with them. She showed off her hard–earned muscles. "Feel how strong my arms are, Lyssa!" she said, thumping down the heavy water jug. Lyssa good–naturedly put aside the pile of figs she was dicing and squeezed Ansel's bicep. "Ei, a true Emetchi you will be, my girl!" she said. Ansel grinned and found she really was proud of herself. The physical labor felt good. She enjoyed the new strength of her body. She found she looked forward to her time with the village cooks as much as to the peaceful time alone at the tarn. As Cronetide deepened, Ansel and the kitchen women joked together each early morn and each afternoon after classes as the women prepared the evening meal, sharing scraps with the village cats who gathered round. After her water bearer chores were finished for the day,

Ansel studied until long after the sun went down and the golden beeswax candles flickered in the Priesera village.

Chapter 29

Ansel was not quite sure what she thought about her advisor. The brash Diatima was so outlandish and impulsive, Ansel found her disconcerting, yet it was clear the rest of the novice Priesera loved her. Several were envious that Dia was her mentor.

"So, Ansel," Dia began one day, her heavy leather boots leaving large muddy imprints on the wet garden path, "How are you liking your first turn as a novice Priesera? I remember staying up all night talking and laughing with all the other novices. It was such fun." Dia smiled broadly and whumped Ansel hard on the back. "You can share everything with me. There is likely nothing I have not done myself."

Ansel merely mumbled some reply. The truth was she spent her days going to classes, doing her chores, studying, and then sleeping. Her life was boring. Other than the companionable kitchen women, she had made no friends at all. She was not ready to share that with the popular Dia, at least not yet.

Luckily, Dia was as interested in telling Ansel about herself as she was in learning about Ansel and did not seem to mind, or even notice, Ansel's reticence.

"I am a Muse Priesera, my primary instrument is my kithara," she said indicating the ever present stringed, hollow box flung over her shoulder. "I sing too. It is the best vocation I can think of. I travel around Kriti, the islands, and even to other nations playing my songs, entertaining people, and learning."

"Have you ever been to the Agronos Knossos?" Ansel asked.

"Yes, a few times. It is magnificent. That is where you are from, is this right?"

Ansel sighed deeply and nodded. "Yes. I miss the Agronos. I miss my meter. Perhaps you have met her, the Elder Escort, Mistress Phoebe?"

"Yes, I have met your meter once or twice." Dia raised an eyebrow and directed her crooked grin at Ansel. "She and I are doing similar work though hers is much more intimate, of course. I, on the other hand, usually travel as a boy. Yes, really," she added, chuckling at Ansel's surprised expression. "Since I am so tall and flat–chested it is easy for me to fool people when I want to. A little glamour magic and no one even suspects I am anything but a young man." Her mischievous light blue–gray eyes twinkled at Ansel's discomfort. "I can obtain information I would never be able to get otherwise," she explained.

They stopped together at the end of the path. Dia laid a friendly hand on Ansel's shoulder and said, "I think we will get on well together, Ansel. Let us meet each quartercycle or so. Go on to your class now."

Ansel nodded and waved as Dia turned and strode toward the Elder Priesera's home office.

At least Ansel's classes were not boring. The novice Priesera had classes for three turns, called Spirals, then at least one apprentice turn, depending on their interests. Some Kore knew what they wanted to do before entering the University and continued upon that path. Others changed their minds after a time. Still others had little idea what they wanted to do. Ansel fell into this last category.

To Ansel's relief, there was no need to worry about specialization during the first turn because the education was very general. Several of the subjects were ones she had already studied with Vasilissa: basic reading and writing, the history of Kriti, and the geography of the surrounding nations. Ansel was not excused from these classes; she was given more advanced material to learn outside the formal classroom. She was surprised to find herself only in the company of Uazet. The girls of the crafts guilds and agrarian families had not had the luxury of leisure time to learn their letters previously and likely never would have at all if they had not been called to the Priesera. For the first time, Ansel began to consider how privileged a life she had lived at the Agronos. As much as she had sometimes disliked her instruction with Vasilissa, she did receive a basic education. She began to understand why the other girls felt resentful of her. Of course, Ansel mused, those girls are not spending their afternoons shaking olive trees in the cold either.

In deep Cronetide the olives were ripe for the harvest. The Cronetide rains sometimes turned to snow in the mountains. It was a heavy soggy snow that made Ansel shiver in her leather boots even under the occasional sunny sky. The boots were the first she had ever owned. They were a marvel of suppleness; hand–tanned and sewn with sinew at the University itself by a leatherworker Third Spiral Priesera a couple of turns older than herself.

"You should consider teaching or perhaps scholarship, Ansel," the history teacher, Priesera Naya said one day, after Ansel finished an oration comparing the shared government of Kriti with the monarchy of Athena and the Achean peoples of the North.

Ansel thanked her teacher and said, "At the Agronos, I had the fortune to observe some of the results of a hereditary monarchy and so I knew some of the pitfalls. However, I can also perceive some of the advantages of a monarchy. Certainly decisions can be made more quickly and efficiently."

"Ah yes, but to what end?" Naya replied.

"Indeed." Ansel agreed, thinking about Demetria's sodden display at the Festival feast. "The fate of so many is dependent upon the talents and temperament of a single individual."

Ansel's favorite classes were those that allowed her to discover and develop her psychic talents. Her new found ability to see the Radiance of others around her, especially when doing magic or ritual, was not as common as she imagined. Her young teacher, Priesera Ursula, noticed her gift first.

"Ansel," Priesera Ursula said one day during a class demonstrating how to use one's Radiance to build charged aether, "I have been watching your eyes following the circle of Radiance. Tell me what you can see."

Ansel replied, "I see a glowing circle as it moves from girl to girl. It looks like the morning mist from the sea, only moving in a directed fashion. I can also see the way it affects each girl's individual Radiance."

"Good for you. The *saria* is a gift not everyone has. Lidah, can you see what Ansel described just now?"

The slight girl shook her head. "No, Priesera Ursula, I cannot. I understand what Ansel means; I can, well, feel the Radiance moving, but I do not see it."

At least once each cycle there was a teaching ceremony or ritual. Some of them were in accordance with the moon, others with the seasontides. These rituals were taught and facilitated by Elder Priesera Aluneia herself, who had been the principal Ritualist Priesera at the University before being elected Elder Priesera. All rituals were enacted in a local cave; the road that bent to the left as one exited the University hillock led directly to it. The cave mouth was at the bottom of the crag where Vasilissa had stopped the girls to have their first glimpse of the University village.

The ritual at deep Cronetide took place late in the evening during the darkest moon. Led by Elder Priesera Aluneia, all the novice Priesera walked in single file down the white road, starting at the loop garden, each clutching a flickering candle. Ansel and the others had to shield the tenuous flames with their hands from the sudden gusts of cold wind. Not a few blew out and needed to be relit. Earlier in the evening, the Second Spiral students had lined either side of the broad main road with oil–soaked torches. Their dancing glow illuminated the way down to the cave. Aside from the sound of cloaks whipping in a sudden wind or an occasional indiscreet giggle when a candle flame blew out again, the night was absolutely silent. The sky was clouded over, and although it was not actually raining, a mist hung in the air making the night thick. Fortunately, it was not terribly cold. The earth smelled damp and rich.

Once inside the cave, the students sat cross–legged in a circle upon bulky wool blankets strewn on the cave floor. In the center was a pottery brazier burning fragrant herbs and incense as well as cypress wood to stave off the damp chill. The cave was softly lit with oil lamps and torches.

"Greetings novice Priesera," Aluneia said quietly as she stood in the center of the circle next to the burner. "Tonight we honor the mystery of the wise Death Hag and honor Her teachings." She gestured around the circle. "I would like to thank the Second Spiral Priesera for preparing the cave for our ritual and the Third Spiral Priesera for assisting me with the ceremony."

"First, the teachings; our foremeters came both from lands to the east and from here on Kriti. Let me explain. When we came from the east, we landed on Kriti and other islands. There were already people here, people who lived in these caves and similar ones around the islands. The native people welcomed us warmly and our wise elders knew that the best way for us all to prosper was to befriend and intermingle with these good people."

"We worked to set aside our fear of each other's strangeness. Those of us from the east taught the native Kritins how to forge bronze and make useful tools of the metal. We taught them to honor the symbol of the Goddess of the Forge, the Labrys of Dictynna, and She in return graciously became the Netted One to the indigenous people. The people of caves taught those from the east to fish and spoke for us to their Goddesses. They taught us how to live on this land, how best to honor its spirit. Our traditions are a blend of the ones brought from the east and those already followed in this land. Therefore we honor the great caves of Kriti and our cave dwelling ancestors by holding our vigils here. We honor Great Meter and her Bull Son. We honor She of Ten Thousand Names, understanding

She appears in countless forms and faces. We honor the wisdom of the elders of both peoples who knew we would all be stronger if we learned to love each other."

Aluneia stood impressive and stern in the torch light, her exposed full breasts adding to her majestic bearing. She paused to accept a rhyton of a bull's head passed to her by a Third Spiral student. "Here, Priesera, is the mystery of the Bull. He exists within Her and each woman." She pointed to her abdomen. Within woman, here under our skin, lies the imprint of the Bull Son. He is necessary for a woman to be fertile. Without him, there are no children. Man, we believe, stimulates the bull imprint, allowing woman to grow the form of a baby. The Son then holds her creation, the baby, as she grows it within her very body. Therefore, on the land both woman and man are needed. He inspires and initiates her into action. She creates while he cradles the creation so it takes the form they both desire."

She stopped speaking and poured a few drops of liquid from the rhyton onto the cave floor. "We honor the Goddess as Kore, the blossoming one, Meter, the fruiting one, and as Bull, Her escort son, the cradling one, for he is of Her and in Her as are Her daughters." She passed the rhyton back to the Third Spiral Priesera, then continued.

"But why is this teaching important during the time of the Hag? Here is the Great Mystery of this season: though women in their Kore and Meter times may grow the body of a baby within their bodies, it is the Sacred Hag who provides the spark of life. From the deathtide of the Hag, during the longest night, she turns the tide of dark and nothingness to become the spark of life that becomes the soul of the baby. Each baby then, contains the soul of one who passed into the underworld at an earlier time. The soul is the gift of the Hag Goddess; She is the only one who brings life from death." Aluneia paused now to hold up a long bone. Dramatically she said, "Hag of Night, Hag of Death, we honor you as ancestor, we know your mystery; that you are us!"

Ansel felt a chill run down her body. She knew most of these basic teachings – all children are taught them each turn from the time they were infants, but hearing them here, and from the Elder Priesera, added power to the sacredness of the mystery. She had a question though, and as shy as she felt, she wanted to ask it. Tentatively she raised a finger. Aluneia nodded to her. "Yes, Ansel, this is a teaching ritual, you may certainly ask questions or offer comments."

Ansel cleared her throat and said, "Priesera Aluneia, if the Hag Goddess brings the soul to each child, then why are we not all female?"

"It is a good question. The answer is that in the land of the Hag there is no male or female, Ansel. The soul has no essential maleness or femaleness, it is the body that determines this. Woman makes in her body a male or female baby, but the soul given by the Hag is both, or perhaps, neither. It is the nature of the Hag."

Ansel decided she needed to think further about this. She wanted to contemplate the implications, the subtleties of this knowledge. She looked around her and saw simple acceptance of Aluneia's answer on the faces of the other novice Priesera. None of the other Kore, it seemed, thought that Aluneia's response might be a point of discussion rather than absolute truth. *Is it wrong to deliberate the Mysteries?* She briefly wondered. *No. I know it is not. Meta and Vasilissa and even Xeronos taught me better than that.* She felt a pang of loneliness to think she was possibly the only one present who would consider questioning the Elder Priesera. Not wrong then, no, but probably another solitary endeavor. Ansel wondered if she was doomed to a life of isolation.

The ritual continued. The novice Priesera stood and took hands in a circle around the smoking brazier. They sang a song to the ancesters of Kriti, honoring them for their wisdom and foresight. Then, each novice in turn spoke aloud of personal ancestors she admired, throwing a handful of sweet herbs into the fire to honor their memory.

Ansel spoke briefly and tearfully of her beloved Uncle Psidoras. "I loved to be with him in his home in Amnisos by the sea," she said. "He always had time for me and was patient with me. He never once compared me to my Meter or my GranMeter, but was interested in who I was, uh, am." She could not bring herself to say more, and she flung the fistful of herbs into the fire, watching them sizzle and smoke as they were consumed by the flames.

Chapter 30

Uazet felt her head grow heavy. Her eyelids slid closed. Part of her fought the sleep; it was not right, she could not remember why, but it was not right. She gave in. A comforting yet unintelligible murmur burbled in her ears, like a stream on a warm Metertide day, the rise and fall in pitch soothing away the aching tension that so often consumed her. Her forehead muscles released their grip, smoothing her too frequently furrowed brow. Her jaw slacked and her mouth dropped open as sleep embraced her in loving comforting arms. Ua sighed, warm and content. Suddenly her chin hit her chest and the part of her who had been screaming for her to stay awake, jolted her back into awareness of her surroundings. She remembered she was precariously perched on a stool, surrounded by other First Spiral Priesera, one of whom was elbowing the girl next to her and smirking at Ua. She fervently hoped she had not snored. Luckily, Priesera Ursula did not seem to notice Ua's lapse. Or mayhap, Ua thought ruefully as she rubbed her eyes, she just did not want to embarrass me in front of everyone for falling asleep in class again.

She forced herself to sit straighter on her stool, stifled a yawn, and tried once again to concentrate on Ursula's presentation of the historic and mystical significance of the "Great Labrys Mysteries."

"Next quartercycle," Ursula droned, "is the night of the turning tides. Since all of you will be participating in the teaching of the great Labrys ritual for the first time, an explanation of the symbol is appropriate . . ."

Priesera Enid, a Third Spiral healer, entered the classroom and, interrupting Ursula with whispered apologies, took her aside and spoke to her. Ua watched them dimly.

Ursula nodded curtly, then, to Ua's surprise, said, "Uazet, go with Enid please."

Ua snatched up her nearly blank clay tablet, clutched it to her chest, and stuck the small inscribing stick she had been using behind her ear. In her haste, she damaged the damp clay, but she doubted that anyone thought she had been taking notes anyway. Silently she rose to her feet and followed Enid out of the classroom.

"We are going to the healing house," Enid said tersely to Ua. They left the teaching rooms, blinking in the bright morning sunlight that splashed the narrow stone lined street. It was early Maidentide; in the lower lands like those where Ua grew up, the land would have sprung to life a full cycle ago. Here now the air was fresh with gentle breezes and tiny pastel blossoms dotted the sides of the road. Ua inhaled deeply, allowing the air to clear her head.

Turning toward the healing house, Enid continued, "We must hurry. A Kore was brought to us a short while ago. She was gored by a bull."

Ua gasped involuntarily. Being gored by a bull was usually deadly. "Where did this happen?" She asked. "Is she a Bulldancer?" The word 'Bulldancer' felt odd in her mouth. In the lands of her birth, people did not dance with dangerous creatures!

"I do not know much. She is a Bulldancer at Agronos Knossos. They were treating her there but her wound became sour and they felt she needed our care. Also, her meter teaches here; she is the daughter of Priesera Vasilissa. Elder Healer Priesera Kai knew she was coming and made preparations for her care."

Ua nodded taking in the information. "Why am I being called?"

"Kai asked for you. We are forming a healing circle to alleviate the festering of the wound. We need many Priesera who move Radiance well and Kai thought you would be helpful."

Ua felt both honored and fearful. She had never been asked before to participate in a healing circle; it was an acknowledgment of the respect the other healer Priesera held for her work.

They reached the healing house to find several Priesera already gathered. Elder Healer Kai, Uazet's advisor, quickly took her aside. Nodding her thanks to Enid, Kai put her hands on Ua's shoulders and began to instruct her in an urgent voice. "A healing circle, as you know, is really just another form of Radiance building circle. We will raise the Radiance level through the healing tones you have been practicing and then, at my signal, direct it through me. I will lay my hands directly on Geneera or around her body essence."

Uazet nodded grimly and hoped it was as simple as Kai made it sound. Kai studied her pupil for a moment, then smiled gently and said, "Uazet, we have asked you to help because you are thought of highly in the healing house. Just relax and concentrate on directing your energy through me. I will be in charge of doing anything else." Uazet closed her eyes as they unexpectedly welled with tears at Kai's kind words and nodded her head.

Several young Healer Priesera entered the room carrying a cushioned board. Upon the board, covered up to her bare shoulders with a woolen blanket was the unconscious Geneera. They carried the plank to the center of the room and laid it on a low rectangular table that reached to about Kai's waist. Uazet looked at the injured girl's face. *Kritin*, Uazet thought, noticing Geneera's long sharp nose, her light olive skin, and the impossibly black curly hair that had been carelessly cropped short. The girl's full lips appeared pale in contrast to the angry flush of her cheeks.

Carefully Kai undraped the injured leg. Uazet bit her own lips hard when she saw the wound. The skin was ripped from just above the knee almost to the groin. By some miracle, the major vessel that ran up the side of the leg had not been touched. But putrefaction had already set in and although the girl might not die from the wound itself, unless the festering was controlled she might die from fever.

Although it was no longer bleeding, the puffy gash wept a milky, foul smelling liquid and crimson smears streaked up the leg from the wound site.

"Yes, it is festering, just as we feared," Kai said. She reached for the hand of the Priesera next to her and then all the Priesera joined hands in a circle. Scrutinizing the faces of the other healer Priesera in the circle, Uazet momentarily forgot the seriousness of the situation as she felt a wondrous spark of recognition. A feeling of rightness and elation filled her body as she pondered the knowledge that since the beginning of time women had joined hands in circles to heal or perform other magic, that all over the land Priesera did the work of the wise by joining together. She felt her heart swell with pride that she had been included in this important work.

Kai addressed the circle of women. "This is Geneera, Vasilissa's youngest child. She grew up at the Agronos. I believe she is about fifteen to sixteen turns old. She is a Bulldancer but I have few details about how she was injured. She was found in a field, gored and her meter had her brought here."

Some of the Priesera nodded, their eyes wide with sympathy. Others were already swaying slightly with their eyes closed as they listened to Kai's words.

She continued, "Though her wound looks bad, she is lucky; the bull impaled her only superficially in her upper right thigh. She has lost much blood though the worst of it is the putrification. The bull dragged her for some small distance and the wound was covered with dirt when she was found. We know that these types of wounds usually fester. We have already cleaned the area and used poultices to draw out much of the poison. Our work today is to cleanse the wound at a level we cannot otherwise perceive. I have done this successfully before. I ask you to build Radiance and charge the aether with each other, then direct it toward me. I will then conduct it to her wound."

Kai signaled for the healing circle to begin. Uazet forced herself to concentrate on the work at hand. She had always found it easy to slip into a trance and, when the toning began, the drone deepened her spell even more. She felt the Radiance begin to rise around the circle and added her own resonant tones. She directed her Radiance toward Kai and could see through closed eyes the stream surround Kai who directed it through her hands and onto Geneera's wound. The gash looked even more diffuse and deep red when perceived with the *saria*, the deeper sight. It throbbed and the red shade was pierced with the black of corruption. Uazet watched as Kai directed the Radiance toward the black streaks and how they threw sparks when the healing aether touched them.

Then, Uazet became aware of something, or rather, someone else. "Who are you?" Uazet heard a weak voice ask of her, but she was too surprised to respond. "What is happening to me?" the voice wailed plaintively.

"Geneera?" Uazet asked mentally to the voice.

"Yes. Why do I hurt? What is happening?"

Startled, Ua opened her eyes and looked at the girl on the table, but Geneera had not moved; her eyes remained closed and it was obvious no one else had heard her words. Several of the other healer Priesera opened their eyes and frowned at Ua since she had disrupted the Radiance circle, leaving a hole where her Radiance had been flowing. Quickly she rejoined the circle.

The weak voice, however, began to sound panicky. "Are you there? Where are you? Do not leave me alone!"

"You will be fine, Geneera. We are taking care of you," Uazet tried to send soothing, calm thoughts to the girl, whose body was now starting to thrash about on the table. Kai reached out to the girl on the table, stroking her. This seemed to quiet Geneera's fears, because she said to Ua, "That feels better, it does not hurt so much."

Uazet mentally sent Geneera a picture of herself putting a finger to Geneera's lips to further quiet her. "Good girl, Geneera. Do not fear, you will be fine, we will help you feel better." Then, because she sensed that the girl needed some more reassurance, Uazet sent her a mental picture of herself holding Geneera in her arms, comforting her.

That night, Uazet tossed about in her bed, too troubled to sleep. A faint glimmer of moonlight peeked shyly through the window of her sleeping quarters in the healing house. Across the hallway, a drugged Geneera mumbled audibly in her dreams. Frustrated at the stubborn elusiveness of her own sleep, Uazet threw back her bed linens and rolled to her feet.

Perhaps, she thought to herself almost hopefully, perhaps Geneera would like a sip of water or a draught for her pain. Uazet stopped herself abruptly from leaving her room to dash once again to Geneera's side. *What is the matter with me?* She shook her head in self–disgust. *This cannot be right. It is as if something is drawing me to her. She is quite ill enough without me pressing myself on her constantly! I must talk to Kai about this.*

Still, Uazet could not deny that she was now wide awake and that to return to her bed would only start her to again thinking of Geneera, or worse, of her sister, why did Geneera remind her of her sister? *How pathetic I must seem to Kai,* Uazet fretted. *Since I have come here I have been nothing but trouble. First I must sleep separate from the other First Spiral Priesera because of my nightmares, then I cannot stay awake in class, and now I become obsessed with a girl probably because I did something wrong in the healing circle.* Uazet shook her uncombed tresses, trying to clear her thoughts. *I will walk to the herbal garden. I can find some peace there.*

Chapter 31

All was a haze for Geneera. Time pulsed as she became more aware, then less aware of her surroundings. An angry bull snorted and pawed the dry soil. Clouds of dust rose like yellow fog around its muscular body. He charged directly for her, his massive head lowered and tilted, gravel scuttling out of the path of his galloping hooves. She gasped in terror, scrambled backwards, then slipped on loose pebbles and fell hard, knocked breathless. The bull smelled of musk as he bore down on her, his breath fetid. She saw and heard the tip of the bull's left horn puncture her leg. As if it was someone else instead of her, Geneera watched as the bull snapped its neck back with her impaled on it. She was thrown into the air behind the beast. Pain seared through her where her flesh ripped. She clambered to roll over and crawl from his path as he turned to face her. Blood gushed from her leg, streaming into the dirt, the earth turning a muddy red–brown as it eagerly sucked in the moisture. Next, he ploughed into her from behind. Her palms, then her knees were scraped raw as she was pushed along the stony field. Suddenly the bull turned and retreated. She collapsed, hugging the ground and howling to Great Meter, praying the bull would not attack again.

Restlessly she tossed in the bed, moaning and then became dimly aware of a gentle young woman, heavy black hair framing a delicate face, eyes the color of amber and flecked with gold, looking down upon her where she found, to her confusion, that she lay on a soft, clean cot. She murmured questions to the strange woman, who shook her head almost imperceptibly while holding a finger to Geneera's lips, quieting her, comforting her as she drifted back to sleep. Only to find herself back on a dusty plain facing a bull she knew was trying to kill her and no matter where she ran she was unable to get out of its path. Her legs, inexplicably painful, were moving slowly as though through water, and she felt mounting panic as she realized she was unable to run. She felt pain, saw blood. In terror she felt herself rise through the depths of the sea to shriek – a sound that came out no louder than a moan.

She was lying on a mattress stuffed with sweet herbs, a clean linen sheet and a light wool blanket pulled over her shoulders. She threw back the blanket and saw her right leg, completely wrapped in clean white bandages, was immobilized by wooden splints. Gasping in relief, she wrapped herself again with the blanket and gingerly laid her head back down on lavender scented pillows. For several minutes, she simply lay staring at the unfamiliar ceiling, trying to make some sense of her surroundings. She again lifted her unaccountably heavy head and squinted in the sunlight that flooded the small room. She stared dully at the cheerfully decorated space, its white plaster walls painted with frescos of people collecting wildflowers. Her tongue felt as rough as the wool of the blanket covering her. A middle–aged woman dressed in a simple white tunic opened the door and entered into the room. Geneera stared at her mutely, finding it hard to focus her eyes.

"You are awake, child?" the woman asked softly.

"I am so thirsty. Have I been asleep? Where am I? Oww, I am so sore!" The last words ended with a grunt of pain and surprise as Geneera struggled to prop herself up on an elbow. It was unnerving that her body felt so clumsy. Her tongue felt swollen in her mouth and her words sounded slurred as she attempted to speak.

The woman smiled reassuringly as she offered Geneera water a cup of water. Geneera greedily swallowed the cool liquid the woman held to her lips. Carefully replacing the cup onto the plain wooden table beside the cot, the healer Priesera replied, "You have been sedated, Geneera. You will feel heavy and dull for a while yet. Do you remember being injured at Bulldancing practice?"

Geneera winced involuntarily, then fuzzily nodded her head and was promptly rewarded with a feeling of nausea. She sank back down on the fragrant pillows to allow the sick feeling to pass.

"You have been quite ill after your accident and you were brought to the healing house of the Priesera," the woman continued. "Your wound went sour, but the fever broke last night. You need to go back to sleep now. In a few hours the herbs we have given you will wear off and you will be feeling much more like yourself." By the time Kai had finished her last sentence, Geneera was lightly snoring.

Uazet was there when Geneera awoke next. Opening her eyes suddenly, Geneera jerked herself to a sitting up position, only to gasp in pain. "Where am I?" she demanded out loud to no one in particular, not remembering her conversation with Kai earlier that afternoon.

"In the healing house," Uazet stated simply as she turned to face her patient from where she had been leaning over a table and grinding something green in a gray stone mortar.

Geneera was even more startled when she was answered by the woman, or, she realized, the girl, who haunted her troubled dreams. Here was the strange delicate woman with the too light eyes, the silky and oddly accented voice. Seeing her standing in the same room was too much for Geneera to comprehend. Troubled but fascinated, she silently observed Uazet's graceful movements as she finished crushing the herbs with a pestle, and then scraped them into a pottery bowl of something thick and translucent. Purposefully, Uazet mixed the herbs with the unguent, her arm making vigorous circles with a carved wooden spoon, and then placed the mixture over some brazier coals to warm it. Geneera thought of asking many questions but somehow none of them seemed to get to the heart of what it was she wanted to know.

The ointment warm, Uazet briskly pulled down the blanket that covered Geneera's torso and legs. "I need to change your dressing." she announced.

Geenera's body was covered only with a short skirt and her injured leg was wrapped from her groin to below the knee. "Wait! Wait!" Geneera cried, pulling the blanket back up over herself. She feared seeing her leg, facing how badly hurt she really was. In a flood of words, Geneera asked, "Who are you? How long have I been here? Am I going to be all right?"

Uazet faltered, nearly dropping the ointment. Then as if collecting her thoughts, she stepped backward, and cleared her throat. Brusquely she replied, "Your leg is injured, some of the muscle in your thigh has been torn. You will most likely regain use of your leg, but will always limp and it will never be as strong as it originally was." She paused and bit her lips as Geneera digested that information.

"I will be able to dance the bull again though, yes?"

Uazet shrugged and looked uncomfortable. "I do not know. I am sorry, it would be better for you to ask these questions of Elder Healer Kai. I believe she will be here soon, perhaps right after the evening meal."

But Geneera just stared at the healer girl, silently pleading to hear that her brief time in the troupe was not over, that her very life was not over.

Uazet looked nervous and plunged on. "You have been here for three nights. You do not remember because you developed a high fever and were delirious at first. You have also been given herbs to make you sleep, which is no doubt why you feel so confused."

The door to Geneera's small room opened and the middle–aged woman, whom Geneera vaguely recognized, entered. Uazet sighed in obvious relief and said, "Priesera Kai, this is Geneera. She has questions." She thrust the bandages and ointment into the hands of the healer Priesera and fled the room.

Kai turned and watched Uazet's rapidly retreating back with her mouth agape, then looked back at Geneera and shrugged her shoulders.

"Why does she not like me?" Geneera asked blinking rapidly in surprise.

Kai grimaced and replied, "Oh, that is just Uazet's way. I would not take it personally." Kai began to change the bandage on Geneera's wound, using the poultice Uazet had carefully prepared.

Chapter 32

Ansel took a deep breath before knocking lightly on the door-frame to Geneera's little room in the healing house. "Hoi, Geneera, if you wanted to visit an old friend, you could have just made the journey. It was not necessary to hurt yourself, but then, you always did have to do everything the hard way." Ansel leaned against the open door frame and smiled faintly at her own joke.

Geneera turned her head toward Ansel and after a fleeting pause, smiled back. "Hoi Ansel," she said, her voice rough. "Yes, I do everything the hard way do I not?" The attempt to be playful failed and Gen collapsed into tears. Ansel strode to her bedside, dropped to her knees and hugged Geneera fiercely. Cheek to cheek, they wept for several moments.

"I have been so worried about you, Gen. The healer Priesera would not let me visit you before today. They tell me you will be well," Ansel said finally, pulling her wet face from Geneera's neck. She dabbed her face with a linen square, then gently stroked Geneera's riot of curls.

"Of course I am going to be well." Geneera replied with some of her old bravado, dismissing her friend's concern with a clumsy wave of her hand. "I am just bored. They told me that I cannot even get up for another quarter turn. You know how much I hate to sit

She Who Walks the Labyrinth

still." She gave a snort that was half sob. "I do not know what to do with myself."

"Well," Ansel pretended to muse, stroking a non–existent beard. "Since I know how much you love to read," Ansel's smile widened as Geneera stuck her tongue out at her, "I brought you a tile game."

"By the Meter's teats; my favorite game!" Geneera exclaimed as Ansel produced a small wooden board and a package of inlaid wooden tiles from a black leather pouch she had slung over her shoulder. "Thank you, Ansel. This will help."

For an awkward moment, Geneera looked like she was going to cry again, then instead, she wiped her cheek with the back of her hand and deftly set up the board on the small table next to her bed. She lined the multicolored tiles face down and said, "Want to play?"

"I have to warn you that since coming to the Priesera School I have become a consummate tile player, I play almost every day with the kitchen women."

"We shall see!" Geneera challenged.

For the next several minutes, both girls concentrated on the complex game. Their conversation danced around painful, controversial subjects, sometimes nearer to them, sometimes further away. When one or the other became tongue–tied, they stared at the board and played.

"You have heard, I presume, that your meter is pregnant. She is big as the Agronos. There is whispering that she must carry twins."

Ansel giggled. "Can you imagine? I was shocked to hear it after all this time." She shook her head. "I begged and begged her to give me a baby sister when I was little. She told me she could barely manage me. Raising me was not easy for meta."

"I know. I do not wish to say anything bad about your meta, Goddess knows she is a model of understanding compared to mine, but sometimes she seems so caught up in her work." Geneera paused, cocked her head and shrugged.

"Yes. You phrase it kindly. I have come to understand that Meta is self–involved. It was not until I met a friend of hers upon Heria that I realized what I had been missing." Ansel hugged herself around the shoulders in remembrance. "Nadia is an Escort in the town of Daedalos. She is so loving and comforting, but not at all beautiful like Meta. To be honest, I would choose warmth over beauty in a meta anyday." Ansel's fingers flew to her mouth, then she deliberately dropped the hand and said more softly, "I did not mean that, Gen, I love my meta."

"I know, *mellia*, I know."

After several moves with the tiles, Ansel asked, "Are you still sharing a room with Carea?"

It was Geneera's turn to wince. "I am or was," she faltered, then blurted, "Carea must always win; she always wants to be the best. Part of me loves her for it, but she can be so cruel. I found myself thinking cruel thoughts too when I was around her. I do not like that. I do not want to be like that." She caught Ansel's hands in her own and met her eyes.

"Ansel, I am so sorry. I said nasty things about you that I knew were not true. I wanted Carea to love me. She seems to thrive on making other people wrong. I was going to speak with her about it when my accident happened."

Ansel nodded, blinking away tears. "Garin?" she asked softly.

"No news. Ganymede's GranMeta finally returned to Phaistos late Cronetide. They say Garin's Meta has taken to her bed and refuses to leave it."

They were silent again for a while.

Biting her lips, and after a few false starts, Ansel asked, "Can you tell me what happened with the bull? Or do you not want to speak of it?"

"To be honest, I do not remember exactly what happened. In my memory, I am alone with the bull, but that is not possible. None of us are ever alone with the bull. I just remember thinking it wanted to kill me. I can see its eye staring at me, and I think, oh, this beast wants me dead. Then, I am lying in the field with the Bulldancers all around me and Carea is screaming for a healer. I remember thinking about my brother; that I would see him. I think I must have fainted."

Ansel put down her tile and leaned over the board to hug Geneera. "After Amnisos, my memories were so strange I thought I would never be right again, Gen. It gets better though. You will get better."

Geneera pulled away. "But I will never dance the bull again, Ansel. I will never have the strength in my leg again. Everything I have ever wanted, everything I worked so hard for, it is gone now. I cannot even think what my life will be like when I leave this place."

"There is no need to leave here for a very long time. I am here. Do you know, come third cycle Metertide, I will be a Second Spiral novice and will move to a double room? I need a roommate. You can stay in my room with me, just like we used to at the Agronos. Your meta is here too. She was really worried about you, you know."

Geneera stared at the the board for a long time. Her next move was clumsy, and she knocked the tile off the board. Looking up, she caught Ansel's eyes, then looked down again and shrugged.

"Not so worried that she came to visit me," Geneera replied flatly, pretending to return her attention to the game.

After several minutes, Ansel tried again. "She did not think you would want to see her."

"She is right." Geneera closed her eyes briefly and sighed, then said, "Ansel, my mother is a brilliant scholar, a renowned teacher. People say she is the finest orator on Kriti. She should not have tried her hand at childrearing. I do not wish to speak of her anymore."

Ansel nodded sadly, wondering why sometimes what seemed so obvious to her was invisible to those she loved. She looked down at the beautiful inlaid tiles thinking, If I tell Geneera her meter sent this game as a gift to her, Vasilissa will have my head.

Chapter 33

The day was cool and clear, but marching around in the hills made Mykalo sweaty and irritable. Why had Theseus insisted his old war band come all the way out here for their midday meal? Surely it was not for old time's sake. None of them much missed life on the road, running from the wrath of villagers and wondering how it would all end. Living in Athena had been the only safety the group of young men had ever known. He glanced over to the slender young man Myko called 'leader' for so many turns. Myko himself was older and possessed a much bigger build, but all of them agreed long ago that Theseus was the cleverest and most resourceful of them all. He was a fair swordfighter too.

Theseus gestured toward a rocky meadow which swept open between the barren hills. "We will stop here. Phillip, unload the donkey."

Obediently the man unstrapped the leather pouch from the huffing beast with his good arm; the withered one hung uselessly at his side. The donkey flicked its tail smartly and tossed its head a few times, but Phillip had no problem sliding the sack of rations from its back.

Myko settled by himself on a flat rock in the shade. He shrugged off the belt of his bronze sword and felt the muscles of his shoulders ease. He rubbed the back of his sweaty neck with one hand.

"So what was so important you needed to drag us all the way out here, Theseus? Plotting to overthrow old hag Demetria?" Myko half smiled and half sneered as the rest of the men guffawed.

Theseus snorted. "Nah, Myko, not yet anyway. Here, have some food, then we will talk." The wiry Theseus personally handed his first man a chunk of cheese and a slab of greasy mutton. Myko grunted and met his commander's eyes as he took the proffered food. Theseus had changed since he returned from Kriti over a turn ago; he seemed less open, more wary. Myko did not like the change; this was not the same Theseus he had trusted with his life a few short turns back. Any change was a thing to distrust.

The men passed the wine around and noisily devoured the food. After several minutes, Theseus cleared his throat and said, "I am going to Kriti. I expect to be gone for at least one full turn, perhaps longer."

Theseus returned to chewing his meat as casually as if he had announced an extra round of sword practice instead of that he was abandoning his lifelong friends. Myko glanced around him, taking in Phillip's shocked face, the confused looks of the other men as they looked one to another. Inwardly he steeled his himself to reveal nothing. He was the first to speak. "Why are you going?" His voice betrayed no surprise.

Theseus narrowed his eyes and looked at Myko. "I go to study at the University."

This caught Myko off guard and he started to sputter. Theseus silenced him with a hand. "I have had a vision that calls me there. You of all people would question my visions, Mykalo?"

Theseus chose such moments to remind Myko and Phillip that they would have died in battle had he had not seen the ambush just before it happened.

"I have never once doubted your visions, Commander Theseus." Myko said sincerely. "But why the University? They do not even take men do they?" The others were nodding, listening intently. It suddenly occurred to Myko that he would be the leader once Theseus left; he rather liked the notion.

"I will be the first man to go. The Priesera is the power behind the government of Kriti. And it is the power of Kriti we are interested in, heh?"

"Why do we not conquer this island just as we have conquered Aegina and Kea?"

"Bah. Mykalo, you show your ignorance. Kriti is not some small backward village that we can overrun and frighten the peasants into submission. Kriti is not a military force, but it is an economic force. She is isolated and she is rich. This is both why she is so desirable and why we must be careful."

Theseus bent closer to his men and spoke more softly. "Rumor has it Demetria will sign an alliance with Kriti. But allies who are really enemies are the most dangerous foes of all, no? By spending time on Kriti, I will know where She is vulnerable when the time is ripe."

Theseus smiled, looking more like the man Myko had pledged his life to.

Myko grinned back. "Ai, Theseus, Kriti would be a fine fish to net; a very fine fish." But something itched at the back of Myko's mind; he just did not trust what Theseus said. He vowed to keep careful watch.

Chapter 34

"Lyssa, your cooking is the best, as always. The honeyed dates are the finest I have eaten since, since, well, I was out east." Dia licked her fingers in appreciation while the plump cook blushed.

The late Koretide sun was setting; the longest day of the turn was approaching, and the women had gathered at the celebration for Diatima. This was her final turn at the University and though she would be visiting the University frequently, she would no longer be a student. A special dinner had been prepared including Dia's favorite sweets, then there would be storytelling, song, and of course, dancing. Everyone at the school was invited and the dining hall was packed and noisy.

"Tell us the story of your trip east, Dia," someone called out. "What did you see? What did you do?"

Dia carefully wiped her hands on a linen cloth and swung her kithara from behind her shoulders. The laughter hushed as the women and girls crowded around to hear her tale.

"Oh," she began in a rich, dramatic voice, "the peoples of the East are glamorous and mysterious. On the coast of Anatolia are the brave Emetchi warriors, tribes of women who wear swords and ride horses." She strummed some chords on her kithara for emphasis.

All the young Priesera, including Ansel, gaped at Dia, enraptured.

"Emetchi? Do they live only with women, like on Lemnos and Delos?"

"Some of the Emetchi tribes are only women, yes. Others are mixed women and men. They live all up and down the coast. They are fierce." More chords and the crowd sighed "ohhhh!" in encouragement.

"Do the women really fight? Just like nomadi men?"

"They fight the nomadi." Dia carefully enunciated each word for emphasis.

Everyone gasped. "They fight the fierce nomadi?"

"Yes. Whenever a village is under siege from the nomadi, the Emetchi take up arms and join the villagers to fight them off."

"They are heras, the Emetchi," Aluneia interrupted. All eyes turned to her where she sat near Dia. "We have never had need of their fighting aid, but at the last terrible chake several turns ago, they sent food and medicines, and they helped us rebuild. They are defenders of Goddess and Meter right."

"Where did they come from Priesera Aluneia?" Ansel asked.

"From many places but especially the northern mainland, up past Athena. They were exiled from their homelands when the nomadi invaded. They bitterly hate the nomadi."

A softer voice spoke into the resulting pause. "Pardon, Priesera, but many also are from the east beyond the mountains, where I grew up." Uazet said. She stood up, blushing, at the encouragement of Aluneia. "My homeland too was invaded. The peoples who escaped fled to the coasts and now guard them. They are courageous in their defense of She of Ten Thousand Names."

"Yes, indeed," agreed Dia, refocusing the attention onto herself. "Further east, one enters the lands of the sacred groves. I saw the temple women there dance like no others."

Impulsively, Dia grabbed a large table linen and drew it up to just below her eyes. Extending her arms from her side, she wiggled her eyebrows up and down as she held the cloth taut. Behind the semi–transparent fabric she began wiggling her hips in a semblance of sensuality. Dia was not a curvaceous woman and the sight was ridiculous. Her audience shrieked in delight.

Uazet clapped, then laughingly said, "Really, I should be insulted. You poke fun at a very sacred dance of my people. Would you like to know about it?"

When everyone nodded or exclaimed, 'Yes, tell us!', Uazet continued.

"This is dance of the veils; the story of our Goddess Inanna's descent to the Underworld where she meets her sister and gains power over life and death. Inanna is the Queen of Heaven and of all the Sacred Grove lands. She must pass through seven challenges and the dance therefore requires seven veils."

She snatched the linen from Dia's grasp and wrapped it over her torso so that it covered one shoulder. "The other veils are placed to completely cover the body, even the head and face, excepting the eyes. Each veil represents a challenge for Inanna to meet. She must give up every part of her self to enter the Underworld."

She allowed the veil to slip down from her torso with a quick flick of her hip. "By the end of the dance, the dancer is completely unveiled to symbolize Inanna's naked soul. The dance is very old and very sacred to us. We only perform it for women in the temples."

"What happens to Inanna when she reaches the Underworld?" Ansel asked.

"She is hung on a meat hook."

As a group the young Priesera gasped.

"No, no," Aluneia laughed. "Not by the neck, by the foot. It is a common symbol in the east. To hang upside down is to see things differently, to allow for transformation. In a sense, it is similar to the Labyrinth journey that each of you will undergo while you are here at school, no Dia?"

Dia passed her fingers through her thick red hair and looked thoughtful. "I think I see the similarity. Through the Labryinth journey, we are transformed. We see it as a journey to ourselves though, not to the Underworld."

"Well, then it is indeed similar," Ua said. "For what is the Underworld if not a place where the soul is transformed? Innana and her sister Erishkegal are two faces of the same Goddess. The dance makes it very clear I think."

"Could you perform it for us, Ua? We would love to see the dance," Lidah asked.

"Oh, I have no veils and really, it is done only by the Temple Dancers, those dedicated to Inanna."

"In these times, though Ua, the knowledge of the dance is threatened if not shared with others," Aluneia said.

"Yes," Uazet said. Her eyes grew large in her tiny face and reflected vast sadness. "My Temple is no more. My people are scattering." She looked as if she might say more, but then instead she smiled warily. "I would be honored to perform the dance to please Inanna and also to please my new sisters. I will do my best," she said finally.

Veils quickly were created from scarves and linens. Aluneia produced a drum. She placed it under her left arm and began to beat out a heartbeat rhythm with her right hand. Ua took her place in the center of the audience and began to dance.

To Ansel, Ua appeared to be a skilled dancer. As shy as Uazet was in her everyday life, she was exceedingly charming and expressive as she danced. She thrust her hips and torso quickly and then slowly, the muscles of her abdomen writhing sensuously and snake–like. She smiled flirtatiously and gazed directly at many of the women, her slender arms and hands moving sinuously.

Ansel was amazed at how much she understood just from a dance. Inanna faced challenges in her journey to the Underworld and each time she passed another gate, a veil was removed. Dancing was a passion on Kriti, but usually it was to induce trance and raise Radiance or to celebrate the fertility of the land. To use dance to tell an entire story was new to Ansel. Geneera, sitting next to Ansel, her crutches across her lap, stared open–mouthed. When Uazet finished, stripped of the final veil, the entire room rang with cheers and applause. Abruptly the timid face of Ua returned as she snatched up the veils and fled the room.

The party continued for several more hours with Dia leading bawdy songs and ending finally with ring dancing as Dia strummed her kithara, Aluneia beat spirited rhythms on her drum and a Third Spiral Priesera Ansel did not know played lively melodies on a double pipe.

The next morning came far too soon for Ansel; now that the olive harvest was over, she was back to lugging water for the kitchen morning and afternoon.

Geneera joined Ansel where she sat on the back step outside the kitchen area. Gen was finally off of bed rest and onto wooden crutches and she made it a routine to visit Ansel every morning before breakfast. This morning when she greeted Ansel, Gen was frowning and muttering to herself. "I passed my meter this morning. I swear to you truly Ansel, it took only one minute before she began to harangue me about becoming a teacher again." She shook her head. "To change the subject, I asked her about her relationship with Uncle Niko. Do you know she lied to me about it? She said they were merely friends." She chuckled suddenly. "She is such a bad liar; I do not know why she even tries with me. Her face gets all red and her voice goes up several tones. I did however, manage to fluster her enough for her to stomp off. Honestly Ansel, I just avoid her as much as I can."

Ansel shrugged. "I am sorry your meter is so difficult, Geneera. Perhaps in time you two will work out a way to relate to each other."

"It is not at all important to me," Geneera said holding her hand up and pursing her lips.

The girls fell silent for a few moments, and then Geneera said, "Tell me everything you know about Uazet." Geneera's voice was suspiciously nonchalant as she reached out to pet a striped marmalade tomcat she had taken to feeding out behind the main kitchen. Ansel was immediately curious.

The cat, whom Geneera had named 'Melagori', sniffed Gen's outstretched fingers thoughtfully before rubbing the side of his white muzzle against them, purring loudly. Ansel, seated on the stone step next to Geneera, paused before replying.

Ansel herself did not much like Uazet. Earlier in the turn, Ansel had made friendly overtures toward Uazet, which the girl had rejected rather soundly and for no apparent reason. "I do not know her very well, Gen, but then, I do not think anyone has been able to get close to her. She seems strange, maybe even conceited. She is quite a dancer though. Why do you ask?" She looked over at Geneera with a raised eyebrow.

But Geneera did not look at Ansel. Instead, she cooed at the big cat who had climbed into her lap. He looked into her face and purred loudly, his big paws clenching and unclenching the fabric of her skirt to the rhythm of his own inner dance. Geneera squinted back at the tom, stroked his thick fur and quietly called him a pretty baby.

"Why do you think she is odd?" Geneera finally asked.

Ansel shifted uncomfortably on the step. "Well, she either will not look you in the eye or she holds your gaze overlong. She does not pay attention in class. The teaching Priesera will not even call on her anymore because she does not hear them until they have said her name several times." She leaned over to stroke the cat who now lay curled up in Geneera's lap. "People have tried to be friendly to her but she does not care. She spends all of her time at the healing house, even eating there, and Joli told me that she goes into the gardens there and talks to the plants all the time. I know that her specialty is healing with herbs, but honestly, she seems to have no awareness of other people at all. Why are you so interested in her anyway?"

This time Ansel stared at Geneera in silence until her friend finally looked up into Ansel's eyes. Geneera gave Ansel a rueful grin and shrugged, blushing deeply. Clearing her throat, Geneera replied simply, "I think she is the most beautiful girl I have ever seen."

Chapter 35

The ceremony of bees took place on the longest day of the turn. The young Priesera were led to the loop garden at the end of the whitestone road by Aluneia's office. The sun was high in the sky.

"First," instructed Aluneia, "just wander the garden watching the bees. I will call you back in a few minutes and you will tell each other what the bees have taught you about themselves."

The breeze was glorious high in the mountains and the meadow smelled of green herbs and flowers. Ansel meandered in circles for a while, then sat on an outcropping of rock to more closely observe the bees as they visited nearby flower blossoms. One landed on a stalk of bright red flowers. The chosen blossom bobbed up and down as the engrossed creature nosed deeply into its depths. Ansel listened to the bee's quiet buzz and wondered just what the bee was doing. Soon the insect launched itself from the blossom and landed on another where it repeated its actions. Its behavior was not particularly interesting to Ansel, but she felt happy just to be outdoors.

Soon enough, Aluneia called the Kore together in a circle. They sat in the grass and began to discuss bees.

"What did you each notice?" Aluneia asked.

Joli raised a hand and replied, "The bees land on flowers and stick their heads in the blossoms. My bee found a whole shrub of flowers she liked and was really excited. She flew away and then returned with a whole group of bees. She must have told them about the bush."

"My meter told me the bees collect something from the flowers that they bring back to the hive," Beryl volunteered.

"Where do bees live?" Aluneia asked the class.

"In hives," several girls responded.

"We call ourselves 'the People of the Bees'. Why do you think that is?"

Ansel thought about this for a moment, then raised her hand. "Well, many of us live together at the Agronos. It is sort of like a hive. The Agronos itself even looks a hive with the way the rooms are all connected."

Aluneia nodded. "We bury our dead in hive–like tombs, too."

Lidah shyly raised her hand and said, "Bee communities are organized around a queen. We are organized around our Goddess."

The girls nodded. Uazet said, "I have noticed that your artwork sometimes makes the people all look like bees with the tiny waists and all. Even the long skirts of the Priesera look like the stripes of bees."

Aluneia smiled. "That is a wonderful observation, Uazet. Anyone else?"

Beryl raised her hand again. "My meter is the leader of our farming guild. Whenever they have a meeting, she wears a brooch with two bees on it."

"Oh," Ansel blurted. "My GranMeter wears one like that too."

"What do you think that brooch represents, Beryl?" Aluneia asked.

The girl shrugged. "My meter told me it is what makes her the leader of the guild. It represents her leadership somehow."

"The symbol," Aluneia said, "is of two bees head to head, holding a drop of honey between them. Has everyone seen this symbol?"

Everyone nodded except Uazet. Aluneia drew out a wax tablet and stylus from a pocket in her skirt and quickly sketched the symbol to show Uazet.

"It represents community working together for a purpose. In the symbol, the bees toil to make honey. This reminds us of the sweetness and abundance of life. We Kritins work together too to bring to ourselves and each other a good life."

"Now let us explore the Mystery," continued Aluneia, "Here is another symbol you all know." She gestured to a Third Spiral Priesera who brought a small golden double–bladed axe from behind her back and handed it to the Elder Priesera.

"The labrys of Dictynna is a symbol of our strength. It is always made of bronze to depict our industry or gold to represent our wealth. We were the first people to forge bronze from copper and tin, as you know. But why did we choose the double–axe to represent our civilization?"

The First Spiral girls all shook their heads, eyes wide, while the older novices grinned. Aluneia said nothing, forcing the girls to think. Then Ansel saw it. She raised her hand.

"They are the same symbol," she said. "The backs of the bees curve and their limbs reach to the center. The labrys is the bee symbol in shape, but without the details.

"Good Ansel. Can the rest of you see this?" Some of the girls shook their heads. Aluneia this time took a piece of charcoal from her pocket and, crouching down, drew on a large flat rock:

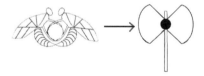

"See, here?" she pointed, "the handle of the labrys is there so it can be held."

"So then, the labrys is not a weapon?" Uazet asked.

"No, it is never used in such a way," Aluneia replied standing up again and wiping her hands of charcoal. "It is a symbol of ourselves, our culture, our civilization. We would never want to desecrate it with violence."

Aluneia motioned for the girls to circle again. "Let us take hands and honor the mystery of the bee people." The novices took hands as Aluneia began a hum that vibrated through her nose. It sounded like the buzzing of a bee. The older Kore joined the hum, and then the First Spiral students joined in. They staggered their breathing so the sound was continuous as they increased in volume and pitch. Together, the People of the Bee buzzed, delighting in their sense of community and purpose on the longest day of the turn.

Chapter 36

Even high Metertide was delightfully cool in the mountains. During her breakfast, Ansel was given a message to attend Priesera Aluneia directly after the midday meal. She had not spoken with Aluneia privately since formally beginning her First Spiral turn. She found the door to the Elder Priesera's office open when she arrived.

Ansel seated herself across from Priesera Aluneia's desk, then lowered her eyes in respect. "Ansel," Aluneia began, "since Dia will no longer be living at the University all the time, I have decided to be your primary advisor. She will advise you when she is here at the village." Ansel nodded, feeling both relieved and anxious. She still found the Elder Priesera intimidating but she felt she and Dia had never really understood each other. "I have an unusual assignment for you, but I think you will find it suits your gifts." Aluneia continued while Ansel squirmed a bit in the hard chair. "We have a student coming who will need tutoring. You are fluent in Greek, is that right?"

Ansel nodded, not certain if she should speak or not. She did not wish to appear presumptuous in front of the Elder Priesera.

"This student speaks Greek fluently, but Kritin barely. Since you are already ahead of the rest of your class in schooling, we would like you to spend your afternoons during your second turn helping this student with his studies.

Ansel looked up sharply.

"No. I did not have a slip of the tongue." Aluneia chuckled at the look of shock on Ansel's face. "The student you will be tutoring is a male."

"Not the consort from Athena?"

"Yes. You know of him?"

"He once spoke to me about men entering the Priesera. At the last Seven–Turns Festival," Ansel added.

Aluneia paused and lowered her voice as if sharing a confidence. "The circumstances are extremely unusual and we do not intend to allow the University to be open to men in general." Aluneia sighed and rubbed her eyes. Ansel suddenly noticed the Elder Priesera looked tired. "The reasons he is here I cannot reveal. It is enough for you to know we consider allowing him to join a necessity. You understand, Ansel, do you not?"

Ansel nodded. One could hardly grow up at Agronos Knossos and not understand that certain things could not be discussed with just anyone.

"He will be allowed to attend morning classes with the First Spiral group. In the afternoon on most days, you will tutor him in Kritin, both the language and our culture. Your tutoring will be considered your village work. It will not be considered his. He will need to make up the time in the evenings and the afternoons he does not study with you."

Keeping him good and busy, Ansel thought to herself. Aloud she asked, "When do I start, Priesera Aluneia?"

"He has already arrived. The tutoring will begin tomorrow after morning classes."

Ansel's second turn at the University began in difficulty. The buzz about a young male at the school was the only topic of conversation for the first few quarter turns. When it became known that Ansel was tutoring him in the afternoon, some of the old resentments returned and Ansel once again found herself the object of mistrust and envy. Ansel herself felt it was only a slight improvement over harvesting olives in the snow.

Theseus stood with his back toward Ansel, looking out the one small window of his tiny private cottage. Parchments lay strewn across his unkempt cot and across the square cypresswood table.

Ansel paused in the open doorway and knocked on the doorframe. Theseus did not look around. "Come in," he said over one shoulder.

"What is so interesting outside?" Ansel asked in Greek.

"I have never before lived in a place with only women. I am watching them work." He turned around, "Also, I study the mountains. I have never been so far inland that I could not judge where the sea lay." His eyes rested upon her. "I know you, do I not?"

"I am Ansel. Phoebe, my meter, escorted you at the Festival."

He smiled a little, showing straight teeth. "The beach. You walked onto the beach and I thought you your meter. Still I see the resemblance."

Ansel felt a flush rise upon her cheeks. His eyes reminded her of the deep sea. One could lose themselves in his eyes, or crash upon hidden rocks no doubt, she thought to bring herself to the work at hand. Shaking her head imperceptibly, she said, "I am your tutor. I am to help you learn our language and tell you what I can of our culture."

In halting Kritin, Theseus said, "How do thee fare, Mistress Ansel?" Then in Greek he added, "I suppose the first thing you would tell me is men do not belong in the Priesera, no?"

"Consort Theseus, my task is to be your tutor, not your judge." Ansel answered first in Kritin, then in fluent Greek.

Chapter 37

Devra stumbled into Rheana's apartment at Knossos, her square face smudged with dirt and her dun–colored hair lank. She hung her head as she stood towering over petite Rheana. She clasped her large chapped hands in front of her belly. "My apologies, Mistress," she began. "I have searched and searched. I believe they are either far from Knossos or they are in a very obscure area that I do not know. I did not find any caves being used for sacrifice either."

Rheana sighed and nodded. "I know you have done your best, Devra and you have my thanks. I know these mountains well and did no better. Go now and find food and rest. I will make sure you receive your pay."

"I am sincerely sorry, Mistress Rheana. It is not often I cannot find what I am looking for. It makes me wonder," Devra paused, her mouth drew into a tight line.

"Yes?" Rheana asked.

"Is it possible they were taken far from Knossos, or even from Kriti somehow?"

"I do not know how that would be possible, Devra, but at this moment, we should consider any possibility." Rheana shook her head, more to clear her thoughts than from any disagreement with Devra.

"It would require someone with a boat, Mistress. There were many boats here during the last Seven Turns Fest, yes?"

"Yes, there were." She paused, nodded thoughtfully, then said, "I will bring your thoughts to Mistress Phoebe. Thank you, Devra."

Phoebe was still resting in bed after some seventeen hours of labor had produced healthy twins. The little girl she named 'Phaedra', the boy she called 'Damarin'. The healer/midwife, Priesera Eida, was a young woman who hovered incessantly over Phoebe. She was in Phoebe's room again when Rheana appeared, fussing over young Damarin who was red–faced from wailing.

"Rheana!" Phoebe exclaimed. It was an obviously sincere delight. "How lovely to see you. Eida, would you please give Rheana and me some privacy? I will be certain to call you if I need you."

"The babies will need to be fed again soon, Mistress Phoebe. Shall I come back then?"

"That will not be necessary, Eida. I can handle the babies with Rheana's assistance. Please do not come back until I call."

Phoebe eyes followed Eida as she left the room and then she gave a sigh of relief. "She will be back in here again on some premise long before I call," she said sidelong to Rheana. "Thank you so much for coming. She was infuriating Damarin." Indeed the baby stopped howling the moment Phoebe hoisted him from his little wooden cradle and snuggled him in her arms. "I must insist that Eida leave the children and me alone for a while. She is exhausting and she does not take a hint well."

Rheana suppressed a smile. "When will you be able to leave your bed?"

"Within the next few days, I hope. I am feeling restless and bored. I need to get back to work, though I expect I will not be able to do much for a while. I have decided to nurse these babies myself. I gave Ansel over to a wet nurse almost immediately so I could resume Escort duties. I regret that for so many reasons. I am older now, and wiser, I hope."

Phaedra awoke and was screwing up her face for a yowl. Rheana scooped her up and gave her to Phoebe who had already offered one nipple to Damarin. Phaedra eagerly began to suck on the other. "Look at me, I am a dining hall." Phoebe said with a smile.

Rheana returned the smile quickly, then felt her face become grim. "Devra is back from the mountains. She has given up, Mistress Phoebe. She suggests that the boys may have been taken by boat either to another part of the island or possibly even off Kriti."

"An interesting thought, that. If true, we may never find them." She dropped her eyes and shook her head. "Ach, my heart aches for their meters."

Phoebe shifted young Damarin a little, then said, "With so many people at the Fest perhaps someone saw or heard something they did not think important in the moment. I will send inquiries with the next boats out to Phaistos and Zakros."

The younger woman bit her lower lip for a moment, then said, "I hope I am not being alarmist, Mistress, but Trader Alekki did mention seeing the boat of Iphikeles leaving the bay of Amnisos. Is it possible, I wonder? I dread . . ." But Rheana could not bring herself to complete the thought aloud.

"This might also implicate Kourete Nikolas." Phoebe shook her head. "I pray to Pasifae that it is not so. How brazen would that sacrifice religion have to be to snatch two Kritin boys from under the eyes of their meters?"

"They would have to be brazen or desperate. Certainly they must have noticed that the tremors are getting worse, not better. This threatens the very core of their beliefs, does it not?" Rheana reached out to stroke the rosy cheek of Phaedra. So innocent, she thought.

"I should have paid closer attention to what Alekki said at the Fest. I am slipping, Rheana."

"No, Mistress Phoebe. You were busy with the Athenian Consort and we do not even know exactly when the boys went missing. You should not blame yourself."

"Perhaps not, Rheana, but nevertheless I do not have vital information that Knossos needs and here I am in bed with two babies, feeling useless." She shifted the now drowsy Damarin off her nipple and into the crook of her arm. Phaedra lifted a tiny hand and squeezed Phoebe's breast so hard she winced. Gently she redirected the baby's hand to her index finger. She smiled at the infants and thrust her face down to plant an impulsive kiss on her baby daughter's head. "I do not regret my decision though. I just need help. Rheana, have you thought about my request that you stay here with me indefinitely?"

Rheana shifted her feet. "Yes Mistress Phoebe. I grew to love Phaistos in the time I was there and am flattered that they would like for me to be among them, but I believe I am more needed here. I will be glad to stay, at least for the foreseeable future."

"That is all that anyone can ask." Phoebe inhaled deeply and flashed a wry grin at Rheana.

Mykalos thought surely the thin stretch of lips over Polymachos' teeth was meant to be a smile, but it made him look like a death's head. There he stood at the side of his sister, that hag known as Helen Demetria, as the pronouncement was made. Mykalos understood very well the peril he and the others of his war band now faced.

"Polymachos is the new Royal Consort. I will make it official within this quartercycle. You will follow his lead or you will leave Athena. Choose now." Demetria looked as if she were several hundred turns old. The poppy will do that to you old sow, Mykalos thought.

He spit on the ground near his feet. "I speak for the rest. We leave. We follow Theseus, never that seilos brother of yours.

Polymachos put a hand on his sword, but hesitated at Demetria's glance. "Theseus is dead. He met with an accident on Kriti." Demetria said. "You will be off Athenian land within the day. Take nothing more than your horses and the arms you had when you arrived. If you are found within the boundaries of Athenian territory after moonrise, the army of Polymachos will have orders to run you through. All of the folk as far as our boundaries will be warned not to give aid to you."

"Boundaries that we helped expand," Phillip growled under his breath.

Mykalos grabbed Phillip's arm. "Be silent," he murmured. "We must get out of here alive. We will have our day."

Taking little more than their horses and battered swords, Theseus' war band followed Mykalos and left Athena behind.

Chapter 38

The breeze of early morn was growing cooler as Metertide waned and Geneera found herself shivering on the back stoop of the main kitchen area alone. Ansel had some sort of early morning Priesera duties and so Geneera was on her own to feed her cat companion. The orange–striped tom was late, which was unusual. Geneera called repeatedly for Melagori to come get his breakfast and after many minutes, she was finally rewarded with a weak "Rwow" followed by a coughing, choking sound. Melagori crept from the brush that grew by the side of the kitchen. Every few steps, he squatted to his haunches and made whooping, hacking sounds. Upon reaching Geneera, he threw himself at her feet with his sides heaving and his breathing labored. His normally clean and soft orange fur looked dull and was dusty on one side, as if he had been lying in the dirt for some time. His white muzzle was flecked with foam and his eyes were glassy.

"Oh Meter, Melagori!" Geneera said, "Are you sick or hurt or what?" The big feline just thumped his tail in reply, then rolled to a squat and began gagging again. Geneera stroked the cat tenderly while trying to think what to do. When Melagori laid his chin in the dust, closed his eyes and seemed to stop breathing, Geneera panicked. Scooping him in her arms, she limped toward the healing house, cursing the stiff, sore leg that caused her to jostle the semi–conscious cat in her arms.

Geneera burst into the healing house. "Is anyone here? This is an emergency!" Uazet rushed out of a back room.

"Geneera," Uazet said, "is it your leg?"

"My cat!" Geneera said. "He was making terrible choking noises. Can you help?"

"Have you looked in his mouth?" Uazet asked. The shy, otherworldly girl suddenly became a directed, focused young woman who knew what questions to ask and how best to get the answers she needed for a diagnosis. After carefully listening to what Geneera observed, Uazet had no trouble deciding the most probable source of Melagori's problem.

"He likely has a bone or somewhat in his throat, Geneera. Put him here on this table."

Geneera gently placed the big cat down on the table. Conscious again, he crouched on his haunches and began wheezing loudly.

"I need your help. Wrap your arm around him like this." Uazet leaned over the table and secured the cat's chest to her own torso with her right arm. "Then place your other hand behind his ears and force his head straight up. See how his jaw drops open? That is what I want."

Geneera nodded and did as Uazet directed. Melagori wiggled and thumped his tail but otherwise accepted Geneera's manipulations. Ua pried open the cat's mouth wide with her fingers and peered in.

"Oh my, yes, poor boy. A big splinter of bone is lodged in his throat. That must hurt. Probably it is a bird bone. They are hollow and fracture easily, you know. Keep him in that position for a moment more, Gen." She stroked the cat who seemed to understand the girls were trying to help and did not struggle overmuch.

Ua whirled around and shuffled through a shelf over the wooden counter. "Ah, here. This will help." She displayed a small copper tool with long tapered ends. With the cat's mouth open, she reached in with the pinchers and tugged, then drew out a ragged and bloody bone. "Here we go. Hopefully there are no more fragments lodged further down his gullet."

Geneera let him go. Melagori blinked at them, then wrinkled his nose, shook his head, and let out a big juicy sneeze. "There you are, baby." Uazet murmured softly to the tom, stroking his head. Melagori shook himself all over, blinked at the girls again as if to ask what all the fuss was about, sat and began to lick a paw.

"Thank you so much," Geneera said effusively. Suddenly she felt more self–conscious now that the crisis was over. She looked down at her sandals and scuffed a toe on the floor.

"You named the cat Melagori? Well, he is indeed a pretty cat." Uazet asked, still stroking him. She seemed lost in thought. "You really like animals, yes? He is very trusting of you. You have a way with them. I had a sister who was good with animals too." Abruptly Uazet stopped petting the cat. The warmth that flooded her voice was replaced by professionalism. "I am glad I could help Geneera. Now I really need to get back to tincturing herbs." Without another word, Uazet turned her back to Geneera and strode to the back room of the healing house.

Chapter 39

In the darkened room, Geneera flung back her linen sheet in exasperation. This was the fourth, maybe even the fifth time she had wakened tangled in it from tossing and turning in her restless sleep. Her dreams were dark and strange – nameless men in foreign dress walking the streets of Knossos, threatening people with bright swords, and Geneera frantically looking for, and being unable to find, Uazet, or maybe it was Ansel, or even Jerid who cried out her name.

She squinted into the dim of her room. In the bed on the other side of the studio, Ansel slept peacefully. It was still deep night, hours before dawn. *I need to walk,* Geneera decided. Quietly she slipped from the bed and pulled on her short skirt and tunic, finding them rumpled on the floor where she had left them earlier. Geneera tiptoed down the stairs and out into the clear, starlit night. She breathed in the cool night air and wished briefly she had thought to grab a cloak.

Heading no where in particular, she found herself drawing near the central training house, in which candles and torches were kept lit all night. In the front room was a sanctuary where Priesera often went to meditate. Even though she herself was not Priesera, Geneera liked the sanctuary with its huge purple gypsum altar adorned with candles and crystals and other beautiful objects.

It took a moment for Geneera's eyes to adjust to the faint flickering candlelight of the sanctuary. She found that she was not alone; an unrecognizable figure knelt directly in front of the altar. Geneera heard the unmistakable sounds of sobbing. She stood in the doorway, fingers to her mouth, feeling awkward. She was about to turn away silently when she realized it was Uazet whose sobs grew louder until she was very nearly wailing. Geneera thought her own heart would break listening to the other girl's anguish. Before she had really thought it through, she hurried to kneel at Ua's side, whispering "What is wrong Ua? Was somebody cruel to you? Is there anything I can do to help?"

Ua, obviously startled, drew in her breath sharply. "Who are you? What are you doing here?" Then, a look of recognition crossed her face and she relaxed slightly. She groped in the sleeve of her dark robe and brought forth a square of cloth. After blowing her nose, her voice sounded impersonal, but quavered. "Oh, Geneera, you frightened me. I am fine, nothing is wrong at all, I just could not sleep and decided to meditate on a healing technique I am developing with Priesera Enid."

Geneera stared at her silently for a long moment. Finally, Ua crumpled up her wet handkerchief in her palm and bowed her head. Tears splashed down onto her knees.

"Ua," Geneera said softly. "You do not have to tell me what is wrong if you do not want to, but I would be honored to be your friend. Everybody needs someone to talk to and you do not have to be ashamed to cry in front of me.

"I thank you, but," Ua began, but the words seemed to stick like bone fragments in her throat and in another moment she was weeping again. Geneera put her arm around the slight girl. Ua threw her arms around Geneera's neck and wept uncontrollably. Geneera stroked Ua's thick dark hair and murmured "It will be fine, just cry. All will be fine." Ua sobbed harder and Geneera found her own heart ached in sympathy. She wondered how long Ua had been silently bearing such a burden of grief.

After several minutes of bitter tears, Ua began to quiet and pulled away from Geneera's arms. "I am so sorry," she stammered. "I did not mean to involve you in my problems."

"No, no, please," Geneera replied quickly, gently holding Ua's shoulders and looking into her amber eyes that glittered like a wild animal's. "I do not mind. Honestly."

Ua sighed and said softly, "I have been reluctant to let anyone near me since, Setha, my sister, and my meter were murdered." She looked down at her hands twisting the soaked cloth handkerchief. When she looked back up, tears slid down her face. "I do not know how much you know about how I came to live here," Geneera shrugged.

"Obviously, I am not from Kriti; I can barely even speak your language. I grew up far to the east of here, outside of Babylon. My Meter came from Egypt originally. She was sent to marry a wealthy man in Babylon. She was a follower of Sekmet, the great lion. This is why I am so familiar with cats; we lived with many. My sire had several wives and though I never knew him except in passing, he was generous and kind with all of us. When our neighbors invaded our lands, they tried to convert all the people to their god, Marduk. Any men who refused were killed, as were most women over a certain age. I had a twin sister, Setha, and we were both training to be Priesera of Bast, the cat daughter of Sekmet. Setha could talk to all animals, especially the sacred cats. The invaders raided our household and, and," Ua faltered, then began to weep again, curling her legs up under her body, her arms wrapped around her torso, hugging herself and rocking.

Geneera shook her head slowly, watching Ua. "You lost your whole family."

Ua nodded. "I have some distant relations in Egypt still, but after my sister . . . died, one of my sire's wives who also escaped the invaders hid me. We ran and ran to the west until we were deep in the mountains. She was injured though and her wounds soured. She died one night as we hid in the cave." Ua paused, then took a deep breath and continued. "Then, somehow, Diatima found me. She said a Seer had a vision and that she was to bring me to Kriti. I knew she was right, that I had to come here. And where else did I have to go?"

Ua looked up at Geneera and uncurled her legs, dropping her hands to her lap. "I often come here at night because I cannot sleep well. I feel so old inside, like they murdered me too, just not my body. I dream of my sister, that we are in the temple room together, talking about our studies. The invaders enter and she pushes me under the altar table. I watch through the drapery as they drag her away and I wake up screaming because I know I cannot stop them and I know what they will do to her."

Ua covered her face with her hands and Geneera thought she would cry again, but after a moment, she ran her fingers through her tangled hair and said, "That is why I sleep at the healing house instead of with the other novice Priesera. I have such terrible nightmares and no one could sleep if I shared a room with them. Sometimes I think I shall never again be able to sleep through the night; that I will never again be whole." Ua was silent for a long time.

"I know what it is like to lose someone you love." Geneera said at last. "I lost my brother. I loved him very much." Her voice cracked and she bit her lips hard to keep the tears that suddenly gathered in her eyes from running down her cheeks.

Ua must have seen through her. "So," she said, reaching out to take Geneera's hand in her own, "We have a grief in common. What was your brother's name?" Geneera drew in a deep shuddering breath. "Jerid," she said, and then was silent again as she fought to maintain control. "There, I said it. That is the first time I have said his name aloud since his death. He died in a bulldancing exhibition at a Seven–Turns Festival many turns ago." Geneera spoke through clenched teeth and the muscle of her jaw twitched as Ua gently stroked her hand.

"So, and you danced the bull to honor and remember him." Ua nodded thoughtfully. "Look at me, Geneera," she said meeting Geneera's gaze. "I am honored you told me of Jerid and it is a gift to me to offer you some comfort. It allows me to look outside of myself and remember that I too have something to lend to others." Ua actually smiled gently then, her huge golden eyes looking deeply into Geneera's face. Geneera found she needed to break her gaze with Ua because she was seized with an almost overwhelming desire to kiss her. Shifting her weight carelessly, she suddenly gasped aloud in pain as her still stiff leg muscles protested their cramped position. The muscle of her injured thigh began to spasm painfully.

"Oh," Ua exclaimed, "Is your leg hurting? How thoughtless of me! I did not even ask why you were up in the middle of the night – is it your leg? Do you need a pain draught?"

Geneera shook her head. "No, no, my leg is fine, it barely hurts at all." She nevertheless rubbed at it and began to gingerly straighten it out, grimacing, and hoping that Ua would not be able to see the pain on her face in the candle light.

Ua shook her head and scrambled to her feet. She then grabbed Geneera by her upper arm and urged the injured girl to lean on her while getting to her feet. "You always pretend that nothing hurts you, but I can tell you are in pain. You must be after sitting so long in that cramped position."

When Geneera started to protest, Ua put her finger to Geneera's lips and continued, "Let us go for a short walk into the herb garden. It will stretch out your leg and I can pick some leaves there that will help relax your spasms. Come on now, put your arm around my shoulders and lean on me, just until the cramps let up a little." Geneera did not protest the opportunity to put her arm around Ua, although she did wish that she was the one offering strength. Together Ua and Geneera slowly hobbled to the garden.

The moon was nearly full and her shimmering light reflected off the flat, mica flecked stones of the path into the healing gardens, illuminating the way like a sparkling stream of water flowing through the scented darkness. It seemed to Geneera she could even hear water tinkling somewhere in the distance. She smelled the sweet and spicy fragrance of herbs and it surprised her to see some of the plant blossoms were in full bloom. Ua paused at the entrance to the herbal garden and inhaled deeply. "I love to come here late at night," she told Geneera softly. "Many of the plants speak to me directly at this time and sometimes their little guardians will come to talk too."

Taking Geneera's hand, Ua led her onto the garden path. They had walked but a short way down the trail when Uazet turned to her left and knelt to a low shrub that grew to the side. Geneera watched as the girl whispered softly to the plant, then gently plucked a handful of leaves from it. Ua thanked the plant and turned back to Geneera. Rolling the leaves rapidly between her palms, she said, "The juice from the leaves of this plant contains an agent that will calm the spasms in your leg. Just ahead in the center of the garden is a bench. We can sit and I will rub the bruised leaves on your leg."

The garden path widened into a circle. At center was a pool with a spring burbling up from the middle. Surrounding the bath were several ornately carved stone benches. Ua led Geneera to one. Pushing her onto the seat, Ua first smelled the leaves, then began rubbing them firmly but gently up and down Geneera's upper thigh. Geneera found herself needing to talk.

"Who are the plant guardians?" Geneera asked, hoping Ua would not think it was a stupid question.

Ua shrugged. "I see them as small, winged, human–like beings. Some talk to me about their particular plant. They can tell you amazing things really, although I suppose knowing exactly how many bees visited a particular blossom in the past three days can be of rather limited value." Ua giggled a little, a high pitched laugh that sounded to Geneera like the tinkling of little bells.

"They also tell me how the plant is faring; things like whether its root system is healthy, how many flowers it will have this season, if the plant liked the nutrients I gave it, things like that."

"Oh," Geneera replied. She felt awed by Ua now. "You talk directly to the plants too? What do they tell you?"

"Yes," Ua replied, "Although 'talking' is not precisely what I do. The plants communicate differently. Usually I touch a leaf or stem or berry and see a picture. If I ask what medicinal value it might have for a human or an animal, I get a sensation, like warmth, in some part of my body. Sometimes it can be rather unpleasant," again

Ua laughed her tinkling laugh, "like when I asked a shrub what it might be good for and it made me sick to my stomach."

"The plants see themselves in terms of how they can help humans?" Geneera asked.

"Oh no!" Ua replied. "They are beings on their own journeys. Some have agreed to work with humans, though I do not know why. Perhaps they learn from us just as we learn from them. But I know their work with us is only a small part of why they are here. Once I asked a great old tree what it felt was its purpose and it showed me images that I did not comprehend at all. I hope someday to understand more."

An awkward silence ensued as Geneera sought the courage to ask Ua the question that most burned at her heart. At the same moment, both girls started talking. "Ua, I was wondering," began Geneera while Ua said, "I am not usually this comfortable . . . ,"

They giggled as their words rode over each other's, then Geneera said, "Please, you go first."

Ua smiled shyly and said, "What I was going to say is that I am not usually very comfortable with people, especially since my sister . . ."

Ua paused and Geneera encouraged her, saying, "Go on."

"But I have really enjoyed talking with you tonight and I want to thank you for being patient with me. You probably think I am strange, talking to plants and all; I know that the other novices think me nixed."

Geneera shook her head. "I think what you have told me is fascinating, Ua. I have never in my life met anyone like you, anyone I like quite as much as I like you. I would consider it a privilege to talk to you anytime. Really," Geneera added when she saw something that could have been mistrust enter Ua's eyes. Geneera impulsively grabbed Ua's hands, noting how small and delicate they were in comparison to her own larger ones. She looked deeply into Ua's eyes, trying to ask the seemingly otherworldly girl the silent question directly from her yearning heart.

For a moment, it seemed that Ua understood and would respond in kind, but then the moment passed and Ua released her hands from Geneera's grip saying, "Do you know what I think would be good for your leg? A dip in the warm springs." Ua answered herself before the disappointed Geneera could open her mouth. Raising herself from the bench, Ua pulled a reluctant Geneera to her feet and led her to the pool.

Ua pulled off her cloak and the tunic underneath revealing her small, well–formed breasts, and the outline of her firm buttocks covered only by linen undershorts. Geneera, stricken with uncharacteristic modesty, turned her back to Ua and half–heartedly began fumbling with the ties of her own tunic in the overly revealing moonlight.

Geneera heard a splash as Uazet jumped into the waist deep pool. "Come in, Geneera," Ua called, "this water is always warm. It will be good for your leg!"

Setting her jaw, Geneera resolutely pulled her tunic over her head, slipped the skirt over her slim hips, turned toward Ua in the pool and awkwardly lowered herself in. Indeed, the water was pleasantly warm and smelled faintly of sulfur.

Uazet ducked her head under the water and then waded up to Geneera who leaned back at the pool side. Stone benches lined the inside of the pool; Geneera slid onto one. Seated, the water just covered her breasts, leaving her shoulders exposed. Ua drew herself up next to Geneera on the seat. The water covered Ua up to her collarbone and Geneera was not sure if she was disappointed or relieved that so little of Ua was actually showing. "There, that feels good on your leg, no?" Ua said, sounding stiff and formal again.

Geneera admitted that it did. She looked down into the gently rippling pool, refraining from looking into Ua's eyes, afraid of what she might find or, more precisely, what she might not find reflected in them. But sometimes in the night, even the shyest of lovers will not be denied. Soon Geneera's curiosity and longing won out over reticence. She looked up into Ua's eyes and to her everlasting wonder, Ua's walls crumbled like so much eroded stone. Geneera glimpsed the sensitive, lonely girl Ua tried so hard to hide and Geneera was no longer so afraid.

Taking Ua's hand in her own, Geneera whispered, "Did you really just bring me out here because I am your patient or is it more than that Ua? I think you know that I would like more from you. What do you . . .?" Geneera did not finish her query as Ua placed a slender finger to Geneera's lips, quieting her, and then brushed back an unruly curl from Geneera's forehead. Ever so lightly, she brushed her lips against Geneera's mouth.

Geneera grasped Ua's fine boned hands, kissing them eagerly, first the open palms, then the wrists and forearms. As she pulled Ua into her arms, she parted her lips, and kissed Ua hungrily. Ua responded to the caresses with an intensity that matched Geneera's. Leaning back in the shelf ledge, she pulled Geneera closer, straddling her, their breasts touching, until Ua's head rested on the pool edge, her thick dark hair flowing into the water behind. Geneera's arm encircled Ua's waist, and her other hand slowly began to explore Ua's body. Ua's breath became short gasps and she trembled as Geneera first caressed her small belly, then her soft breasts. Her fingertips lightly brushed Ua's nipples, teasing them gently until they stood hard and erect from her body. Ua moaned softly, encouraging Geneera to caress her breasts with her full hand. Geneera nuzzled, then gently nibbled at Ua's neck and ears with her tongue and teeth. Her hand left Uazet's breasts and lightly traced a path down her ribs, across her belly, and down to her warm vulva. Ua parted her thighs invitingly at Geneera's probing touch. Ua shuddered in pleasure as Geneera's fingers began to explore her depths. Geneera inhaled deeply of Uazet's scent, sandalwood mixed with a deeper subtle musky scent and the faint sulfur of the water as both girls immersed themselves in pleasure.

Chapter 40

Ansel was spending yet another afternoon tutoring Theseus. In spite of herself, she had to credit him; he was working hard despite the overt flirtations of Joli and several of the other young novices. "You are learning quickly, Theseus. Already you can speak to me mostly in Kritin and mostly you make sense." Ansel said slowly in Kritin. She sat in a chair at his desk sideways, one elbow resting on its arm while he sat across the room from her on top his bed, legs crossed.

"Kritin is similar, but not identical to a language I heard spoken many times upon Paros as a boy." His speech was measured and his accent heavy, but certainly understandable.

Ansel nodded. "The people of Paros have origins similar to the Kritins. We all came from the east and settled on different islands. Did your meter speak Kritin then?

Theseus winced. "I do not know; my true meter died when I was little. I was not originally from Paros. I was brought there from the coastal town near Trozaen by a trader woman." Something about the tone of his voice convinced Ansel to keep the conversation with Theseus at a more impersonal level.

"We have always traded with those who live on the other islands and on the mainland. We are closely related," she said.

"Why then do most speak Greek and not Kritin?"

Ansel raised her eyebrows. "I am surprised you do not know the answer. Long ago, light–skinned people came from far north of Athena and took over the mainland and some of the more northerly islands. You surely have the blood of these people yourself; see how your skin is much more golden than mine and your hair, though wavy, is lighter in color and texture?"

Theseus pulled at his shoulder–length hair and examined the strands while Ansel continued. "These people spoke Greek and made it the official language. It seems to happen every so often. Armed bands migrate down from the north to settle here. Legend says that this is why we fled the east originally, to escape the invaders."

Theseus let go of his hair and frowned. "Why did your people not fight back instead?"

Ansel shrugged. "Why not indeed? We are a peaceable people; perhaps our ancestors were not even armed. She of Ten Thousand Names condemns killing except when desperately pressed. Also we have seen what happens when nations take up arms. They change."

"So it was easier to just leave?"

"Sometimes Goddess asks us to leave." Ansel paused and stared into space for a moment, then added more quietly, "My meter tells me we may have to leave again. We may have to pick up everything and leave this whole area."

Theseus leaned forward, uncrossing his legs. "Why would your people leave Kriti? Are you afraid of invasion?"

Ansel covered her mouth with her hand. She was not sure how much she should confide in this young man. Finally she said, "The fire mountain on Heria is restless. Our seers may tell us we must leave. I do not know any more." Briskly she changed the subject. "Let us talk about Kritin guild structure now. What can you tell me about guild families and how someone outside a guild family can join a guild?"

For a moment it appeared Theseus would argue, but then he sat up straighter, clasped his hands together with his fingers interlaced and said, "Men from the Monastera often join guilds after they finish their studies. Sometimes children who exhibit interest in a craft they were not born into are sent to Guild families."

Chapter 41

"Come quietly, Priesera." Aluneia said to the girls and Theseus, beckoning to them. "Look, over the hill down into the marshy area; do you see them?"

Ansel and the other novice Priesera peered over the edge of the hill. Below, Ansel could see the long–legged, slate–gray birds with striped black head feathers and a red spot on the top of the head. The cranes! She smiled. There was a flock that passed through Knossos too on their way south. She had loved to watch them when she was a child as they grazed around the river. They were often so loud that sleep was impossible in early Cronetide.

On the north side, the University hillock was abutted by wetlands created as the mountain stream fanned out on the flat delta. The cranes, some twenty or more in this flock, were knee deep in the marsh. They rambled with backward knees about the fen, their heads bobbing as they foraged for plants and frogs that lived there. As the novice Priesera watched, one crane threw its neck back and called loudly with a throaty trill. Others answered and soon they were making a constant raucous noise.

"We are very lucky here at the University that this flock comes to this marsh each turn during early Cronetide. We will go down to them now and do a ceremony of honoring."

Ansel remembered this from the previous turn, her first at the

University, but she knew at each turn the novice Priesera participated at deeper and deeper levels depending on the Spiral they were in. She looked over her shoulder and saw Theseus still gazing down at the cranes. "Do your people dance the cranes, Theseus?" she asked.

"Yes, though I have not often participated." Ansel had to be content with that enigmatic answer as Aluneia was waving all the Priesera down the road that led past the tarn and into the wet lands. She threw the hood of her cloak over her head as it began lightly drizzling.

Once they reached the edge of the marsh, Aluneia held up her palm to stop. The cranes were tall birds; their long necks made them appear even larger. They stared at the line of humans, but did not seem particularly frightened. A couple trilled and purred while a few others thrust their beaks in the air, batting their wings up and down, as if inviting the girls to dance. One turned its back to the girls and began swinging its plume of wing feathers back and forth at the Kore in what was an almost seductive step. The novice Priesera laughed in delight.

"These birds know us," Aluneia said. "We dance with them every turn. See how eager they are?" She smiled, then turned to the Priesera and said, "But first, the teaching."

"Cranes aid human souls as we pass from this world to the underworld and back. When we dance together, we both honor their service and tell them of our relationship to each other and the land." She paused, turning toward the flock. Ansel saw that a number of the birds were watching the humans as if listening closely.

Aluneia continued. "When our ancestors came from the east and mingled with the people of the caves, we all danced together with the cranes so the birds would understand that we have become one people; that our ancestors should go to the same place and our spirits should come back here to this land. This way, our ancestral lines were co–mingled and we became one people both in the future and in the past."

Beryl raised a hand. At Aluneia's acknowledgement, she thrust her thumb in Theseus' direction and said, "Should he be here for this ceremony? Do we want to co–mingle his ancestors with ours?" She glared openly at him. Theseus said nothing, but his lips were set in a thin line. Beryl had been particularly sour regarding Theseus ever since he had arrived and Joli began flirting with him.

Aluneia grimaced slightly. "Anyone who comes to the Priesera mingles with us, just as Uazet did last turn at this time and countless generations of Kore before her. It is part of being accepted here."

Beryl looked irritated and mumbled something under her breath, but Aluneia either did not notice or did not chose to notice. Several of the other girls shifted their feet. Ansel felt the tension growing. Apparently Beryl was not the only one who felt disturbed.

Since Theseus arrived, the Priesera, both novice and ordained, had split roughly into "pro–Theseus" and "anti–Theseus" camps. Predictably, Vasilissa was the most vocal of the Priesera who thought Theseus belonged nowhere near the University. Ansel was surprised at her own feelings. She did not particularly like Theseus, yet she felt sympathy for him as his tutor. Whatever his motivations, he was truly working hard to learn the language and understand the culture. She had decided privately that she belonged to no camp; she would trust to She of Ten Thousand Names that all would work out regardless of her personal feelings.

Aluneia lined up the girls along the edge of the marshy area. Ansel and the others slipped off their leather sandals and their toes squished into the soft, wet, grasses. The birds lined up too, facing the Kore.

Then, Aluneia began an elegant dance. Stretching out her cloak, she lifted her arms out from her body and mimicked flight with bent elbows and outstretched fingers. Her arms did not flap wildly, but instead, she controlled the up and down movements as if she could feel strong air currents buffeting against her muscles. The light cloak filled with a slight breeze. Her face, expressionless with her eyes closed, was a mask of dignity and reverence. She picked up her feet carefully in the same controlled manner, as if lifting them out of deep water. Her knees bent, she strolled a few steps closer to the watching birds, then, a few steps back.

One bird whooped a greeting and began to mimick Aluneia's movements, gently flapping wings partially spread, feathers like long delicate fingers, a bent–kneed step or two toward the Priesera, then back. The crane bent back its head and so did the Elder Priesera.

The girls and Theseus followed Aluneia's lead. They tilted their heads, their faces serene, eyes closed, and stepped elegantly once, twice, three times toward the line of birds, then back. The birds grew excited and began an awe inspiring hooting, trilling, trumpeting ruckus as they began their dance.

Aluneia increased the speed of her steps slightly, as did the Priesera. The birds followed suit. Soon the humans began a sensuous, controlled forward and back waving, flapping movement with their cloaks, as if to embrace the air with their "wings". The birds responded with small leaps and hops as their wings lifted their lithe bodies from the ground. Many dipped their beaks into the marsh, then flipped grass and mud into the air. They kicked out their legs and in response, so did the Priesera.

The birds then formed a semicircle that almost, but not quite, met the humans. The Priesera stepped forward to complete the circle. The half bird, half human ring waved their limbs, leaped, and danced, the birds trilling loudly, the humans humming and grunting, all hopping and stretching, kicking their legs and tossing grasses into the air. Faster and faster they danced as the Radiance built between human and bird. Hop, kick, flap, leap. Finally, when Ansel thought she must collapse, the birds all screamed a tremendous shriek and as a group took wing, a spectacular flutter of white and black, beating the air, lifting off, black legs tucking under gray bodies, flailing to gain height and speed, and soaring over the tree covered mountains.

Some of the Priesera dropped to their knees in exhaustion, overcome by the shock of the emptiness left by the departing birds. Others panted and yipped in exhilaration. Ansel just stood in silence, watching the Radiance of the great flock as it flew away, taking with them an imprint of the Priesera carried between their great wings.

Chapter 42

Today, the most amazing thing happened; Aluneia had me hold a meeting involving all of the Priesera. Here is how it all started. The tension concerning Theseus erupted during the mid-day meal. He usually just eats in his cottage away from everyone. But today, he came into the dining hall and ate with the rest of us.

Priesera Vasilissa was sitting with many of the novice Priesera. Theseus came in, got some food, and then was looking for a place to sit. Priesera Vasilissa stood up and said to him, "You think you belong here at this University, but you do not. It is an atrocity that you are allowed to even live here. Go back to your cottage and do not make us see your face." Many of the novices giggled and nodded in agreement.

Theseus just froze. I think he wanted to throw his bowl of stew at her but knew if he did it was him who would be in trouble, not her. No one, not even the silly novices who spend all their time trying to get his attention, would say a word on his behalf.

I felt enraged. I do not particularly think Theseus belongs here either, but no one deserves to be humiliated unjustly in public like that. I know what that feels like from when I was a little maid. I refuse to just sit back and watch it happen to someone else. Besides, the Elder Priesera and the Elder Council themselves decided to allow him to enter the University; Vasilissa was cruel to attack him.

I stood up from across the room and said as calmly as I could muster, "Priesera Vasilissa, with all due respect, you are not being fair to Theseus. He has been accepted into the Priesera and has as much right to be here as any of us do."

Priesera Vasilissa just glared at me for several moments with those cold eyes of hers, but I would not back down. The whole room was tense and silent. Then Elder Priesera Aluneia came in and demanded to know what was happening. Vasilissa told the Elder Priesera said that I was being insolent to her. I felt afraid, but I told Aluneia exactly what happened. The other novices agreed with my version. I was surprised that Vasilissa lied about me, but Geneera told me that her meter lies often and is very bad at it. I never had her lie about me before though and it was unnerving.

Anyway, Priesera Aluneia asked Theseus to leave for a few moments and then told everyone that we all needed a formal meeting; the hostility was interfering with normal operation of the University. Then, she turned to me and said that I was to facilitate the meeting. I was stunned. Vasilissa was spitting mad. Aluneia took me aside later and assured me that I was quite capable, that she *would be there, but she wanted me to gain experience in having people listen to me.*

So, this afternoon, Priesera Aluneia cancelled everybody's chores and called a meeting of all the novices and all the Priesera. Theseus was not invited because Aluneia said that the meeting was really less about him than about having faith in the decisions of the Elder Priesera and Council.

The meeting was held in the dining hall, since it is one of the few rooms big enough to hold all of us. I sat at a desk in the front of the room where everyone could see me. Everyone else sat at the long tables. First, Priesera Aluneia spoke. She told everyone that she personally had been involved in the decision to allow Theseus to come to the University. She explained about seeing the Mark of the Chosen on him and talked about the message of the Eilithyliad. She then had me talk about tutoring him and how well he was learning Kritin. Since Priesera Aluneia is Theseus' advisor, she told everyone how well he was progressing in his studies and how hard he was working. She emphasized that it was not important for us to understand exactly why She of Ten Thousand Names chose Theseus, but it was important for us to trust that the Seer, the Elder Council, and the Elder Priesera herself had all decided it was appropriate he be here. Vasilissa made sure everyone understood that she had not approved of him being admitted but had been overruled by the rest of the Council.

Then, Priesera Aluneia opened the meeting to questions and comments from everyone else. It was my job to keep track of who wanted to speak and in what order. As it turns, I also needed to keep the conversation from erupting into a fight. I am surprised that people were actually willing to follow my direction. Twice I had to stop Priesera Vasilissa from interrupting and shouting at Priesera Ursula. Priesera Ursula says that Theseus has many intuitive gifts; she strongly believes he belongs here. Priesera Vasilissa is still very angry even if she eventually agreed that she could not did not have the authority to throw him out of the University. She still does not want Theseus here, but I think she will not dare to challenge him again. Everyone knows that Elder Priesera Aluneia would not approve.

After the meeting finally ended, Elder Priesera Aluneia rubbed my back and said, "Ansel, you are a courageous girl. Always follow your heart and spirit."

I told her that I was not very courageous, that I felt afraid much of the time. But then she smiled at me and said, "Having courage does not mean you are unafraid, Ansel. It means that you do what you believe is right despite your fear."

Chapter 43

Middle triad Cronetide was rainy and chill and the people used it for rest and inner reflection. It was a time to evaluate the achievements and disappointments of the previous turn and a time to shed them both in preparation for the coming of Maidentide.

All of the people walked the labyrinth together at this time. The public labyrinth walk was not the same as the private labyrinth walk each novice Priesera would attempt when it was her time. The public labyrinth walk was a community event; some mysteries can only be grasped when people are gathered together.

This turn Ansel understood this proverb better than any time before. Each Cronetide previous, the public labyrinth had appeared as if by magic, either ephemerally sketched in the great cave the Priesera used for so many of their ceremonies, or before that, in the cave used by the people at Knossos.

As a Second Spiral novice, Ansel, for first time in her life, helped in the creation of the great labyrinth. The novices and Elder Priesera Aluneia had gathered during the brightest part of the day, though of course, it was still dim within the cave itself. The torches that always lined the cave walls were lit and Aluneia sketched the outline of the labyrinth right onto the expansive cave floor with white limestone chalk. Next, dozens of sturdy bronze columns, each reaching as high as Ansel's waist, were positioned along the chalk lines.

These metal pillars were heavy and required two novices to put them in place. Finally, huge fat beeswax candles were set onto the columns. The candles would be lit by the Third Spiral Priesera just before the ritual started.

That evening it rained a cold, steady downpour. Though the weather was uncomfortable, it was expected this time of tide and considered good fortune. The people understood they needed the rains of Cronetide. They knew that the Crone was sometimes harsh, but She did what needed to be done, simply and matter–of–factly.

All of the people wore their warmest clothing. Their cloaks of heavy wool, now damp, released a pungent, though not unpleasant odor. Almost one hundred people slowly trod the labyrinth at the same time to a slow heartbeat drummed by Aluneia on her largest instrument, made from the hollowed trunk of an ancient cypress tree. Its heavy thud sounded dull from moisture. Another hundred waited patiently huddled in line under the long overhanging lip of the cave for their chance to enter the labyrinth. Most were women, many of them Priesera and novice Priesera, but many others were workers from the village: cobblers and tanners, weavers and herders.

The labyrinth ceremony began directly after the evening meal and would last late into the night. Ansel arrived somewhat later than she had planned; she waited for nearly an hour for her chance to enter the labyrinth. Theseus, she knew, would arrive even later as he was still out on the hill tending the olive grove. It was time to surround each tree with oiled cloth to catch the first of the olives as some ripened and fell from the trees. Ansel was relieved to be excused from the olive harvest this turn. It was cold and dirty work even when it was not raining, which was rare.

She finally reached the front of the line where she was granted entrance onto the path by a Third Spiral Priesera. Inhaling deeply of the incense that perfumed the thick air, she allowed herself to slip into a light trance state, facilitated by the flickering flames and the deep throb of the huge drum. She had been walking the enormous public labyrinths since she was a small girl and was first taught to step with the sonorous beat of the drum.

The labyrinth walk represents the journey of life and Her passages. Always I am moving toward the middle, but the path is never direct. I have to trust that the road is taking me where I need to go, even if sometimes it seems I am heading the wrong way.

Beginning the journey, Ansel followed the path is it appeared to lead directly to the center, but then turned abruptly to her left. She skimmed around the the center. Looking over her shoulder, she saw the people who had been walking longer than she, yet appeared to be further from the center. They passed her going in the opposite direction. Occasionally she met eyes with someone she knew and smiled. She contemplated the labyrinth lessons she had been taught over the turns, both by the Priesera at Knossos and also here at the University; some of them spoke to her heart.

The labyrinth teaches us that we pass each other on the journey of life and may even look as if we are heading in opposite directions, Ansel thought, yet ultimately we walk the same path.

This turn I completed the First Spiral of my training, and endured the rejection of many of the other novice Priesera. I not only survived, but some of them even respect me now. Ansel's heart warmed to that thought, then she sighed. I still do not know the direction in which I am called. I will meet with Aluneia soon and she will want answers from me. Ansel shuddered a little.

The upcoming appointment with Aluneia was an important meeting. They would discuss when Ansel would be ready for the other labyrinth journey; The labyrinth journey. It was rumored at the University that no one emerged from that journey unchanged.

Ansel paused from her musings and saw that she was now walking almost side by side with Geneera with Uazet right behind her. The slight girl with the golden eyes stared straight ahead, her pupils in the unfocused state indicating deep trance. Geneera was walking with the help of a stout polished wooden stick. She would always walk with a limp, the healers said. She wore a leather tunic, possibly one she had helped to make. Geneera was accepted into the University leather worker guild and now spent her time stirring huge vats of agents that softened the hides. Geneera looked cheerful. *Love will do that for you,* Ansel thought as she smiled widely at Geneera, then rounded a bend that took the them in completely different directions.

My friendship with Gen was given another chance and I am grateful. She is in love with Uazet and I need to be happier for her. Just like the Labyrinth journey, sometimes one walks hand in hand with another only to have a curve in the path send you far from each other. She resolutely repressed the grief that accompanied that thought. *It is the way of life and I cannot change it. I would not change it.* Briefly her thoughts flickered to the catastrophe of Amnisos, but she did not allow those to burble all the way to consciousness.

She was on the portion of the path furthest from the center now and soon the path would make a turn that would bring her much closer to her destination. As she made this turn, she saw Theseus walking another section of the maze. He did not seem to see Ansel. His expression was thoughtful; his eyes soft, his focus inward. Ansel wondered briefly what he was thinking so hard about, but then she once again glimpsed the center and resumed her own personal journey.

I learned much from my First Spiral of studies and also from the community. Altogether, this time has been both challenging and good. She sighed deeply. *I am ready to let this turn go, to dissolve into the void, to become one with She–Who–Walks–the–Labyrinth,* she thought. Grief encircled her heart in a heavy embrace. *I need to melt into the arms of Great Meter and cry for a long while.*

The final section of the path, the one finally leading to center, was strewn with symbols of death. Animal skulls and dried flower heads lined the way between the candles; dead branches intermingled with bones and finally, stones. Ansel felt the last remnants of the past turn drop from her like the shedding of old skin. The exhilaration and the triumphs, the grief and the fury were left at the entrance to the center of the labyrinth.

In the middle was a large clay pot underneath which a fire

danced. Many people knelt before the fire, the hoods of their cloaks pulled over their heads. A few Third Spiral Priesera sat quietly to the side on cushions, waiting to offer comfort or cloths to wipe the eyes of the participants. Ansel knelt in the dimness. She felt the warmth of the fire, the envelopment of the dark, the sense of being embraced by the nameless and faceless people in the center with her. *Safe,* she said to herself. *Here, we are neither boy nor girl, old nor young, Priesera nor village cook. Here we are all simply children of Her, a bit of Her, entwined with Her and each other.* She felt the tears begin to flow as she allowed herself to dissipate into the warm stream of community.

Chapter 44

Ansel clenched her hands into fists and commanded herself to relax. In as calm a voice as she could muster she said, "You tell me you think Kriti should take up arms? Ridiculous. No one can compare with us in culture and civilization. We are the most advanced nation in the world."

"Precisely." Theseus answered. "Therefore Kriti is the object of envy and lust. And she is vulnerable too." He opened his arms wide, palms up. No doubt he hoped to keep this debate amicable, but Ansel was feeling peevish.

"No one would dare," she insisted. She wrapped her arms about her slim waist in an effort to comfort herself. "Besides, we are an island; how could any nation bring enough arms and warriors?" Ansel started tapping her foot and stared at Theseus as if she thought him slow of mind.

Theseus snorted. "Ansel, I have given this much thought. You are naive. The cities are not fortressed and it would take no more than several dozen well armed and seasoned warriors to create havoc. Trust me, Ansel, I know."

"Several dozen? Havoc they could create, but how could they possibly maintain control?"

Theseus shook his head slowly and pursed his lips. "You tutor me of the history of your people, yet you do not comprehend it yourself. Invaders need only institute their own rules of governance. Tell me, why does Athena have a hereditary monarchy while Kriti does not?"

"Ha." Ansel pointed a finger at him. "You did not know that when you first came here. I taught you that myself. Athena was conquered long ago by the nomadi. They instituted the monarchy, but over time, the Priesera regained control and established rulership."

"Yet, is it the same? Is Helen Demetria Priesera?"

"No." Ansel admitted. "Well, she has authority of the Athenian Temples, clearly. But she is only called 'Priesera' as an honor because she inherited the throne from her meter, obviously not because she had any special leadership skills. I doubt she even understands who the Priesera really are."

"Do you not understand the implications? Has a hereditary monarchy made the civilization of the Achean people better? Demetria is a direct descendant of the nomadi. So what that she is female. Does she have more talent in governance for it?"

"Well, she, at least, is in the image of Goddess." Ansel thrust her fists on her hips.

Theseus grunted. "You allow yourself to be ruled by your prejudices. She is a terrible leader. If I say that in Athena, however, I risk death. Here your citizens take for granted that they may challenge the Elder Council."

"I would rather die than take up arms." Ansel looked up at the ceiling and crossed her arms, feeling self righteous.

"Again you show your ignorance. You would be fortunate merely to die. The men, perhaps, would be killed outright. Vasilissa and women of her age, past the first bloom of youth and fecundity; they might have the blessing of death. You, lovely Ansel, you would become the slave of one of the nomadi, forced to bear him children, isolated from other women for fear of revolt, your name and your ancestresses denied and forgotten."

"Suicide then." Ansel felt her lip curl. She forced herself to breath more deeply. How this arrogant boy got under her skin!

Theseus glared at her. "The easy way out for you. Death and enslavement for your sisters and your nation. How proud of yourself you must be, Priesera."

Ansel winced at the truth of his words. She remained silent for a long moment. When she next spoke, the anger had drained from her, leaving only sadness and fear. "But, to take up arms, to train our people for the military, it eats at the very soul of a nation. You call me ignorant, unappreciative of the very history I tutor you in, but this I have gleaned; in the nations that institute a military, Goddess there becomes secondary to killing, hateful, vengeful gods. Men seem more attracted to the armies and the fighting. I am not sure why." She flung herself onto the chair next to where Theseus sat on his cot.

Theseus breathed in. "Brute strength is a factor, dear Ansel. Have you ever tried to swing a full blade?"

"No, of course not."

"Bronze blades are extremely heavy. Some of the nomadi use blades of another metal which is even heavier. The majority of women can not wield them with as much skill."

"Women would not want to."

Theseus laughed. "Tell that to the Emetchi nations. Do you know who they are? Legions of women who have learned to fight as well as any man. They once came from nations such as Kriti, nations invaded by nomadi. They are women who chose to learn to fight rather than be enslaved or choose suicide. They are much admired and much hated."

Ansel felt anger stir in her belly again. "I do not want Kriti to become a nation of warriors like Athena or even like the Emetchi. We spend our lives dedicated to She of Ten Thousand Names and to beauty and life. To become a culture of war and death is to become the antithesis of who we are." Angry tears welled up in her eyes.

Theseus lowered his voice and his eyes became soft. "To not take up arms is to die, perhaps not in your lifetime or mine, but someday surely. It seems to me the choice is to live enslaved or to live free."

"And to me the choice seems between to die a thing beloved or to survive but become what is hated."

"What a sad and difficult choice than would seem to be. I am sorrowed that you think this is true," Theseus acknowledged as he awkwardly patted Ansel's back.

Surprised at the surge of genuine compassion she sensed from Theseus and perhaps even more startled at her own overwhelming physical response to his friendly touch, Ansel jumped to her feet.

"I, uh, I must leave early. I have an important appointment with Priesera Elder Aluneia later today and need to prepare for it." She grabbed her cloak and rushed out of the doorway and into the cold wet street.

Chapter 45

Ansel stared out at the steady rain thinking about the question Elder Priesera Aluneia had just asked. "What do we mean when we speak of Mysteries?"

The office of the Elder Priesera was warmed by a cheery fire in a large copper brazier in one corner. Aluneia, looking stern, or perhaps just thoughtful, sat across the cypress wood table from Ansel, her hand cupping her chin. The window was behind her head, the thin hide lifted to allow the dim light of the rainy day to illuminate the room. The wooden chair was hard on Ansel's backside. It was a simple chair with no arms, and Ansel tucked her hands under her thighs to keep from chewing her fingernails.

Finally Ansel began to speak. "I was going to give you a simple answer," she started, "but the more I think about it, the less simple the answer seems to me. Obviously, we think of Mysteries as something hidden or unknowable. But then, I should feel that there are no Mysteries any more for me because I know them. Yet, I feel even to the depths of my bones this is not true."

Aluneia nodded but said nothing. Ansel paused, unsure how to give words to the concept. A hand crept to her mouth seeming of its own volition. Ansel jerked the fingertips out of her mouth and stuffed the disobedient hand back under her leg. "My words are so inadequate. If talk about my experiences of the Mysteries, perhaps I will stumble on the underlying meaning." She allowed the mischievous hand to scratch her forehead with a ragged fingernail.

"When we do the rituals of the Blood Mysteries, for example, we speak about cycles; the cycles of nature, of woman, of She of Ten Thousand Names, my ears understand the words but it is my heart and my spirit who respond, who really know deeply how these things are related. I mean, I feel Maidentide within myself; the newness, the joy of living. I genuinely understand the goat kid who kicks up her heels in celebration of green grass. Even though I am no longer a Maiden in body, just like the turnings of nature, I can re–experience the spirit of the Maiden."

Ansel paused again, but Aluneia continued to say nothing though she nodded.

"Of course, I am Kore now, the time of fertility, and just like the Koretide of nature, I can feel within myself the desire to blossom. I find I seek new experiences, which is really very unlike me since I have always feared change. I am sorry, Priesera Aluneia, I do not know if I am making any sense to you."

"No, I think what you are saying is important, Ansel. Please go on," Aluneia encouraged.

"The Mystery of it all, what makes it a Mystery, I believe, is not that the knowledge is hidden, but that it is not experienced at the level of talking. I think perhaps I could shout the Mysteries from the roof of my GranMeter's apartment in Knossos, but until one feels the Mystery in her body and spirit, the simple knowledge of it is not the Mystery itself."

Aluneia smiled a little. "I have a parable I often use. One may find herself walking one of the many paths to the Underworld and on the side of the passageway she finds a beautiful gemstone. It is magnificent; everything she hoped to find and more. She admires it, picks it up, and brings it back from her long and difficult journey. But then, when she tries to show this marvelous jewel to someone else, someone who has not trod that particular path, it looks just like an ordinary stone. It is only the women who have also traveled that path who know it for the precious gem it truly is. Do you understand?"

Ansel nodded thoughtfully and dared to meet the eyes of the Elder Priesera. "I think I grasp what you are saying. I remember when we danced with the cranes this past late Metertide, I came to understand that perhaps when we dance, we also do a service for the cranes, though I do not know what that service might be. I just knew, somewhere deep inside myself that the dance fulfilled needs both within the humans and also within the birds. Yet, as strongly as I felt this insight, I could not put the words together to convey the meaning to the other novice Priesera. It was something that needed to be sensed at a different level than just in conversation."

"So you would say that what makes something a Mystery is that it is felt or known somewhere special, deep within the place of sacredness?"

"That is my best answer, I guess." Ansel said, pursing her lips and shaking her head slightly. "I know it is inadequate."

"No, I believe you grasp this well. Part of why these are called 'Mysteries' is that no one can explain them." Aluneia actually looked amused, her eyes twinkled and her lips curved into a grin. Ansel found herself chuckling just a little in relief.

"Now, what other things have you learned here at the University? I do not mean in your studies, I have the other teachering Priesera to report to me how well you learn, I mean, about yourself and your path of service.

Ansel drew in a deep breath. She had been dreading this question. "To be honest, Priesera Aluneia, I do not yet know what my path of service is to be. One thing I am learning is that I only like being around other people for a short time and then I am exhausted. It is ironic; all my life I thought I wanted people to like me, to be popular, but now I find that I do not so much. I fight with Theseus as much as tutor him." Her body unexpectedly filled with warmth when she said Theseus' name. No time to think about that yet. She pressed on. "He says things I find ridiculous and I cannot bite my tongue fast enough to avoid telling him what I think. I do not like the chatter and silly gossip of many of the other novice Priesera. Perhaps I am in danger of becoming the arrogant know–it–all I have been accused of being all my life."

Aluneia smiled in a genuinely warm manner that Ansel found surprising. "So," she said, "we can count out Escorting as your service, then."

Something about Aluneia's droll style suddenly struck Ansel as intensely funny. She slapped her forehead lightly with the palm of her hand and laughed ruefully for several moments. Finally, she put her hand over her mouth and said, "I just had a picture of my own meter as a novice Priesera. She told me she had been far more interested in cosmetics and gossip than in her studies. She is likely one of the novices I would disdain, no?"

"Your meter was already in her apprenticeship by the time I entered the University, but I think it is safe to say you are quite unlike her."

"And my GranMeter, I wonder what she was like as a novice."

Aluneia shook her head. "Some of the Priesera here are old enough to remember, I am certain. You should find someone and ask."

"I believe I have learned to not take myself and everything so seriously." Ansel said suddenly.

Aluneia nodded, encouraging Ansel to go on.

"I thought the world ended when I had to fetch water and harvest olives during my first turn, but it did not. Instead, I made friends with the kitchen women and looked forward to the time alone." She smiled thinking about the women teasing her about her muscles.

"Yes, that was a test of character for you. You could have felt humiliated and gone home; some of the Agronos girls before you have done just that."

"Honestly? It never occurred to me to leave the Priesera. I think, well, I did not have anything better to go back to. I was unhappy at the Agronos during the last tides I was there."

"No, instead you persisted here and then you took on the very unusual assignment of teaching our first boy Priesera."

"Yes, Theseus." Again that unsettling flood of warmth occurred when saying his name. "He works very hard, but he is a challenge."

"Indeed. Ansel, since Diatima left on assignment and I have been your advisor, I have seen much growth in you. You have become more thoughtful and less self–involved. I am not overly concerned that you do not yet know what it is you are called to do. Often this becomes clear after your labyrinth journey. I will provide opportunities as they arise for you to explore your options after your journey."

Ansel nodded and was silent for several moments. Finally she said, "Priesera Aluneia, I am concerned that Goddess has not again appeared to me since I came to the University. Is it possible She has changed Her mind about me?" Ansel held her breath and awaited Aluneia's answer.

"Ansel, in all my time as a Priesera, I have never heard of She of Ten Thousand Names changing Her mind about someone. It is far more likely to happen in the other direction; a Priesera decides the service is too demanding for her. Do you know that some of the Kore here have never had an encounter like the ones you have had? They were chosen and marked in different ways – some in dreams, some who just called to Her in their hearts and knew they were answered. Do not fret, daughter. She will make Her presence known to you again in the proper time and place." Aluneia looked down at a wax pad she had been taking notes upon and added some. After several moments of silence she said, "Ansel, I believe you will be ready to take the Labyrinth Journey by late Maidentide. It is only a few cycles away now, and you need to prepare yourself."

Ansel nodded and leaned forward in her chair. "First, I want you to become more of a leader among the novices. I want you to become more involved in the ceremonies both during both preparations and the rituals themselves. I will assign you these tasks."

Aluneia handed Ansel a bundle of scrolls. "I also want you to write your thoughts and dreams regarding your Priesera path."

Ansel chuckled. "I have always done this Elder Priesera. I keep journals and have done so since I was a young maid."

"I am not overly surprised. You learned to write early in your life. Still, these scrolls also contain questions and observations for you to ponder and answer. Perhaps you would be willing to share some of your writing with me."

Ansel nodded and took the proffered bundle of scrolls. She unrolled one quickly and looked over the several pointed questions before allowing it to curl back in on itself. She laid them all across her lap and redirected her attention to Aluneia.

"Finally," Aluneia said, "You must listen to your inner voice for the proper timing. Unlike the public labyrinth, the private one is always prepared for our use. It is used periodically by Priesera who feel they are embarking on a transformation or feel they have lost their way. Travel through the labyrinth is never to be undertaken lightly, but must be prepared for, both in body and spirit. I have here another scroll that you are to read about the Labyrinth Journey. It tells you where to find the path inward and what you may expect when you enter. No one can tell you exactly when it is your time to enter the labyrinth. That is between you and Goddess."

Ansel took this new scroll and balanced it on her lap next to the bundle she already had. Aluneia stood, signaling that the meeting was at an end. Ansel stood also and was surprised to find that she was almost as tall as the Elder Priesera. Aluneia had always seemed so tall. It was true that Ansel had a growth spurt in the past few turns, but perhaps it was also true that she had been guilty of seeing some people as far more intimidating than they actually were.

When she glimpsed Geneera and Uazet, the ancient woman stopped dead in the middle of the whitestone road, rain pouring down her already drenched hair and into her unblinking eyes. She stared at them so intently, her head swiveling on her wattled neck as they scurried by together trying to get into the shelter of the herbal house, that Geneera felt obliged to say something. Wrapping a protective arm around Ua, Geneera said, "Can we be of assistance in some manner, Priesera?"

The woman pointed directly at Ua. "You speak the language of the caves. I have been searching long for you."

It was Ua's turn to stare, and Geneera suddenly felt as if she looked at her friend and the old woman from a great distance. "GranMeter . . . ," Gen began, but Ua placed a hand on Geneera's arm and interrupted saying, "I have seen you in my dreams, Eldest. What have you come to tell me?"

"They call to you. How can I not know this? I, too, hear them." As the hag spoke, Geneera felt a surge of terror pass through her; she had no idea why. Apparently Ua was not frightened in the least.

"Tell me more," Ua urged.

"No. Not here. Come to my cottage. Ask any of the Priesera, they will know how to find it."

"Wait, GranMeter, who are you?"

Although Geneera had asked the question, the answer was directed toward Ua alone. "I am the Eilithyliad, the Seer at the cave of Skoteino. Come as soon as you can. I await you."

After she left, Geneera remarked, "What an odd woman. She makes me shiver, Ua. Maybe you should not go see her."

But Ua just looked thoughtful and did not respond.

Chapter 46

Maidentide weather came early that turn and the days became warmer and sunnier almost a full half cycle before normal. When Dia saw that the bird migration to the north had started and the winds had truly shifted from the south, she started on her long journey. She was at sea for three full quartercycles when her destination finally came into view. Her little vessel floated toward the shore.

"Dia!"

"Alekki! Such a wonderful surprise! What are you doing here?"

The big man thrust his hands towards Dia, hauling her by the elbow out of her tiny sailboat and into the clear knee–deep water, then enveloped her in a huge bear hug and sloshed several kisses on her cheeks. "Welcome to Athena, wandering one. I have spent over a full turn here with my meter and brothers and my sister's sons. Did you come all the way from Kriti or from where?"

"Straight from Kriti."

"A long journey in such a puny boat. Lucky for you the winds have been so favorable."

"Yes. I must admit I am happy to have my feet on soil again."

Alekki nodded. "What brings you to fair Athena? And how is your beautiful meter? Is she coming to visit Athena soon? I have some wonderful bracelets to show her; silver from Troy with black wood inlays. Very exceptional. I will be here for at least another few cycles, perhaps longer."

Chuckling, Dia hauled her boat onto the golden sandy beach of Athena's bay with Alekki's help. She squatted to tie her boat to a stout stump. Over her shoulder she said, "I am in Athena on business and Meter is fine, Alekki, as always. But no, I do not think she is coming this way anytime soon." Dia finished her knot and stood; the top of her head reached to the man's nose. "She has given the business over to Brita and Karakos." Dia shrugged, then added. "She has settled upon Delos."

"Ah. Now that is a shame." Alekki shook his head. "Always did I look forward to trading with Melodia. She was a haggler, your meter, may Goddess smile upon her. And she did not even think to say farewell to her old friend. That aches my heart."

Dia laid a hand upon his arm. "It was a sudden decision on her part, but I will tell her you asked of her. Perhaps I can bring her to visit with you in Egypt when you return or you can visit Delos. After all, she has only quit trading; she has not dropped off the end of the world."

Alekki's expression brightened. "Perhaps so. Now, Mistress, no *Priesera* Dia, seeing as your meter is not here, you will, of course, have to substitute for her and join me and the boys for supper."

"Ey, I would be pleased to accept. I am sorely in need of a wash and a warm meal! Of course, I will be happy to provide some entertainment, if it pleases you. I have picked up several new tales since last I was here." Grinning, she patted her kithara which hung in its usual place across her broad shoulders. "Also, old friend, I have a favor or two to ask of you."

"Granted. For the daughter of Melodia I would be pleased to offer any assistance I can."

"I need directions and the loan of a horse for a quartercycle. Do you know where lies the village of Paradisos?"

"Pah. Indeed I do. Run by a leader not fit to muck out a stable. Fancies himself a warlord, too."

"Oh? This is why I was sent here by Elder Priesera Aluneia; to investigate a rumor. Tell me what you know."

Together they turned toward the harbor and fishing village where Alekki's meter made her home. Already it was late in the afternoon, and Dia's stomach growled loudly. The soft sand was warm and pleasant on her feet. She paused to put on her sandals where the beach gave way to stones and rock.

Alekki politely waited for her to wipe the sand from her feet, wrap the ties of her shoes up around her calves, and re–hoist her pack. He resumed speaking once they were again upon the path to the villa.

"Paradisos was united with Athena until recently. Cannot say as I blame the villages for not being pleased, seeing how Athena took taxes and returned little. Well when that Polymachos took over the army, Paradisos pulled out. Seems the leader there managed to hire his own little war band. There have been some skirmishes at the border, but somehow that gang of warriors in Paradisos holds the Athenians at bay. Must fight like the Erinyes themselves, I guess. It has got the other annexed villages grumbling and the army's had to divide itself to keep order."

Dia shielded her eyes from the sun with the palm of her hand. It would set soon enough and the air was beginning to cool. "I have heard not much good about the leadership of Polymachos either."

"Ey, that is the truth. All I know is what blows on the wind," Alekki leaned closer to divulge the gossip, "but I hear tales of re-volt stirring. The last consort, that Theseus, he was well loved here, especially by the army. They do not much care for how he was replaced. He was the one who united the villages for Athena. I hear the army hates Polymachos so much they do not care to hold the borders in his name. Rumor has it Theseus was murdered by either Polymachos or the Helen herself. Polymachos does not command much loyalty, I surmise."

Dia was silent for several moments. She decided to take her me-ter's old friend into her confidence. She lowered her voice and said, "But Theseus is alive and on Kriti. He is hidden away with the Priesera, believe it or not. I need not tell you that this is news to keep close to your chest, Alekki."

Nodding, the man massaged his rubbery beige lips with the fingers of his left hand. He mused, "Now if that is not an odd thing for a warmonger."

Dia nodded. "My thinking exactly. It is why I am here on the northland. Tell me, is there a taverna in Paradisos?"

"Yes, a small one, hardly fit for a dock brat, but it is all they have."

Midmorning of the next day, a much cleaner and well–fed Dia trotted out upon a shaggy grey mare up the northwest road to find Paradisos. She was dressed in trousers and a simple tunic with a knotted sash. Her shirt fell open to her waist yet it still carefully covered her scant breasts; Dia looked for all the world like a young boy. She had subtly encouraged this by choosing clothing that emphasized her broad shoulders and slender hips. A bit of glamour magic helped too.

The road was rugged with many turns and inclines and the sun was already edging westward when she finally trod the village outskirts. Riding into the center of town, she located the inn marked with a small wooden sign rudely cut with the word 'Taverna'.

The taverna was dimly lit and smelled none too clean, but it was blessedly cool compared to the direct sun out of doors. "Midday meal is over, son. We reopen tonight," a woman wearing a coarse brown linen robe said. Her upper arms jiggled as she leaned over to wipe a nicked and gouged wooden table.

"Are you the proprietor of this taverna, Mistress?" Dia asked.

The woman straightened. "Yes. Are you looking for someone lad?"

"I am a traveling muse and storyteller, Mistress, looking to exchange a night's entertainment for a meal and bed for me and my horse." Dia indicated her kithara to illustrate the point.

The woman sucked in her cheeks and cocked her head, appraising Dia. "Are you not too young to be out and about as a story-teller?"

"No Mistress. I am older than I look. Seems the heritage of the red hair does not grow much beard." Dia had no idea if that particular bit of information was in fact true, but she figured no one else knew either.

The woman seemed satisfied. "Good enough lad. Been a long time since we have had a muse through here. I wager the villagers be glad enough to hear a tale or two. Be you any good?"

"I am very good Mistress."

"The woman laughed, her ample breasts heaving. "Sure enough you would tell me that regardless. Well, I will get the word out. The Caster Herself knows we could use the business."

When the night was full dark, the farmers and crafters could no longer work and so looked for entertainment. News of a muse spread even into the next village and the little inn soon was filled to capacity. The owner and her two young children, a girl and a boy, were busy filling mugs and bowls with a deep golden ale. At the long plank tables sat scores of folk all cheerfully clamoring for more ale, wine, bread, fish, olives and cheese. The crowd did not smell all too good, but they were good people; the type Dia loved to perform for. Traveling as she did, she always had a supply of tales that folks had never heard before. They always loved her as much as she them.

She began her first tale, a rowdy sea chant filled with blatant sexual innuendoes. Halfway through it, a group of young men entered and pushed their way through the crowd to the front. An undercurrent of grumbling ensued as the youths claimed a front table that had been occupied, but it was exactly what Dia had hoped for; the war band had arrived.

She ended the first tale, greeted with cheers and good natured hoots, then launched into a second; a song so bawdy that even hardened travelers sometimes blushed to hear it. "This one is just for you boys," she said, lifting a mug of water beside her stool towards the war band in a toast. The crowd roared and howled at the tale, the warriors stomped their feet and raised their mugs back to her.

After a few more stories, Dia announced, "I am fair parched, good audience. I take time now to drink some ale. I will pass a cup for tips. Please remember I am just a poor traveling lad who is trying to help support his sister." She grinned so saucily that the crowd laughed. Who knows what the people thought was the truth of her tale, so long as they put copper into the mug.

Deliberately, she walked to the war band's table and sat down as they made room. "Mind if I join you for a minute?"

A deeply muscled man, who looked slightly older than the rest and was clearly the leader of the group, offered a half chuckle and whopped Dia on the back. "Glad to have your company, muse, The name is Mykalo, Myko my lads call me."

"Diotemos. Call me Dio."

"Where do you hail from, Dio?" asked a sandy haired youth with a lame arm. "And where do you get your stories from? My brother always told stories though I have not seen him in many a turn . . ."

"Cut it, Phillip. For teat's sake, give the lad a chance to drink his ale in peace."

Phillip shrugged. "Many apologies, Dio. Myko always tells me I prattle."

"Not at all, Phillip. A muse is a lover of words or he is no muse. I hail from Delos and my meter is still there. I come from a family of traders though, so I picked up many of my tales just listening at marketplaces. Now tell me your tales, friends. It is clear that you are fighters and a muse is always in need of fresh stories."

"Ei, and tales we could tell you." Phillip said. "Right now we are at hire for Paradisos, but before this we were in Athena."

"Indeed. Were you a part of the Athenian army then?"

"Yes, before that bottom feeder Polymachos took over. We came to Athena with the consort before him, Theseus."

"Yes, I have heard tale of him."

"Ei, a more ruthless and shrewd leader there never was. Compared to him, Polymachos is but a little maid."

All the men chuckled. Dia said "You speak of Theseus in past tense. What happened to him?"

"He last went to Kriti to study at some school or so he said. But now he is dead. Those fancy *kakopoios* killed him on their treacherous island."

Dia swallowed hard to hide her response to this piece of news. Demetria no doubt delighted in spreading this lie. Phillip however, was continuing.

"Hoy, I have a tale for you. Theseus was really planning to invade Kriti. Now we are going to continue his plan and avenge him."

"Phillip, you are too deep in your cups and talk too much." Mykolo growled.

"Ai! I have been to Kriti. They are a wealthy people. How would you invade them?" Dia opened her eyes wide and carefully kept her tone of voice a mixture of awe and innocence.

Myko answered, taking over for Phillip. "Theseus told us of their unfortressed cities and dandy manners. At night, with no warning, the island would be vulnerable to a well–planned attack. No offense, lad, but I will talk no more about this since I mean you no harm, it being foul luck to harm a muse anyway." The brawny man met Dia's eyes and made sure she saw the implied threat there. "We will now talk of something else."

"Good Myko, never would I make a tale from an action in the planning, though of course, once it is a done deed I would have it ready for telling." She grinned in a way she hoped would appear conspiratorial. "I must return to my old tales now anyway. I thank you for the company, kind sirs." Rising, Dia walked to the front of the taverna. The crowd cheered at seeing her. She sang and told stories well into the night, then slept in the stable with her horse where no one would think to look for her had they any reason.

Chapter 47

Ansel recognized the voice of the veiled Priesera who stood at the entrance to the dark labyrinth; Aluneia. The Elder Priesera was dressed in her formal ritual garment; a sea blue collared blouse open at the waist exposed her full breasts and her long wasp–waisted skirt was decorated with a contrasting apron of moon gold. *How did she know I was coming this night?* Ansel wondered to herself, *I did not tell anyone.* She remembered then, that Aluneia's gift from Ariadne was to know when people with whom she was connected were transformed in some way.

"Why have you come to this place of transformation?" Aluneia asked. Ansel inhaled and closed her eyes, then gave the proper answer, "I seek knowledge."

"And what will you do with this knowledge?"

"I will use it to aid my people, my nation, and myself."

"Then enter, daughter."

Aluneia lifted her arm and Ansel passed under it. Aluneia's voice drifted eerily after her, "Extinguish your candle at the bottom of the stairs."

No going back now. Her heart thumped in her chest. Drawing up the hem of her long robe, Ansel descended the stairs almost on tiptoe so as not to disturb the grave silence of the ancient ritual. At the bottom of the staircase there was a turn and she pinched out the flame of her small candle. She saw the flickering then; two huge pillar candles framed the entrance to the dark labyrinth room. At the doorway was a wooden pillar on which balanced a silver chalice and a papyrus scroll.

Ansel unrolled the scroll. It made a scratchy, crinkling sound. 'The Labyrinth Journey is a path to transformation as old as the civilization of the people from which you hail,' she read. 'Greetings to you, fated one, who stands at this precarious entrance. No one leaves unchanged. Before entering, drink deeply from the cup. Know that the ThreadHolder traces your steps. Pray to Her whom you wish to meet, then enter."

Ansel grasped the cup by its stem and looked in it. It was about a quarter full of a thick brownish–green liquid with tiny green flecks suspended in it. A mixture of herbs, Ansel supposed. *Just toss it down your throat. It cannot be any worse than some of that turned wine you and Geneera drank once.* She swirled it and gulped it in one swallow. Green. It tasted green like grasses and new leaves with perhaps a hint of something more acrid underneath. Her senses were sharpened from the two days of fasting she had done in preparation for this journey and the drug to dissolve the veil hit her hard. Within moments, her knees felt weak and she nearly collapsed. She was prepared to expect this and quickly grasped the pillar at the entrance. *The weakness is momentary* she whispered to herself, hearing Aluneia's voice in the words. But it sounded like Aluneia was right in her own head. The ThreadHolder! Wonder overtook her fear. Aluneia's voice whispered right in her head. Relief washed over her. Truly she was not alone.

Ahead, the slick walls of the labyrinth gleamed in the shadows of eerily dancing torch flames before disappearing completely into darkness. As she crept into the entrance, Ansel perceived that the walls themselves reached amazing heights. At first, she was careful to walk straight down the middle of the hallway. If she reached out her arms, her fingertips would just brush the smooth walls on either side. She could not even guess how high above her the ceiling was.

She noticed fragrance; amber, so heavy its taste lay in her mouth like sweet sticky honey. In the sputtering dim, she could just make out strategically placed pillars from which heavy smoke was emanating. She pressed her hand flat against one wall and glided it over the wall in a spiral pattern. How silky it felt. In fact, she observed, the very air felt like being bathed in slick drapery. Or like heavy soft sea water that one could breathe in. She fancied herself immersed in the sea; she extended her arms into the dimness and swam through it like a great seamaid. *I swim,* she thought, then said aloud. "I swim in the waters of the Great Goddess. I am her fish child of the sea." She saw bubbles come from her lips as she enunciated her thoughts. They floated toward the ceiling shrouded in darkness high above her.

The darkness grew; it became a radiating, pulsating, throbbing creature with a great shadowy heart. *It is the drug* Ansel thought to herself. From somewhere, exactly where, Ansel was never sure, a reassuring nod from Aluneia intruded into Ansel's awareness – *yes, the drug alters your senses. Do not fear, child, go forward.*

Ansel reached the end of the first straight corridor and followed as it sharply turned left. She gasped and halted. Ahead was the courtyard at Knossos, and there were girl children, each no more than six turns, standing in a circle. It was as though Ansel was standing both in the hallway, but also floating above the scene. There was a solitary small, dark girl in the middle of the circle. She held her hands over her face, head bowed. Her shoulders shook as if she were crying. As Ansel watched, the girl in the center dropped to her knees. With a shock of recognition, Ansel realized she knew this scene. She knew each girl in the circle – there was tall, muscular Lydia, who was the daughter of one of the cooks. And her disdainful best friend, Thais, at her side. Ansel realized she knew who the girl was in the middle of the jeering children, too. She knew why this girl knelt sucking one thumb, holding her stomach with her other arm, as the singsong taunts rose to her ears.

"You are so ugly, Ansel, your Meta had to ask people to play with you."

"Yes, she begged us talk to you. We did not want to, but we felt sorry for you."

"You always think you are so great and beeeuuuutiful because of your clothes, but you are ugly and stupid."

"You look just like one of those ugly slimy snails. Your eyes bug out just like a snail and your ears stick out just like snail feelers."

Gleeful laughter followed and the girls began chanting, "Snail ears, snail ears!"

"Look at her suck her thumb, just like a baby!"

Ansel watched as her younger self struggled to her feet and tried to break out of the circle of tormenters. The girls joined hands and rebuffed her efforts. She fell hard on her backside.

"Go on and cry, baby. Go run to your Meta. Even she does not want you."

Finally, the girl Ansel burst through the ring of bullies and ran as fast as she could, stumbling out of the courtyard.

The Kore Ansel, still in the labyrinth, gasped at the memory of years of mockery this scene brought back. "It was so unfair," she exclaimed aloud to no one, to everyone, to anyone who could hear. "It was so unfair. They all hated me because I learned to read and write and they could not go to classes like me. I was so shy, I did not know how to make friends. Meta asked them to include me and be nice to me, but that made it worse. Finally, Meta sent for Vasilissa because I was so far ahead of all the other girls and I was so miserable around them."

A voice, not Aluneia, but from within Ansel herself asked, *Do you forgive her?*

"What do you mean, forgive? Those girls? No, I do not. My Meta? I never blamed her really, well, not much anyway." Ansel heard the sadness and anger in her own voice. *I sound young even to my own ears.*

No; do you forgive her, the little girl you once were, Ansel?

"Forgive myself? Forgive myself? For being ugly and stupid and shy and clumsy?"

Was she all those things, that little girl in the center of the circle?

"Yes! Stupid for wanting friends! And ugly next to beautiful Meta! Wait, no, I do not know. I always thought so, but seeing her there, she was so sad. It was just all so unfair." A sob escaped from her throat, and Ansel began to weep for her younger self.

Ansel babbled through her tears, "She did not think she was better, she was just shy and awkward. I mean, I did not think I was better, I was just shy and awkward. I was five turns old, for Goddess sake! Just a little girl. Of course she, I mean I, did not deserve to be treated like that. That was cruel. I was so lonesome. So alone. Meta was busy, I visited my uncle as often as I could, but he was out in Amnisos. It was too far for me to walk by myself."

Her voice growing softer and quivering, Ansel gave in to her tears and wept bitterly for several minutes. When she finally dried her eyes on her robe, she understood that the little girl she had been was neither ugly or stupid nor undeserving. An empty spot in the very pit of her stomach, one she realized had been with her for a very long time, was suddenly not quite so empty. She placed a palm just beneath her ribs and took a moment to marvel at the miracle of healing that had begun.

But the journey was far from over. Ansel trembled as she peered down the dark hallway in front of her where moments ago she would have sworn was the courtyard at Knossos. She both dreaded and yearned for the fathomless hallway to end at center.

She now walked less steadily and clung to the right side of the passageway. The walls were a strong smooth support. Another sharp bend appeared, this time to the right. Ansel hesitated, then set her chin and deliberately turned with the path.

There stood her Meter, and next to her, Ansel's GranMeter, Thesmas. Both women bore deep frowns and had their arms crossed over their chests. They stood preternaturally large over Ansel, casting immense shadows. Ansel stopped and gaped up at them.

"Meta?" she asked.

Phoebe looked down her nose at Ansel and said. "I am the most beautiful, elegant and graceful woman on all Kriti." Ansel, her mouth open in surprise, continued to stare up at her very large meter. After a moment, she laughed. "That is nothing my meta would ever really say."

She turned to Thesmas. Her huge GranMeter looked down her long nose and said, "I am the wisest and most important woman on Kriti." Ansel shook her head and snorted. "That may be true Gran-Meter, but my, have you grown in stature!"

The voice from within Ansel said, *Yet, this is what you tell yourself about them. Their size is your creation. What else do you notice about them?*

"Well, they are big. Huge!"

You stand in the shadows they cast.

Ansel looked around and realized it was true. She was standing directly in their shadows. "Well," she said, "they cast huge shadows too."

Step out from their shadows, Ansel.

"You mean right here? Right now?"

Aluneia the ThreadHolder answered. *Symbolic steps are powerful, Ansel. This is why we perform ceremonies, the symbols help create the reality.*

Ansel nodded, feeling the truth in the statement. This was another Mystery then; symbols and symbolism speak deeply. With concentration and careful intent, she stepped out from the shadows of her Meter and GranMeter. It was as if a heavy yoke lifted from her shoulders. She marveled at the lightness she felt. "I did not know," she mumbled. "I really did not know."

Ansel stepped around the next corner, and then stopped dead. One more length and she would have fallen off the cliff overhanging Amnisos. She pulled her foot back as she saw and then felt the linen bandages around her ankle. With both trepidation and resignation, she peered over the cliff down to the beach. People stood on it, calling to the boats where they bobbed. Her dread suddenly overcame her conscious knowledge that this was a hallucination. At the top of her lungs she screamed, "Run! Run! The wave is coming!" As before, a couple of men broke from the mob and turned, racing for the cliff steps. Even knowing what happened next, Ansel shouted encouragement to them, "Run! The wave is coming!"

And then it came, higher than she had even remembered, pounding the fisherfolk's boats that lined up at the crest in an onslaught of death. She heard the water, terrifying in its roar, saw the moment just before it crashed upon the beach wiping out the people in slow motion. But then, the water of her vision turned into a giant human fist, immense fingers curled so tightly they were whitened. It hammered the beach, smashing people, village, and sand alike. Ansel's knees gave way and she collapsed, her eyes never leaving the gruesome scene. The fist receded in a wave of smoke; the beach was empty.

The Caster of Nets appeared, as Ansel somewhere deep inside knew she would. Again, the giantess who gathers the dead looked directly at Ansel and into the girl's soul.

"See, little one. There is more here than water. The fist of the dominators has appeared, lo even here in the lands of She of Ten Thousand Names. As I speak to you now paths are being taken, destinies set, and She–who–stands–at–the–Cross–Roads likes not the road chosen. But we may not interfere. It will be long ere the children of the Great Meter can rest safely in Her blessed arms again on this land. I grieve for the children." A large tear fell down the deeply wrinkled cheek of the Caster. She laid down her glimmering net before Ansel and vanished.

Ansel cried out, "Wait, Goddess, do not go! Tell me more!"

A male voice replied softly, right next to Ansel, "She has gone, Ansel. She has told you all She can." Garin stood next to the startled girl.

"Garin! Garin, how are you here? We have looked and looked for you, how can you be here?" But then she realized this was not the flesh and blood boy Garin. Garin was dead; it was his specter who had spoken. She saw now that he stood next to another boy whom she did not recognize. Vaguely she perceived the shades of an entire group of young men standing behind Garin.

"Garin," she choked, her voice lowering a pitch, "What has happened?" She felt herself swallowing convulsively.

The ghost of Garin nodded at Ansel's recognition of his state. "Yes, we are dead, all of us, myself, Ganymede, all the rest. We were sacrificed to the Bull God. It is a terrible force, birthed in obscurity, which grew slowly, hiding in desolate places. But now it is a great power and a fell one. It must be stopped, Ansel. Shedding the blood of innocents brings forth brutality. That which is kindly and loving is repelled. All that is joyous is silenced. All that is good becomes perverse. A shadow falls across the lands. We have come to tell you, Ansel, it must be stopped. You must help stop it, you and your Priesera sisters, your daughters, your descendents. "

"How, Garin? How can I stop it? What must I do?"

"I do not know, Ansel. I only know that it is up to the Priesera and you must lead them. She of Ten Thousand Names bids you to stand in your power now. It is She Herself who calls. If we are to again stand in the loving embrace of Great Meter, you must act."

Then, Ansel was again alone in the labyrinth. No, something moved at her feet – a small snake. It gleamed with green luminescence as it wriggled before her, leading her on the path. *Snake omen,* Ansel thought with a hint of weariness. *The wise say to watch for change when the snake appears. I think it comes overlate this time.* She felt drained, but willed one foot in front of the other. The snake skimmed the floor sinuously leading Ansel onward. A turn, Ansel held her breath. *No more,* she pleaded. The hallway was agreeably empty.

The snake slithered along at a leisurely pace. Slowly, Ansel felt her strength return. Another turn, and Ansel saw the center of the labyrinth. She stopped, the snake continued the last remaining paces into the very middle. It coiled itself into a circle and bit its own tail. Suddenly, a vortex of dust blew up and where the snake had been stood a tall daunting woman, both great and terrible. Her long, black, curly hair was blown from her shoulders as though she stood in a brisk wind. Indeed, there was a gust of sea air and Ansel involuntarily shuddered, clasping her arms tight around her shoulders as she stood in awe. The woman wore the gown of the Priesera – long flounced skirt, rolled at the waist with a blouse completely open exposing prominent full breasts. Her arms were extended and in each hand She held a snake. Her face was grim and terrible. The effect was commanding, even frightening. Ansel dropped to her knees.

"Get up, Ansel. We have no time for frailty. It is already late," the Goddess said in a booming voice.

Ansel gulped, but found the strength to arise to her feet. "Goddess," she said in a voice she hoped did not betray her terror. Ansel recognized Her as She who had marked Ansel at the beach that night so long ago. "I have come to you."

The Goddess smiled a little as she regarded Ansel. "My visage shocks you. You knew not who called you that night. I hid my full countenance so I would not frighten you then. Tonight, you must know."

"Snake Goddess, She–Who–Brings–Wisdom–Through–Change, The Caster's daughter, Akakallis. of the Underworld, of course I know you. I am humbled that you chose me."

"And also frightened."

"And also frightened," Ansel agreed.

"Change is coming, Ansel, my chosen. I am Goddess of Wisdom, yes. But tonight I claim my new title, Goddess of Meter Right. You are the first of my chosen who will bear my new standard. Others will come. I chose you because you love what is. You will ensure that the changes include She of Ten Thousand Names. We will be called the Erinyes, the Gorgons, the Furies, the Andromache. In time, we will join with other women from other places."

"The Emetchi?"

"Yes, the Emetchi and others. Already the change begins. Sides are being chosen. You must bring clarity, Ansel. You must be firm in your loyalty to Kriti and the life Kriti represents."

"I could be nothing otherwise."

"Daughter," said the Goddess, "To lead, you must serve. To inspire trust in others, you must live utterly in faith. The mountain crumbles to sand, then the Great Meter pushes it up again. The rain drop becomes one with the mighty oceans, then draws up to the clouds again. In this life, you have chosen to dance with the Underworld Maiden. This opportunity is at hand. Trust in the path of your heart and others will follow."

Chapter 48

Everything had changed, yet nothing had changed. Ansel was exhausted after her time in the labyrinth. The next day she was excused from classes but not from tutoring. She slept all morning and then made an appointment to talk with Priesera Aluneia that evening after dinner. She felt on edge with Theseus; she was exhausted from her Journey and there was so much to think about, so much to absorb, so much to understand. It was hard to concentrate, let alone show understanding. She repeatedly snapped at him for minor mistakes. When he again expressed his opinion that Kriti should formally arm, the distress she felt boiled over into querulousness.

"Have you learned nothing, Theseus? I have told you repeatedly; we wish not for an army. We wish not for fortresses! You come to the most sacred place on Kriti to make mockery of us. May Goddess dash your soul against the rocks." Ansel glared at him.

Theseus clutched his hair within his fists. "Ansel, you are wrong. I speak only of protection. I know the ways of the outside world. You do not. You think Goddess will lay Her arms about this island and save her from invasion. I only wish it were so."

"How do you know She will not? She has fierce faces too. And protective ones. She is called The Goddess of Ten Thousand Names. Some are capable of brutality. Why would She allow Her own people to submit to cruel and evil invaders?"

"Look to history. Does She protect Babylon? What of Macedonia? Even Catal Huyuk, from where your people originally hail. Your ancestresses migrated here from a nation invaded."

"To here. To Kriti, where we are isolated, where we are safe. We are the most advanced civilization in the world." Her lower lip curled and she thrust her fists upon the waist of her skirt.

"Which makes Kriti even more susceptible to envy." Theseus sighed and dropped his hands next to his knees on the mattress. "Ansel, all wars are holy wars and none are. Goddess is on everyone's side and no one's. Kriti is the last vestige of the old religion, therefore by definition Kriti is the enemy of the new."

Ansel crossed her arms in front of her chest. "What of the Emetchi nations? Are they not another vestige?"

"They are armed, their settlements are scattered across large areas of land, and none of them promise the wealth of Kriti. As a target, they are far less attractive. Ansel, you need to understand this; it is not a matter of if, but of when. Kriti must prepare herself."

Ansel stomped a foot. "How can you say this, you who claim yourself a hero of noble and honorable intent. What is honorable about self–destruction? What is noble about becoming that which you most hate? Where is your faith in She who loves Her children? What you claim to love about Kriti is exactly what you seek to destroy. To arm her, to fortress her, is to glorify all which you claim to have laid aside."

"Your meter understood, as does the Elder Council. Do you think I do not know the trade they made? I am here at this University only because Kriti desired alliance with Athena and this alliance is only advantageous to Kriti because Athena possesses an army. Ask your meter. She at least understands. She is as realistic as she is beautiful."

"Implying, I suppose, that I am neither." To compare Ansel unfavorably to her meter was exactly the wrong thing to do when she was in such a foul mood. She felt her eyes blacken with outrage. "Do not think you understand the first thing about my meter. Do you think she has any true feelings for you? You were her assignment, nothing more. You have been here long enough to understand. Do you not know the truth about Escorts yet? She manipulated you to tell her everything she wanted to know then reported every word you said to the Council. You probably do not remember even half of what you told her."

Theseus fell silent. He stared out the window across the room from where he sat on his cot. Ansel shifted from foot to foot, beginning to feel guilty that she had thrown this into his face. Probably he had figured it out. Probably he had not wanted to think about it over much.

"I am sorry," she began, but Theseus thrust out his palm and stopped her. "I know," he said simply. "I know about the connection she made to me. I know I behaved like a love sick fool. I have known now for many cycles, ever since I was instructed how to throw forth tendrils of energy myself. I knew what she had done. I felt ashamed."

His frank confession startled her. She felt her anger and self–righteousness drained away and she sank slowly onto his cot next to him. Suddenly she felt merely tired. "It was cruel of me to be so blunt," she said finally. "I am sorry. I stood in the shadows of my Meter and GranMeter so long. Until now, I had no clear idea of just how resentful I am to be compared to my meter." She blinked back tears. "Please forgive me. It is difficult to be the ordinary and grace-less daughter of such a, well, of my meter."

"You? Graceless? How is it possible that you consider yourself so? You are as beautiful as your meter, if not more. You are a Grace Herself when you step into the room. Ansel, how is it possible you do not know this?"

But Ansel could not take in his words. They bounced away from her like pebbles off armor. She dropped her gaze and began picking at her fingers. After several moments, she looked up again and said, "My Goddess calls me to defend Her, to fight the changes to come. But how can I do this? What if some changes are inevitable? I know that some forces are far too large for one human, even any group of humans, to overcome. Yet, this is my charge. How can I safeguard the nation I love when the very threat of change triggers that change?"

"Ansel," Theseus said, his eyes deep and soft, "I have no answers. What you say is undeniably true. But what I have to say is true also; my heart is here now and I would defend Kriti, but I grieve for the destruction that will come of such defense."

"I wish that Kriti could remain isolated," she replied quietly. "Perhaps it will, Theseus." She turned toward him fully, searching his eyes for any sign of hope. But she found none and her courage failed. Impulsively, despairingly, she threw her arms around him, pulling him close, seeking the comfort of a friend.

The shock of the touch was startling and Ansel pulled away clumsily. Theseus caught her shoulders and looked into her eyes with a probing expression. "I . . . I have to admit that in part, Ansel, my heart lies in Kriti due to your presence."

Ansel felt her heart thump. "I do not know what to say. I do not know what I feel," she stammered, twisting to escape his grasp.

But Theseus grabbed her hands, held them hard, and would not let go. An unfamiliar thrill surged through Ansel's body in response to his touch. "Say aloud how you feel," Theseus urged. "Say it aloud to me. We will work to understand it together."

"I am your tutor."

"I know there is more."

Ansel wrested her eyes from his and glanced down at her lap where his hands clutched her own. She was trembling. "I do indeed feel something," she whispered. Wondering, she looked back into his eyes. "Yes. I do. I do feel something more for you."

Theseus eagerly jerked up one of her hands and kissed her fingers roughly. She felt drawn deeply into his large dark eyes, a force at once magnetic and penetrating. He leaned forward and kissed her lightly, then more forcefully upon the lips. She was surprised at the intensity of her reaction. A jolt, like a bee sting or perhaps more like a bolt of lightening, surged through her. She parted her lips and pressed them passionately against his. He wrapped his arm around her shoulders, then their mouths separated and he hugged her close to himself.

"I have longed to hold you thus." He murmured into her ear. She pulled back, then touched his cheek. She smiled slightly.

"You are very beautiful, Theseus. Your skin is soft." She giggled at her own brazenness, feeling giddy. "Your eyelashes are so long." Bravely, she kissed each eyelid lightly.

He leaned toward her and kissed her deeply again, this time placing his hand first on her shoulder, then sliding it down slowly. Ansel gasped a little when he began to cup her breast first through the robe, then as he slipped his palm underneath the cloth. She felt her thighs grow moist as Theseus gently fondled her nipple between his fingers.

He kissed her neck as he gently slipped the robe down from her shoulders. Gazing at her naked breasts, he said. "You are lovely, just as I imagined you would be." He then lowered his mouth to a nipple to gently suck at it while caressing the other. Ansel could not restrain a soft gasp of pleasure.

Pushing him back gently, Ansel said, "I have not been with a man, or really, anyone, before. I think I know now why I waited. I was never certain who I was and therefore was very certain that no one else knew me. I did not want to share intimacy as my meter's daughter or as the granmeter of the First Elder. I wanted to love as Ansel and know that my lover knows I am Ansel and no one else. Does that make any sense to you?"

Theseus nodded. "And now you have found Ansel?"

"Now I know she exists as an independent person, anyway. I am finding her . . . me, as I go along. I know an Ansel who is more than daughter and grandaughter. I was not sure of that before."

"Congratulations." Theseus grinned.

Ansel returned the grin somewhat ruefully, then loosened the knot of her own robe and pushed it completely free of her body. Naked, she rolled to her knees on the bed and guided Theseus to his back. At his side, she gently worked loose the knot of his robe. He slipped it open and Ansel straddled his hips, gliding her moistness against him, coupling with him.

Chapter 49

Later after the evening meal, Ansel once again sat across from Aluneia in the Elder Priesera's office. This time, she found herself looking directly into the deep eyes of the older woman, no longer as afraid. After facing Akakallis, Elder Priesera Aluneia seemed merely human.

The outer edges of Aluneia's eyes crinkled, hinting of a smile. "I see the changes in you Ansel. I followed your journey into the labyrinth and heard your thoughts, but tell me, what did you learn?"

Ansel shook her head slightly. "Elder Priesera, I am to serve the Maiden of the Underworld, Akakallis of the snakes. I am stunned and honored beyond my comprehension. "

"Yes. I understand. Akakallis has called few to Her service. Times are changing and now She is intent on gathering Priesera. Do you know what you are to do next?"

"Not clearly. She said there would be others called to Her. I do know I will have to journey to Knossos to tell my meter and the First Elder about Garin. I will know when the time comes. For now, I will return to my studies and look within."

Aluneia nodded. "That seems wise to me, Ansel. How different your path will be from that of your meter and granmeter. It seems to me that Akakallis has chosen well."

Tears sprang to Ansel's eyes and she restrained herself from hugging Priesera Aluneia. "Thank you for saying that, Elder Priesera. I will do my best to serve Akakallis and the Priesera well."

"One more thing," Aluneia said as Ansel stood to leave. The Elder Priesera took a linen–wrapped bundle from her desk and handed it to Ansel. The novice Priesera unwrapped the gift to find a wide silk sash sewn into a looped knot – her sacred Priesera knot.

"Sew it yourself onto your formal robe during a dedication ritual to Akakallis, Ansel. You enter your Third Spiral as an Initiate."

Iphikeles was not impressed with Helen Demetria. It is no wonder the Bull Son, Great Minotaur, scorns the worship of His Meter. Look what it has done to this woman

Still, Iphikeles maintained careful control of his true feelings; it would not do to allow the powerful ruler of Athena and the surrounding areas, including the mighty city of Mycenae, to suspect that she was the object of scorn. This was especially true given the nature of the visit; to obtain aid in their quest. No, it would not do to alienate this wealthy personage who also wanted Theseus captured and killed – even if for entirely different reasons.

"I have been sorely betrayed by Kriti." Demetria began as the men, including Nikolas, Iphikeles, and several other members of the sacrifice religion of Heria, bowed to her. "I was promised by the Elder Council that they would get rid of Theseus for me. Yet, I am told he lives."

"Sadly, this is true, My Helen." Nikolas said. "I have it on impeccable authority that he is hidden in the mountains of north central Kriti, at their Priesera University." He shook his head. "I am saddened and angered by this treachery, Helen Demetria. The worthy nation of Athena does not deserve this duplicity. It is as a citizen of Kriti that I make the offer to finally and utterly rid you of him."

Helen Demetria glowered at the group, but Iphikeles intuited that it was drugged fury at Theseus and Kriti and not directed at the men before her. She continued in a slurred voice, "I feel no further obligation to ally with Kriti, regardless of your actions. However, I will offer help. It is my understanding that you wish to capture him unharmed so that you may turn him over to the Bull God, is that correct?"

"Yes, Helen, that is correct. We seek to offer perfect sacrifices to Him whom we call Minotaur. We believe the offering of Theseus will assuage his rage at our people for not worshipping Him properly. Then, He will stop seething and we will again live as we always have."

"So, you desire resources to assure a quick and quiet confinement, and to spirit him back to Heria."

"Yes, Helen. We need our activities to remain unknown to the rest of Kriti, at least until the sacrifice is done, otherwise the Priesera will try to stop us." Iphikeles sighed, thinking about the limited understanding of the Priesera. "When Minotaur is appeased," he continued, "the people will understand that we were forced to perform sacrifice, that it is a sacred act to Minotaur and not an affront to their Great Goddess." He gestured toward the monarch with open palms. "It is known that you keep a supply of mekoi. This is something we cannot purchase in quantity without rousing suspicion. You, however, can." Demetria nodded. "We also ask for the use of a sturdy boat that holds up to ten men that will be unrecognizable to our own fisher and trader folk," Iphikeles finished.

Demetria's expression was inscrutable, but she waved a hand to an assistant. "Track Alekki. Tell him I need to see him as soon as I may. He spent Cronetide at the shore here and I believe has not yet returned to Egypt." Turning her attention back to the men of Heria and Kriti, she said, "I will have someone notify you when I have what you need. It may take up to several quartercycles. Prepare yourselves for launch by early Metertide. If I can get the resources to you earlier, you shall have them. Every moment that Theseus lives is another moment too long for me."

Iphikeles bowed low. "May Minotaur smile on our venture," he said humbly.

Chapter 50

There was no joy in the Maidentide for Geneera. Nothing, nothing was the same. No ephemeral flowers, no cheery birdsong, no goat kids leaping in circles, kicking up their tender hooves to the bright sun, nothing touched the dread emptiness of her darkened soul. Ua had changed. After her visit to that hag, suddenly it was as if a different person inhabited a familiar and beloved body. No more was Ua the gentle, smiling companion with the bell–like peal of laughter. No more was Ua the passionate lover whose body trembled at Geneera's touch. She was replaced with a stranger, someone Geneera did not recognize, someone who did not love her anymore, someone who was taken by the song of the caves. And Geneera was cut adrift at the University, a sad crippled figure who haunted the herbal garden and stared at worried friends with empty eyes.

After Ua went to see the Seer, she had gone directly into the Labyrinth of the Priesera. Several hours later, she was carried out by the healers; her lovely dark hair had turned completely white. For a full quartercycle, Ua screamed in delirium. The Eilithyliad, who had been Ua's ThreadHolder, would not explain. "It is our way," is all the answer she would provide to the distraught, pleading Geneera.

When Ua came to herself, she did not even ask for Geneera. Since earning her Priesera knot, she only wanted to speak with the Seer. A full cycle passed before Geneera could even bring herself to confront Ua. She just could not drift anymore, lost at sea. She needed words with Ua, even if they were not words she wanted to hear. One morning, having spent the entire night before summoning her courage, she burst into Ua's room at the healing house, but then stopped short in surprise. Clothes were stacked into neat piles on the bed and Ua was packing some of them into a leather travel sack. Ua stopped as she looked up at Geneera.

"Ua, where are you going?"

"I am leaving tomorrow morning with the Eilithyliad to visit the sacred cave of Skoteino."

Geneera felt her knees tremble. "Were you not even going to tell me?"

Ua dropped her eyes. "I was undecided. I thought I would just pack first. I was afraid you would want to stop me."

"I do want to stop you."

"You must not. This is my calling. Please do not interfere, Geneera." Ua wore the formal open–breasted robe all the time now. Geneera gazed sadly at the tiny, firm breasts that she had once known and loved often as Ua resumed folding her few articles of clothing and sliding them carefully into the leather sack. When Ua turned her back, Geneera stared morosely at the new Priesera Knot between the Initiate Priesera's shoulder blades. The heavy silk ribbon seemed to have bound her lover's heart.

Geneera's legs gave out and she dropped heavily onto Ua's bed. "I will not try to stop you then. When will you be back?"

"I do not know exactly. But the Eilithyliad spends the Crone season here every turn."

Geneera rose to her feet again abruptly. "Are you telling me you will not be back until it turns cold again? Ua, how can you do this to me?"

But Ua's eyes had turned cold themselves and her lips formed a thin line. "You see why I hesitated to tell you."

"Tomorrow? You are leaving tomorrow?" Geneera's heart grew heavy in her chest and her vision became blurry with unshed tears.

Ua bit her lip. Her voice was softer. "Tomorrow, yes. First to Knossos for a quartercycle or so, then to the cave."

"Knossos. Can I come with you as far as Knossos? When you leave, I have no reason to stay here. It hurts too much. Maybe Ansel's meter can find something for a lame girl to do in Knossos."

Ua shrugged. "Do not expect I will be able to spend time with you. I will be busy attending the Eilithyliad."

Geneera could not stop the tears from silently sliding down her cheeks, but she refused to give in to the release of a sob. Instead, she shrouded her heart in deep empty shadow, finding some strange comfort in the emptiness she found there.

The journey back to Knossos was lonelier than Geneera could have imagined. On the first day, a cool drizzle made her leg ache constantly, but her heart ached even more. Although Geneera's eyes followed her every movement, Ua paid little attention. Instead, she spent every moment hovering around the old Seer. The Seer did not speak a word to Geneera, though she did not seem in any way hostile toward her either. She seemed utterly indifferent and so did Ua. That night Geneera laid her sleeping blanket away from them and quietly cried herself to sleep.

When they arrived at Knossos the following afternoon, Phoebe stood at the southern entrance of the Agronos, holding the hand of a toddler on each side, awaiting them. She always knows, Geneera thought, and somehow she found this idea mildly comforting, or at least familiar.

But even Phoebe did not seem her usual self. A furrow had appeared between her brows and she murmured something privately to the Seer and by default, Ua who stood close by. Geneera, a few paces back, did not hear the exchange. But when Phoebe turned to Geneera, she wore her customary smile and said warmly, "I am glad you have returned to Knossos, Geneera. We will talk later. Right now I need to confer with the Seer, but I promise I will speak with you at dinner. Do you need to rest? The room you shared with

Ansel is aired out and a bed freshly made up. You can stay there for now."

Geneera nodded numbly and trudged up to the room she shared with Ansel only a few turns ago. It seemed as if lifetimes had passed. Dropping her small bundle on the floor next to her old bed, Geneera limped to the window and looked out over the courtyard. Familiar sounds drifted up to her ears. The Bulldancers! They were practicing just on the other side of the Agronos walls – she knew the noises of the calls and grunts well though she could not see them from where she stood. On impulse, Geneera hobbled down the stairs and out the west entrance, just as she had even before she joined the dancers' troupe. She tried to jog to the side of the Agronos, but her leg would permit only an awkward, shuffling gait. She slowed to a walk, surprised to feel slightly winded by her effort.

She watched the dancers practice for about half an hour until they took a break. Fatima was the first to spot Geneera. She waved and yelled something to the others that Geneera did not hear. Soon most of the team were running over. "Geneera! How good to see you! How is the leg?" Carea hugged her hard and for a few moments Geneera could almost believe nothing had really changed. But when the coach again signaled for practice to begin, the young dancers called their farewells and jogged back to the training without her. Geneera had not thought it possible to feel more alone than she did before. She hobbled slowly back to her room in the Agronos.

When dinner time finally arrived, Ua actually sat next to her. "Where is the Eilithyliad?" Geneera asked.

"She and Mistress Phoebe are still talking. Mistress Phoebe asked me to tell you that she regrets not speaking with you this evening, but something important has come up to which she must attend. She asks that you come to her study in the morning and share breakfast with her."

"What is happening?" Geneera stared at Ua's white hair, longing to touch it. Ua frowned.

"Mistress Phoebe is worried about omens she has received from the fire mountain on Heria. She is afraid a great crisis is coming. She has asked the Eilithyliad to search for vision regarding it."

"Can she do that away from her special cave?"

"It is difficult, but not impossible. She will go into the great underground dark beneath the Agronos this evening to search the Underworld for messages. I was excused to eat, then I must return to tend her."

"How did she ever get along without you?" Geneera asked grumpily, then regretted it when she saw Ua's offended expression.

"She honors me to allow me to be her apprentice, especially since I have not even finished my training. I need her teachings much more than she needs the bit of care I provide."

At the chastisement, Geneera dropped her head to blink back the tears she refused to let Ua see.

Ua pursed her lips. "Geneera, I need to tell you something. I am also a Seer. We are different than the other Priesera. Our relationship is only with Goddess. There is no room in our hearts for more. I may return to the Priesera village in Cronetide, or even earlier, but I can no longer be in a relationship with you."

Geneera gasped at Ua's bluntness, though her words were hardly a surprise. "You are saying you will never be able to have a partnership with someone outside of the Seer Priesera?"

"Even maintaining a relationship within the Seers is extremely rare. Often one does not enter the Seer path until one is quite old; past their time of child rearing and of love relationships."

"But not you."

"No, not me," Ua agreed. "I feel the call powerfully, though I am young. Once the caves call, there is no returning to a normal life."

Geneera shook her head. "How can you know? What of everything you are forsaking?"

"The Seers foresaw my coming. They sent Dia to find me, to save me from my homeland. The caves themselves told them I was a Seer. It is my destiny. It is also what I most want."

And no one knows better than I what it is like to know what you want most, Geneera thought to herself. *Or to have it denied you.*

After gulping some food, Ua rushed back to serve the Seer. Geneera found herself sitting alone. Her own food lay virtually untouched in her bowl; it was tasteless in her mouth, the textures vaguely irritating. She gave up trying to eat and decided to return to her room. The slick stairs up to the apartment seemed especially difficult to manage and she finally gave into an urge to drop to her knees, crawling up the last few steps like an infant. She sat on the cold marble top step and holding her face in her hands, leaned against a featureless limestone base, shutting her eyes against the garishly painted cypress pillar.

I will not cry. I am finished crying, she insisted to herself, but the tears heedlessly rolled down her face. *Maybe I can apprentice with one of the crafts here in Knossos. I could speak with Phoebe about the leather guild.* The thought sparked not even the remotest ember of interest in her breast. Her heart was cold ash. *I am too old to be learning a craft. The only craft I ever cared about was Bulldancing.* She snorted softly to herself. *How ironic; I am educated more than most of the populace. I could teach. I would rather be dead.*

Some part of her seized hold of this taboo, unspeakable thought. *I would rather die than teach. I would rather die.* The thought echoed in her head softly, quietly, like a secret whirlpool, spinning in a distant sea. *I would really rather be dead.* She dismissed it harshly, but then there it was again, like the smile of a new friend, like a comforting whisper, a siren's song urging her to dash her life against the rocks. *I would rather be dead. Ua would grieve. She would hurt like I hurt.*

There was little movement about the Agronos. Below, a handful of kitchen workers were busily cleaning after dinner, others were outside basking in the warm air. The far away murmur of voices rose to her ears like the drone of bees; exhaustion clouded her thoughts. She must have fallen asleep she decided, for suddenly she jerked her head up and it was quite dim where she still sat at the top of the stairs.

The staircase appeared elongated from the top, the bottom lost in curved shadow. Geneera yearned for the sunlight but instead a long, lonely night loomed ahead; morning was a long time off, if indeed it ever came at all. She grasped the pillar and awkwardly pulled herself from the step, her woolen robe catching under one heel. She was unsure where to go. The room she had shared with Ansel was so full of memories and old dreams. She dreaded returning there. *I know,* she thought suddenly, *I will go down to the ocean. It is not very far to Amnisos.* The thought cheered her so that the stairs did not seem so hard to hobble down, nor was the walk across the Agronos, down the path and out to the beach so difficult. She met no one; the moon was incongruously bright and full and the path lit far into the distance from the reflection of the white, flat stone slabs. She was weary when she finally reached the ruined town built into the stone jutting up from the shore, but the cyclic rush of the waves as they journeyed up and back was comforting.

The sand sucked softly at her feet, her leg ached and she sat down hard. The dry beach sand snuggled against her bottom and she gave into the space, stretching out full length. Yesterday's clouds had cleared and the stars shone brightly through the moonlit sky. Some few were especially bright. Geneera liked to think they were her special stars. "So you are still there are you?" she said aloud to them. "Why do you watch and not help me? I have lost everything: Bulldancing, Ua, Jerid, Carea, meter, even Ansel." Through her tears, the stars seemed to twinkle even more brightly.

Then, the Thought returned abruptly, unbidden. It was like a voice breathing seductively in her ear. *You could end it all. It would be so easy. How far do you think you could swim with your leg?*

Geneera shook her head to clear it. The sand crunched as she shifted her legs. "No," she spoke aloud. "I do not want to think this."

But the voice continued, ignoring Geneera's protest. *Ua would be sorry. She would cry. So would your meter. They would realize how much they had wronged you. How badly you were hurt. They would be sorry. They would cry.*

"No." Geneera repeated, but this time the quality of her voice was a little less adamant to her own ears.

The pain would be gone. Do you wish to spend the rest of your life watching the 'dancers, knowing you can never be one of them? Do you wish to watch Ua, knowing you can never again have her?

"No! No!" Geneera cried aloud, confused, not really sure anymore if she was agreeing or disagreeing. The relentless voice persisted. *You will never have to miss Jerid again. You will never have to hear the voice of Meter in your head again, knowing she was right the whole time. You will never have to teach. It would be so easy; just look out at the ocean, Geneera, just look out over the Meter Sea. She will take you home in her arms and you will never have to hurt again.*

Geneera did look out at the ocean. Rising to her elbows, she looked. The air carried a sweet yet faintly fetid scent, the salt felt sticky on her body, the spray cool, the sound mesmerizing. It was like breathing, almost exactly like breathing; in and out, the water like thick, dense air. Just like breathing. Inhale a little water; a quick way to end the pain. She rose, against her own volition it seemed, to be closer to the ocean's edge. *Just to look,* she told herself. *Just to look.*

The water rushed to greet her feet and lapped at them hungrily, caressing each toe like an eager lover, sucking them tenderly. She waded in slowly, felt the playful waves swirl around her calves, kissing them, pulling and pushing, inviting her deeper. It felt cold, but cold was exactly right; exactly how she felt inside. Icy. Bitter. Empty. She allowed herself to fall to her knees on the soft sandy bottom, the water swelled around her, catching her gently, rising to her shoulders, eddying about her thighs and arms and breasts, then retreating coyly. The cloth of the heavy robe she wore weighed greatly on her, clinging like a second skin. She crawled in to where the water became deeper. It was a thing alive, the ocean, and it loved her, She loved her, Geneera was sure, more sure than anything she had ever known. She called. She called. Perhaps this was what it was liked to be summoned by a Goddess. Perhaps she had been a Chosen One after all. Geneera pushed off into the deep and swam out far as she could manage, to where the bottom was out of reach of her feet. She felt gratitude that she was special, marked; Priesera–lover of the sea, giving in to the fluid embrace.

Chapter 51

Dia felt as irritated as a pinched puffer fish. For three solid days she had been stranded on Heria in the storms. "My news does not help anyone when I cannot get the message to Aluneia," she fumed.

When the weather finally cleared, she had insisted upon sailing out even if it was late in the afternoon. "I am a meter–suckled good sailor and I can find my way home to Kriti even in the dark," she had snarled when Nadia, who had offered Dia shelter, tried to convince her to wait until morning. "I remember many times my Meter swore up storms of her own when she was delayed. Do not try to stop me." In the end, even the powerful escort Nadia could not stop the head–strong Diatima.

The winds were favorable and in an evening several days later, Dia pulled into the mouth of Amnisos. Dia had to get to the Priesera Village quickly, so she chose to land in the harbor closest to Knossos.

The water sparkled by moonlight and though the shore itself looked dark as a cavern, the moon overhead allowed her to see clearly where the water ended and the beach began. Looking toward shore, she caught glimpse of a shadow of someone standing in the water. Then, she watched the person kneel. *Oh for Goddess' sake, who would be out swimming at night this early in Maidentide? The water is cold!* But something about the person, a woman, Dia decided, caught her attention. In her haste, she might have let it go without further thought, but something about the woman's stance, the somnolent movements, gave Dia pause. She decided to trust her instincts.

Swiftly but quietly, she pulled her little sailing boat in to get a closer look just as the woman splashed and went under water. "Goddess, something is not right over there," Dia muttered aloud.

She waited for the woman to re–emerge, but there was no sign of her. Alarmed, Dia jumped out of the boat into the cold water and swam swiftly to where she had seen the woman go under. It was not very deep; hardly even completely over her head. She ducked under and opened her eyes to look for the woman, but all was blackness. She broke the surface of the water and looked around. No woman. She definitely had not come back up. Dia took a deep breath. Desperate now, she groped blindly in what she hoped was the right location. She grabbed a fistful of material! Gripping it with all her strength, Dia surfaced, pulling the cloth with her. Something heavy was attached.

She kicked the short distance to the side of her boat and grasped the edge. With a mighty tug, she lifted the waterlogged cloth above the surface of the water. A shoulder emerged. She had a hold of a sleeve of a robe. A thrill of strength coursed through Dia and she pulled as hard as she could; a head surfaced, but it lolled. She flung the woman's listless arm over the side of the boat and hooked the sopping robe on a wooden hook lodged in the hull. It was only strong enough to secure a coil of rope, but might hold for a moment or two. The woman's head was now entirely out of the water, but Dia could not tell if she was breathing. Cursing like the Trades-Kore's daughter she was, Dia ducked under the water, sprang off the bottom and with a strength belying her slenderness, shoved the woman's body upward. The top half of the woman now hung over into the boat. Dia swam around the little vessel, where it listed out of the sea from the weight of the unconscious woman. She managed to grab the side and pull herself into the boat. Quickly she slid to the other side, and hauled the body fully onto the deck.

A woman all right. Just Kore probably; not much more than a girl. Her body lay akimbo in a puddle of water and there was no sign of breathing. Dia pushed her onto her back, straddled her belly and began pushing upon her chest using knowledge learned from the beginning of time by all peoples of the sea. In a moment or two, the girl coughed and sputtered, violently expelled seawater from her lungs, then vomited on Dia, herself and the deck. Dia sobbed with relief. Then in the next moment, she spat in fury.

"By the Furies themselves, you fool of a girl, just what were you doing in the water like that? By the Goddess, I should throw you back in."

The girl murmured something incoherently. It sounded like "go ahead." Dia trembled with exhaustion and fear in the aftermath of the excitement. She restrained herself from grabbing the girl by the shoulders and shaking her hard. In the darkness, Dia could just make out her face. She felt a shock of recognition.

"I know you," she said, "from the Priestessing school. You were always around Uazet, that girl I rescued. You are the one with the bad leg."

The girl groaned, tried to sit up, then laid back down again clutching her stomach. Then she curled onto her side and began to sob uncontrollably, Dia's heart softened in spite of herself.

"Hoi, do not try to sit up yet, you will just feel more sick from swallowing all that salt water. Here, let me move you out of that puke." A dripping Dia scooped up Geneera as if she were a small child and slid across the deck with her a few feet. She grabbed the blanket she normally slept upon and placed it over Geneera's quaking body.

Not knowing what else to do, Dia sat down and reached out to stroke the girl's dank hair. Soon, she cradled Geneera in her lap like a baby, murmuring soft words as the lame girl cried herself into an exhausted sleep. Dia leaned back against the mast of her boat, and allowed herself to be lulled to sleep by the gentle rocking of the Sea

Meter. The warmth of Geneera's body kept Dia from becoming too cold. She decided she might as well stay where she was. There was no way she could carry the girl all the way to Knossos and Dia was as comfortable in her boat as she was on the beach. She cursed softly to herself; Great Meter had spoken and Dia's news would have to wait yet another day.

The early morn sun shone in Dia's face. She opened her eyes and shook her head to clear it. Her arm, still cradling Geneera, was all pins and needles. She extricated it from around Geneera as gently as she could.

Geneera woke anyway. Groaning, she covered her eyes and blinked as if the sun hurt her eyes. She pulled herself jerkily away from Dia and cursed. Then she said, "I am sorry."

"As well you should be." Dia cocked her head and raised an eyebrow. "Bet you have got one furious headache. Your stomach settled?"

Geneera nodded, but said nothing.

"Just so happens I have got some willow bark on hand." She reached for her pack, rummaged around in it, then pulled some bark from its cloth wrapping and handed it to Geneera. The girl obediently chewed it, though her distaste was obvious on her face.

After a couple of minutes, Dia asked, "Want to tell me why I had to pull you out of the sea last night?"

Geneera grunted and lowered her eyes. "No."

"You going to try that again?"

"No."

"Good enough, then. I need to dock. I have important information to get to the Elder Priesera. Coming with me?"

Geneera looked up and stared into Dia's face for a long moment, then shrugged and mumbled, "Sure. Nothing better to do."

Dia nodded curtly. "That is what I reckoned."

Geneera's exhaustion and injured leg made the walk towards Knossos slow going. When they finally reached the outskirts of the Agronos, Dia said "I must get back to the Priesera village just as quickly as possible. I have got things to tell Priesera Aluneia. Can you ride a horse?

"A horse? I have never ridden one."

"Well, you are about to learn."

"How in the name of She of Ten Thousand Names did you get a horse? I do not think more than a handful of people on this whole island have a horse."

"Well, uh," Dia cleared her throat, "I won him. When I travel, I usually disguise myself as a boy. It helps me learn things a Priesera might not otherwise discover. I am no threat as a boy, you see. Anyway, there was this man in Ubad who wanted to play tiles with me. If I lost, he could, uh, have me for the night. If I won, I got his horse.

Geneera's eyes were wide. "But what if you had lost? Would he not have killed you when he found out you were a girl?"

Dia chuckled. "He had no way of knowing I am the best tile player in all the islands. Luckily for me, he was a man of honor."

Geneera giggled with just an edge of hysteria.

"Anyway, the other horse belongs to Priesera Aluneia. Luckily she keeps Orimos stabled at Knossos most of the time. Mine is a fury on four hooves. Aluneia's is a regular Grace. I think you will catch on pretty fast. Even at a walk we can cover ground more quickly than on foot. Hoi, how well do you know the Agronos?"

"I grew up here."

"Really? That is good fortune. Do you think you could sneak into the kitchen and get some food? I am in a hurry and want to avoid a formal consultation with Phoebe. She nets me every chance she gets."

Geneera gulped. "I was supposed to meet her for breakfast this morning. I wonder if she is worried about me."

"Not that she should be, right? Well, you missed your meeting, old girl. It is well past breakfast time now. My guess is that she is so busy snooping and chasing her twins that she is not even thinking about you."

"What do you mean?"

"You mean to tell me you grew up at the Agronos and you do not know how Phoebe spends most of her time? She is busy spying on everyone here and at the other Agronos' finding out everything there is to know. And it just so happens I have a piece of information she will want. First, though, I tell Aluneia. Now, about that food."

Geneera nodded.

Chapter 52

Geneera was astounded. Who knew how differently one might feel in such a short span of time? Who knew that it was even possible to fall in love with a member of a different species?

After riding astride Orimos for just a few minutes Geneera was enamoured. *How could I not be?* she thought. Orimos was beautiful with her huge brown eyes, her soft grey muzzle and whitish mane. And the dappled mare was patient with Geneera. She seemed to understand intuitively that Geneera not only did not know how to ride, but that she was lame. The mare stood still as a statue as Dia gave Gen a leg up onto her blanket covered back, then took directions from Geneera as if the horse spoke Kritin herself.

Dia talked to the horse while she slipped a soft leather harness over Orimos' nose then handed the long ends to Geneera. "Here is Geneera, old girl. She does not know about horses, but I know you will treat her with kindness and that she will be gentle with you in return. She will not need to tug hard if you pay attention." Orimos snorted, blowing air out of her great nostrils and whickered softly as if agreeing with what Dia told her. Dia dug a small wrinkled apple from her pocket and held it while Orimos crunched it noisily.

"There now Geneera, Orimos has agreed to carry and listen to you. She is a lady. You keep your end of the bargain and you two will get on fine. She behaves as if she understands words, but you are better off using your body to communicate. Lean in the direction you want her to turn. Press your knees into her sides gently if you want her to go faster. Only use these laces to tell her it is time to stop munching grass and get going. She is a sensitive animal and responds best to kindness. Now Hades," she said, jerking her thumb at the big black stallion whose lead she was holding, "he is another animal entirely, and luckily for you, he is my problem." Hades whinnied loudly, jerking his head up and down as if laughing in agreement with Dia's assessment. Dia thumped him affectionately on his shoulder.

Orimos *was* a lady. She walked gracefully, trotted daintily, even ate with little nibbles, her soft pliant lips extending little kisses to the plant leaves as she brought them closer to her teeth. Hades was graceful too, but he would never be called dainty. He was completely black except for a white star on his forehead and another white blotch on the back of his left hind leg near the hoof. His was a fiery personality – high strung, athletic, and mischievous. He was a perfect match for his human companion. Geneera could imagine red–haired Dia and shining black Hades galloping along beaches laughing together, mane and hair flying, as they leapt over any obstacles in their path. It was fun for Geneera to imagine that someday she too would have a horse of her own to ride and love. As she and Dia rode the path to the University, Gen daydreamed about her perfect horse. It would be deep red–brown, she decided, a big female with tremendous liquid eyes and an outgoing loving, personality. Together they could do anything. Gen suddenly realized that lameness need not be an obstacle to her happiness anymore. She nearly wept at such a possibility.

Riding allowed them to reach the University in one long day's journey. There were many more hours of sunlight this time of the turn and there were a couple more hours of light remaining when they rode up the University hill. They first passed a few lone cottages – those used for the Seers in Cronetide and the one used now for Theseus, Gen knew. They were almost past his cottage when Dia suddenly reined Hades to a stop.

"Wait here. I want to check something." Without further explanation, she jumped off Hades, handed his lead to Geneera, and strode to the front of Theseus' cottage.

Dia told herself that she just wanted to be sure Theseus was still at the University, but as she approached, she simply followed her intuition as it pulled her toward the door."

"What is going on here?" Dia roared when her eyes adjusted to the dimmer light of the cottage she had just barged into. Ansel and Theseus, together in his bed, clearly preoccupied with each other, froze at the same moment. Then they both moved at once. Ansel jumped out of the bed, grabbed her robe, and hurriedly tried to throw it over her naked body. She settled for holding it in front of herself. Theseus meanwhile, wrenched the light wool blanket from his bed and wrapped it around himself.

"Dia!" Ansel finally found her voice. "What are you doing here? I tutor Theseus every afternoon. You know that."

"I do not think this is what Priesera Aluneia has in mind as tutoring, do you?"

Ansel frowned. "I spend much time teaching him. We are not breaking any rules. Why did you just disrupt us and why are you upset?" she demanded.

Dia lost her temper at Ansel's self–righteous manner. "You little fool. What do you know about this boy? Do you know I just came back from Athena? You should be interested to know what I learned there about your lover."

Theseus interrupted. "Athena! Why did you go to Athena? And what do you think you found out about me there? Tell us both."

But Dia knew she needed to tell Aluneia before anyone else, certainly before wasting another moment on this traitorous and dangerous boy–man. Pointedly ignoring Theseus, she said, "Come with me Ansel. Put on the robe, quickly. I am taking you to Priesera Aluneia. We will see what she thinks about your tutoring of 'Priesera Theseus'," she added with a sneer.

For a moment, Ansel looked defiant, but then she slipped on the robe, and said to Theseus more calmly, "I had better go with Dia. Priesera Aluneia should hear about this from me, not her."

Theseus looked sour, but nodded his head in agreement.

Outside, Ansel was startled to see two horses and Geneera atop one of them. Without any explanation to Ansel, Dia took the long thin leather strap tied to the black horse's harness and led them both to the road with the click of her tongue. She jerked her head to indicate for Ansel to follow, glaring openly at her when she did not walk quickly enough to suit Dia. Gen smiled at Ansel gamely, and said a faint "Hoi there," but when Ansel just scowled, she looked straight ahead. It took little time to get to Priesera Aluneia's office

"Hoi, Priesera Aluneia!" Dia called into the office. Ansel thought grumpily, *At least Dia is polite to the Elder Priesera. If she had not just barged into the cottage, Theseus and I would have at least had time to put on our clothes!*

Aluneia came to the door. "Dia," she said, then, looking from the surly Dia to the horses to a scowling Ansel, she said, "Well, it appears we need to talk. Come, I will ask my apprentice Phidra to look after the horses." Ansel watched as Aluneia hugged the pretty grey mare before leaving her to usher the women into her office. Ansel noticed that Geneera too hugged the grey horse and whispered something into Orimos' ear before limping through the doorway.

"I caught her laying with Theseus." Dia said pointing at Ansel before Aluneia even had time to invite them to sit.

"Hmm," Aluneia began.

Ansel interrupted. "If Dia had shown the common courtesy to call out or knock, we would have been dressed and happy to greet her. Instead, she is making a fuss."

"You do not know him, Ansel. He is not to be trusted!" Dia began to shout. Seated between Ansel and Dia, Geneera swiveled her head first to Dia, then back toward Ansel, her mouth open in obvious confusion.

Aluneia raised her hand. "Stop, Dia." Ansel opened her mouth to retort. "No, you stop too, Ansel. One of you speaks at a time. Dia, you start. Report Priesera; what did you learn in Athena that makes you not trust Theseus? Then, Ansel, you can speak next."

Ansel crossed her arms in front of her chest. *What business was it of hers who Ansel took as a lover? Dia had no right to humiliate her this way.*

Dia took a deep breath and leaned back in the chair. She crossed an arm over her chest and shoulder to pat at her ever present kithara. Ansel realized Dia comforted herself by checking that the instrument was still there. "I found Theseus' old war band. Helen Demetria kicked them out of Athena just as soon as she could. No surprise there. They felt no loyalty to her or her brother."

"Did you speak with them? What did you find out?" Aluneia asked.

Dia nodded. "They think Theseus is dead. No surprise that old Demetria told them lies. But here is the treachery; they say he only came here to learn our weaknesses." Dia looked sidelong at Ansel. "They say he had a plan to invade Kriti. Now they believe we killed him and they just might avenge his murder."

"Treachery? That is not possible." Ansel said, sitting bolt upright in her chair. "He loves Kriti. He told me!"

Aluneia again raised her hand for silence. "You will have your turn to speak, Ansel. Let Dia finish her report."

"I think they are only dreaming right now and that we are in little danger from this war band, especially as they are no longer affiliated with Athena. They hated Polymachos more than they longed to conquer us, which is our good fortune." Dia pressed her fingertips together and was silent for a moment, then she continued. "Still, it does not speak well of our boy Priesera, does it? How do we keep him from letting his band of ragtag warriors know that he is alive and well? And since he is the clever one of the group, could he not encourage them to go back to Athena, swallow their pride and await his return? Even if we do not allow him to leave while he is a novice, we cannot force him to stay here in the mountains forever, can we? Was the Elder Council not shortsighted in letting him come here at all?"

"It was not just the Elder Council, Dia, as you well know. I advocated for him too. And the Seer spoke for him."

"But why, Elder Priesera? Why? Though you know I honor your decisions and choices, this is one I never understood." Dia's anguish was clear in her voice.

Aluneia sighed. "There never really was a choice, Dia. The Council, the Seers, and myself – we all knew he was coming anyway. His exact face, his exact name, his exact quest and the time of his coming we could not predict, but we knew he–who–would–force–the–change would come. The question always was, would he come as a lover of Kriti and Her ways or would he come to destroy Her? We gambled that the best chance for Kriti was for him to live here for a time and learn of us so that he could fall in love with us. Our heart is our worship of She of Ten Thousand Names. We know She chose him and the question has always been, will he choose Her too? We could only give Her, and him, this opportunity.

All eyes turned to Ansel, but suddenly everything she thought she knew, all the arguments she was prepared to make, turned to ashes in her dry throat. Dia scrutinized her as they all waited for her to speak.

"What is next?" she finally asked.

It was Dia who replied. "I need to return to Knossos, I believe, to confer with Phoebe." She glanced at Aluneia. "I am hoping you will come too."

But Aluneia shook her head. "No. I think it is Ansel who must go. I trust her."

Dia chewed the inside of her cheek, her jaws moving slowly and deliberately for a time as she considered, and then finally she nodded. "Agreed then. Ansel, we must leave in the morn." To Geneera, Dia thrust out her chin and said, "You coming along, friend? Orimos will pine if you do not."

Geneera smiled grimly and shrugged.

Chapter 53

Several hours before the dawn, the screaming started. Startled from a sound sleep, Ansel bolted upright before she remembered where she was. In a moment she realized that she and Geneera again shared the same set of rooms they had lived in growing up in Knossos. Geneera was already on her feet, throwing on her short skirt.

"That is Ua," Geneera whispered harshly. Without even looking to see if Ansel followed, she hobbled into the dim hallway, stopping only to light a candle from the flickering torch outside their suite.

Ua screamed again. Ansel scrambled from her bed, threw a loose robe around herself and trailed Geneera up the hall. The apartment Ua shared with the Eilithyliad was jammed with people, all crowding in to peer at the shaking girl. The Seer sat in the middle of a cot rocking and muttering something too low to be heard. Ua's eyes were open, but it was not clear that she was truly awake. She trembled and began to shout. "Fire! Smoke and fire! People are dying, can you not see them? Help them! For the sake of the Goddess, HELP THEM!" she shrieked at the top of her lungs.

Phoebe rushed into the room, followed by the healer Priesera Eida and Rheana. Upon recognizing the Elder Escort, the crowd parted, allowing her to draw close to the shaking girl. Rheana grabbed a blanket off the bed and handed it to Phoebe. "Ua, *mel-*

lia," Phoebe said softly, "Ua, can you hear me? It is Phoebe. I am just going to wrap this blanket around your shoulders." The girl made no response as Phoebe gently draped the wrap over her thin, trembling shoulders. Rheana calmly positioned Ua between herself and Phoebe. Unobtrusively, she placed a light hand on Ua's back. Ansel opened her *saria* and saw that Rheana was brushing down the girl's frenetic Radiance.

"I see fire," Ua said suddenly. She looked directly at Phoebe, obviously seeing her for the first time. "There is fire, Mistress Phoebe. I smell smoke. Oh, Mistress Phoebe, I am so sorry. I am so sorry." The girl collapsed into Rheana's awaiting arms. Dia, who had just arrived, pushed through the crowd and together with Geneera who had been hovering close by, lifted the girl and placed her gently on her bed. Someone swathed Ua in another blanket.

Phoebe sat next to the Eilithyliad who was still silently rocking. "Are you well, GranMeter?" Phoebe asked. When the Seer nodded, Phoebe beckoned Priesera Eida to her side. Eida took the Seer's hand and began speaking to her in a low tone. Phoebe stood up and said, "Please, everyone, go back to your beds now. We will attend the Seer and the girl. All is well. The girl has frightening dreams. We will tend to her."

No one was satisfied, but they grumblingly obeyed Phoebe. Ansel, Geneera, and Dia hung back as the crowd dispersed. The Seer still would not speak; Eida stroked the crone's arm and rocked gently in rhythm with her.

"If I am not mistaken," Phoebe said quietly, "it is time to call the entire Elder Council together again. Rheana, send out the message to Phaistos and Zakros. I will send someone to convey the message to Priesera Aluneia and Vasilissa at the University. First I must tell the First Elder the time has come; the Seers' visions have cleared."

Ansel could not return to sleep after the excitement. She wandered down to the open kitchen area for food and found that many others had done the same. The kitchen workers were bustling around hours earlier than usual. The brazier fires were hot and many people already held warm cups of herbal teas sweetened with honey.

The buzz, of course, was about Ua. Some openly complained that she was a nuisance or perhaps jinxed by the Underworld. Geneera, seated on a bench at the side of the patio with Dia, glared at those who dared insult Ua. Ansel feared her old friend would start a fight. She joined them, deliberately pulling up a chair to block Geneera's view of an Agronos weaver who was being particularly vocal in her opinion of Ua. As she passed the woman, she said "Shh. The girl has friends here. You show your ignorance." Ansel marveled at her own boldness as the woman stopped complaining and looked down at her tea.

"Greetings, friends," Ansel said. "I hope you do not mind if I join you? I could not sleep and see that others felt the same. Dia, I hear that GranMeter has sent for Devra, the Emetchi tracker. We are hoping she can discover what happened to Garin. Do you know her?"

"I met her once when I was traveling east." Dia began, launching into a story of her many adventures. The women chatted lightly until the sun rose.

In the time since Ansel, Geneera and Dia returned to Knossos, Ansel had only seen Ua a few times. When she had related her Labyrinth experience with the shades of Garin and Ganymede to First Elder Thesmas, Xeronos, and Phoebe, they wanted her to also tell the old Seer. Ua attended along with the Eilithyliad, and while she anticipated the hag's every need, Ua had not even acknowledged a passing acquaintance with Ansel. Ansel, however, knew to not take it personally. Geneera had warned her; it was not just Ua's hair that was different. When little Damarin ran to Ua knees demanding to be picked up, Ua would have stepped right on him had Phoebe not quickly intervened. Whatever veneer Ua had once been able to display in social settings had disintegrated, leaving only the oddness that so many intuited lay just beneath the surface.

Ansel was concerned for Geneera at first, but it seemed her old friend had found a way to cope with her loss. She spent nearly all her time out riding on a gray horse with Diatima on a huge black one. Geneera had found her grace and athleticism again, and for this, Ansel was glad.

Ansel herself spent much time playing with her little sister and brother. To her surprise, she found she enjoyed talking with her meter and Rheana. She had left Knossos a child and a daughter. She returned a peer and a valued member of the Agronos. She was Priesera now, even if still in training. She wore the Knot between her shoulders and that changed everything.

Late that morning, while Ansel was back in her apartment writing in her personal set of scrolls, Rheana appeared in the doorway. "Priesera Ansel, Mistress Phoebe desires your company if you are available. Priesera Ua and the Seer are with her."

In Phoebe's suite, Ua, looking disheveled, sat slumped on a bench. The Seer sat next to her and stroked the girl's hair.

"Ansel, thank you for joining us." Phoebe said. "The Eilithyliad and Ua planned to leave this morning for the cave of Skoteino, but they have cancelled their journey, at least temporarily. The Seer wants to tell us what she and Ua have seen."

Ua looked up and stared at Ansel. "Greetings Ua," Ansel said tentatively, not sure what to say. Ua just stared and Ansel realized that the girl might not even see her.

"You must excuse your friend," the Seer said. "It is challenging to live with one ear to the cave song and the other in this world. It may be many turns before Ua will be able to make sense of her life. Some of us never do. Imagine having many voices and visions in your mind at all times. It is difficult even to be sure where you are. Many of us do not even attempt to leave the caves or interact with other people. We are never completely sure if someone is a vision or really there. She of Ten Thousand Names lends us these gifts but She demands a high price. We can no longer live as others do. It is a lonely and demanding life."

Ansel nodded. "I thank you for your words, it makes it easier for me to understand."

"There is fire," Ua interrupted. "It is coming. The earth shakes.

The Bull is bloody, bloodied. It burns." Abruptly, Ua placed her hands over her ears and shrieked.

The Eilithyliad took the girl by the shoulders and said gently, "Ua, this is a vision. It is not happening in present time." She turned to the other women and said, "I share some of what she sees." "Let me tell you about it. I believe Ua needs a sleeping draught. We Seers have one we use prepared from the resin of poppies that allows us peace of mind. Ua cannot determine what is happening and it is upsetting her."

Rheana offered to prepare the draught, then left the room leading Ua by the arm as if the young Priesera were blind. The Eilithyliad continued, "I see the Agronos in flames. There has been a tremendous shake and many have died. Ah Phoebe, especially you must beware. I do not know why precisely, but I see you wailing, wailing. Your heart is breaking."

"My babies?" Phoebe thrust a hand over her heart in alarm.

"I do not know. Many are dead. I am sorry I cannot tell you more. I keep hearing in my head the words, "Know thyself, Phoebe, know thyself, be true to yourself."

"But when is this going to happen? How long do we have?" Ansel asked. "Meter, you have called for the Council. Are you thinking it is time for us to leave already?"

The Eilithyliad sighed. "We have some time, I think, but time moves differently in the place of visions."

Phoebe said, "Seer, when the First Elder called for the Elder Council to come, she sent a code word so they will know it is urgent. They knew they would have to make a decision, but I think we all hoped it would not be so soon. May Goddess grant that your visions have come in time for us to save ourselves."

Some things change rapidly and thoroughly, others not at all, Ansel mused. Frustrated, she punched at the unyielding, uncomfortable and completely non–sleep inducing herb scented pillow several times before acknowledging that once again, she was doomed for a restless night at Knossos. Kicking at the scratchy wool blanket she felt certain had bunched around her legs with intentional malice, Ansel sat up in bed and huffed. *My mind is racing and I cannot calm it.* She ran her fingers through her tangled curls and then rubbed her face with her palms. *I have not visited Amnisos in many turns. Perhaps a brisk walk to the beach will help me.* She grabbed a light wrap to break the wind, slipped on her sandals and left the suite, while Geneera snored softly across the room.

Ansel thought it possible she could walk the path in her sleep. How many times had she followed the glittery white stone slabs behind the Agronos north past the outskirts of the town. She could almost believe she was a maid again, so much was the same. Beyond the Agronos were the individual dwellings that became sparse further from the center, then the familiar small trees with their thick bark and thorny leaves to protect them from the goats. The goats themselves, though not visible, still made their presence known with an occasional "blaaaaaah".

Ansel allowed herself to sink into trance as she walked. With the passing of each well–known and well–loved landmark she felt her Radiance swell, reaching out to the trees and the stones, the goats and the houses. It was not long before she was again on the lonely stretch where the path led to the cliff edge. She thought her heart might burst out of her chest with grief and joy.

Again she thought, *So much has changed, yet so much has not. This another Mystery,* she realized ruefully, *the bittersweet experience of life.* Somehow the terribly painful times, the ones that left her on her knees gasping with a crushing sorrow, had also taught her to appreciate the smallest, most mundane joys. Her heart soared just to hear the bleat of a goat, the sigh of the ocean, the wail of a sea bird. Ansel knew in the depths of herself that not one of these things could ever be taken for granted. Every moment was sacred. Each touch, each song, each natural thing was a holy sacrament, each instant filled with wonder and awe. Yet, the grief and loss was always there too, just underneath the surface. Nothing could ever be pure joy or pure pain again. Laughter cycled round to grief, tears cycled round again to elation. It was the way of life, and one could fight against it or embrace it as a most holy Mystery.

Before descending to the beach, Ansel looked over the cliff edge to where Amnisos had once nestled. She had heard the rebuilding of the village had begun, but the darkness hid any trace of the destroyed town. At the bottom of the repaired stairs, she trod carefully on the rocky soil toward the sea, then slipped off her sandals when she reached the soft sand of the beach. The water sparkled where the moonlight reflected off the choppy little waves. Still She inhaled and exhaled, Great Meter sea, a Goddess who gave and who, just as easily, took away.

"Akakallis, Maiden Goddess of the Underworld, who came to take me that night so long ago, I greet thee." Ansel said aloud. Somewhere out in the shoal, a sea bird shrilled a lonely greeting. Ansel sat down on the sand facing the sea, just eluding the grasping waves as they rushed up to inspect the intruder. Disappointed their prey was out of reach, they retreated regretfully, leaving shimmering white foam in their wake. Ansel crossed her legs, wrapped her light cloak around her shoulders and began a breathing practice she had been taught at the University. *Goddess of Ten Thousand Names,* she thought, *I long this night only for peace.*

Abruptly she heard the breathing of another person. Startled, she opened her eyes and looked around, but she was quite alone. The breathing continued; it was heavy, almost a panting. A thought erupted into her mind, but somehow she knew it was not her own. *How long does it take for the drug to take effect I wonder?*

"Hello?" Ansel said aloud, puzzled.

The ThreadHolder! came a surprised response. *Ansel, are you my ThreadHolder? When did you get back to the University? Hoi! These hallways are dark. The walls are so high. The darkness is so thick, I think I could brush it aside with my hands. My legs are wobbly, is that from the drug?*

"Theseus?" Ansel said. "Theseus, where are you? I hear you in my mind. I am not at the University; I am at Knossos." Then suddenly, Ansel understood. "Theseus," she said, "what are you doing in the Labyrinth? You are not supposed to go in there for another turn at least!" But scolding him would not change anything, it was already too late; Theseus was in the labyrinth and she had somehow become his ThreadHolder.

Chapter 54

Everything Ansel knew about threadholding rushed back to her; it was not much. "Almost nothing is as life transforming as the Holy Labyrinth Journey of the Priesera, and Holding the Thread, it is an ancient term for a timeless tradition." Vasilissa had once said. "Literally, the ThreadHolder holds the force of life of the Walker in her hands. It is a profound responsibility. The one who Holds the Thread and the Walker are bound together for the rest of this life."

I must not falter. I must find the Thread beyond the veil and make sure it does not become entangled or snap. He could die in there and it would be my fault. Ansel shook her head trying to clear her thoughts. *It is a binding. Between Priesera, it has always been a commitment of close friendship for life. Theseus and I will be forever bound together in our lives. It is almost a mating. Can this possibly be right?*

But she knew she did not have a choice. Whether Theseus had chosen her or whether it was a deed of the Fates, Ansel could not refuse to be his ThreadHolder. She quickly realized that in his drugged state, he could not read her thoughts, but heard only the words she spoke clearly aloud. She was not certain what she was receiving from him; his thoughts, his words, some vague feelings, perhaps a jumble of it all.

Ansel decided her best strategy was to put aside her fear and increase her trance state. Just as she had been trained by Priesera

Ursula, she took control of her breath, intentionally inhaling, holding it in, and then exhaling. She visualized her breath as a circle, half the arc within her body, half the arc without. Her training took hold and she soon felt less panicky. Opening her *saria* vision, she looked down at her lap. A glowing ball of woolen–like string rested between her crossed legs. From the ball, one glowing strand emanated and disappeared out into the darkness of space. This, she knew, was the Radiance of Theseus she was to watch and guard while he took the Labyrinth Journey.

The words of the ThreadHolder oath came to her. Aloud she said, "I have the Thread, Theseus. I protect you with my own life as you make the journey. I promise I will unravel the Thread gently and surely as you go deeper and deeper in." She was grateful that he could not feel the fear that coursed through her. She resumed her breathing practice as she felt him nod in the darkness.

"I am having difficulty walking." He said. There was a note of alarm in his voice.

"Reach out and touch one of the walls. Allow it to support you until you are accustomed to the effect of the drug on your body. The unsteadiness will pass."

She saw with her *saria* vision that he was now leaning against one wall. "Ansel?" he said aloud. "Are you still there?"

"Yes, go forward. I will not let you become lost."

Instinctively, she began to hum softly, a soothing atonal sound, while she carefully placed her hands around the ball of Radiance in her lap. All went smoothly for several minutes as Theseus adjusted to his drugged state, then Ansel noticed a small fray appear on the Thread. Just at that moment, Theseus turned the first corner in the Labyrinth. Ansel focused her attention on the ball, surrounding it as best she could with comfort and warmth.

Someone stood before him. *Goddess?* Ansel heard him ask. But it was a man. Theseus recognized him as the consort of Kriti. "Consort Xeronos?" He asked aloud.

Then the face changed to Helen Demetria. Shock bolted through him as her heavily bejeweled, deeply wrinkled face glared at him.

Demetria said nothing, but turned away and led down the passage-way. Theseus had to follow or be left in the dark. He regained his voice. "I am not afraid of you, hag," he said. But Ansel felt a sensa-tion of fear she knew was not hers. So, Theseus was indeed afraid of Demetria. Ansel allowed the thought to drift out of her conscious-ness and watched it float off into the ethers of her deep trance state; it would be invasive and distracting to feel everything Theseus felt. Her job was to guard the Thread, not to judge, not to wonder, not to interfere in any way; only to protect.

"Are you not afraid of me? Then you are twice a fool, young The-seus, for the wise know when it is prudent to fear." The deeply lined face of Demetria morphed into the more angular one of Vasilissa, her haughty expression twisted into a mocking snarl. "You think you belong at the Priesera school, do you?" She laughed a horrible, derisive cackle that echoed into the ears of a drugged Theseus.

He started to defend himself, to sputter that of course he be-longed, but she had turned her back on him again and was now several paces further down the path. She called behind her, "Fol-low me closely or you will never make it further than the entrance way." He followed, knowing he had no choice. Ansel continued her gentle hum, watching closely as the frayed section of thread played out from the ball.

They walked the outer curve of the labyrinth in silence, but with each step it seemed the form changed, distorted, until Theseus felt utterly confused. "Vasilissa" had developed a pronounced limp by the time they reached the first turn toward center. She abrupt-ly stopped and turned to face him. "Sit," she instructed, her face hidden in the shadows of the torch flames that flickered along the walls. A bony finger pointed to a bench that had materialized.

"Now, son of the water and the air, let us have a conversation." The figure grew larger, with broad shoulders and a long cloak.

Theseus sat, swallowing convulsively. "How did you know I called myself thus? Did Phoebe tell you?"

"I know many hidden things, boy. Phoebe did not need to tell me." The voice deepened to a rich baritone, "Was I not there myself in my vineyard in Portulos, tending my grapes when you screamed those very words at me just before you slit my throat?" The figure abruptly knelt in front of Theseus who recognized him as one of countless number of men he had killed. In front of Theseus' eyes, the death replayed itself. The man's great bulging eyes first registered surprise and then suddenly, nothing at all. He was hideously dead. A knife dangled, its blade suspended across the man's throat, and Theseus knew it to be his own. Blood spurted from the man's neck, splashing onto Theseus' tunic. But the man, his eyes now sickeningly flat and dead, continued speaking. "My sister and two of her children found me lying in the dirt. There was no need to kill me. I would gladly have given you food."

"I killed you in battle." Theseus sputtered. He winced at the memory.

"No. You killed me in ambush. I was unarmed."

"It was for Athena. I was in the army. We were taking over Portulos, teaching the villagers to fear us. We wanted your village. We wanted as little trouble as possible."

"Ay then. Less gladly would I have given my land and freedom to Athena, but for my family's sake I would have surrendered. I was armed with nothing but a wooden hoe. You attacked me from behind. Do you know the fate of my kin?"

Theseus shook his head. "No." The word sounded impotent in the endless dark hallway.

"Nor do I. I departed for the Netherworld after they found my body."

"I will find them, I promise. I will look after them."

The man jerked to his feet as the face transformed again, the figure changing into a huge man who stood toweringly over Theseus. "Then you will spend the rest of your cursed life looking after the kin of those you killed dishonorably," this one snarled.

Theseus rose too. "But I did not kill dishonorably. I killed to live, then later, I killed for Athena."

"Do not lie. You slew for enjoyment."

He remembered then, the gut thrill of stalking another man

through the brush, the satisfaction when his victim had no time to make a noise, the look of surprise upon a dead face, many dead faces including the face that now stood before him. So many men. But never women. Never children. "I am honorable" he said aloud. The words thudded dully in his ears.

"My family was left destitute when your noble army confiscated our land. My sister's children died because there was no food to feed them."

The face shifted rapidly again and again, but slowly enough so that Theseus knew these to be the faces of all of the people he had killed. He stopped even trying to count.

Something grabbed at his entrails like a great hand. Leaning against the wall he bent over and fought the urge to vomit. "Ah Thea, Ah Thea, what have I done?" he said.

Ansel, rocking to and fro on the beach, tears streaming down her face, blew softly on the ball of thread, watching the frayed section glow; it became stronger and less frayed.

The face of the man changed once again, but this one spoke more gently. Theseus did not recognize him. "Go on, son. There is more you must learn. A noble man claims his actions. A hero faces his challenges."

Another shift, but this face was not human. The lower body remained human in form, but the torso and face, those eyes with their odd horizontal pupils, were definitely those of a goat. Theseus snorted in surprise. "I had heard rumors of people meeting the Bull Son in here, but surely you are a goat–man."

"My appearance is as necessary. To you I am goat. Follow me."

The goat man drew out a cudgel from beneath his cloak, turned his back to Theseus, and hobbled ahead, leaning heavily on the stout wooden branch.

Ansel drew a deep breath. The thread now looked strong as it played out between her hands. Gratefully, she wiggled her toes in the sand to restore the feeling in them. She watched as, for many minutes Theseus followed the goat–man deeper into the labyrinth.

Another fray appeared. Ansel inhaled sharply and prepared herself to envelope the ball with her own Radiance, protecting the Thread against snapping; Theseus in the labyrinth turned another corner.

The goat man stopped and turned to face Theseus. "I am not here to be your goatherd," he said. "I am here to drive you to remember." With that, the goat creature reached out and touched Theseus at his breast bone with a sinewy arm that ended in a cloven hoof. The touch was like the sting of a thousand bees. Theseus felt a shock run through his chest and course through his body. His eyes rolled up his head. The goat pushed Theseus to the floor and commanded in a half–bleating voice, "Remember now."

Theseus floated somewhere above the earth, watching. He saw a slight boy standing in a field, surrounded with goats. The boy appeared to be about seven turns or so, but Theseus knew him to be older. He recognized the meadow, then himself. He was swinging a staff made of wood over his head; it was exactly like the one the goat man shuffled along with. The boy was shouting. Theseus knew the words, "Bow to me, goat." He watched, sickened as the boy clubbed a young goat with all of his strength. Blood spurted in the air, on the boy's face, splattering his shirt. He remembered what came next too: his adoptive family finding the goat, cutting its throat to put it out of its misery, the suspicious looks they gave him when he said a wolf had mauled the animal, their disgust at the blood spatter on his shirt. *Of course they did not believe me*, he thought. *A wolf would have ripped out its throat, not bashed in its head.*

"I remember." Theseus whispered, closing his eyes against the memory. But it would not disappear. Opening them again, he shouted aloud to the goat–man. "I remember. I am sorry. I cannot change what I did."

The goat merely stared at him dully and said, "That memory

was not buried deeply." He extended the cudgel and another jolt struck Theseus. "Remember!" the goat commanded.

In place of the goat–man, another man stood before Theseus, a man with a leering face and several blackened teeth. He seemed far taller and bigger than Theseus and he hunched over the boy; the stench of his breath made Theseus gasp for air.

"I know you. From my nightmares." Theseus whispered.

The man bent over Theseus and snarled, "Earn your breakfast, boy." He raised his arm as if to slap him and Theseus prepared to take the blow. Then, the man unbuckled his belt and made to drop his trousers. Theseus' knees gave way and he was beset with nausea, choking, panting for breath, a vile taste of salt in his mouth. The full content of his nightmares vomited into his consciousness. He remembered this man. How had he ever forgotten? It was not a dream. He screamed and screamed, until his throat was aching and his words incoherent. Salt. Salt in his mouth. Salt in his blood. Gagging.

Ansel cupped the ball of Radiance with gentle hands, allowing the warmth of her palms to pulse into the ball, surrounging the frayed area. "I am with you," she whispered. "I am with you."

Another memory came unbidden then. He remembered a woman, a gentle woman who held him. He remembered her strong arms cradling him. "I am with you," she whispered. Words of a song came to him, one he had heard many times.

> Festival child,
> of luck and dreams,
> impetuous child,
> of the wind and sea,
> I love thee,
> I love thee.

He saw her before him, cradling a toddler, a baby who could only be himself.

"Meter," he murmured. Her eyes were huge, sleepy and dark

like his own, her hair a tangle of soft black curls. She looked little older than he knew himself to be now. He crawled to her down the hall of the labyrinth while she floated just out of his reach. Finally, after many lengths, she stopped. He was at the center of the Labyrinth.

He watched as a group of men came in. He knew what would come next. They were burly and blond, in short leather skirts, gleaming metal daggers hung from their sides; nomadi. He watched helplessly as his young self tried to hide beneath the skirts of his meter, but one man swept him aside with a strong blow. His meter struggled against them. He howled as they overpowered her and she grabbed for one of their knives. Stabbing one of them awkwardly in the thigh, she angered the rest and sealed her fate.

"Meter! Meter!" The little boy screamed. Theseus watched as they plunged the knife into her over and over again, then violated her bloody body. The shrieks of his dying meter rang in his ears like some great keening, howling beast. Theseus rolled himself into a ball. The screams would not stop. In time he realized they came from his own throat.

Ansel fought to maintain control. The thread was frayed thin and appeared bright red with black patches. She watched in horror as an angry swollen knot appeared. The string snagged and would go out no further. As the tension increased, Ansel panicked, afraid the thread would snap. She reached out and wound her own essence around the knot, reinforcing it. *Breathe,* she told herself. *Breathe calmly. Oh Goddess of Ten Thousand Names, help me now!* Not knowing what else to do, she prayed aloud. "Goddesses who tend the life force, Akakallis who Gathers, Ariadne who Weaves the Net, and the Caster, please help me with this thread of life. Please do not allow it to snap here in my hands. Strengthen this thread, untangle the knot."

A golden glow appeared and laid itself over the girl. Ansel suddenly remembered seeing Aluneia overtaken with the Radiance of Pasiphae at her Koretide ritual and knew this to be happening to herself. Gratefully she allowed herself to be guided, expertly pulling back on the strand and releasing the tension while Otherworld hands laid themselves over her own. An ethereal scissors appeared, the Thread was cut and then, by a magic greater than that of any human, the ends were annealed. The injury was gone and still the life force remained. Ansel wept in gratitude for the miracle.

Arms were holding him. Love surrounded him like a healing poultice placed upon his very soul. Theseus felt the grief ease and peace replace it. He opened his eyes to blinding Radiance. Through his tears the light broke into shimmering rainbows. He blinked, shielding his eyes. She was there standing over him. "I am Pasiphae, She Who Shines For All. I have shone my light into your being, for the truth could no longer remain a shadow over your soul. Your truth was painful, Theseus, but the past is a memory which can hold little power over you now. It is yours. As is the future. You now have what you need to move forward."

She touched his forehead. He winced in anticipated pain, but the touch was soft. The open wound that was his heart healed under her tender touch. "Never again will you forget and never again will these memories hurt you this badly. Invoke The Caster. She loves the true heroes, those who possess the courage to face Truth. She has chosen you to lay down the net of destiny. May you choose wisely and grant to others the compassion that has been granted to you."

Chapter 55

Aluneia knew Theseus' cottage was empty even before she tapped lightly on the doorframe. Though it was only mid morn, the essence of life, the trace swirls of Radiance that clung to a room for hours after it had been occupied, was not there. The room felt bereft. Pushing in the door, Aluneia looked around.

A light woolen blanket lay crumpled in a pile on the cot, the sweet grass stuffed head cushion askew at one end. Scrolls lay bound upon the small wooden table that served as Theseus's desk, the ink pot tightly corked, the feather pen clean and laid neatly beside the ink. Aluneia could sense the precision of the occupant, his keen, careful demeanor, his cat–like grace.

Closing her eyes, she widely opened the sight that was without eyes. The force within the room was muddy, murky . . . but there had been movement near the bed. She walked over to inspect it more closely.

"Aluneia, if you are looking for the boy, he is not here." Startled, Aluneia turned around sharply. Priesera Vasilissa, the hood of her cloak drawn up over her grey streaked hair, stood in the doorframe with her arms crossed in front of her chest.

"Vasilissa, you startled me." Her concentration interrupted, Aluneia shook her head to clear it and walked back towards the door, and asked, "Where is he?"

"Early this morning I sent him on an errand for me. I need saffron from the mountain crocuses for the Metertide ritual. I sent him to fetch it. He will be absent several days." Vasilissa stared at Aluneia as if daring the younger woman to challenge her, even if she was Elder Priesera.

Aluneia frowned, puzzled. "I sensed a transformation approaching for him. I am not close to him so I cannot be sure when it is to be. I thought I would warn him."

Vasilissa barked a laugh. "Ah Aluneia, for once you are too late. He has had his 'transformation' as you call it. He dared the Labyrinth Journey last night. He looked as if he had seen a shade or two while in there too!" she smirked.

Aluneia could not figure out why she was so disturbed by Vasilissa's demeanor. The woman's Radiance was red and swirling, but then, Vasilissa was often agitated. She said, "And yet you sent him out this morning on an errand? Vasilissa, that was unkind."

Vasilissa drew herself up and snorted. "He disregards our traditions at every turn. He knew he should not attempt the Holy Journey yet. I felt it was only just that he serves the Sisterhood after he threw dirt in her face."

Aluneia felt troubled. "I wonder who held the Thread for him. I presumed that when the time came, it would be me. I never dreamed he would take it upon himself to enter the labyrinth without proper instruction. Did you look at him closely? Was he truly well enough to go on such a long trip?"

"He was fine, Aluneia. You worry about the boy overmuch," Vasilissa replied with a high pitched laugh.

The sun was streaming into a west–facing window by the time Phoebe finally woke Ansel. She sat on the bed next to her daughter, and gently touched her shoulder.

"I have been waiting for you all morn, Ansel. Did you forget we were to meet?"

Ansel heard her meter's words as if through deep fog. She had been in the midst of a dream. Theseus was in trouble and needed her to guide him, or maybe it was to find him. He was being held against his will, a man with fetid breath leaning over him, threatening him, a goat–man with a cudgel was going to hit him over the head. Shaking herself from the mists, Ansel became aware that her head was throbbing painfully. She looked blearily into her Meter's face; Phoebe's eyebrows drew together in an expression of concern.

"Meter," she mumbled finally, "I had the most extraordinary night." The sunlight was bright and Ansel cupped her hand over her eyes. "I wish to tell you about it, but oh, my head aches."

Phoebe nodded and said, "Come to the dining area with me and we can have some tea. I find if you slip the willow bark into mint tea, it does not taste so wretched." Phoebe slipped an arm around Ansel, helping her sit up in bed. Ansel appreciated the help – she felt weak as a mewling kitten. It was pleasant to be cared for.

"Thank you for your kindness, Meter." Impulsively, Ansel grasped her Meter's forearm and squeezed it lightly. "I am sorry I have taken your kindness for granted. I will do better. Honestly, I am well. Where are the babies? Do you need help with them?"

Phoebe smiled and gave Ansel a quick hug. "No, but my thanks. They are with Xeronos. He loves to play with them whenever he gets the chance." She chuckled. "He carves the most extraordinary wooden toys for them. Who would have thought he would develop such a nurturing side after all these turns?"

Ansel pulled herself up from the bed, smoothed her sleeping tunic, and shuffled to a dressing table where she picked up a shell comb and began pulling the tangles from her hair. She turned to face Phoebe who was still watching her from the bedside.

"Meter, last night I was ThreadHolder for Theseus. He decided to enter the Labyrinth early. I do not believe he told anyone he was going to do it. It was . . . ." She searched in vain for words, then finally shrugged and said, "Have you ever Held the Thread?"

Phoebe blinked. "No. I have not. Usually that is a role only the Elder Priesera or a very few seasoned Priesera ever fill. How did this happen?"

Ansel spent the next several hours with her Meter as she first had a meal, then went to the baths to wash the sand and salt from her hair, all the while explaining how she had been selected, then much of the journey itself. She did not tell all the details of Theseus' experience; she sensed this would be a violation and even Phoebe did not press. Instead Ansel spoke mostly of the necessity for focus and calm and how difficult it had been to sustain.

"I was frightened, Meter," Ansel admitted. "A few times I thought I would fail and Theseus would be lost forever in the labyrinth." Ansel let the water sooth her tired body.

"He was a deeply injured young man, Ansel. You must know that. I believe I would have found Holding the Thread for him a challenge myself, and yet you have done it successfully. I am impressed that you were able to do this."

"He was indeed deeply injured, Meter," Ansel nodded as she wrapped her long hair into a length of cotton toweling. She wrapped the cloth around her head, twisted it firmly around the hair, then folded the end of the towel back over her head. "At one point, I encountered a tangle in the Thread. I almost lost him. I prayed to the Fates and a miracle occurred. Goddess Herself intervened." Ansel felt a renewed sense of wonder and hugged herself at the memory.

"Was he healed?"

"Yes, I believe so. It was so powerful, Meter. I felt humbled to be part of such a healing."

Phoebe nodded. "The Eilithyliad told me that the healing of one soul is as holy as protecting an entire nation." She hugged Ansel close to her.

Ansel was exhausted all that day and returned in the early evening to her rooms to sleep. As she laid her head on her now friendly and perfectly soft pillow, she suddenly remembered the dream from which she had been awakened. Theseus had been calling to her, telling her he was in trouble. She dismissed the dream as understandable after the experience they had just had together. Surely he was as at least as exhausted as she and was safely taking as much rest as he was allowed at the University.

A quartercycle later, Ansel awoke with a start from yet another dream of Theseus calling for help in the dark. She sat up in her bed and shook her head. From across the room, Geneera said softly, "Ansel, are you well?"

"Gen, I keep having these dreams. I hear Theseus calling to me, begging me to help him. He is foggy and does not seem to know where he is. It is dark and hard to breathe. Sometimes I get a sense of motion, swaying back and forth, and nausea."

Geneera pulled herself to her elbow. "Have you spoken to your Meter about the dreams? You were his ThreadHolder. Perhaps he is sick after the Labyrinth Journey and you are sensing his illness?"

"I do not know. I have been thinking and I believe I need to travel back to the University to see if he is well. I finished what I needed to do here at Knossos; Meter and GranMeter know about Garin. Once Devra arrives she will surely find the cave upon Heria. I wonder if Dia will let me go back though."

"She too is finished with her reports to your Meter. She might well be ready to return to the University."

It did take some effort from both Ansel, and finally Phoebe, for Dia to be persuaded to return to the University, especially on behest of Theseus. Dia clearly did not think Ansel should have anything more to do with him.

"Ansel, do not allow your feelings for him dim your wits. He is not to be trusted. He told his warband he was here to learn of the weakness of Kriti. How can you still care for him?" Dia frowned down at Ansel from the back of Hades.

Ansel kicked the grass with the toe of her sandal for a moment, then said, "Dia, I know you find it hard to believe, but I do not want to go back because I want to be with him. I fear for his safety. I think he is in danger and calling to me for help. I need to find out."

Dia snorted. "What sort of danger could he possibly be in at the University? Perhaps he is in danger of succumbing to another novice's advances?"

Ansel felt her cheeks flush and she grew angry. "That was unfair and cheap, Dia." She crossed her arms in front of her chest. "I am going back to the University; you cannot stop me. I will go alone if I must. Something is wrong. You may think it is simple longing or jealousy on my part, but it is not." She bit her lip, then added, "I do think you are wrong about him."

In the end, both Dia and Geneera accompanied Ansel back to the University. Dia said she wanted to keep close watch on Ansel and besides, she was handed the assignment of telling Priesera Vasilissa about the Elder Council meeting by Phoebe. Geneera just went wherever Dia went these days. Or more precisely, if Geneera had a chance to ride Orimos, she took it, and that meant being with Dia. It had been almost a full half cycle since Theseus' Labyrinth Journey and Ansel was nearly frantic to arrive. She had begun to hear him calling out to her even when she was just in a light trance and her dreamtime was filled with nightmares. Always it was the same – Theseus was in the dark, drugged nearly to incoherence, and needing her to find him.

Chapter 56

Ansel was alarmed if not entirely surprised that Theseus was no where to be found in the village. Her stomach knotted when the kitchen women confirmed that no one had seen the boy for at least a quartercycle. She, Dia and Geneera proceeded to the end of the loop road to Elder Priesera Aluneia's study and residence. Dia went in alone and after a moment, Aluneia herself appeared at the doorway with Dia at her heels. Aluneia wore a frown, but her face softened when she glanced at her horse, Orimos.

"Greetings Ansel, Geneera." She said politely before turning to stroke the horse's neck. Orimos nickered softly and bumped Aluneia's shoulder with her head. She turned to Ansel and said, "Dia tells me you are concerned about Theseus, Ansel. Geneera, your meter sent him on an errand almost two full quartercycles ago. I agree he should have returned by now." A worry line creased her brow and she squinted into the sun over the mountains to the north.

"Elder Priesera, I was Theseus' ThreadHolder," Ansel said. She noted the look of shock on Aluneia's face. "I know something is wrong. I can feel him calling to me in distress."

"You can feel him even though he is not in the labyrinth?"

"I think he must be ill or even drugged. He is confused and shows me darkness and movement. He is afraid."

"If he is in *eukinthos* it is possible he can contact his ThreadHolder, especially so soon after his Labyrinth Journey. Still, the labyrinth drug wore off within hours of his taking it. Unless, he has had a bad reaction to it?"

"I do not know, Priesera Aluneia."

"Vasilissa might know. If she sent him off on some silly errand while knowing he was ill . . . ." Aluneia did not complete her thought, but Ansel heard the displeasure in it.

Dia went to find Priesera Vasilissa. Geneera led the horses around to the back of Aluneia's cottage. There she allowed them their heads to crop the green meadow grasses. As they followed, Ansel told Aluneia about her experience as ThreadHolder. Within several moments, Vasilissa and Dia joined them at the back of Aluneia's cottage. Vasilissa's voice could be heard as she spoke to Dia.

"I do not wish to make the journey all the way to Knossos at this time, Dia. The Council shall have to meet without me." She shook her head and put up a hand. "Yes, yes, I understand you think it urgent, but honestly, Phoebe can be so irrational. She overreacts and gets the First Elder upset." What other opinions she was going to share with Dia were cut short when she caught sight of Ansel standing next to Aluneia. When she glimpsed Geneera, her eyes turned hard and unreadable.

"Vasilissa," Aluneia began, "Ansel is concerned that Theseus is hurt or unwell. She was his ThreadHolder in the labyrinth and has had some continued contact with him. He is overlong now in returning and we fear he has perhaps reacted badly to the labyrinth drug. Did he seem ill to you when you sent him out to gather saffron?"

"No," Vasilissa shook her head brusquely. "Even I would not have sent him if I thought he was ill." She turned to include Ansel. "You are mistaken, I am certain. He has likely just decided to take a little break from his studies."

Ansel could not be certain, but something about the way Vasilissa's eyes glittered felt wrong. Her entire demeanor seemed evasive. Ansel softened her own eyes and looked at Vasilissa through the *saria* for a moment. Yes, something looked wrong too – Vasilissa's

Radiance did not flow freely as it should, instead it was constricted and swirling. And the color was off; it appeared a murky, muddy red. Ansel did not know precisely how to interpret what she saw. "No, Priesera Vasilissa," Ansel repeated. "I keep getting visions of him in a dark place and he seems lost. He cannot think clearly. He is frightened. I am quite sure something is wrong."

Vasilissa snorted loudly and waved her hand dismissively. "He will be back soon enough, Ansel. He is not worth worrying about."

Geneera stared at her meter with a puzzled expression. She frowned. "Meter," she said. "Why would you say such a thing? Ansel is worried. Why would you send him on a long journey when you clearly do not even trust him to return? This is unlike you."

Vasilissa's face turned red and she began to laugh almost hysterically. Her voice raised a pitch. "Even *he* could retrieve a little saffron."

Now Geneera looked concerned. "Meter, you are a bad liar. What do you know that you are not telling us? Was Theseus ill when you sent him?"

"If he has disappeared, I am sure it is of his own choosing. Perhaps he decided to go on an extended hike in the mountains," Vasilissa said, her eyes suddenly blazing. "He was not ill, Geneera," she added.

"Yet he is now," Ansel said. Suddenly her heart sank; someone else she knew had gone into the mountains on a hike, but he never returned. "What do you know, Priesera Vasilissa?" she asked with growing boldness. "Has Theseus disappeared like Garin?"

Geneera gasped. "Not like Garin! Garin is dead, Meter. They took him. They sacrificed him."

Vasilissa laughed loudly again, her voice nearly a shriek. "You have such wild imaginations."

But Ansel knew down to her very bones that Theseus had been taken. *It explains everything: the drugged state, the fear, even the darkness. They could have him hooded or covered. The motion! Oh Goddess, is he in a boat?* She snapped her fingers. "That is it. Priesera Vasilissa, how could you? They are taking Theseus to Heria." She turned to Dia and Geneera, "Please, we must find him before they kill him!"

Nikolas jerked his thumb toward the dilapidated cart covered with a leather tarpaulin. "He is getting restless again, Kel. We better pull off the trail and put him down before he wakes up any more."

Just then a groan loud enough to be heard over the clop of the donkey's hooves emanated from somewhere inside the clapboard cart.

Iphikeles nodded, grabbed the leather harness and led the donkey to the side of the path. He reached into his rucksack and grabbed a lumpy bundle of linen. Unwrapping a sticky brown glob of resin, he pinched off a chunk and placed it on a red hot coal in the small brazier Nikolas held. Immediately smoke began to pour from the lump of mekoi. Briskly Iphikeles raised the leather cover and stuck the smoldering brazier under it. He stole a quick glance at the boy. Theseus was tied-up and semi–conscious; from the glaze over his large dark eyes, Iphikeles saw that he was in no position to yell or struggle overmuch. He pulled the leather back down over the top of the cart and waited for several moments. When he again raised the oilcloth to retrieve the brazier, the boy was passed out. Iphikeles chuckled. "He is so doped he has no chance of even remembering this journey. Mekoi is the perfect tool – the boy will arrive uninjured, yet he gives us no trouble."

Nikolas grunted. "And a useful thing, too. The road is rough and long through these Southern mountains. We should have gone north and around Knossos. We could have evaded Phoebe somehow." He mopped his brow with a square of linen. "Ai, I will be glad when this journey is over."

"A few more nights and we will reach Hagia bay and the boat, brother Niko, my good man. Then, my men will take over and your part in this will be over. Stop looking so nervous. You will be safely home in Phaistos before Theseus and I even arrive at the cave. We have passed only a few folks and with you clean shaven and dressed like a farmer, no one recognizes you." He narrowed his eyes, thinking for a moment, then said, "My only worry is that Vasilissa will not play her part well. She needs to delay the Priesera long enough for us to get off Kriti."

"Oh, she will. She quite hates the boy and is happy to do anything that I ask of her," Nikolas assured his brother.

Chapter 57

Ansel clung to Dia's waist as together they rode Hades through the mountain pass back to Knossos. Ansel wished they could go even more quickly, but a horse could only move so fast on these narrow rocky paths. Although they had left the University that same afternoon, they had to stop at the halfway point for the night. The horses could not continue safely in the dark. Ansel begrudged the time lost even as she tossed and turned in a fretful sleep. Her nightmares took on a new sense of urgency. She was sure now that Theseus was on a boat. She could almost smell the sea. She felt as nauseated and helpless as she was sure Theseus felt.

The next morning, they were up with the dawn and reached Knossos by mid morning. Fortunately, Devra had arrived and was in the Bulldancer meadow with her big horse, Dolphina. They greeted her and told her what they learned.

"Yes, if they have taken Theseus, they will be heading to Heria with him, I am certain." Devra grunted and scratched her head. "But where precisely are they taking him? Where do we start the search? I found that cave above Daedalos, but I hear tell that the most important sacrifices are made somewhere around Atalancia. Who are these people who took Theseus? Do we know?"

"If anyone can tell us who might be involved, it will be my meter." Ansel said.

They found Phoebe in her apartment with Rheana. She was trying to have a conversation above the din of the twins shrieking and chasing each other around her desk. When the four women entered her office room looking serious, she asked Priesera Eida to see if Xeronos could please watch the children for the rest of the morning. Phoebe's eyes followed her babies as Priesera Eida obediently scooped up Phaedra, then took Damarin's chubby little boy hand into her own and marched them out of the office doorway.

"Now tell me what you have learned," she said, brushing back a stray tendril of hair. Ansel noticed her meter did not keep herself as meticulously groomed as she had before the arrival of the twins. She seemed happier though.

Ansel quickly told Phoebe and Rheana her suspicion that Theseus had been abducted. Devra then asked if the Elder Escort might give them direction in tracking him. It was Rheana who answered.

"Mistress Phoebe," Rheana breathed. "I think I can help. Remember I told you I recently received puzzling news from TradesKourete Alekki?" Briefly she explained to the others. "When I was at Phaistos, I befriended another Priesera there who, it turns, is the sister-daughter of the opium trader, Alekki." Her eyes sparkled. "Well, Thalia sent me a message from Phaistos just this past cycle with news from her uncle. She said Alekki saw Iphikeles and some of his followers, including Kourete Nikolas, visit Helen Demetria. Shortly thereafter, Demetria purchased a large quantity of mekoi from him." She turned to face Devra squarely and continued. "Normally, he said, he would not be suspicious of Demetria buying more mekoi, but she had just procured her usual stock within the last quartercycle and Alekki needed to make a special trip to Egypt to fill this order. He supposed it might be that she was just planning to entertain another devotee of the poppy, but it also made him suspicious enough to want to pass the information on to us."

Geneera looked puzzled. "So, how does this relate to Theseus?"

Phoebe answered. "Demetria. If Demetria has learned that Theseus lives, she may have enlisted the help of the sacrifice religion to get rid of him. Iphikeles is the leader of that religion on Heria."

"And Iphikeles is from Atalancia," Devra finished for her. "My thanks to you, Mistress Rheana, Mistress Phoebe. I believe I now know where we should begin our search." She turned to the others and said grimly, "We need the horses. It is a long journey."

"And of course, you also need a boat," Phoebe added. "No matter how swift your horses, they will not swim to Heria. I am just the woman to get you that boat."

First Elder Thesmas immediately granted use of the largest and swiftest sailing vessel available. It was still cramped quarters for the four women and three horses.

The horses did not like to travel by boat. The motion of the waves upset them. Dia and Devra led them to the center of the deck by the biggest mast, where the vessel rocked least and tied cloth strips around their eyes. "They relax more if they do not see the water." Dia explained. Still their hooves slid with the larger waves and they whinnied nervously. "There, there, Dolphina," Devra crooned. "We have been through this before. We will be on land again soon." Dolphina neighed loudly, ending in a loud snort of protest. Hades and Orimos echoed his displeasure.

In Dia's small boat, it would have taken several days to reach Heria, even with the most favorable of winds. In this many-sailed boat, it took only two.

They landed at a different harbor than on Ansel's trip to Daedalos. This one had deep water right up to the shore and was lined with flattened hand-chiseled rocks. The already edgy horses were not pleased to make the small leap from the deck to the rocky ledge of the harbor, but with encouragement from Devra and Geneera, each made it safely. Still, the whites of Hades' eyes were showing even after he was well onto solid land. "There, there, big boy," Dia said softly to him, stroking his flank tenderly.

It was too steep to ride in many places and Ansel cursed their slow going. She knew Theseus was still alive, but she dreaded feeling the moment he would no longer be. "He is here. We are closer," she confirmed to Devra when asked. "I feel him strongly now, but he is still drugged and I do not get a clear picture. I wonder how long they will keep him alive once they arrive at the cave."

"I doubt they realize they are being followed," Devra said. "They will take their time and do whatever preparations they feel are necessary." Her jaw was set in a stern line; Devra was tracking. She was going very slowly, bending over every disturbed rock, inspecting every broken twig. Ansel found it infuriating, but she knew it was important not to lose the correct path.

"They are very sure of themselves and are not taking care to cover their tracks." Devra muttered. "They clearly do not fear being stopped," she shrugged. "It is a fortunate turn for us."

Dia shuddered. "This has been going on in the open then? Why would the governors of the cities allow it?"

"Perhaps they feel self-righteous and then again, perhaps they are well armed," Devra suggested.

Geneera spoke up then. "And perhaps the governors themselves take part in it."

"Not in Dadalos, certainly," Dia answered. "Nadia would have known. She did not have anything good to say about what was happening in Atalancia. Perhaps this is why."

Devra shrugged again. "I prefer to track than to speculate. We must be prepared to fight them. Dia, are you as skilled with that knife as you are with your *kithara*?"

"Somewhat," she replied.

"I am not skilled with a knife, but I can wrestle," Geneera added. "I am stronger than I look."

"I am worthless, I fear," Ansel said.

"You are the one who will ultimately lead us to him, Ansel. And you are the one who will know if he still lives."

Atalancia was in the high reaches of Heria, closest of all the cities and towns to the ash throwing peak, Herilia. Nadia had told Ansel that the once great city in the clouds with its famed gilded gates and sparkling whitestone streets was partially abandoned. People were afraid of the fire mountain now, where they once reveled in its glory. The women did not go into the town proper. They skirted the city, looking for paths leading out to the caves they knew were located nearby.

"The ritual caves the citizens of Atalancia use routinely are not going to be the ones we want," Devra said. "These people would not dare defile caves dedicated to Great Meter with their bloody offerings to Her Bull Son." She halted the small party, her hand held out, as she inspected what looked like a narrow goat path that veered off to the right and up. "A group of people passed through here recently," she said. "See this scuff?" She pointed to the edge of a flat rock. "Someone slipped here and left a mark from his shoe. And here," she said, peering over the edge of the rock a foot length down to the soil. "Here is where he landed." Ansel saw that some small rocks were depressed into the soil. Devra pondered aloud, "I cannot tell exactly when this happened, but let us hope we are on the right path."

They turned onto the small trail. A few paces further and Devra pointed to a pile of dung. "Look, here is their donkey." To Ansel's disgust, she touched the mound. "Still warm," she said, smiling. "They are not moving very quickly. No doubt they cannot travel fast with a drugged prisoner. They had a longer and harder road than we did getting off Kriti and a farther sail from the Southern Shore. They have to tend to their prisoner every few hours. If they overdose him, they will kill him. They need him alive for the sacrifice."

Ansel shuddered. Dia laid a hand over her shoulder. "We will reach him in time, Ansel, and we will save him too." She placed a hand over her knife hilt.

Ansel could hear him faintly now all the time, whether because they were close or for some other reason, she could not say. She tried to send him reassurance that they were coming, but did not know if he could hear her at all.

They continued to tramp upward and climbed back on the horses as the path leveled out. Single file they walked steadily up the long winding path.

A line of caves appeared. Ansel knew they were close now. She could almost hear Theseus calling to her. But from which cave?

Devra turned to Ansel. "Are they here?"

"Yes," she answered, her jaw clenched. "He is really afraid now." Suddenly she nearly blacked out. A fiery spasm of anguish bolted down her arm "Oh Goddess, there is blood!" she moaned.

"Which cave, Ansel? Which one?" Devra took Ansel by the shoulders, not allowing her to collapse in pain and fear.

She pointed to a small entrance. "I think that one, but I am not certain. It may be the next one."

Devra whirled to see where Ansel pointed. "I am heading into that one. Dia, you and Geneera try the one next to it. Ansel, stay here and watch the horses." Tossing Dolphina's lead to Ansel, she drew her knife and began climbing the rocks up to the cave entrance. Dia clambered after her while Geneera quickly looped the reins of Orimos and Hades around a stunted tree branch. Even with her injured leg Geneera proved to be quick. She swiftly caught up to Dia.

Ansel felt sick in the pit of her stomach. Theseus was injured, stabbed. She felt him struggle and knew he was tied up. His terror was almost palpable to her. She could not just wait. She tied Dolphina's lead around another sturdy branch. Then, she crawled over the loose rock up to the cave Devra had just entered. Ansel took a deep breath to gather her courage before plunging in. It took a moment for her eyes to adjust to the darkness and she cursed herself for her blindness. She could see, just barely, that there were several small chambers toward the back. Following the scuffling sound from one, she peered in. Devra was battling two men. Ansel did not recognize either of them, but behind them all, lying spread out on an elevated flat stone slab, his forearm sliced open and bleeding profusely, laid Theseus.

The men were armed with short daggers. Though Devra's knife was longer, she was having trouble holding off both men. Ansel ran out of the cave and screamed, "Dia! Geneera! Over here!" then sprinted back into the cave. She did not know precisely what to do, but when one of the men had his full back to her, she thrust her right shoulder down and galloped at him, throwing her entire weight into the small of his back. To her surprised gratification, he fell flat onto his stomach and his dagger skittered across the cave floor. He was not a particularly agile man, but he was stronger than Ansel. He rolled to his back and kicked at her ferociously, catching her in the stomach. Ansel flew across the floor. *At least I distracted him from Devra,* Ansel thought through a winded haze of pain.

Dia and Geneera rushed into the room. Dia flourished her long knife at the man whom Ansel had tackled. He thrust his palms up in a gesture of surrender. This took the heart out of the other man whom Devra swiftly disarmed. While Devra and Geneera held the two men at knife point, Ansel scrambled to Theseus' side. Dia cut his ropes and Ansel helped him sit up. He was clearly still drugged.

"Ansel, I kept trying to reach you," Theseus managed before he collapsed. Dia flung the slight man over her shoulder and carried him out into the sunshine. Laying him in the grass with surprising gentleness, she inspected him for broken bones. After a few minutes, she said, "He is ill from the mekoi and weak from hunger, no doubt, but other than this nasty gash on his arm, he is well enough."

Chapter 58

Killing Polymachos was pathetically simple. Even his so–called first man would not rise to his defense. He was given the chance to leap onto a horse and gallop away. Instead, Polymachos fell to his knees and begged for his life like a child. Myko yanked back his head by a hank of hair and slit his throat without a second thought. The blood welled and spilled over from the deep gash. The eyes of the dead man went vacant in a most satisfying way.

Standing upon the chest of the Consort's corpse, Myko roared, "We are now the power of Athena! Come with me. We march upon the city center."

Helen Demetria was waiting, but there was little she could do against the men whose job it had been to protect her and her holdings. A handful of loyal guards stood round her, but they were dispatched quickly at Myko's signal. Still, the Queen stood unwaveringly before him and he grudgingly admired her for that.

"I am Athena now, Demetria."

The woman was visibly pale yet her eyes were fierce and her jaw set. Finally she said, "You think you can rule here? There is more to governing a state than by force and violence."

Myko supposed she was right. He had thought only of the glory of conquering Athena, not of what would follow. He had little knowledge of the affairs of state and even less interest; his eyes were set upon Kriti. Thinking fast, he said, "I offer you exile and safety in exchange for knowledge. I will take your daughter in marriage. I will not be consort, but King. She will teach me what I need to know about running a state.

There was silence for many moments. Then she said, "I accept these terms."

"Demetria, you have no choice," Myko replied. She turned her back to him haughtily to leave. Myko nodded to one of his men who stepped behind the Helen, grabbed her by the hair and slit her throat in one smooth motion. As she sank to the floor of the throne room, Myko's men cheered.

"Better to start fresh than to rule as she ruled," he announced. "Now, we turn our thoughts toward Kriti and revenge."

Chapter 59

The return trip to Knossos was arduous. The jumpy horses were difficult to control and Theseus was ill. He sweated, scratched, complained and paced, annoying everyone around him. It was a relief when he slept for short times, though he moaned and tossed fitfully even then. His arm was sliced cleanly, but there was always the concern of the wound turning sour. Ansel was glad it was not the arm he used to eat or write; he was already intractable enough.

"Whatever is the matter with you?" Ansel finally asked in exasperation as Theseus began complaining once again about the food. "We are all tired of salted fish and dried fruit, but this cannot possibly be worse than what you ate on the road with your army nor the scraps you must have eaten recently."

"I am irritated with everything and ill of the sea," He snapped through gritted teeth. "If this is poppy sickness, I understand Demetria better now. It is miserable." He scratched at his arm furiously, causing it to bleed again.

"Stop that. Your arm is trying to heal and you will cause it to sour."

"Go away, Ansel. Leave me alone," he said leaping to his feet to pace around the deck of the boat once again. As she picked up his abandoned dinner bowl, she saw the horses prance nervously as he passed them.

"Even the horses are upset by him," Devra observed dryly.

"We should have left him to the Minotaur," Dia grumbled. "Fine, fine, I did not mean that seriously," she added when Ansel glared at her.

Still, even Ansel was relieved to leave Theseus behind at Knossos with the healer Priesera while she and the other women rode off to the University. Dia had asked Devra to report to Aluneia before leaving. Devra had become fast friends with Dia and Geneera and for her part was pleased to stay for a while. The women rode companionably, Ansel trading mounts with Devra and Dia. Dolphina and Hades were happy to carry her as long as they were not on a boat.

Now that Theseus was safely at Knossos, Ansel enjoyed the journey and noticed it was not nearly as long as she previously had thought in her panic, nor were there nearly as many places the horses could not maneuver as she remembered. They arrived in the late afternoon of the morning they left Knossos, then immediately reported to Aluneia, who ordered dinner be brought to the women while they told her of the rescue.

"They both had short iron knives," Dia said between bites of roast fowl. "I picked one up after the men surrendered. It was marked with a seal I did not recognize. It looked like their Bull god with blood dripping from his flanks."

"Charming," Geneera said.

"Did you just leave the men then?" Aluneia asked.

Devra answered. "They surrendered. We tied them up loosely with rope we found in the cave, but we did not want to kill them. Truly, we did not know what to do with them." She shrugged her shoulders. "We concentrated on getting Theseus back to Knossos. He was injured, but we wanted to get him off Heria. We just retreated back to the harbor and the boat as fast as we could."

"Probably wise. You did not know if these men would regroup and come after you to retake him. Did you recognize either of them?"

"I believe the taller man, the one Ansel thinks actually slashed the boy, is Iphikeles, a well known follower of the Bull Son."

"Yes, I know Iphikeles. He is the elder brother of Kourete Nikolas of Phaistos."

Dia nodded. "TradesKourete Alekki warned me about him when I was in Athena. I wonder how the man knew where to find Theseus."

Aluneia's eyes glittered. "I know the answer to that. I am sorry, Geneera, but your meter is involved more than she is admitting. Mistress Phoebe warned me that Vasilissa told Nikolas where Theseus was. It would be no difficulty for Nikolas to pass that information on."

Geneera looked troubled. "Are you saying she deliberately sent Theseus out on an errand knowing he would be captured?"

Aluneia slowly shook her head from side to side. "I do not know precisely what occurred or what her role was, but somehow Iphikeles came either near or even into this village undetected and knew how to find Theseus. Someone here helped him and your meter is the most likely candidate."

Dia put an arm around Geneera's shoulder. "We need to get the truth, Gen. Do you want to go somewhere else while we question her?"

"No," Geneera said. "I have been a part of this. I helped rescue Theseus. Meter does not lie well in front of me. I would prefer to be there while you question her, even if it is painful."

The confrontation with Vasilissa was not long in coming. Aluneia summoned her to the Elder Priesera's office the next morning. Ansel, Dia, Devra, and Geneera were already seated around Aluneia's big wooden table when Vasilissa arrived. Her face was stone cold with one eyebrow raised as usual, as if she were asking an unspoken, but no doubt haughty, question. All the women rose, and Aluneia gestured for Vasilissa to sit in an empty chair.

"Vasilissa," Aluneia began. "Here is Devra, an Emetchi woman who makes her living through tracking and travel preparation. She and the rest of these young women," Aluneia paused to sweep her arm indicating the rest, "are just back from Heria. Theseus was abducted out of our village or the surrounding area, Vasilissa. They found him, fortunately, before he was badly injured or killed. How did Iphikeles of Heria find him?"

"Goodness, why would I know?" Vasilissa asked, raising her chin so that she appeared to be looking down at Aluneia. She carefully did not look at, or even acknowledge, Geneera. "Perhaps Iphikeles was in the area and Theseus had the misfortune to run into him. For all we know, the boy could have volunteered to go to Heria not knowing the danger he was in."

"Priesera Vasilissa," Ansel said, "do not take us for children or fools. We know Theseus was calling out to me for more than a half cycle. This is why we knew to come here to check on him in the first place."

Vailissa narrowed her eyes at Ansel. "Ansel, it is completely improper that you have become involved with the boy. You think you know him, but clearly you do not know what he might do. None of us do. Yes, I do think you are a child who is rebelling against the Sisterhood and making poor decisions based on lust. Dia, you agree with me, do you not?"

"I do not trust Theseus, that is true." Dia covered her mouth with her hand. "He was quite sick from poppy essence. Ansel, is it possible he was lured to Heria, perhaps with the poppy?"

"No. He is disgusted at what it has done to Helen Demetria." Ansel frowned first at Dia and then back at Vasilissa.

Aluneia interrupted. "Why would Iphikeles have been in the area anyway? If he is looking for young men to sacrifice, why would he be in the neighborhood of the University?"

"There are young men here too. Kai has a son, as does Lyssa. Many turns ago, I had my Jerid here, before he sacrificed himself to the Bull." Vasilissa spat the last.

"Meter," Geneera interrupted, "for Goddess sake, have you lost all sense of decency? I can see you are lying to us. Tell us the truth."

"Geneera, you are hardly the standard for truth. Aluneia, I have told you everything I know. If you are finished with me, I plan to enter a time of meditation for several days and would prefer to not be disturbed." Vasilissa swept quickly from the room leaving the women to look at each other in distress.

Chapter 60

A quartercycle passed and, except that tutoring Theseus was no longer her chore for the afternoon, all was returning to normal for Ansel. She joined Dia, Geneera and Devra as they were sitting around a bench laughing and eating a midday meal of grilled vegetables and goat cheese. Devra planned to leave the next morning to return to Heria; she intended to discuss with Mistress Nadia what should be done about the sacrifice religion. The women dreaded saying goodbye and all were lingering over hot tea. Suddenly, their cups began to rattle. Ansel looked up sharply and felt a chill streak down her spine. She gasped involuntarily. "Shake," she managed to utter.

But then it stopped and she gasped in relief while Dia continued eating as if completely unconcerned. Geneera thumped her on the back. "Just a little tremor, Ansel."

Ansel giggled nervously. "A bit jumpy today, I am afraid. I saw three snakes over the ground this morning and I think it sets my nerves on edge."

Devra put her cup down and stared at Ansel intensely. "Snakes above the ground? Not just sunning?" She thrust her hand over her chin and mouth and muttered, "The horses are uneasy today too."

No sooner had Devra made that observation when the ground began to shake again, this time in earnest.

"Out! Outside, away from the kitchen, now!" Devra shouted, knocking the plank table away from herself in her haste. Dia grabbed Geneera's arm, pulling her towards the exit while Ansel fell to her knees, hands over her head. "Now, Ansel, now!" Devra shouted, grabbing her arm and dragging her toward the door. Chaos erupted as people realized what was happening. The tables were bucking, spilling their contents onto the floor. Someone started screaming and everyone rushed for the door. Devra, still dragging Ansel, arrived at the exit just after Dia and Geneera. Outside the earth groaned and shook. The air thickened with soil and plaster dust; women pulled their tunics over their noses to breathe. The noise was deafening; rocks crashed down the side of the nearby mountains, window frames creaked and splintered, the ground rumbled and jerked so fiercely that no one could stand. Ansel collapsed onto jagged rocks that bit sharply into her flesh. She rolled into a fetal position, covering her head with her arms as best she could, whimpering and muttering prayers. All around her women shrieked, pebbles flew and debris rained.

Finally it stopped. Ansel, trembling, moved her arms from her head and face and brushed copious dust and rubble from her body. In an act of will she fought her panic by gulping air. She looked around and saw Geneera, Dia, and Devra close by, all looking dazed. She exhaled with a huff. "Hoy, Geneera!" she called, "Are you all well over there?" All around her, people were sobbing and calling for assistance.

Geneera blinked at her, then said, "Scratches. Bruises. I think Dia may have twisted her knee."

But Dia shook it off. "I am fine. I will wrap the knee." She scrambled to her feet, but leaned on Devra's shoulder where she knelt looking out over the fields.

"The horses have run off," Devra said.

Ansel said. "There are people trapped in the buildings."

"I wonder where Aluneia is," Dia said suddenly. "Goddess, I need to find Aluneia." Without another word, Dia ripped a length of cloth from her linen tunic with her teeth, knotted it tightly around her knee and limped off to find Aluneia.

Devra was on her feet, flexing her legs to see if she was hurt. "I need to find those horses. There will be aftershakes and they could be hurt."

Geneera nodded. "I will help you."

"What is the matter with you?" Ansel said. "People are hurt! We must help them."

"There are many around to help you rescue people, Ansel. We are the only ones who will go find the horses." They turned away from Ansel and trotted toward the meadow.

Seeing that no one else was taking up the slack, Ansel began to coordinate the rescue. Everywhere people were milling around aimless looking for leadership. Many were dazed and hurt. She heard cries from within the damaged buildings.

She found Kai already helping a woman who had obviously broken a leg. "I need cloth and a flat board, Ansel, and herbs from the healing houses. Find me women who know anything about the healing arts and send them to me here. We must form groups to find people who are hurt."

Ansel called people together who were unhurt and formed rescue teams. "We will bring everyone we can here to Kai and the healing women." Seeing their dazed faces, she reminded them, "We must get people out of the buildings. There will be aftershakes and it is not safe. It is warm now, but we will need shelter for the night. You, little ones, you can find us blankets and linens. We must keep the hurt ones warm." Soon, Ansel was the woman others came to for direction.

The long afternoon wore on. The sun hung innocently in the western sky, oblivious to the carnage below. "Kai!" Dia shouted above the din. She hobbled over to the healer woman, a limp body thrown over one shoulder like a sack of grain. "I have Aluneia. She is hurt."

Aluneia was unconscious, though Kai could not tell anyone why.

She did not appear to have a head wound of any sort. Her breathing was shallow, but otherwise normal. Her robes were torn and her hair matted with dust, but other than some bruising, she looked to be in better condition than many other women Kai was tending.

"I found her in the sanctuary," Dia explained. "It held well through the shake. She was like this in the middle of a pile of rubble. I do not know what is wrong with her. Kai, do you know?"

The healer brushed a lock of hair from her forehead and pursed her lips. "I cannot tell, Dia," she said. "However, there are several people who need immediate care and I must tend to them. Lay the Elder Priesera over there on a cot; I will tend to her as soon as I can." Tenderly Dia carried Aluneia to an empty cot in the meadow. There, the healers were sorting the injured; the more grievous the injury, the quicker they would be tended.

Kai checked on the Elder Priesera several times over the course of that exhausting afternoon and evening, but there was little she could do. "We need a healing circle, Dia, even to diagnose her injury," she said, biting the side of her lip and looking puzzled. "She looks to be well except that she cannot respond to us. Until we have several women with time for a circle, I must continue to care for those who are more gravely injured, though I hate to leave the Elder Priesera." Kai's face was drawn and dark circles rimmed her eyes.

"I will stay with her, Kai," Dia assured her.

The healer nodded silently and hurried away. Dia did not envy the healer women; there were so many injured people, so many difficult decisions. Her choice was so much easier. She would stay loyally beside her mentor even through the long night; there was no greater priority for Dia.

Evening finally came and the sun began to dip behind the mountains. "Priesera Ansel said to bring these to you, Priesera Dia," said a young girl who carried a stack of neatly folded blankets.

"My thanks to you and to Prisera Ansel," Dia replied, shaking loose the folds of the first one and tucking it around Aluneia's shoulders. Still the Elder Priesera did not respond. Another youngster, this time a boy, brought around soup and hard bread.

"My thanks, Castor," Dia said as she accepted the food. "Lyssa is raising a fine son." The little boy blushed to the roots of his dark hair and ran off.

Geneera and Devra had found the hysterical, wild eyed horses and returned them to the meadow. It was not until the next afternoon, however, that Geneera realized her meter was missing. First, she looked through all the workers Ansel had coordinated, hoping to glimpse Vasilissa among them.

"No, Gen," Ansel said, a frown crossing her face. "I have not seen your meter since before the shake. I did not think to look for her either, I am sorry to admit." She brushed her tangled hair back from her smudged face. "Perhaps Dia has seen her, or Kai."

Geneera fought a growing sense of unease as she scanned the meadow full of injured women and every person tending them. Still she did not see Vasilissa. "Dia," she said, "I am searching for my meter." Geneera stopped and looked at the woman on the cot where Dia knelt. "Is that Aluneia? What is wrong with her? Is she injured?"

"We do not know, Gen," Dia answered anxiously. "I am looking after her until Kai can learn what is wrong. I am sorry; I have not seen your meter. I have been right here next to the Elder Priesera since I found her early yesterday."

Finally, Gen forced herself to look over in the other meadow; the one across the white stone road, behind the sanctuary to the right. Here people were crying and wailing over their dead. Already some of the bodies were starting to turn foul in the warm sun. A group of hardy women were discussing the fate of the bodies.

"We could build a new hive tomb. There are many stones."

"Burning would be faster, but could we make the fire hot enough, and how will their families feel about this?"

"Digging a pit would be much work in this stony ground, though it would be a good solution."

"Nah, Melina, there is not enough soil for a pit. This hillock is solid stone a few lengths deep. That is where they have the labyrinth for the Priesera, right underneath this hill."

Geneera did not hear the end of the conversation. She drew the neck of her tunic over her nose and mouth and forced herself to search through the laid out bodies. There were many; at least three times ten. She did not know how to feel when Vasilissa was not among them.

Luckily, the expected aftershakes did little more damage. Everything that was to collapse had apparently already done so. Several days passed and still Aluneia did respond. Dia and several other women moved her to a large bed in a tent that had been hastily erected in the meadow behind the herb gardens.

Kai drew together five Priesera, including Ansel and Dia, to form a healing circle. Together the women took hands and began humming through their noses. Then they dropped their jaws and toned a long "Ma". Ansel still did not take seeing the Radiance of the others for granted. She was fascinated to see that Dia was surrounded with shades of yellow, orange and pink.

Kai directed the aether and began to whisper softly to Aluneia while the other women held the energy of the circle.

"Aluneia, come back to us," Kai said. "Do not walk the paths of darkness, Sister. We need you to return."

After several moments, Aluneia began to gasp and sob. Her eyes flew open and she thrust a hand to her heart. Sitting up, she said, "The Thread broke. The Thread broke. Oh Goddess, Vasilissa, my friend, my sister, I am so sorry, so sorry." She began to weep bitterly.

Breaking the circle, Dia rushed to Aluneia's side. The Elder Priesera wrapped her arms around Dia who held her while she keened as if her heart had shattered into a thousand pieces.

In the end, it was Ansel who told Geneera that her meter was dead, lost in the labyrinth that had been damaged from the great shake. The young Priesera organized a group of women to enter the holy site under the hillock, but at the very entrance a huge pile of rocks had caved in. After several hours of excavating with hands, picks and levers, the women encountered a slab of rock so large that even if every person at the University tried to push it at the same moment, it would not have budged. Dirty and exhausted, the team had to abandon its effort. Aluneia assured them that Vasilissa was beyond rescue; the ThreadHolder always knew.

Ansel dreaded meeting Geneera's eyes when the women abandoned their efforts. Geneera had insisted on being part of the team, even though her leg allowed her to be only so much help. Valiantly she had pulled rocks and rubble from the blockage, using stout branches as wedges to move the heaviest stones. When Ansel finally gave up, calling out to the group, "I am sorry, we can do no more here." Geneera first argued, then sobbed and stumbled away, her fatigue evident in her gait. Ansel wept as she wondered if she and Geneera could ever again mend their friendship.

Several more days passed before Aluneia was well enough to resume some of her duties. She called Ansel, Geneera, Dia and Devra to her office. "Geneera," she began, "I am so sorry for your loss. I want you to know that your meter found peace. She entered the labyrinth, as many Priesera do, to find Truth during a time of darkness for herself and I believe she did find it. I know this is little comfort to you, but for my part, I forgive her for what she did. I hope she can rest peacefully. It is you I am concerned about now."

Geneera's eyes looked haunted. She said, "I cannot believe she is gone. I thought I would have time to make things right with her." She looked as if she had not slept well for days. Ansel was not certain where Gen had been sleeping. Ansel, still busy organizing the cleaning of wreckage, had been simply throwing herself onto any empty cot she could find when she was too weary to go further. This morning she had been preoccupied solving a possible food shortage and a contaminated water supply; she had been feeling nauseated for several days and worried that perhaps the water had turned sour.

Devra patted Geneera on the back and said, "Geneera is coming with me, Elder Priesera. She is a fair hand with horses, as you know, and my tribe south of the Emetchi Sea breeds and raises them. I have invited Geneera to join us. We always need women favored by horses."

Ansel blinked in surprise. Geneera was leaving Kriti!

Aluneia, however, smiled. "That is the best news I have heard in many days, Devra. And Geneera, my gift to you then is both fitting and a way of wishing you well. I am giving you Orimos. She has grown to love you and I know you love her."

Geneera gasped and her eyes suddenly cleared. "Priesera, uh, Elder, Aluneia! I do not know what to say. My everlasting thanks to you. I will treasure her and be the best companion to her I know how to be."

Aluneia turned to Ansel and said, "I hope I have not done ill, but I have waited to tell you this because you were so needed in leading us after the earthshake. You have my gratitude for serving while I was not able. However, you must now go back to Knossos. Your meter is in a time of change and crisis, and I sense that she needs you. You must go quickly."

Chapter 61

Agronos Knossos burned. Soot and plaster and burning scraps of debris rained down upon the heads of stumbling, numb, desperate people. But worse was the terrible stink from the pyre that was once a home.

Who would have guessed at the multitude of horrific odors possible when fire engulfed matter never meant to be burned? There was wood burning yes; the mighty cypress pillars supporting the main entrances to the Agronos were scorched as was the vibrant paint on those pillars and the wooden doorframes and those around the windows too. The hide window shades – those had their own distinctive reek as they were consumed by flame and they crinkled up like skin, revealing that they were just bits of charred flesh after all. The intricate tapestries hung on the walls, the wool that had been so lovingly woven into patterns, the dyes so vivid, all left a unique stink when devoured by an inferno.

There were worse things too; things like hair and clothing and Oh Goddess, Phoebe could not bear to think of the other horrible odors, where they originated, and what must have burnt to create the stench that clung over the ruined Agronos like a sodden Cronetide fog.

It had come so quickly. Phoebe and Rheana chatted in the courtyard together while the babies laughed in delight playing a game of 'find me'. There was a little tremble, just enough to shake a few blossoms off the blooming fruit trees. Phoebe and Rheana looked at each other in alarm for a moment, then smiled in relief when it subsided.

But then, the ground began to buck and roar in earnest, and the two women could do little except fall to the ground. Phoebe screamed for the twins to come to her, though the ground was shaking so hard no one could walk or even crawl. Rheana cried out in pain when a branch cracked off a tree and hit her across the shoulders. Phoebe threw her arms over her head and flung her body toward where she had last seen her babies. The courtyard stones heaved. Phoebe struggled to find a foothold, but nothing held still.

Then came the deafening crash of falling stone, louder even than the roar of the convulsing earth, and a huge cloud of plaster dust erupted from the Agronos while flames shot high above them. Phoebe and Rheana were blown flat and all around them people screamed. Then, she felt Xeronos. His life force was expelled violently from his body, the cord of love and energy between them yanked from her inner depths, leaving in her spirit a gaping, bleeding wound as surely as if She of Ten Thousand Names had reached into her very chest and ripped out her heart in some bloody sacrifice. Phoebe knew in that instant that nothing would ever be the same for her.

After an eternity, the shake subsided, though the screaming did not. Phoebe arose then like a specter from a tomb. She did not shriek aloud, immersed as she was into an endless internal keen. She wandered through the ruined walls, not really seeing the utter destruction, not really smelling the charred flesh of burning bodies, not really noticing the black soot on everything, her face, her clothes, her children.

Her children, the one consolation. They lived. They lived. Desperately, she grabbed their hands. Damarin's face was so coated in soot he was unrecognizable except, of course, his Meter knew him from his cry, his Radiance, his, Oh Goddess, his life force which was still there! *Oh She of Ten Thousand Names, thank you for sparing the babies.* He had been knocked senseless for several moments when the ceiling of the SouthWest wing collapsed, taking with it the entire Elder Council and the authority of Kriti. He was almost hidden in the plaster dust and a layer of grit and rubble on top of that, but he revived screaming at the top of his lungs. His sister knelt beside him sobbing, blood streaming through her beautiful fine baby hair making it lank and slimy, her palms scraped red, her knees raw and oozing from sliding across the jagged, tortured slabs of stone in the courtyard where the blast from the collapsing ceiling had flung her little body across the space like a bird in a wind storm.

Phoebe scooped them in her arms and held them so tightly they needed to wiggle loose for breath, then grabbed them by the hands in a vise–like grip, leading them with singularity of focus around the screaming and dying and injured and crushed people reaching out to her for help, pleading for her to save them, to lead them. Together they picked their way around the fires where the torches had lit huge cracked jars of oil, avoiding the ruptured slabs that once were walls or floors or ceilings or stairways, taking them away, away. That was all she knew to do. Take her babies away from the grasping hands and gaping mouths and screaming of the multitudes of injured people.

Phoebe did not respond to the desperate pleas of her people. Phoebe did not give orders to those who begged her for guidance. Phoebe did not take charge to help her people in their time of need. Phoebe was sightless except for her babies. Phoebe was pitiless except for her children. Phoebe knew herself at that terrible moment, and acknowledged in her soul a dreadful, perhaps unforgivable truth; she had never desired to be First Elder. She had never desired even to be on the Council. Now, as her heart lay broken and buried under the ceiling with her dead lover Xeronos, she only had room in her world for those babies. No one else mattered. No one else even existed.

Rheana intercepted Phoebe with her children as she crossed the ruined courtyard. "Mistress, we must help people out of the Agronos, more stone may collapse on them. You must take charge. There is no one left alive of the Elder Council."

But Phoebe's eyes were utterly vacant and Rheana realized she was alone.

She knew she had to take action, but no one it seemed was inclined to follow her lead. She called out to several strong looking men, "Come with me, we will go inside and bring people out." They stared at her and then dispersed as if she had not even spoken. She went to the kitchen as it burned and tried to organize people to throw sand on the oil fires. But after tossing a few feeble handfuls from the sand mounds kept by the huge brazier, they became distracted and moved on to something else.

Theseus emerged from the remains of a healing house, holding his arm. Blood stained a strip of cloth he had wrapped around his wound when flying shards of pottery reopened it. For a moment, he gazed at the chaos surrounding him blinking, his jaw clenched, but then he appeared to make a decision. As Rheana watched, he straightened and appeared to grow at least a hand length taller. Many people stopped what they were doing and turned to look at him. At last Rheana saw the hero within the man.

"We need to take action here," Theseus said. Rheana strode to his side, finding even herself drawn to listen to him. His voice was resonant and kindly, yet commanding. Clearly, here was someone who was used to being in charge.

"Who here is unhurt?" Theseus asked. "We need you to help the others. Who here knows any of the healing arts? You are a healer?" He pointed to a woman who had raised her hand. When she nodded, he said, "find linens for bandages. "You, you and you," he continued, pointing to various people, "help her and form a group who can tend to injured people."

And so the work began and Theseus became its leader. Rheana placed a hand on his uninjured arm. "Theseus, the people have been looking to Mistress Phoebe for guidance, but she is not able. I am afraid in the shock of losing Xeronos and her meter she has shut out everyone except for her children. Go to her, I beg you, and allow the people to see her bestow her blessings on your leadership. They need guidance and you are capable. She can convey the authority you need. The people are alarmed that she has abandoned them. They do not understand."

Theseus and Rheana found Phoebe and the twins in the meadow. The children clung to her, each sucking a thumb.

"Phoebe," Rheana said, "I have brought Theseus. He has been sending people to find the hurt ones and give them aid."

Theseus knelt to look into Phoebe's eyes. "I can help, Mistress Phoebe if you will permit me. Tell the people that I am acting under your guidance while you care for your children." Phoebe simply nodded.

And so, for a full quartercycle, Theseus, with the help of Rheana, restored a semblance of organization to the lives of the people. The fires were contained and in time would burn themselves out. The aftershakes did little further damage and the people were out of the Agronos. Phoebe slowly became herself again, but she continued to rely heavily on Theseus. She came to love him in those days, as did the people around him. He was confident and calm; he began to be seen as something of a hero.

No one noticed the boats sailing into Amnisos and the peril from the North fell on them more suddenly than the great shake.

"Theseus!" a baritone voice barked. Theseus whirled around from where he stood in the central courtyard of the ruined Agronos. He had been instructing a group of men to gather rocks for a great hive tomb.

After a pause, he said, "Mykalo. And Phillip. My men! What? How?" His voice drifted off in surprise.

"Yes. What. How. We would ask the same questions of you." Mykalo's voice was not warm. He glared down at Theseus.

Theseus heard the implied threat and drew himself up straight. His smile vanished. "You knew I was on Kriti. Why are you surprised to find me here? There has been a terrible shake." Suddenly, a look of comprehension crossed his face, and he lifted one eyebrow. "Ah. But that would be why you have now come, would it not be?"

"Yes."

"We were told you were dead, Theseus." Phillip interrupted. "We came to avenge you."

"But clearly, I am not dead, Phillip," Theseus said. "There is nothing to avenge."

"Is there not, Theseus?" Mykalo growled. "Perhaps you do not know that we were exiled from Athena after you left. We were forced back to living in caves, robbing and killing for our bread."

"No, Myko, I did not know that. That hag. May the Goddess of Poppies take her soul."

"Indeed She already has. Demetria claimed you were dead and put her brother Polymachos to head the army. We were run out of Athena." He leaned toward Theseus, every muscle tensed.

"My brother, I did not know."

"No, you were not there. Instead you came here, leaving us to fend for ourselves. Would a true brother have done such a thing? And now we find that you were not tricked into going to Kriti and killed, instead it appears you thought you could trick Demetria and us, your 'brothers', too," he spat.

"I told you the truth. I am sorry for what Demetria thought and did, but . . . ."

"Did you tell the truth to us, Theseus, that you were here to learn the weaknesses of Kriti, to lead an invasion? If so here is your chance. Your only chance. You will lead our invasion, now, or you will die." The watching crowd stepped carefully backward, never taking their eyes from Mykalo.

"Wait, Myko," Theseus began, but Mykalo would not wait.

"No!" He roared. "No! For over a full turn we scrabbled off the land plotting to avenge Demetria's treachery. Revenge is the only thing that kept our bellies full. Show us Theseus, show us you have not betrayed us. Show us or die at my hands!" Myko drew his sword.

Theseus threw up his hands, "I am unarmed, Myko."

"Phillip, throw him his sword. Do you see, my brother," he snarled, "we brought your sword? We came to avenge you with your own sword."

Phillip threw a sheathed sword at Theseus' feet.

"Pick it up, Theseus. Pick it up and defend yourself or I swear to all the gods I will run you through in the name of brotherhood!" Myko howled. His face was red and he screamed in fury.

Myko made to rush Theseus, who snatched up his sword, jerked it from its sheath, and crouched into a fighting position. He tossed the empty sheath behind him. "Myko, do not do this," he said in a low voice.

But Mykalo was beyond hearing. His eyes were blazing, fierce and dark. He gritted his teeth in a grimace. "I should be the leader, Theseus. It is because of me that we now rule Athena, not you. I will kill you in front of these men and they will know the gods favor me."

He lunged for Theseus, who danced out of the larger man's way. The people lined the perimeter of the courtyard, watching intently as Theseus and Mykalo circled each other warily.

"We both know I am the better swordsman, Myko. Do not make me kill you," Theseus said.

"Are you still? How much practice have you had in the past turn, Theseus? I have had much. I have had to earn any bread I got by my sword."

Again he lunged. Theseus struck back this time, turning Mykalo's sword aside, then scurried out of the way. "Do not make me kill you Myko," Theseus repeated.

Myko laughed and ran for Theseus. He brandished his blade, shoving Theseus' sword arm aside and then knocked him to the ground. "Who will be killed?" he raged, plunging the tip of his weapon toward Theseus' chest.

Theseus rolled nimbly aside and jumped back onto his feet, but Myko's sword edge caught his wounded forearm. The wound began to bleed freely.

Myko and Theseus were again circling each other. Myko was

sweating heavily. Blood dripped from Theseus' forearm leaving drops in his path. Several more times Myko lunged for Theseus and each time Theseus dodged the flailing sword. It was obvious that Myko was tiring. "Fight like a man, Theseus!" Myko bellowed.

"I do not wish to kill you, Myko," was the only reply Theseus would give.

It ended so quickly, so violently, so finally. Myko, pushed beyond his ability to reason, ran full out at Theseus who danced back, but then slipped in his own blood. Myko slipped too and fell on top of the slender man. But when he rolled Myko from on top of him, Theseus' sword was lodged upward under Myko's rib cage, and Myko was dead.

Theseus yanked his sword from the man's gut, then threw the bloodied blade by his feet. The metal rang harshly on the stones. Blood pooled around the corpse. Theseus shook his head. "I did not want to kill him," he said softly.

Phoebe rushed to his side to hand him a square of cloth to stanch the blood flowing freely from his wound. She stayed at his side. He turned to Phillip, "Tell the men to stand down Phillip. Go back home to Athena. Kriti is not yours to take."

"No," Phillip said, his voice cutting the air. "Myko was right. You are a traitor. Prove yourself. Be our leader again or die. You can kill some of us, but you cannot stand against us all. We cannot return to Athena empty handed. Myko was our leader. Now you must be." The other men stood by Phillip's side, nodding in agreement.

Theseus stood silent for several moments. Phoebe tensed wondering what he was thinking. She feared for his decision. It seemed that any of the possible outcomes would be bad; that Kriti was the prize regardless of any decision by Theseus. The true question, Phoebe knew, was whether his love for Kriti and She of Ten Thousand Names was worth his life. But surely Great Meter would not require that sacrifice, would She?

Another solution came to Phoebe. It was a terrible compromise born in the depths of the Underworld itself, but it was one where she could be true to Kriti and to herself and to her babies, and Theseus could live.

"Wait, wait," cried Phoebe. "There is another way." Phillip put up his palm to stop her, but Theseus turned to her and said, "Mistress Phoebe, tell us your thoughts."

"Kriti needs the alliance with Athena now more than ever. Instead of sacking her and leaving her open to invaders, why not take her as your own, like the cities of Eleusis and Mycenae. Let Kriti become a member of the nation of Athena. Kriti's riches will be yours. Our wealth and position, our knowledge will all become part of Athena, under the rule of Theseus, first king of the unified lands." She turned to him. "I can help you rule. I will be your consort and advisor."

Theseus blanched at Phoebe's offer. After several more moments of silence, his eyes unfocused, his jaw muscles working steadily, he finally said, "I would accept this offer with gratitude, Mistress Phoebe." His voice cracked. Turning to Phillip he asked, "What say you, Phillip?"

Phillip considered it. "Theseus, the peoples of Athena will follow your lead and would no doubt consider it a victory to take Kriti. We will not leave this land until we have assurances that it will be done exactly as this woman has said." He turned to the rest of the men, several of them nodded. "You will be ruler of all Athena with the island of Kriti and this woman, if you so choose, as your consort." He continued, warming to his words. "You must come back to Athena to lead the army and take the throne. This woman, representing her people, must agree to give a token of substantial wealth, and we take her to Athena to assure the good behavior of the people of Kriti. Kriti becomes a vassal of Athena and the Achean people. In return, we will not destroy the cities nor rob and plunder them."

Theseus glanced at Phoebe, who pleaded silently with him to agree. He looked at his gory, bloodied sword staining the white stone slabs of the courtyard, then at the ruins of the Agronos, the rubble and the blackened blocks of what had once been so magnificent. "Agreed", said Theseus softly, "Agreed".

"NO!" cried a voice from behind him. Ansel strode into the courtyard from where she had just arrived. "No," she repeated, facing Theseus, her eyes meeting his, glaring. "I will not have this." Theseus could not hold her eyes. He looked down at his feet.

"Meter," she turned to Phoebe, "what folly is this. How do you think to hand over our land to these people? How can you even believe you have such authority?"

Phoebe solemnly answered her daughter. "Ansel, I do have the authority. Look around you, child. Somewhere underneath all this," she gestured feebly with her arm, "lay the bodies of the entire Elder Council. All are dead. All. Even my meter and Xeronos." She choked up for a moment, then continued. "Just this past morn have we confined the worst of the fires and only because Theseus was willing to lead us. Agronos Knossos is in ruins; we hear it has survived better than others . The people turned to me as First Elder." A look of pain crossed her face and she exhaled sharply. "Ansel, I have two young children. I never desired to be like my own meter. Leading Knossos, perhaps all of Kriti, it is not a responsibility I can bear."

"Meter," Ansel breathed, not knowing what to say in the face of her meter's grief.

She whirled on Theseus. "You." She pointed her finger in his face. "This has worked to your advantage, I see. I see also that you still kill." She pointed to the lifeless body of Mykalo, his thick life's blood still seeping out onto the white stone. "You bring murder to the very heart of the Agronos. Did you learn nothing then from your journey in the labyrinth? Did you enjoy killing this man? Was he a brother to you? Did that make it all the more pleasurable to plunge your sword through his belly?"

"Stop, please, for the love of all the faces of Her, please stop!" Theseus said.

"Oh Ansel," Phoebe said, tears streaming down her cheeks.

But Ansel allowed her fury to carry her. She clenched her hands into tight fists and spat words at Theseus. "How dare you tell me to do anything, murderer? How dare you mention She of Ten Thousand Names in my presence? I trusted you. I saved you from sacrifice to the Minotaur on Heria. How bitterly I regret it. You knew my heart. You knew I did not want Kriti to die a slow death at the hands of invaders, and behold, who is that invader? At whose hands does Kriti die? Yours."

"No, Ansel," Phoebe interrupted, "listen to me. Sometimes, there are no good solutions. Sometimes all the possible endings are unhappy ones. I promise this to you: Kriti and all she stands for will never die. I will make certain we will never be forgotten. You do not know what happened. Ansel please . . . . "

But Ansel did not hear her meter's words. "I see," she raged on, "you have managed to get everything you ever desired, yes Theseus? You will become king of nations, leader of a great army and even have my meter as your consort. Am I to believe this came about by the hands of the Fates alone? You expect me to believe in the sincerity of your love for Kriti when you have betrayed her? You must think me a fool and indeed I have been one. I thought you a good man. I even thought myself in love with you. No more."

She walked directly to him and slapped his face with all her strength. "Know this Theseus, false King of Kriti. From this moment on I swear to Akakallis of the Underworld that I am your enemy. Never will I bow to you as ruler of any land. Never will I cease to fight to regain sovereignty of Kriti and the nation I love."

Ansel turned her back and strode to where Geneera, Dia and Devra stood. Phillip made to stop her, but Theseus shook his head, signifying to let her pass. To Devra she said, "I would choose to leave this land now, Devra. Please, may I come with you and with Geneera to the tribes of the Emetchi? I am ready to pledge my training, my knowledge and my loyalty to those who fight for She of Ten Thousand Names."

Devra nodded somberly and said, "You will be welcome among us Priesera Ansel." Together the women and horses turned and left the ruined Agronos and courtyard with the echo of Phoebe's loud sobs following them. When they were safely out of earshot, Devra stopped the group. As they mounted the horses, Devra offered to let Ansel ride behind her on Dolphina.

Ansel laid a hand on the Emetchi's arm and asked quietly, even reluctantly, "I need to know something, good woman. Will riding a horse overmuch endanger a child in the womb? I do not know much about riding horses, and, well, it seems that I am carrying a child."

Ansel ignored Geneera's gasp and out of the corner of her eye saw Dia thrust her hand over her mouth and turn away. The unflappable Devra, however, simply nodded and said, "Priesera, our women ride almost until the time they labor. It is quite safe."

Ansel smiled grimly. "Then an Emetchi woman I shall be. I shall ride until I am too big and clumsy to mount a horse. It is not the future I envisioned, but it is the future I now choose for myself and for the daughter Akakallis tells me I am carrying." Resolutely, Ansel straightened her shoulders, then stepped a foot onto Devra's cupped hands, allowing herself to be hoisted onto Dolphina.

"To the Emetchi lands then," she said. "Perhaps there are no good answers, but surely we can find one more honoring of Akakallis and Great Meter than simply handing Kriti over to invaders. I am called to defend Meter Right and I dedicate my life to this cause wherever it takes me. May we now and forever be blessed by She of Ten Thousand Names."

Glossary of Terms

Agronos – community center, civic center, central living area of the people of Knossos.

Bull, Great Bull – moon bull son of the Great Meter, sometimes depicted as a human baby or calf, other times as an adult bull.

Bull Son – although usually analogous to the Great Bull, sometimes depicted as a half–man, half–bull (Minotaur), especially in the sacrifice religion.

Cronetide – Approximately October through January, Roman calendar. The rainy season, winter.

Cycles – lunar cycles, also called "moons". Each cycle is approximately 28 days.

Helen – title meaning "Queen" as of the city–nation of Athena.

Kore – young woman between the ages of menarche and first Saturn return (first Saturn return occurs during the first twenty–seven to thirty years of life). Also used as a general term of respect (as in TradesKore = Trades Kore).

Koretide – Approximately May through July, Roman calendar. Late spring through mid–summer.

Kourete – title "Sir", man, a title of respect. Sometimes used in the context of a trade or guild association (TradesKourete, GuildKourete).

Krikri – native mountain goat.

Maidentide – Approximately February through April, Roman calendar. Early through middle spring.

Mellia – "sweet one", sweetie, affectionate term. Literally refers to "honey".

Mekoi – opium resin, raw opium.

Meta – mom, diminutive of "meter".

Meter – mother, mother Goddess (Great Meter).

Metertide – Approximately August through September, Roman calendar. Late summer.

Moons – as in "How many moons?" Lunar cycles, also called "cycles"

Quarters, quartercycle – refers to the four time periods between (respectively) new to first quarter moon, first quarter to half moon, half to three quarter moon, three quarters to new moon. One quarter equals approximately 1 week.

Seasontides – The four tides: Maidentide, Koretide, Metertide, and Cronetide. "High" season refers to: New moon in initial (first cycle) Maidentide, full moon in mid (second cycle) Kore– and Meter–tides, dark moon in final (third cycle) Cronetide (also called the time of the Death Hag). The solstices and equinoxes are also noted although the ceremonies are primarily noted celebrated via lunar time.

Triads – the three moon cycles within each "seasontide" (i.e. Maidentide, Koretide, Metertide, Cronetide). First triad corresponds to the first moon cycle within a given season, second triad with the second moon, third with the third moon.

Turn – one year.

Whitestone – gypsum, commonly used in the Agronos, native stone to Kriti. Similar to marble.

About the Author

Kassandra Sojourner is an ordained Priestess of the Re-formed Congregation of the Goddess, International. A former scientist and therapist, she finally found her niche as an author, and as cofounder and production manager of the feminist and Goddess spirituality press, *Creatrix Books LLC*. She and her life partner, Carol Marshall, live outside Madison, Wisconsin with many beloved critters. She is dedicated to bringing back She of Ten Thousand Names.

To Contact the Author

Contact Kassandra through the publisher, information below. Kassandra encourages all interested readers to check out the websites of the Re-formed Congregation of the Goddess, International at www.rcgi.org and of The Temple of Diana www.templeofdiana.org. Kassandra is available for workshops, performance work, signings and discussions. *Creatrix Books LLC* will forward all correspondence directly to Kassandra.

About *Creatrix Vision Spun Fiction LLC*

She Who Walks the Labyrinth is the second invaluable addition to the *Creatrix Vision Spun Fiction LLC* imprint. The first addition, *The Planting Rite* by Kip Parker was released in the summer of 2006. For further information about either of these books, please contact us through *Creatrix Books LLC*, information below. *Creatrix Vision Spun Fiction* is a Wisconsin Limited Liability company and a *Creatrix Books LLC* company.

About *Creatrix Books LLC*

Creatrix Books LLC is woman owned and operated and was founded to give a voice to Goddess and her children via the written word.

Creatrix

Creatrix Books LLC
PO Box 366
Cottage Grove, WI 53527
www.creatrixbooks.com